SEPTEMBER
BLUE

SEPTEMBER BLUE

Cat Whitney

Published by Scriptfire Publishing

www.CatWhitney.com

Poems by Julie Ann Cook used by permission.
Gratitude to the publications where these poems first appeared: "Advanced Life Drawing and Anatomy," *The Anthology: Centesimus* (Winthrop University, 2002); "Always Slightly Naked," *The Best of the Final Friday Reading Series, Vin Master Anthology* (Main Street Rag Publishing Company, 2013); "I Do Not Love You," *Love Like Weeds* (Main Street Rag Publishing Company, 2013)

ISBN: 0-9977048-0-2
ISBN 13: 978-0-9977048-0-8

Cover design by JulieAnnCook.com

Printed in the United States of America
Revision #4 July 2023

For all those whose lives have been divided into
The Day Before and The Day After.
For the ones who had to start a new book.
For the ones in the dust, and those who love them, still.

1
Gathering Grey

The winter wind is loud and wild,
Come close to me, my darling child;
Forsake thy books, and mateless play;
And, while the night is gathering grey,
We'll talk its pensive hours away...

—From "Faith and Despondency" by Emily Brontë

The Quill and Fiddle was the quintessential English pub. It sat in the tiny hamlet of Chatfield, in Warwickshire. Near the intersection of the M1 and the M6, Chatfield was just a speck on the map east of Coventry. The pub was built of stone and worn, wooden beams, hinting at a history reaching back hundreds of years. The corner lot allowed it windows that let rare morning sun flood the polished wood floor with thick bands of misty light. When it rained—or even just threatened—the fireplace glow brought out the knots in the wood panel walls and cast shadows from the beams in the ceiling. The chairs were made of uneven wood worn smooth, and the booths were on their sixth or seventh layer of ugly upholstery. The bar was wide and the stools sturdy. On the bar, near the cash register, sat a day-to-day calendar turned to 29 November, indicating the year 2010 had almost run out. The rooms upstairs were once rented by travelers making their way from the north down to London or Bristol. Though the rooms were mostly unused now, the renters' stories seemed to hang in the air.

For Cameron Burke, this was the place he came with his father for his first official drink at eighteen. He was lanky and self-righteous back then. It was the place where he earned his first hangover and nursed wounds of rejection. This was where he came between terms during drama school, celebrated his sister's wedding, and eventually mourned his parents. This was his respite from the chaos, his landing place. He could drop the plastic smile and gracious confidence his career required here. The booth in the far corner gave him peace and privacy. It was *his* booth. All the locals knew it. Yet, this morning, *she* was sitting in it.

The woman occupying Cameron's booth was entirely absorbed in a book. Her hair was half pulled up and half spilling around her shoulders like a rust-colored nest. She wore no makeup, and her skin was pale in the dim light. She was tiny, no more than five foot one, and her legs were tucked up underneath her in the narrow booth. Her small hands turned the pages of a ragged book gracefully. She had delicate features, like an antique china doll with a perfect, pinched nose and fine, thin lips. Cameron's closer examination revealed that she wasn't exactly young, either. Her complete lack of makeup revealed faint lines around her mouth and her eyes—hatch marks tracking a journey where youth had been left behind. She wore old tracksuit bottoms and a jumper that surely must have belonged to a father or older brother at some point. Her shoes were on the floor as though she were at home, rather than in a public place. Cameron stared at her, then cleared his throat, not wanting to be rude.

She looked up, gave him a half-hearted smile, and went back to reading.

Cameron stated, "Good morning."

"Morning," she offered without looking up from the book.

Completely baffled by her lack of recognition or interest, he struggled ahead, stating, "Although, the morning has almost run out, hasn't it?"

She glanced around, looking for a clock. According to Cameron's phone, it was almost noon.

"I suppose so," she mumbled.

At this point in his career, which included some thirty films and an Academy Award, Cameron Burke was not used to being ignored. He considered going back home, but with his limited cooking skills, this was the only place to get a hot meal for lunch. He also didn't want to wake his sister, who worked nights and slept during the day.

Since the mystery woman showed no signs of leaving soon, Cameron resigned himself to sitting elsewhere. He crossed to the bar and perched awkwardly on one of the stools.

Flora approached from behind the bar and Cameron asked, not unkindly, "Who is she?"

Flora shrugged. "I dun't know. She's been comin' in for abou' a month now."

Cameron shifted on the stool. He was not happy, and his first instinct was to pout.

Flora smirked. "Yer see what 'appens when yer go off and leave us fer so long?"

"I suppose," he grumbled.

After a few minutes, he couldn't tolerate the bar stool anymore and, moreover, he didn't *want* to tolerate it. Cameron got up and crossed the room. Today, the sunlight was watery and pale, and it cast a beam that led the way toward the back corner of the pub.

Exasperated but still a gentleman, he asked, "Do you mind if I sit here?"

The redhead raised her eyes and looked him over, finally truly seeing him. For a moment, he thought she would recognize him and make her apologies. He thought she would swoon a little then vacate his seat. Instead, she just stared at him, sizing him up with wide, glossy eyes—mostly brown but flecked with green. They stood out from her otherwise messy plainness. Still, they held no recognition.

After thoroughly studying him, she said, "Sure. Have a seat."

She was American. She'd finally said enough for him to be sure. He sat down opposite her. Flora Walker, who'd been working at the pub for decades, came and brought him tea in a mug. She refused to use good cups and saucers with him, claiming he was like family to her, but Cameron was certain it was also her way of reminding him where he came from. She'd also ruined him years ago for anything other than Yorkshire Tea. Flora glanced curiously at his table companion but said nothing. He worked on adding just a touch of milk to the tea, noticing that the messy redhead was sipping from a mug as well.

They sat together in silence for some time. He wanted to ask her to leave, or for her to take the hint. Cameron was used to getting his way, but he was too English to be impolite to a stranger. He finally conceded to make the best of it. He pulled out his phone and started scrolling while working his way through his tea. He had emails that needed checking, but he got lost in social media instead. If there was one thing that belied Cameron's age, it was his ever-present iPhone. He was given one as part of a swag bag three years prior and had faithfully upgraded every year since.

While he scrolled, the woman across from him kept reading, oblivious. He ordered some of Flora's hearty soup. Not wanting to be rude, Cameron asked her, "Are you planning to have lunch?"

She shook her head. "No. But go ahead."

"Would you like more tea?"

She made a sour face. "I hate tea. This is coffee. With a ton of milk and sugar because you don't have French vanilla creamer."

She went back to her book.

Cameron tried to hide his disbelief. He often forgot that the whole world wasn't raised drowning their tears, or any other emotion, in tea.

This mystery woman had piqued his curiosity, so he questioned, "Might I ask your name?"

She looked up from her book again in doe-eyed surprise. "I'm sorry?"

"Your name." He tried again, "Could I ask your name?"

"Delilah MacClare."

"My name is Cameron," he offered, extending his hand in hopes of eliciting some sort of reaction. "Cameron Burke."

The woman hesitantly shook his hand. "It's nice to meet you." She flashed a tiny smile.

"Do you mind if we share the booth?"

"Not at all."

Still dumbfounded by her lack of recognition, he pressed, "I'm sorry, but have we met before?"

He watched as her eyes focused on him. She cocked her head slightly. "You do look a little familiar, but I don't think so."

Cameron was floored. It had been so long since he had a cold introduction that he forgot what to do. So he stared. Then he realized how duplicitous he was being. Had he not decided to come here to get away from the constant attention for a bit? Wasn't he frustrated with people thrusting things in his face to be signed? Hadn't he occasionally asked what it would be like to have people take him on his own terms and forget the gossip? Here, in front of him, was someone who truly had no expectations, and he was upset because she wasn't giving him his favorite seat in a mostly empty pub. Cameron realized he was acting like a self-centered celebrity and, at the very least, he prided himself on having outgrown being downright obnoxious.

This time his smile was genuine. "Again, I'm Cameron Burke. I grew up here, in Chatfield."

She sipped her coffee. "It's nice to officially meet you."

"You're American?"

"Guilty."

"What brings you to Chatfield? In my mind it's not on the usual tourist circuit."

Glancing at her phone, she said, "My father owns an apartment, or a…flat? Here. He's letting me use it. Because he lives in the States."

"Are you visiting other family here?"

"No. I'm afraid they're long dead."

"Are you working?"

"No."

He was perplexed. What exactly was she doing in his pub? In his town?

Her eyes flicked away, and she laid her hand on another raggedy book. Then she half-answered his unspoken question. "Right now, I'm reading. And what do you do?"

Cameron's eyes crinkled as he laughed. She was either very much enjoying feigning ignorance, or she'd done a smashing job of living under a rock for quite some time. She appeared to be baffled by his laughter, though, so he sobered.

Taking a sip of his tea, he replied, "I'm an actor."

"Ah." She went back to her book yet again.

Cameron felt annoyance creep in again. Here was this woman who had invaded his space, and yet she was the one acting entirely put off by his presence. His *name* had no effect on her. His *smile* had no effect on her. Talking to her was making him realize he might be as spoiled as his sister insisted he was. Still, he was annoyed, because if this woman was going to occupy his spot, she could at least engage in polite conversation.

After another few minutes of watching her read, he asked, "Do you enjoy films?"

Not looking up, Delilah answered, "Not really. They were never my thing. And I don't go out much now."

"I see." Cameron sat back in the booth.

Flora crossed over to them. She refilled Delilah's coffee and brought more milk. Then she looked back and forth at the two of them and stated, "I see the two of ye 'ave finally decided to talk. No consensus yet on who gets t' booth?"

Cameron started to deny her implication, not wanting to be rude, but Delilah raised her head and finally looked present.

She asked, "Is there a problem?"

Cameron looked apologetic as Flora explained, "I'm afraid this is where Cameron likes t' roost after he's been out flyin' 'round t' world. I'm not sure if he's fonder o' t' seating or my cottage pie. I'n't that right, luv?" She asked, adding the obligatory question that was the way of northerners.

Delilah asked Cameron, "If this is your favorite spot, where have you been for the last month?"

He chuckled. "The last thing I did was attend a film premiere. In London."

Delilah cocked her head. "Were you *in* the movie?"

"Yes."

"What was it?" Delilah's question was entirely genuine.

Still sure she was faking ignorance, Cameron answered, "It was *Heir of Taivas. The Seven Summits.*" He waited for her to admit she'd been having a go at him.

Instead, she said, "I've heard those movies are really popular."

Flora laughed this time. "Have ye not seen *Heir of Taivas*, luv?"

Delilah shook her head.

"Ever read t' books?" Flora pressed.

"No."

Silence followed. Oblivious to Cameron's shocked reaction, Delilah stated, "We can split the booth. I'll take it 'til noon every day. Then it's yours for tea or whatever."

Cameron watched as she poured the rest of her coffee into a well-loved travel cup, picked up her bag, and slid out of the booth.

He sat there, baffled, as she walked away.

After a minute, Flora returned, taking advantage of the fact that she now owned the pub and could do as she pleased. In the thick dialect of a person born and raised in West Yorkshire, she asked, "She 'ad no idea who ye are, 'ad she?"

Cameron shook his head, shocked. It was the first time in at least ten years that he was a stranger to anyone.

For the next few days, Cameron felt the arrangement worked rather well. Delilah faithfully vacated the booth at eleven each morning, and he was able to eat lunch in peace. He promised himself he was going to use this holiday to take a break from social media, so he tried to read during lunch. But he found himself arriving early enough each morning to watch Delilah gather her things and leave. From the bar he would watch her pack her bag and take the remains of her coffee. Her clothes were consistently baggy and drab, varying only in color. She always looked the same. It was the only thing he could say he knew about her—she was consistent.

On Friday morning, five days after their first meeting, Cameron watched the redhead walk out of the pub again. He lingered at the bar for a minute, watching the door where she'd gone. He wasn't sure why she still had his attention. She was out of his booth, and she was the least personable woman he'd ever met.

"She's a strange bird, i'n't she?" Flora asked from behind him.

He turned around to see her wiping the counter. Flora was work-worn, with strong hands and an abundance of freckles. She stood at average height, with bombshell curves that had amplified over time. Her frizzy, russet hair was carelessly tied back. Although her beauty had faded a bit with age and labor, she still had striking, dark blue eyes. Eyes that could look right through to your soul. Cameron tended to notice eyes first.

Answering Flora, he said, "I don't know if she's strange. She's just…unexpected."

"If she were twenty years younger, I'd say she's typical. That bohemian, hipster nonsense is all t' rage. But she's too old for all tha', i'n't she?"

Cameron shrugged. "Perhaps she's starting over. Trying to find herself or make a statement. An ex-patriot rejecting loud, American idealism?"

"Maybe." Flora leaned on the bar. "But I've seen people who want to make statements. Those people *talk*."

He gave a wry smile. "I suppose we do, don't we?"

Flora smirked. "I knew yer'd be famous t' first time ye started blathering on about actin' school. You 'ad fire. Ye were annoying, but you 'ad fire."

Cameron chuckled. "I suppose this is why I come home. So you and Mara can take me down a peg."

"Yer sister's a saint. I'd tell 'er, if I ever saw 'er," Flora grumbled.

"Mara doesn't drink much so she has no use for a pub. No use for sleep either, apparently. The hospital is her life."

Flora softened. "But she does a lot o' good, dun't she?"

"And I only sell film tickets, yes?"

Flora smiled. "We all 'ave our own way, Cameron. An' who knows? Maybe yer booth-nicker will eventually say summat worth listenin' to."

―――――――――――――――――

The next Monday, the sixth of December, was bitterly cold. A blanket of mist fell, and the sky nearly screamed its desire to turn the rain to snow. Inside, The Quill and Fiddle was quiet during the morning hours and warmed by a well-stoked fire. A young man hauled in fresh logs from behind the kitchen, wiping sooty streaks across his face as he fed the flames. Flora cleaned tables and brought out hot stew to patrons wearing heavy sweaters and drinking frothy ale despite the cold. In the corner, Delilah was curled in her booth.

His booth. She caught herself.

Today, her feet were shod in worn, suede boots with fur at the edges. They were too industrial to be pretty, but they kept her feet from freezing. Her leggings were nearly covered by a long, faded sweater. It might have been blue once, but now it was closer to gray. Her hair was pressed down under a black knitted hat with wild, rippling strands pouring out below its edges. She stirred the drink in front of her. It was barely coffee. It was mostly milk and sugar, but it was warm. Delilah sipped and turned back to her book. When she read, she fell into books the way a caught fish falls back into the ocean—with great relief, like she could breathe again.

He held her despite the rain, shaking off its stinging cold and kissing her upturned mouth. He pushed back her hair, its heavy wetness winding around his fingers. She wrapped her arms around his neck, and he lifted her so she could wrap her legs around his waist.

There was warmth between them in spite of their soaked clothes. There was wanting. There were too many layers of fabric between them.

The sound of a clearing throat interrupted the story. Delilah looked up, annoyed at the distraction. Then, she realized it was *him* standing beside the table. Tall. Dark hair. Complicated eyes. Expensive black coat. Some years past fifty? Or sixty?

"Delilah?" Her name rolled off his lips in a rich baritone. His voice was like warm tea laced with honey and spiked with the bite of whisky. His voice almost made her forget how much she hated tea.

Cameron.

His jaw was set. Confident. He wasn't chiseled like the dashing man on the cover of her book—brawny and bare-chested. But he held himself like he owned the room, like he owned the world. He looked down at her expectantly.

Glancing at her phone, Delilah saw the time and muttered, "Sorry. I got distracted."

She started to gather her things, but he sat down across from her. "It's all right. It's absolutely frigid outside. Stay."

"Are you sure?" She quirked up an eyebrow. "You know what they say. Two loners cannot occupy the same space at the same time."

He volleyed back, "I believe it's, 'Two objects cannot occupy the same space at the same time.'"

Delilah rolled her eyes and went back to her book. She chewed a fingernail as she read. Cameron scrolled through his iPad with one elbow on the table, leaning his chin on his hand. He ordered then sipped tea, as usual. Delilah was about to start reading a new chapter when she noticed him staring at her rather than his tablet.

"What?" She asked.

"I know it's terribly forward of me, but based on how many hours Flora says you've been sitting here, you must have read twenty books by now. Is this author paying you to review their work?"

She caught his hint of snark and snapped, "Cameron?"

"Yes?"

"Is this what actors do when they're not acting? Sit down with strangers and critique their reading choices?"

"I suppose so. We go home to places where no one is asking us to sign things, and we try to take refuge in our favorite booth in our favorite pub."

She caught his implication with a lift of her chin but refused to apologize.

"So. Since you are in *my* booth, what are you reading that's so interesting?"

With a sigh, she dropped her book on the table for him to see. It was a modern romance novel she'd had for years by author Isabella Loren. The cover featured a couple kissing on a windy beach. Cameron picked it up and stared at it with obvious disdain.

"You enjoy this…drivel?" He raised one eyebrow.

Delilah nodded.

"But…is there even a story?" He scoffed, studying the cover again.

She crossed her arms in defiance. "Of course there's a story."

"If you say so," Cameron grumbled, but his melodic accent took some of the sting out of the words.

Delilah considered leaving. She had no desire to defend herself to an almost-stranger. Instead, she shrugged her shoulders. "To each, his own. I'm not asking *you* to read them."

Cameron conceded, "You're right. You did not."

She tried to go back to reading, but he stopped her. "So, you're Delilah, a visiting American who reads romance novels in a pub in Chatfield. You're not here as a tourist, and you have no other plans?"

She shook her head. "Nope."

Delilah decided he must be a successful actor to be so brazen. She wanted to ask him to leave her alone, but she lacked the necessary malice. Any strong reactions had long since been medicated.

Instead, she tipped her head to the side and said, *"Men of few words are the best men."*

He caught her implication and merely raised a brow.

She explained, "That's from Shakespeare's *Henry the Fifth*. I can quote a dozen more classics, if you'd like."

"All right." He threw up his hands in surrender. "You win. You are more than the sum of your romance novels. But, you've now begged the question…why is someone who can quote Shakespeare reading rubbish in a pub?"

There was a prickly silence.

"Cameron? You said you were in *Heir of Taivas*?"

His chest swelled with pride. "That I was. That I am."

Delilah was aware that the wildly popular fantasy book series, *Heir of Taivas*, by Joseph Warwick, had recently fallen victim to the idea that every book should be made into a movie. Or lots of movies. She also knew she was in the minority, not having read a word or seen a minute of it.

Studying his face, Delilah stated, "You must play a villain. You definitely look like you'd play a villain."

He tipped his head to the side, not answering.

"So, are you?"

He answered, *"If you see me as evil, then I am already condemned. If you see me as good, then I have much to live up to."*

It was her turn to look confused.

"That's Warwick. From *Heir of Taivas: The Acclans*." He smiled. "You see? I can quote things, too."

Delilah crossed her arms. "Fine. You win."

"I'd say we've merely tied up the score." He took a sip of tea.

"So…are you a villain?"

"I think," he responded, "you should decide for yourself."

Delilah was annoyed and not in the mood for games. "You won't even tell me what character you play?"

He glanced down at her smartphone in the turquoise case lying on the table and said, "I think you can sort that yourself."

Gathering her things, she stated firmly, "I don't watch movies."

As she stood up, he suggested, "Then perhaps try the books?"

"Are they better than the movies?"

Cameron smirked.

"Are you always this ambiguous?"

"Maybe."

Delilah rolled her eyes and walked away.

The next afternoon, Cameron sat in the kitchen of his childhood home—a terraced house amidst a hundred others just like it at the north end of town. It was a standard two-up-and-two-down. The ground level was comprised of a tiny front room, a kitchen, and an extension to the kitchen off the rear that was added during a good year. The tiny dining area where Cameron now sat was the same space where he ate breakfast before heading off to school decades before. After more than sixty years, the pictures chosen by his mother still hung over the ancient wallpaper. Scattered rugs made the stone floors tolerable. The narrow, central staircase led to the bedrooms upstairs. It was the same as always, but time had changed the residents, halving their number and leaving, for Cameron, only an air of sad reflection.

Several years ago, Cameron and Mara buried their parents in rapid succession and, according to their will, Mara inherited the house. Wilfred and Theresa Burke were now just smiling portraits on the walls and memories in an old, wooden chest full of faded letters and trinkets. Wilfred died two years before his wife, his body worn down from years of breathing coal dust. Their mother suffered a stroke and went quickly while holding Mara's hand. Later, after the subsequent, rather unexpected death of her husband, Mara moved back into the family home and took over the bigger, front bedroom upstairs. Bigger was a relative term, since these old, brick houses were built to allow as many miners as possible to live on one street, close to the pit head of the mine. The other bedroom, the one Cameron and Mara shared as children, was divided into two small spaces, one of which now accommodated an indoor bathroom. The back bedroom was barely big enough to fit a bed and a dresser, but Cameron appreciated that Mara reserved it for him despite his lengthy absences.

Glancing up at one of the portraits on the wall, he couldn't help thinking of his mother. Theresa Burke was almost as saintly as her namesake in the eyes of her children. She cooked, she cleaned, and she eventually took a job at the library in Rugby to make ends meet. She was loving yet demanding, and she gave her life to her children. Cameron remembered her reading to him from Dickens and C. S. Lewis when he was a boy. Being surrounded by books at the library reinforced Theresa's love for literature, and she was determined to pass that on to her children. Cameron felt, however, that his career was not exactly what his mother had in mind when she read him *Hamlet* by the lamplight.

Their father, sitting stoically beside his wife in the portrait, worked odd hours in the mines. Then, when they shut down, he retired, bringing in a small pension. It was hard work, but Wilfred Burke wasn't one to complain, often covering his aches and pains with a hearty laugh. They were simple people who lived simple lives, and Mara followed in their footsteps. She'd been a nurse for nearly forty years now, selflessly giving to those in need. She had a son who now lived in London working as a lawyer for charitable organizations to support his wife and young daughter. They were a family of givers, of servants and, somehow, from this lineage came Cameron. He knew Mara found his profession to be self-serving, and he hadn't helped that image by being absent for years at a time while his family saw him only in magazines. Since their mother's death, Mara used every opportunity to remind Cameron squarely of his roots. His sister had three years on him, but she acted as though it was twenty. He both loved and despised her for it.

"So, how long will you be home this time? Two or three days?" Mara came into the kitchen and stood with her hands on her hips, demanding. Her accent was distinctly Brummie, with rounded vowels and clipped consonants, whereas his was refined by drama school and the desire to be more posh than his upbringing allowed.

Cameron glanced up from the table. It was Tuesday, and he'd been home a week. He had already outstayed her assumptions. But he didn't say that to his sister. She stood tall, thin, and hawk-eyed, just like him. Her features were softer, however, with less nose and more smile. Her silver-streaked hair was pulled back in a knot and her scrubs were impeccably pressed. She was ready to humbly save the world for another night, right after she got what she wanted out of her younger brother.

Countering her gaze, he answered, "This time, I am here…indefinitely."

Mara raised an eyebrow. "Indefinitely?"

Cameron sighed. "Don't wheedle, Mara. We're too old."

"It's just a bit difficult to believe you don't have someplace to flit off to in less than a week."

He rolled his eyes. "I've just finished shooting a film and premiering another. I think I can afford a short holiday. It's only going to start up again in the spring, so I may as well lay low now."

Mara gave him a little smile. "I've been trying to make you take a rest for years. But I guess you're right about the timing. I just hope you *will* stay. Don't run off after some other project this time. Actually rest."

"Yes, *mother*."

She ignored his subtle dig as she gathered her things. Bag in hand, she stated, "I'm off. I work all night, per usual." She started toward the door then stopped to throw back, "You're not here because you met some girl on that film set who just happens to find

Chatfield appealing? Are you? Because you're too old. It's officially manky, now."

Cameron wasn't sure whether to deny the charges, to scoff at the assumption, or to be offended at her candid discussion of his sex life. So he just stared at her, annoyed.

Her tone softened as she added, "I know it's not my business. But you know I've made it my job to keep you from falling arse-over-elbow all the time."

"And I've tried to sack you from that job for years!"

Mara shook her head and breezed out the door.

The following morning, Delilah left home just as the rest of Chatfield was heading out of town to work. She was a little later than usual, but she had a restless night. Her father's apartment was located on the edge of town, less than a mile from the pub. It was actually part of a larger, sandstone house that was divided and sold in parts. It made her a little sad to see such a beautiful piece of history carved up and rented out, but she was grateful just the same. It was a place to stay, and Delilah liked to lie in bed in her tiny room and imagine the people who used dine, sleep, and live in the house as it once was.

Walking down one of the two main roads that intersected to create Chatfield, she took in the same terraced houses she passed each day. It was almost nine, but the winter morning was still dim and new. The patches of grass in front of the houses were impossibly green despite the cold. The street was narrow and painted with markings she was only starting to understand. The handful of cars that passed her was as much traffic as the narrow road ever saw. She passed the one inn, which was across from the local drugstore, or chemist's. Just before the side road where she turned to reach The Quill and Fiddle, Delilah stopped to sit and rest on a crumbling stone wall. The wall was part of the grounds of an eleventh century castle that dominated the landscape of the village. Nestled among the undulating green hills was this piece of history, older than anything within a hundred miles of where Delilah was born. She was raised in the mountains of West Virginia, in a small town like this one. She was normally grateful for the similarity, but as she caught her breath this morning, she appreciated the differences. The rain was more frequent, but softer here. Quaint, walled gardens took the place of picket fences. The residents were quieter but no less kind.

She continued her walk, noting the sky was irritable gray, making it a struggle to find the sun at all. The ground was damp from rain the day before. The air felt oppressive, like the heaviness of secrets. Delilah tried to walk more quickly, wanting to reach the warmth of the fireplace in the pub.

As she reached the last leg of her journey, Delilah felt a change in the air. Just outside a shop that sold antiques, she stopped and watched the fog roll in. And roll it did. It poured in quickly, blanketing her in quiet blindness. Suddenly, Delilah could barely make out the street in front of her. The other side was lost in nothingness. She looked at the familiar path before her, but it was enveloped by the murky gray.

An older man walking ahead of her slowed his pace but kept going. On the road, the cars continued to pass her carefully, their fog lights showing the way. Delilah, however, was frozen. The panic took her suddenly, before she could use her carefully rehearsed breathing exercises or take her medicine. She backed up against the window of the antique shop and felt a familiar ringing in her ears. The shrill sound of it was drowned out only by the pounding of her heart. She put her hands over her face to try to shut it out, but her breathing was too fast. Her chest heaved, and she tried desperately to slow it down. She started to tremble, and she sunk down onto the sidewalk with her back against the glass storefront.

Breathe. Slowly. Breathe. Slower.

She forced herself to focus only on the words. She grit her teeth, scrunched her eyes closed, and made herself think only about the exchange of oxygen. She took in air and made herself slowly let it back out. She emptied her mind. She counted to one hundred. Then two hundred. Eventually, she could take a deep breath. Then another. But she didn't move.

After several more minutes, with her eyes still closed, she said to herself, *It's only fog. It's only fog. You're okay right now. You're okay. It's only fog.*

It took another fifteen minutes before Delilah was able to stand. All she wanted was to be off the street, so she went into the antique store and pretended to look around. She browsed until the fog lifted, unable to force herself back out into it. Then, realizing how late it was, she decided to go back home. It was nearly Cameron's turn at the table, and she was in no condition to be in anyone's company this morning.

2
Till Winter Comes

Love is like the wild rose-briar,
friendship like the holly-tree
The holly is dark when the rose-briar blooms
but which will bloom most constantly?

The wild-rose briar is sweet in the spring,
its summer blossoms scent the air;
Yet wait till winter comes again
and who will call the wild-briar fair?

Then scorn the silly rose-wreath now
and deck thee with the holly's sheen,
That when December blights thy brow
he may still leave thy garland green.

—"Love and Friendship" by Emily Brontë

"You're early. It's ten-thirty," Delilah stated flatly.

Cameron stood next to their booth, looking down at her as she spoke. It was Friday, and she was strangely absent from the pub for the past several days.

Tossing his winter wear in the booth, Cameron sat down without asking. "It's supposed to snow. I wanted to get here before it really got started."

Delilah scoffed, "So…you wanted to get stuck in here, instead of at home, should this blizzard materialize on what appears to be the first truly sunny day since I've been here?"

Cameron had no rebuttal. He was shocked at how fast she not only saw through his thin excuse but tore it apart and discarded it.

"Fine," he acquiesced. "I hoped to catch you because I brought you this."

He pulled a worn hardcover book from his coat and dropped it on the table.

Pulling it toward her, Delilah read aloud, "*Heir of Taivas: The Perquisition.*"

"It *Ty-Vas*," Cameron corrected her pronunciation of the fictional realm.

Flora brought coffee and tea, glancing at the two of them without speaking.

After she walked away, Delilah asked, "You really have all these books? And you've read them?"

Taken aback, Cameron replied, "For someone who claims to be ignorant of all things pop culture, you certainly seem to have a lot of assumptions about actors."

Delilah shrugged. "I don't care much about the habits of actors."

Cameron tried not to be offended. He explained, "I would never take on a role without reading all the source material, whether I like it or not. And I only have one condition for loaning it to you. Well, two."

She cocked her head, listening.

"First, this copy is my sister's. So be careful with it. Secondly, no romance novels until you've finished the whole series."

Pulling back defensively, Delilah demanded, "And who are you to tell me what to read?"

Cameron gave her a withering look. "Because you need to clear your mind of it. I have only had the opportunity, if you could call it that, to read that drivel once. And I have to say, it read like the script to an ill-conceived, pornographic film."

Delilah squared her shoulders. "Are you also a professional book critic?"

Cameron watched her, fascinated. No one spoke to him like this. People hung onto his words or read between them, but they didn't volley the conversation as though they weren't afraid of him walking away or ending the interview.

"Ok. You're right," he acquiesced. "I'm no literary scholar. But if you're so well read, how can you read that implausible drivel?"

With less hostility, Delilah explained, "Romance novels aren't about reality. They let you escape into a fantasy where everyone is beautiful and love always prevails."

"That sounds a bit…banal," Cameron stated sourly.

Delilah threw back, "Good grief! They're romance novels! I never said they were Shakespeare! Stop making me defend my hobby!"

Cameron could tell by the smile playing at her lips that she was only slightly annoyed.

Still defensive, she added, "Although, I do have a list of words I really don't like to see in the books I choose."

Now he was even more intrigued. "Really? Do you have a list of these words?"

"Oh, yes," Delilah snapped sarcastically. "It's laminated. I keep it on my refrigerator."

Cameron wasn't exactly sure how their conversation had taken this turn. It was a bizarre topic, but he was enjoying it. He hadn't talked about anything this wonderfully silly in a long time. It was an unexpected reprieve from a continuous barrage of interviews with the same questions over and over.

Leaning on one arm, Cameron teased, "Could you bring me that list? I think it would be worth seeing."

Delilah gave him an incredulous look. "I don't really have a printed list. Imagine what would happen every time a guest looked at my refrigerator and saw the word 'cock' in fourteen-point type and preserved in plastic."

In a throaty way that was pure instinct when talking to women, Cameron purred, "And what are the rest of the words?"

"The only other thing I will admit is that I have a love-hate relationship with the word 'fuck.'"

Cameron sat up straighter, unexpectedly thrilled at hearing the word "fuck" come out of her mouth. Then he chastised himself. He was acting exactly the way his sister disdainfully expected—as though people existed only to cheer for him, to make money for him, or to be fucked by him. Out of sheer spite, he was determined to prove Mara wrong this time.

With more honesty than he intended, he said, "I think a lot of us have that sort of relationship with that word."

Delilah's expression was hard to read as she stated, "I will read your book, Cameron Burke. If you read mine."

"Which one?" He asked. She had a couple of books on the table. He picked up a raggedy paperback with a cracked spine.

She snatched it from him. "Not that."

From his glimpse of the cover, he saw it was some sort of poetry anthology.

Clasping the worn book to her chest protectively, she pushed another paperback toward him. "I'll read yours, if you read this."

He grimaced. "You're putting *Heir of Taivas* up against," he took her book from her, "*Secrets of the Shore?*"

Her confidence faltered briefly as she quietly answered, "No. But if I have to try something new…so do you."

Cameron considered the idea for a minute before giving in. "All right, but only this one. And only because I promised my sister I would stay in Chatfield and there isn't much else to do."

Delilah smiled, but not as brightly as he'd hoped. She clenched her jaw as she stared at the cover of the book he'd given her.

The next day was Saturday, and the promised snow arrived. It was no blizzard, but it covered Chatfield in a thin layer of pristine white. Delilah liked the cleanness of it. She liked the look of the world after it was gilded with a coat of delicate, white perfection.

Looking out her living room window, she watched the flakes fall soundlessly to the ground.

The place where she was living was hardly big enough to call an apartment. The exterior color reminded her of the butter-colored sand at Virginia Beach, a frequent summer vacation spot for her family when she was a child. The front of the house was square and symmetrical, with stone steps leading to a large, wooden front door. Some generations ago, Delilah assumed her relatives lived in it and managed the few acres that surrounded it. They might have had sheep, but she wasn't sure. All she really knew was that her grandfather broke down the home into several apartments and sold most of the land around it after her grandmother passed away. Chatfield expanded over the years, and the house was now on the edge of the town rather than nestled in the privacy of the countryside. On some level, Delilah thought all of it must be a loss, but she didn't feel it. Her grandfather, Gregory, was a stoic man, so if any emotion was wrapped up in this property and its subsequent sale, he never showed it. Her father, however, was a more sentimental person. Stephen MacClare refused to let go of his parents' home, even though he lived his whole life in the States. It was a nightmare, Delilah was told, sorting out her grandfather's estate when he died and putting the property in her father's name, but Stephen persevered. Now, Delilah was reaping the benefit while she occupied flat number three, just off the main entry hall.

The living room where she sat held only a tiny sofa and a worn recliner, both facing the modest stone fireplace. Delilah sat curled up on the sofa, watching the snow through the tall window that faced south. To her right was a kitchen that wasn't even big enough to fit a table. Up the steep staircase behind her was the only bedroom, which was more of a loft, and the bathroom was truly the definition of a water closet. Once, this space might've been the maid's quarters. Small as the apartment was, however, it suited Delilah.

Pulling her attention from the snow, she focused on the book in her lap. She started reading Cameron's book mostly out of a desire to best him, but now she was glad she gave it a chance. The first in the *Heir of Taivas* series and subtitled *The Perquisition*, the book was turning out to be rather addictive.

The story was set on a fantasy version of earth and in the fictional realm of Taivas. Accessible only from the highest points on earth, it was inhabited by a myriad of fantastic creatures, including a human-like race called the Citizens. Representatives from every species ruled Taivas as a group, and together they were called the Arches-Asterion. At the beginning of the first book, Earth and Taivas are cut off from one another. A bitter civil war thousands of years ago ended with their separation. Guards were placed at the entrances to Taivas, and the Acclans were formed on earth to keep the history and the existence of Taivas secret. However, the occasional determined Citizen or human would discover a gateway and cross over, and some of them bore or sired children. On earth, they were quickly taken from their parents to be raised with no knowledge of Taivas. Those born in Taivas lost their parents to the executioner and lived as outcasts called Eperra. They were denied a family name and were forced to take Eperra as their surname.

As Delilah continued to read, she met Mohara, a young woman born in Nepal, in the shadow of the great mountain Chomolungma, but raised in London. She also met Marcus Eperra, a rejected renegade living in Taivas and searching for a way to overcome his low social status. When Darian, the head of the Arches-Asterion, dies suddenly, Marcus sees his chance. By sheer persistence, he gets the attention of the new head, Jermias. Armed with an obscure prophecy, Marcus convinces Jermias to send him to earth to look for Darian's bastard child—the true heir of Taivas.

Delilah was lost in Jermias' plan and Marcus' search, or perquisition, when her phone rang.

"Hello?" Delilah answered.

"Lilah?"

It was her father. He often called right after breakfast, his time, which was lunchtime for her.

"Dad?" She asked unnecessarily.

"I saw it was snowing there," he stated softly.

She smiled. They might be thousands of miles apart, but she could count on him to check the weather in Chatfield. In that way, he might as well be next door.

"How's the house?" Stephen asked.

"Still old, but holding up. There's way too much furniture in this place." Delilah chuckled.

"You know I'm not much for decorating. I paid someone to make it livable. Didn't think you'd ever be calling it home…"

They both went silent. They'd reached a precipice, a line in the conversation that was hard to cross on the phone.

Delilah cleared her throat. "I like it here. It was a good idea to come."

There was a pause. "Have you opened that suitcase, yet?"

Delilah swallowed hard and shook her head even though he couldn't see her. "No."

Her father's voice lifted. "Well, good."

She wasn't sure if what she felt was good.

"I made a friend, sort of." She changed the subject.

"That's great!" Stephen was a little too enthusiastic.

"He gave me a book."

"He?" His enthusiasm became surprise.

"Dad," Delilah gave a withering sigh. "There was a fifty percent chance that the first person who talked to me here would be a man. It means nothing."

"Ok. Didn't mean to pry."

"I know."

Delilah was calmed just by talking to her father. Stephen's voice rumbled with a twang forged in the mountains of West Virginia. Delilah remembered him calling to her through the trees in the woods behind their house when she was a child.

Come home, Delilah! Sun's nearly gone. Come home!

His voice always called her home. Even now, she might run home if he gave her permission.

But he didn't. Instead, Stephen asked, "So he gave you a book?"

"Yes," her voice lifted, "a good one."

"Melville? Steinbeck?" His well-read status showed through his Appalachian accent.

"No," Delilah answered. *"Heir of Taivas."*

There was silence.

Finally, Stephen found his voice. "I suppose…if that's what you like."

"It's good. I'm starting to understand the appeal."

"Well…I'm glad. I'll let you get back to it."

"Thanks, Dad."

"Do you have plans for Christmas?"

"I plan to call you," Delilah teased.

"I guess that will do. Just, don't spend the whole day by yourself. *Do* something."

"Dad," she returned, "I'm okay."

"Then I guess I'm okay, too."

Understanding passed between them.

They said their goodbyes and Delilah fell back into her book. She couldn't put it down until she had read the last word at nearly midnight.

The next Monday, Delilah waited for Cameron at the pub. The book she borrowed sat on the table. She was trying to figure out how to check her email on her phone, but her attention was divided between its screen and the door of The Quill and Fiddle. Finally, just past eleven, Cameron entered. She noticed he always moved with purpose, like he was the missing piece from wherever or whatever he was heading toward. Cameron Burke did not walk. He strode. When he reached their booth, he shed his winter apparel, this time dusting snow from his coat.

When he sat down, Delilah stated, "I finished the book." She pushed it toward him.

He looked momentarily surprised. Then his features settled into curiosity as he asked, "And?"

"I concede the point. It's a good story."

"Far better than the rubbish you gave me."

She countered, "Maybe."

"Delilah, there is no way that that drivel…"

She cut him off. "Are you paid each time you use the word *drivel*?"

Cameron stopped, stared at her, then laughed.

She wasn't amused.

Still laughing, he said, "Fine. You win this round. Now tell me your thoughts on the book."

Delilah softened. "Like I said, it's a good story. The characters are real, and I love that they're not perfect. Jermias is stubborn and Marcus, well Marcus is kind of an ass. And I'll admit, I did not expect this 'chosen one' to be a woman. Not from a male author."

Cameron nodded. "Ah, yes. Every fantasy story must have a 'chosen one.' This one has Mohara, the Bohemian, Nepalese beauty who paints her dreams. She is the reason girls all over the planet are wearing ponchos and taking art classes."

Delilah went on, "I like that she paints what she sees in her dreams. And I love that she's not sixteen years old. An adult heroine is a nice change. She does have that whole 'my parents died tragically' backstory, but she is otherwise…different."

"I had a feeling you would like her." Cameron's eyes glinted with unspoken pride.

"Well, I do." Delilah went on, "It definitely sets things up for more. I would read the second one."

"You would?" He smirked in satisfaction.

Delilah cocked her head. "You're certainly smug. Did you think I would hate it?"

"No." Cameron looked slightly less satisfied.

"I mean, you handed a *book* to a person you've seen do nothing other than *read* for three weeks."

"Well, I assumed your standards were set at *Secrets of the Shore* level, so…"

Delilah crossed her arms over her chest. "So…you read mine?"

His gaze dropped to his hands, and she knew he had not.

He argued, "Did you honestly expect me to make it through that-"

"Drivel?"

Cameron didn't argue. "Do you know another word to describe it?"

Miffed that he hadn't held up his end of the bargain, she gathered her things and started toward the door.

From behind her, Cameron called out, "I'll bring you the next book."

Delilah kept walking, too annoyed to respond.

―――――――――――――――――――

Delilah avoided him for three days. She stayed home, certain she didn't want to argue with someone over what she loved, however silly. Delilah felt she had as much of an appreciation for literature as anyone. Her father made sure of that. She had a decent eye for art and her favorite book was a collection of poetry, but she also liked sappy romance novels. She was certain Cameron had his own eccentricities that were less than noble. So, she would not apologize for hers.

On the fourth day of her anti-Cameron protest, an icy Thursday where the rain mixed with the snow to create a gray, slushy mess, Delilah caved to her desire to eat something other than canned soup. She shuffled into the pub just after eleven. Crossing to the booth in the back corner, she noticed that Cameron was not only there, but he had a book sitting on the table.

Looking up from his tea, he smirked. "I knew you would be back."

She ordered some food to take home, laid the book she brought on the table, picked up the one he brought, then left without another word.

That night, in the wee hours, Delilah was still reading. She took a break for dinner but otherwise read for hours straight. It was no different than her usual routine, but it had been some time since a book kept her up this late. For all the years she spent wondering what all the fuss was about regarding *Heir of Taivas*, she finally understood. In this volume, Mohara was introduced to the Acclans, a group who passed down the knowledge of Taivas through generations and worked to keep its existence a secret from Earth's inhabitants. Warwick introduced two more characters, Amy and Alex—identical twins who were both Acclans. Delilah also learned that Mohara's dreams, which helped Marcus find her, were not just the ramblings of Mohara's subconscious. They were caused by memories of the Realm of Taivas she didn't know she possessed.

Delilah's eyes were tired from reading. Sometime after 1 a.m., she set the book down and rubbed her face. Sliding to the edge of her bed, she let herself look in the large, free-standing mirror in the corner of the room. She stood up and stared at her reflection, registering what she saw—curly, auburn hair spilling over her shoulders, faded flannel pants, a worn Journey t-shirt, sharp features, eyes too big for her face. Delilah stared at her reflection until the room started to fade away. Focusing only on the image in the mirror, her throat started to ache. She started to speak, but the phone rang.

Jarred back to reality, she turned back to the bed and answered her cell.

"Lilah?" Her father was on the other end of the call. "I just thought I'd say…goodnight."

She wasn't sure how he could have known she needed to hear his voice. Grateful for the distraction, she replied, "Thanks, Dad. Goodnight to you."

"It's late there," he added. "Wasn't sure if you would be up."

Delilah felt the ache in her throat again. "I was just...I was reading...and I..."

Stephen sensed her distress. "What is it Lilah?"

"I started to talk to her again."

Her father sighed. "It's okay, Lilah. Nobody said you couldn't talk to her. It's just...you have to talk to other people, too."

"I know. And I have been."

"The guy with the books?"

"Yeah. And sometimes others."

Steering the conversation toward a lighter subject, he asked, "What else does this friend do? Besides lend books?"

Delilah felt the tension from so many unspoken things start to dissipate. "He's some kind of actor. His name is Cameron. Cameron Burke."

"Huh. Sounds kinda familiar. Is he British?"

"Well, yes."

"I should've known. I guess most of them are."

Delilah giggled. "Yes, Dad, all of the people in Chatfield are British. Specifically, they are *English*."

"It's good to hear you laugh," Stephen said softly.

"Thanks."

"Can you sleep? It has to be late there."

"Yeah. I'm okay now. I'm just going to finish my book."

"Good. Sleep tight."

"Goodnight, Dad."

Delilah fell asleep sometime later with the finished book on her chest.

───────────────

The following morning, or close to afternoon, Delilah woke to her phone ringing. Pulling herself groggily to the edge of the bed, she reached across the nightstand for it. Answering it, she tried to sound as though she'd been awake for more than a millisecond.

"Lilah?" It was her father again.

"Yeah?" She mumbled.

"Did I wake you up?"

"Ummm…"

"It's okay. You've got a different schedule, and there's the time difference…"

"Aren't you heading to work?" Delilah finally formed a coherent question.

"Yes. But I had to tell you this before I left. Your friend with the books, you said his name is Cameron Burke?"

"Yeah?" She rubbed her eyes.

"He's pretty famous." Her father had never been one to mince words.

"Really?" Delilah was fully awake now. "He hangs around in this pub here by himself. Although, I guess he did say he just went to a movie premiere…"

Stephen laughed lightly. "I've got to head to work. But look him up. I think you've borrowed a book from a celebrity."

"I will. Thanks."

For the second time in twelve hours, Delilah hung up with her father. Dragging herself from the bed, she stumbled to the bathroom, pulled her hair out of her face with a clip, and mindlessly went through her morning routine: Brush teeth. Take medications—four bottles, four pills. Use one inhaler.

She splashed water on her face, then took Cameron's book and headed downstairs. She settled herself at the tiny kitchen counter with a bowl of cereal and her laptop. Opening the computer, she pulled up Google. Between bites, she typed in Cameron's name.

Delilah grew up in a town where television reception was poor and movie theaters were far away, so she spent much more time reading books than staring at screens. The unintended consequence was that she was always a little behind when it came to pop culture. Even when she moved away from home, Delilah was more likely to see a play than a movie.

However, she recognized in one search that Cameron was indeed a celebrity. His filmography spanned some thirty years. She scanned the titles and calculated that his first three major movies came out when she was about ten, which would explain why he was vaguely familiar. It also implied his age, because she was playing on playgrounds when he attended his first premiere. There was a bit of a gap between his initial success and the trilogy that launched his latter career. The internet detailed his films, his accolades, and even his height and family history. She felt a twinge of compassion, because it couldn't be easy to have this much of yourself plastered all over the web. Finally, she looked up his name as associated with *Heir of Taivas*.

Delilah assumed if Cameron had any sort of major part, he would have told her. She also forgot that their conversation about the books came about because he was *in* the movies. Yet here he was—as Marcus Eperra. As she stared at the pictures of his familiar face framed by long, wild black hair and his tall frame outfitted in worn, leather riding boots and a billowing cloak, she felt a twinge of what his fans must feel. She wasn't sure if he could act, but the pictures of him suddenly filled in the outline of who Marcus Eperra was in her mind: The unwanted renegade. The man who needed a purpose. The antihero with a chance at glory. Delilah scrolled further and started to read some of the commentary about his performance but quickly closed her browser. She didn't want to spoil the books.

She also didn't want to know any more about Cameron. As annoyed as she was with his teasing, he intrigued her. He could have told her exactly who he was and everything he'd done, but he hadn't. Delilah wasn't sure of his motive, but she was glad he allowed her to talk to him as simply Cameron. He was the first friend she'd made in years, and she needed to keep him normal, for now. So she shut the laptop and went to make herself decent. Ten minutes later she went out the door, his book in her hand.

3
We Wear Our Words as Armor

We wear our words as armor, weighty and clanking,
and arm ourselves with double entendre'd swords.
We give Arthur a run for his legend, thanking
our stars, our gods, ourselves, our hope, our Lord's
promises, mostly kept, quiet in pockets, clinking
as coins, spare, sparse as change—towards
which we aspire under this heavy metal, thinking
of nothing more than what next: which words
do we give? It is apocryphal. It is revelation
each time we speak, each time we joust, we spar.
It is complex, mismatched metaphors, elation
in secrets, like underwear under which we are
meat and thoughts and blood and breath in skin—
we are words dancing, precious dust, of God and star.

—*"Always Slightly Naked" by Julie Ann Cook*

Cameron didn't see her coming. It had been two days since she walked out on him and, by Sunday, he assumed she wasn't returning. He told himself he was annoyed with her disappearance because she had his sister's book, but he couldn't deny that he wanted her to come back. For the first time in quite a while, he was lonely, or at least aware of being alone. He'd met with a few other old friends since returning to Chatfield, but it wasn't the same. The people he grew up with didn't lose their minds and scream for him like true fans, but he had become Cameron-the-actor, rather than Cameron-the-person. He missed Delilah, with whom he was simply, Cameron.

Suddenly, she was there, having come into the pub through the door at his back.

Delilah set his book down on the table and asked, "May I sit?"

Setting his phone down, as he'd been mindlessly scrolling, Cameron answered, "You may."

She slid into the booth just as Flora brought him fish and chips. They were golden, buttery, delicately crispy, and so terrible for him he only indulged occasionally. The weather was bitterly cold, though, so he opted for food that was warm. He looked Delilah over as she shrugged off her heavy, patchwork coat and pulled her knitted hat off her head. Her hair was positively untamed this morning, with ember-colored snarls tumbling into her face and down her back. The hat had not helped matters, he assumed.

Pushing his book toward him, Delilah barked, "I read it. I enjoyed it. Can I have the next one?"

"Of course." Cameron selected one of the well-fried chips.

While he chewed, Flora brought coffee to Delilah and glanced at the two of them. "I see the two of ye 'ave made up."

Flora missed nothing. Cameron gave her a slight nod before she walked away.

"I'm still mad at you," Delilah stated, pulling his focus back.

"I suppose I can't blame you."

"You made fun of me." She laid his crime out before him.

"I'm sorry. Truly."

After a moment, her expressive eyes softened. As he continued to eat, he watched her fill her coffee with everything but salt and pepper. Then she sipped carefully.

"Don't you ever eat?" He asked without thinking.

"Yes. I ate breakfast an hour ago."

"Breakfast?" He checked his watch. "It's midday."

"Someone's book kept me up until three in the morning." She gave him a hard look.

"Here." He pushed his plate forward as an offering to share. "You look thin, although it's hard to say since your wardrobe might have come off someone three times your size."

She looked annoyed. "Do you want to talk about your book, or do you want to try to feed me like a stray puppy?"

Cameron felt reprimanded. He was glad, however, when she picked up a couple of chips and nibbled gingerly.

But instead of commenting on the book, Delilah asked, "Why didn't you tell me that you're Marcus?"

He leaned back in the booth, wondering at what point she'd figured it out.

"It suits you." She stole another chip.

"How so?"

"You've already got the dark hair and you're tall. Black works on you. You probably intimidate people naturally. But, mostly, it's your eyes. Your eyes are...complicated."

"I'm not the only one who's complicated."

Per usual, the words were past his lips before he really processed them. He saw her recoil then look away.

"I think other people would agree with me," he added, trying to make the comment less personal.

She ignored him. "Well, I don't think Marcus has Mohara's best interests in mind."

"Marcus sees an opportunity and takes it. He's an outcast who wants to find a place in his society."

"It feels a little like he's using Mohara. I mean, he doesn't tell her that if she comes back with him to Taivas, he gets money and status," Delilah argued.

"Possibly. But Mohara wants to explore this world she's being pulled into. She's no prisoner," Cameron countered.

"At this point in the story, it's all a bit...complicated."

Cameron didn't argue.

After a minute, Delilah added, "Maybe you wouldn't come off as a villain if you smiled more. You do have a nice smile."

Cameron started to reply, but her face registered that she inadvertently complimented him.

Delilah looked down at her hands, then up again. "Can I have the next book?"

He nodded, and they faced off, at an impasse over who won this round of verbal sparring.

"Do you have plans for Christmas day?" Mara asked Cameron the next evening as he set the table for dinner.

Cameron tried to eat with his sister before she went to work at night, since it was the only time they saw each other during the day. Sometimes, she cooked. Other times, it was merely sandwiches. Today, it was mushy peas and leftover roast from the Sunday before. He checked his phone. It was the twentieth of December. He thought back to the holiday last year spent in London getting ready for another seven weeks of filming. He went to a Christmas Eve party with a few friends and drank too much wine, then spent Christmas Day watching old films and ordering takeaway. He was perfectly content with the arrangement. The year before that he stopped in to see Mara on his way to Newcastle to shoot another film he was working on. Before that, things got blurry. He probably owed it to his sister to stay home this year.

"I'm inviting some of the nursing staff over for Christmas lunch around one o'clock. It's something of a tradition we've had going these last few years. One of us makes the main dish and the others bring something," Mara went on.

Cameron realized he'd been out of touch with his sister long enough for her to establish an entirely new tradition in his absence. Of course, he couldn't blame her. With their parents gone and him not around, she needed some sort of new holiday ritual.

Coming around the table so he had to look at her, she asked again, "Will you be here?"

"Yes," he answered, "I'll be here."

Mara smiled at him, but underneath the smile he knew she was weighing his ability to keep the commitment.

Tuesday dawned with sheets of rain that melted away the dirty snow from the streets and pavements. However, the cold ensured bits of it remained in the cracks and corners, a token reminder that winter was far from over. It was late afternoon, and Delilah sat curled in a chair by the big, stone fireplace in The Quill and Fiddle. The usual booth was simply too cold today. The frigid air made her lungs hurt, so she sought refuge by the fire. She lost herself in her worn copy of *Words Dancing, Precious Dust: Poetry of Life,* when Cameron's voice pulled her back to reality.

"Delilah?"

She looked up, her mind foggy from reading.

He sat down opposite her in the other wingback chair in front of the fire. He kept his long, black overcoat on.

Delilah shifted in her chair, adjusting her long sweater over another pair of sweatpants. She cocked her head and asked, "Are you not staying?"

"I have to go to a show in London tonight. I promised a friend. And I must leave now so I can stop by my flat and get proper clothes, but I'll be back tomorrow," he explained.

"Have fun," she offered haphazardly. She started to go back to her reading, but she felt his intense gaze. "What?" She asked.

"I wanted to apologize before I go."

Delilah raised an eyebrow.

"In our conversations, I've had some fun at your expense. I never meant to offend you."

Deep down, Delilah didn't care what he thought of her, but she was touched by the gesture.

"Also," he went on, "I hope you have a Merry Christmas."

She smiled in spite of herself. "Apology accepted. And I hope the pub is open on Christmas. Otherwise, it's frozen pizza for me."

Delilah saw his face change, and she realized how her answer sounded. She quickly added, "Which is fine. Traditional Christmas really isn't for me."

Cameron held her in his penetrating gaze as he offered, "My sister makes Christmas lunch. Why don't you come?"

Delilah laughed nervously. "You don't have to invite me over. Really, I'm fine."

He sat back in the chair. "Consider it a peace offering for making fun of you and not finishing your book."

She didn't answer, not sure how she felt about the idea.

Leaning toward her again, Cameron said, "I could use a friend. Otherwise, my sister is unbearable."

He was teasing, she knew, but his use of the word "friend" caught her. It was nice to hear him confirm their relationship.

"Here," Cameron grabbed a napkin and took out a pen, "this is my phone number. Text me what you decide."

She accepted the napkin he had scrawled on and watched him leave.

The next day, she unfolded it from her bag and typed out a simple message:

I'll be there.

Delilah.

A few minutes later, he replied:

Good. :-)

C.

He sent her an address and Delilah saved it, along with his number. Now, she could at least tell her father she had plans. She wondered if he would be pleased, or shocked. Then she shook her head, because somehow her life had taken an inexplicable turn that had resulted in her having a celebrity's personal phone number.

When the first knock came at the door Christmas morning, Cameron and Mara exchanged a long look. He told his sister the night before that Delilah would be coming, and she was more wary than pleased. He supposed he couldn't blame her, but that didn't change his mind. The first guests to arrive were Mara's fellow nurses, Aida and Beth. Both were single and nearly Mara's age. Peter and Suzanne, a young couple who were trainees at the hospital, arrived next. They had no children and, apparently, no time to cook for themselves. The house wasn't big enough to swing a cat normally, and now it was starting to feel claustrophobic with Mara's friends and their chatter. When the doorbell rang for the final time, Cameron knew it had to be *her*. He gave his sister another look, hoping she would behave.

When he opened the door, he noticed Delilah had on real clothes. She wore denims and a soft, blue jumper. It was too big, but at least it didn't look like she'd found it at the bottom of a pile at a charity shop. She pulled off her patchwork coat and hat, revealing a long, coppery braid. She was wearing furry boots again, this time in brown.

Cameron took her coat and offered, "Welcome."

She smiled. "So…this is where movie stars live?"

He returned the smile. "No. This is where I grew up."

Cameron led her to the kitchen where Mara was setting out food. His sister's hair was loose today, falling to her shoulders in black and silver waves, the same as his would be if he didn't color it.

Mara wiped her hands on her floral apron and looked Delilah over. With a hesitant smile, she offered her hand. "I'm Mara Hamilton, Cameron's sister. It's nice to meet you."

Delilah shook her hand and replied, "Delilah MacClare."

Tipping her head, Mara added, "MacClare? That's Scottish, is it not?"

"Yes. My grandfather, Gregory MacClare, was from Perth."

"Really?" Mara glanced over at Cameron with questions in her eyes.

Cameron was surprised, as well. That information was news to him.

"Have you ever been there?" Mara pressed.

"No." Delilah shook her head. "He and my grandmother, Elizabeth, came to the States during the war. The house here in Chatfield belonged to her family. She was an only child, so she inherited the house when her parents died. Now it's my father's."

"Well, Cameron, you didn't tell me that your friend had such deep roots here." Mara gave him a long look.

He shrugged. "I didn't know."

Hands on her hips, Mara retorted, "You know her well enough to invite her to Christmas lunch, but you don't know where she's from?"

"Technically," Delilah interjected, "I'm from West Virginia."

"Really?" Cameron looked at her in surprise again.

Delilah laughed. "Guilty."

"You don't sound it," Cameron stated.

"Well, you don't get very far in auditions if you sound like you just stumbled off a mountain."

He wanted to ask her about her use of the word "auditions," but Mara spoke first.

"What *have* the two of you talked about?"

They met each other's eyes and Delilah said, "Books, mostly. Cameron has convinced me to finally read *Heir of Taivas*."

Mara finally dropped her guard. "Well, that's something he knows a great deal about. I *will* give him that."

The change in subject caused Aida to pipe up with, "My daughter is positively in love with you, Cameron. I don't have the heart to tell her how very boring you really are."

"Boring?" He retorted.

"As compared to being a magical vagabond from another realm? Yes, boring," Aida returned.

"I might be smitten myself, if I didn't know you so well," Beth added.

Aida and Beth were two of a kind. They both had short hair that might've been brown or blonde once. They were built short and sturdy with hands worn from years of caregiving.

"Cameron doesn't need any more admirers," Mara added. Her face smiled, but there was an edge to her voice.

Cameron caught Delilah's eyes and rolled his, hoping she wouldn't take his sister and her friends too seriously.

After a few more minutes, they sat down to eat. Mara fell into easy conversation with her co-workers and Cameron had to admit that they all knew how to make a meal. Delilah seemed to appreciate the cooking as well, and he actually got to see her eat. Her hands gracefully held the silverware, and her slender fingers tipped the wineglass to her lips. He wondered, for the first time, exactly how old she was. Thirty-five? Forty? Her eyes made her look older. Her clothes made her look younger. She didn't say much throughout the meal, but she listened. She smiled at the stories Mara and her friends told, and she listened as they asked him for stories of filming *Heir of Taivas*. Cameron was used to people being in awe of his role in the franchise. He wouldn't admit it aloud, but he was protective of the part he played. He also liked the attention.

Delilah, however, didn't hang on his every word. Occasionally, she looked impressed, but never in the starry-eyed way of his fans. Between his stories and Mara's, she answered the questions she was asked. Cameron knew most of it. Her father was in the States. She had no other family here. She was as vague as always about her reasons for coming to Chatfield. She was determined to give up her secrets slowly, like a puzzle with a thousand pieces and no instructions.

When dinner was over, Delilah stayed for a bit while they all finished the wine. She sipped slowly, watching those around her wind up their conversations as the afternoon sun sank lower in the winter sky.

Before she could say her goodbyes, Cameron pulled Delilah aside. While the others chatted in the lounge, he led her through the dining room and into the kitchen. From one of the cupboards, he pulled a plain gift bag.

"Here. I got you something in London."

Her eyes widened with surprise. It struck him how much taller he was than she. He had more than a foot on her. She looked up and took the bag from him.

"I didn't get you anything," she stated without much apology.

"I didn't think you would."

Delilah pulled open the bag. Her face lit up in the widest, most genuine smile he'd ever seen on her. One by one, she pulled out each of the five volumes of *Heir of Taivas*. She kept smiling as she carefully looked over each, then placed them back in the bag, which sagged under their weight.

"I thought you should have your own," he offered. "So, if you get miffed and storm out on me again, at least you won't have my books."

She looked up, and he gave her a tiny smile. He was, for the most part, teasing.

"Thank you." Her gratitude was sincere.

Cameron half expected her to hug him, because she looked so pleased, but when he started to put his hand on her arm, she backed away. There was no other reaction, and she still looked quite happy. However, he sensed she had drawn a line he couldn't cross. He wasn't sure that she was aware of the invisible defense she'd raised, but it was clear there would be no touching. Knowing better than to push her, he walked her to the door while she continued to voice her thanks. When they had said goodbye and the door closed behind her, Cameron turned to find Mara waiting for him.

"What was that?" She demanded.

Facing off with her over the back of the sofa, he asked, "What?"

"You're exchanging gifts with her?"

Cameron sighed in exasperation. "You and I exchanged gifts this morning. It's Christmas for God's sake."

"We're family." Mara plowed on, "What is she?"

"I gave her *books*, Mara. Why are you interrogating me?"

His sister dropped her shoulders and her voice softened as she answered, "Because I know you. You've been sneaking girls out of that bedroom upstairs since you were barely old enough to pass your A Levels."

Cameron gave her an incredulous look. "I think it has been some time since I have either brought someone into, or snuck someone out of, that bedroom."

"You know what I mean." Mara pushed, "It's not only about the ones here. Your bedroom seems to have a revolving door."

Cameron rolled his eyes and argued, "There haven't been that many, Mara."

"Perhaps. But it's convenient how your partner seems to change as often as your current project changes."

Cameron felt anger boil to the surface. She had no right to judge his behavior. She had no right to force her moral compass on him. He had never *intentionally* hurt anyone, and he didn't intend to in the future.

Sensing his temper, Mara took a deep, calming breath. "I'm sorry. But I've seen how the fans look at you. I've seen them screaming that they love you and I know what they write about you on the internet. With the amount of time you spend on that phone or some other gadget, I would think you would know, as well."

He rubbed his eyes. "Mara, contrary to what you may think, I do not sleep with arbitrary fans from the internet."

She crossed her arms and stared him down. "So you say."

"She's not like them," Cameron shot back at her.

Mara's brow raised, and he knew that wasn't the answer she expected.

"A month ago, when I met her, she had no idea who I was. I still don't think she really knows the public me," he explained.

"And you believe that?" Mara asked carefully.

"Yes," he stated without hesitation.

She didn't argue.

"It's just nice to have a person I can really talk to. And I gave her *books*. What could be less romantic than books?"

With more wisdom than anger, Mara answered, "I would think you, of all people, would know the power of books."

4
Ships in the Night

Ships that pass in the night, and speak each other in passing,
Only a signal shown and a distant voice in the darkness;
So on the ocean of life we pass and speak one another,
Only a look and a voice, then darkness again and a silence.

—From "Tales of a Wayside Inn" by Henry Wadsworth Longfellow

A week later, on New Year's Eve, Delilah was curled in the recliner in her living room reading a book. She had devoured it over the last few hours and was nearing the end. *Heir of Taivas: The Seven Summits* was rife with surprises and new information, and the thrill of the story was the *only* thrill Delilah wanted as she heralded another year. While the rest of the world partied around her, she did what she'd done for the last few years and wrapped herself in the comfort of a good book:

> *Marcus explained, "You are an Eperra, like me, but Jermias believes you are of his lineage. That means you are allowed to sit with the Arches-Asterion as an Heir of Taivas. You can convince the seven sisters to open the gateways to Taivas, but it will not be easy. The Acclans will fight us. And the sisters are not easily convinced."*
>
> *Mohara listened intently.*
>
> *"The gateways to Taivas are found on seven points high in the mountains on Earth. Man calls them the Seven Summits. There is*

quite a lot of interest in them, but most of your people have forgotten why. The seven sisters are: Hekkuma, who lives atop Aconcagua and can be seduced into giving passage; Massyllu inhabits Denali and will move aside at the promise of a feast; Ahnause lives on Uhuru and gives passage for gold; Lyskyinan makes her home on Puncak Jaya and mostly cannot be bothered to block passage at all. Most Eperra make their way to and from Taivas this way. Veeha lives on Alborz and few pass this way because of her vicious anger. Katteous inhabits Vinson and will let you by for the price of one of your most valuable possessions. Then there is Ilpeythis, who lives atop Chomolungma and must be constantly convinced of her own value."

"You expect me to remember all of that?" Mohara asked.

"If you plan to succeed," Marcus snapped.

Mohara's expression turned pensive. "And we must convince them all to open the gateways?"

"Yes."

"Amy and Alex will be our enemies, if we do."

"Hopefully," Marcus stated, "they will come to understand."

Mohara hesitated. "This is a dangerous plan. I know Chomolungma. Many people don't survive it."

Marcus quickly replied, "I will keep you safe at all costs. But you will know what to do. The mountain is in you, because you were born in her valleys. She knows you."

Mohara looked up at him, trying to feel as confident as he sounded.

Needing a break, Delilah stopped reading and dropped the book on the table. At 762 pages, this one was the longest, and the story was weaving itself into complexities that she needed time to absorb. She let it all roll over in her mind, and she wanted to share her thoughts. Looking around her empty apartment, Delilah felt a familiar pang in her chest. She considered calling her father, but he would have no idea what she was talking about. If a book was written after 1970, it was a hard sell to get him to read it. Picking up her phone, she decided to text Cameron. She wasn't sure if she knew him well enough for it to be appropriate, but she decided to take the chance:

> I can't decide whose side I'm on, the Acclans or Taivas. I feel like Mohara is going to have to choose at some point. I feel like Marcus regrets agreeing to find her in exchange for money and a title. There's so much. My mind is full.
>
> Delilah.

A few minutes later, Cameron replied:

And you're only halfway through the story.

C.

> I have about three hundred pages of this one left.

Where are you?

> At home. Where else?

It's New Year's Eve. How old are you?

> How old are YOU?

Touché. But at least I'm out of my house.

Where are you?

The Quill and Fiddle. They
have a New Year's get-
together every year.

Like a party?

The real party is down the
street. Those of us who are
too old for partying meet
here and remind each other
to take our medicine before
midnight.

Hahaha. I hope it's fun. Don't
drink too much. Or break a
hip.

That's just mean.

I'm going to try to finish the
book now.

You should. And then come
down here and we'll talk
about it.

I'm good here. It's cold and
dark outside.

Maybe. But it's warm and
there's wine in here. I even
got Mara to come.

I'd rather just read.

Trust me, you're going to
want to talk about it.

Maybe another time.

Ok. Suit yourself.

Delilah put the phone down, but the smile stayed on her face.
The banter was nice. It felt comfortable and easy. It felt familiar. She

glanced over at the vintage suitcase she kept by the front window. It was locked tight, giving away none of its secrets. She stared at it for several minutes before making herself pick up her book and resume reading. Forty-five minutes later she read:

"I can't travel with you anymore, Marcus. You lied to me! This has all been for your own gain. I have no reason to believe you want to expose Taivas for anything other than spite. You've used me!"

Marcus stared at her, not denying it.

"I have to continue on my own."

"You won't make it," he stated harshly.

"I can call on..."

"Amy and Alex won't help you. They're Acclans to the death."

Mohara took a deep breath, looked Marcus in the eye and said, "Then I will go on my own."

He stared at her then stated gruffly, "So be it."

Mohara watched him go, leaving her alone in the swirling snow.

Delilah set the book down. She was forced to admit Cameron was right. She did want to talk about it. So, in spite of herself, she decided to go out. She wrapped up in her coat, hat, and gloves, leaving everything else on the kitchen counter in her haste.

When she walked through the heavy door of the pub, she noticed a few people turn to look at her. She'd made no real effort to get to know anyone in town, although the owners of the local market had started to recognize her. Some of them were curious about her. The nosy nature of those who inhabited small towns was universal. Delilah wasn't fazed by their curiosity, however.

Scanning the room, she was relieved to find it occupied by people chatting in groups or watching the television in the corner.

There was wine and food, and everyone seemed to be having a very tame kind of fun. Delilah relaxed. This wasn't the wild party she feared. Clearly, that was down the street at the tavern called Hannigan's. She could feel the thrum of the music in the floor of the pub and was glad not to be there. This was enough of a change for her. The chatter and laughter around her were soothing.

Suddenly, a well-modulated voice purred in her ear, "So you decided to give the old people's party a chance?"

Delilah turned and smiled. "The book made me come."

"Brilliant. No one should be alone on New Year's Eve."

"I wasn't alone."

"Books are not companions."

"Yes, they are," Delilah retorted without hesitation.

"All right, point conceded." Cameron pulled her over toward the fire and asked, "What part of the story got you out of your house?"

"I'm halfway through *Seven Summits*. Marcus and Mohara just fought with each other and went their own ways. I'm not sure who I'm pulling for right now. They're all so flawed, so human, even though they're part of this supernatural story."

"Now you see why I insisted you read them before watching the movies?"

"I've always preferred books to movies. I was just surprised to hear an *actor* say that."

"You assume that we are all narcissistic prats?"

"You haven't convinced me you're not...yet."

Cameron laughed. With a wave of his hand, he ordered two glasses of wine. It was then that Delilah noticed other people looking her way. It was subtle, but there were glances and whispered words. Some of them smiled, while others tried to hide their curiosity. She also realized it wasn't her that they were interested in. It was her *with him*.

Turning back to Cameron, she said, "I'm starting to see how very famous you are."

He flicked his eyes around the room then back to her. "Ignore it. Most of them are only interested in us because they know Mara. They know too much about me to really hold me in any sort of esteem. I think they're more curious about you."

"If only I was as interesting as they think," she murmured.

"Maybe you are."

Before Delilah could reply, a waiter brought glasses of white wine. She immediately took a long drink, and it was good. Mara crossed to them then, and Delilah's attention went to her. Once again, there was no denying that this woman was Cameron's sister. With her salt and pepper hair pulled up in a perfectly careless knot, the likeness to her brother was especially obvious tonight. Mara descended on them, with her sharp, hazel eyes taking in every detail. Her flowing black dress made Delilah suddenly feel underdressed. She turned back to Cameron, noting his dark pants and open collar shirt. No one was in black tie, but they certainly weren't wearing sweatpants like her.

"Delilah!" Mara smiled and took her hands. "It's lovely to see you again."

"Thank you. Cameron convinced me to come out."

"Did he?" Mara glanced at her brother.

Cameron shrugged and sipped his wine. "She was reading at home. By herself."

Delilah tipped her head to the side. "Guilty."

"Well," Mara smiled. "I'm glad you came. We want you to have wonderful memories of Chatfield."

Someone across the room called out to Mara, and she walked away. When Delilah turned around, Cameron had secured two chairs by the fire. Grateful, she took one across from him. She slipped out of her coat and winter wear and sipped wine as they talked. When Delilah arrived, it was just after ten o'clock. As they discussed the complexities of *Heir of Taivas*, however, time slipped through her fingers. Before she knew it, someone turned up the television and the wine was replaced with champagne. Delilah started to decline the drink, but Cameron confessed he'd bought the champagne for all the guests.

"Movie star perks?" She quipped.

He shrugged as though buying champagne for a hundred people was equivalent to offering everyone chewing gum.

"To new friends?" He offered, holding up his glass.

She clinked her flute with his. "To unexpected friends."

Realizing how close it was to midnight, Delilah glanced nervously around. The others in the pub were huddling with friends or their significant others. London glittered on the television and occasional laughter trilled over the hum of excitement.

Setting down her glass, she said, "I should go."

Cameron frowned. "It's almost midnight. Stay."

She shook her head, her stomach knotting. "No. I like to be home by midnight."

He looked at her oddly. "Is your carriage turning back into a pumpkin?"

She tried to laugh, but it stuck in her throat.

Softening, he pushed, "Stay. It's a tame party. I promise. We toast the New Year, then we play cards because we're all too old to dance."

Delilah laughed and her worry abated just a touch. She glanced at the clock. She couldn't make it home now, even if she was capable of running. She took another sip of champagne in an effort to calm herself and watched the television. The others around her grew more excited. After several more minutes, she listened as the new year was counted in. At midnight, a cheer arose. Laughter and some singing ensued, but nothing more. Delilah let out a long breath, relieved.

Then, it started. In the logical part of her brain, the part that merely relayed information, she knew it was fireworks. She knew the noises she heard outside were made of light and color, and were part of a harmless celebration. She realized that the revelers down the street were having some harmless fun. However, the part of her brain that responded to it was buried deeper, in a more primal place. Logic was bypassed and self-preservation took over. She started to shake, and all sounds but the boom and crack of the fireworks faded away.

As her trembling grew worse, Delilah sat her glass down on the nearest table. Now shaking violently, she pulled herself deep into the chair. Tucking her knees under her chin, she covered her ears with her hands and squeezed her eyes closed. Fighting the tightness in her chest, she tried to muffle the cracking explosions on the street outside. She tried to mentally go somewhere else, to shut out everything but her racing heart.

After a minute, she realized Cameron was in front of her trying to get her attention.

"Delilah?"

"No!" She snapped.

"Delilah, what's the matter?" He tried again, his voice genuinely concerned.

"Please make them stop," was all she could say. "It has to stop. Make it stop. I can't…I can't…please!"

She shouted the last word, and a few people close to them turned to see who was yelling. But Delilah didn't notice them. Her focus shifted entirely inward, and her eyes were tightly shut. She didn't see Mara come over and push Cameron aside. She didn't know it was Mara holding her arms and softly saying comforting words. Out of habit, Delilah started fumbling for her bag. After several seconds of reaching with her eyes still shut, she remembered she'd left her bag, and therefore her medicine, at home. She put her hands back around her head, covering her ears. She took more deep breaths, trying to find calm, trying to breathe the way she'd been taught.

After a few minutes, the fireworks outside finally stopped. Most of the people in the pub made their way outside to enjoy the show. When Delilah opened her eyes and looked around, she saw that a few people stayed to stare at her. Glancing at Mara, who was kneeling in front of her, and Cameron, who was to her left, she saw the concern on their faces. Trying to hide her trembling hands, she stood up suddenly and reached for her coat and hat.

"I should get home," she threw out, retrieving her coat from the back of the chair. She could barely walk, but her instinct was to run.

"Delilah," Cameron spoke up from behind her, "maybe you should sit down for a bit longer?"

She shook her head hard. She needed to get home to her medicine in order to calm the racing of her heart.

"Please let us make sure you're okay," Mara added, her nurse's training showing itself.

"I'm fine." Delilah pulled on her coat, fished her hat out of the pocket and pulled it on. "But I need to go home."

Putting her hands in her pockets rather than finding her gloves, she headed out the door and into the night. She was still shaking, but out here she could blame it on the cold. Cameron was pulling on his own coat and gloves when he caught up to her. He laid a hand on her shoulder, but she jerked away.

Whipping around, she spat, "I'm fine. I'm not going to die or anything."

Cameron was taken aback. "I didn't think you were going to die. But I also do not think you're *fine*."

She plowed ahead, making her way through the crowd of people who came outside to enjoy the fireworks. They were now hugging and celebrating and singing in the new year in the frigid night. Delilah walked right past them. Cameron kept in step with her, undeterred. His legs were much longer than hers, and her lungs protested her walking faster.

When they turned the corner and left the revelers behind, he said, "It would make me a bloody prick not to walk you home. And I can't have it getting around that I'm a prick, now can I?"

Delilah wasn't ready to laugh, but his usual banter was comforting. They walked in silence the rest of the distance from the pub to Delilah's home. At this late hour, it was bitterly cold. By the time they arrived, she really wasn't sure if the shaking was from her panic attack or from the cold. Her head felt clearer, but her pulse still raced. Taking a minute to catch her breath, she closed her eyes to keep her head from spinning.

On the steps leading to the heavy front door, Cameron turned toward her. Searching her face, he asked, "Are you going to be all right?"

"I'm fine. I just don't like fireworks."

Cameron looked at her as though he knew it was a flimsy excuse. "I know we don't know each other all that well but, if you need anything," he hesitated, "Mara would love to help, being a nurse and all…"

Delilah tried to smile. "Please tell her thank you."

He looked her over again, obviously struggling with what to say. Delilah was grateful he took the time to walk with her. She did feel a little calmer, but she needed him to go. She needed space tonight.

After another few seconds, Cameron turned and walked down the steps. He turned back long enough to watch her open the door. Delilah couldn't meet his eyes, though. She went inside quickly, crossed the hall, and entered the sanctuary of her home. Twenty minutes later, she was in bed, letting the pharmaceuticals numb her to sleep.

Cameron allowed Delilah her space over the weekend. She didn't ask for further help, and he didn't feel it was his place to push himself on her. They had only known each other for a little over a month. He enjoyed her company, but he had no right to her personal life. He also wasn't sure that he wanted her to share her secrets with him. He was afraid he would have no idea what to say.

However, on Monday, when she didn't show up at the pub, he decided to send her a brief text. She seemed to be okay with chatting that way, so he asked:

Just making sure you're all right?

C.

Fine. Don't worry.

Cameron decided to leave it at that. He couldn't press any further without implying she wasn't fine and asking questions that felt inappropriate. So he let her be. Instead, he absently scrolled through different apps on his phone. As a result of his career, Cameron had an active presence on social media. He felt that if anyone should be speaking for him through these outlets, it should be him. He also liked to feel he was up to date on the world. Mara teased him about it, saying he lived for retweets, but he didn't care. As he checked his email, an idea struck him.

Pulling up his web browser, he typed in Delilah's name, guessing at the spelling of her last name. Since she claimed to have direct ties to Scotland, he went with the traditional spelling. He scrolled through the results, finding several other people's Facebook pages and Twitter accounts. There were listings of name meanings and ads for finding long lost relatives. Delilah certainly didn't have any sort of past that was newsworthy. At least, not as far as a basic web search was concerned. She also didn't have any social media accounts of her own. Still, he kept scrolling, looking for even the most obscure mention of her. After several minutes, he stumbled upon something buried many pages into the search. Clicking the link, he found himself looking at an archived magazine article from 1994. It described a music video by a well-known American singer of the time:

> The video features one of the most unique elements to be used as of late, an aerialist. Performing on the Spanish web, aerialist Delilah MacClare elevates this pop single video to something more like art. She takes a sensual ballad and turns it into a thing of beauty. In fact, she runs the risk of upstaging up-and-coming singer Shariah Stone and proving herself to be the real star of this video.

Cameron scrolled down and looked at the photos. There were several grainy images of Delilah hanging by her wrist and ankle from a thick rope. Clicking back, he scrolled again until he found another article. This one was from a few years later and was about the premiere of a show in Las Vegas. There were several professional photos included, and at least two of them were of Delilah. She was younger and her hair was smooth, straight, and pulled into a bun, but it was definitely her. She was wrapped somehow in black fabric and hanging high off the ground. For a second, he thought she was nude, but he realized she had on tan shorts and some sort of tan, cropped tank top. She was posed exquisitely, with her toes perfectly pointed and her arms splayed beautifully. She was tiny, but far from frail. Every sinew and muscle were accented by the light, showing the strength it took to hang so effortlessly. The photographer caught her in the middle of an aerial dance in which she was climbing and twisting herself to music he couldn't hear. Another photo showed her hanging by one bent leg, her face serene despite the obvious physical strain.

Cameron was floored. He never expected this from the girl who read romance novels while wearing ancient tracksuit bottoms. He assumed she had some sort of life outside Chatfield, but this surprised him. He wanted to know this side of her. However, more than that, he wanted to know why she gave it up. Natural curiosity filled him, and he saved the photos. At some point, when she seemed calm, he would ask.

The next morning was a wet Tuesday. Rain was a way of life in this land of lush countryside, muddy streets, and gray skies, but winter rain wasn't just wet. It was cold, the kind of cold that permeated Cameron's clothes, chilled him to the bone, and formed icy puddles waiting to soak through his shoes. As much as he loved home, he would gladly trade January in England for any other month.

Standing just inside the door of The Quill and Fiddle, he shook off his coat and furled his umbrella. Stowing them both by the door, he worked at pulling off his scarf and gloves as he crossed to his booth. His mood improved instantly when he saw Delilah had returned. There was an open book in front of her, but she was staring into the mirror that hung on the wall over the table. That much, at least, was normal. Sliding carefully into the seat across from her, he watched her startle when she realized he was there.

She gave a weak smile. "I guess I didn't scare you away forever?"

Cameron chuckled. "No. This is my booth. You would have to have the plague to get rid of me. The actual plague."

"The Great Plague or the Ebola virus?" Delilah asked with a smirk.

"Does it really matter?"

Delilah shrugged. "Maybe. I'd have to weigh the symptoms and type of death against how much I might want to get rid of you."

Cameron laughed. He was glad to see she hadn't lost her sense of humor. He called Flora over to order tea, and Delilah asked for coffee. She seemed to be back to normal.

Casually, he asked, "What are you reading?"

Glancing at the ragged paperback under her hands, she said, "A book of poetry. I've had it forever. It was the perfect gift for a creative teenager who was also full of angst." She closed the book. "I used to try to write poems, before I realized I was a terrible poet."

Cameron laughed and reached for the book. She handed it over and he flipped through the pages, noting the classical works among lesser-known authors.

Without warning, Delilah bluntly addressed the elephant in the room. "I have panic attacks."

Cameron handed her book back. "All right."

"Does that freak you out?"

He smirked. "I'm an actor, Delilah. I've seen people lose their shit over chocolate biscuits."

She looked confused. "Biscuits?"

"Cookies," he clarified.

Delilah couldn't help laughing. "Seriously?"

"Unfortunately, yes," he deadpanned.

"Well, I have no issues with cookies. Or biscuits," she assured him.

Cameron cleared his throat and grew serious again. "You know, if you need…anything, while you're here," he reconsidered his words, "Mara says you can ring her. The nurse in her wants to fix everything."

Delilah searched his face. "Tell her I said thank you, again."

"So," Cameron quickly changed the subject, "you're still reading my books?"

She pulled her copy of *Seven Summits* out of her bag. "Yes. I'm back at it." She paused. "I have to know if Marcus is good or bad, and if the twins reconcile with Mohara."

He crossed his arms and looked at her, his expression revealing nothing.

"Very good," she teased him. "Perfect ambiguity."

He was glad she was smiling. Whatever her troubles, she appeared to have them under control today. While sharing another plate of fish and chips, they talked for a bit about the last half of the book. She mused about her ideas as to where things were going, and he remained smugly silent. Inside, however, he was enjoying seeing someone travel the journey of *Heir of Taivas* with no preexisting ideas. It was gratifying to see someone else grab hold of and love the story to which he'd committed five years of his life.

When the conversation started to wind down, Cameron decided to ask her about the photos. It seemed like whatever troubles she had were brought on by a specific trigger, the fireworks, considering how quickly she returned to her version of normal. Panic attacks weren't that unusual. He wondered if maybe she had some sort of childhood accident with fireworks that caused them. While wondering those things, he pulled out his phone and scrolled to find the photos he saved.

As she sipped the last of her coffee, he laid the phone down in front of her and asked, "Is this really you?"

Delilah set her cup down. Very slowly, she picked up the phone and studied the photos. Her face was hard to read. She looked at them for a long time, as though she didn't quite believe they were real.

Finally, she put the phone down, slid it back toward him, and asked, "Where did you find those?"

"The internet," Cameron responded truthfully.

She looked down for a minute. When she met his eyes again, her expression was stormy. "Have you really so completely lost touch with how to relate to real people that you resort to digging up information on the internet?"

He wasn't sure what to say.

"Do you see me searching for every article and picture I can find about *you*?"

Cameron felt a twinge of anger, because even though she might have a point, he hadn't intended to be invasive.

"It's from an article in a magazine," he stated. "Anyone could find it."

"It doesn't mean that you *should!*" She retorted.

"Look, you don't have to talk about it. I'm not going to push you. I only found some photos."

Delilah stood up, grabbed her books and her bag, and started for the door.

Cameron stood and called after her, "Wait! I'm sorry! You don't have to…run away again."

But she was gone.

"Brilliant," he grumbled.

Cameron dropped back into the booth, frustrated, annoyed, and wondering why he was bothering with someone who might be certifiably mad.

Delilah fumed all the way home. Halfway down the rain-slick street she pulled on her coat, but not her hat or gloves. By the time she got home, her hands and face were frozen. She spent a few minutes coaxing a fire in the fireplace, then dropped onto the couch, tossing her winter apparel over a chair. She sat there, taking deep breaths, and cursed herself for walking so fast in the cold again. Her lungs felt like they were on fire, so she lay back on the couch and closed her eyes until she could breathe properly. Pulling herself up, she sat down on the rug in front of the fireplace and slowly stretched out each part of her body, making herself focus on her breathing.

Delilah's typical stretching routine was a combination of yoga and ballet exercises she put together for herself. Stretching and deep breathing were the only things that helped her anxiety, other than her medication. Sometimes, nothing but the medicine helped. But, today, thirty minutes of stretching calmed her significantly. Afterward, she sat up and focused on her feelings about Cameron again.

He had no right to pry, she told herself.

Meeting Cameron was such an unexpected surprise, and she didn't realize until now how much she was enjoying being a blank slate with him. He made her laugh at things she hadn't laughed at in years. He had no expectations of her, and his voice wasn't tinged with a thousand unspoken worries every time they talked. He had no underlying motives in making her smile. She didn't know how much she needed a friendship like that until today. Yet today, he broke the spell. She had to admit, he didn't mean to, but he did it all the same.

But you can't have a full-on panic attack in front of someone and not have them look for answers, she reasoned with herself.

Still, he could have asked her questions. He could have let *her* decide what to reveal. He took the choice away from her, and she couldn't help being angry about it. So she sat there and fumed, debating whether their short-lived friendship was now over. Then, an idea struck her. Retrieving her laptop, she flipped it open on the tiny coffee table.

Pulling up her internet browser, Delilah searched for Cameron Burke once again. This time, however, she went past his filmography and press photos. She looked for more detailed articles about him, and the more she read, the more interested she became. Pieces of the articles jumped out at her:

Cameron Burke, up-and-coming star, wed his co-star Marianne Agrietta just weeks after filming of his breakout film completed.

After only five years of marriage, their divorce was explosive and wrought with legal battles.

Tall, dark, and mysterious Cameron Burke has won the heart of another co-star.

It's rumored that no woman who plays opposite Cameron Burke is safe from his charms.

Actress Naomi Ruiz-Sosa speaks out about her stormy relationship with Cameron Burke.

Cameron Burke, who played sexy antihero Cyrus Whitkey in the three Fyrelords films, takes home the Oscar for his work in a brilliant new drama.

…has just come out and admitted his relationship with Broadway-turned-film-star Catherine Beckworth, proving their on-screen chemistry was rivaled only by the chemistry in their bedroom.

Up and coming British screenwriter Selena Bingham refuses to talk about her short-lived fling with Cameron Burke.

Clearly, Cameron made his living playing wild, charismatic leads, and his personal life paralleled his on-screen personas. Each new project ended with him paired with another woman. As she read, Delilah wondered what made him get married in the first place. She wondered why these women kept falling for him, given his history. However, she had to admit, there was something about tall, brooding Cameron Burke that made *her* keep talking to him. But that wasn't enough to make her fall for him.

The next thing Delilah did was look at his fan pages, and they were both impressive and disturbing. He had an almost cult following. There were fan message boards and fan blogs. Women around the world, ranging in age from teenagers to retirees, fawned over him. The last thing she found was a multitude of fan fiction stories featuring him and, after reading a few, they felt far too voyeuristic. So she shut the computer. She finally realized how many people would kill to sit across from him as she did almost every day.

Delilah leaned back on the couch and stared out the window. She thought about what she read and how it colored her perception of Cameron. She considered how she would have felt about meeting him if she watched all his movies or read his fan pages first. She knew, especially ten years ago, that her reaction would have been very different. She also realized that her complete lack of knowledge about him must be part of why he kept coming around. She took him at face value. And that's all Delilah wanted from him. She needed unbiased friendship and, until now, Cameron had inadvertently given her that.

We're good for each other. In a weird way.

The thought hit her quickly, but she held on to it. She rolled it over in her mind and weighed it against how angry she was with him. She felt some remorse for reading gossip about him for the last hour. On the other hand, this made them even.

Delilah was still mulling over it all when there was a buzzing sound, letting her know someone was at the main door. Delilah heaved herself off the couch and went to answer it, wondering if her neighbors locked themselves out again. She was taken aback when she found Cameron on the steps outside the front door.

Standing tall before her, he said, "Forgive me for coming to your home without ringing, but I thought you might not answer the phone."

Delilah started to agree with him, but he stopped her.

"I just want to say...I'm sorry." His eyes flicked away for a second. "I shouldn't have pried into your life. I know how that feels."

She felt her anger lessening as he echoed her own thoughts.

"I meet people all the time who have read all about me and have made all kinds of assumptions."

Delilah felt another twinge of guilt for doing just that.

He put his hands in his pockets and went on, "The truth is, talking to you has been…wonderfully different. And I don't want to lose that."

She just looked at him, trying to decide if she wanted to forgive him.

Cameron glanced down at the ground. "I also want you to know that you don't have to share anything with me. We can just talk about books. Or weather. Or whatever you choose. I won't look you up again. But, your photos are beautiful. And you will always have that moment of beauty. No matter what has happened or will happen, that is part of you, forever. And it was beautiful."

Delilah was taken aback. He said all of that in a very offhanded way, throwing it out there as though she could take it or leave it. Yet he reached something in her that hadn't been touched in a long time. For a second, she felt every fiber of her being light up, and she remembered passion and hope and drive. Just as quickly, she shook it off. What she was left with was the reluctant admission that she wasn't mad at him anymore.

Offering him a slight smile, all she could think to say was, "Thank you. And it's okay. I overreacted."

"Tomorrow, then?" He asked hesitantly.

"I'm not sure. But, maybe."

He started to walk away, but she stopped him by saying, "Cameron?"

He turned around.

"I can talk about me, and my life. I should. And I will. Everything isn't a secret. But I have some things that have to stay locked up for right now. Does that make sense?"

Looking at her with his steely, hazel eyes, Cameron answered, "That's all you have to say."

He walked away, and Delilah watched him go. As he strode down the wet street, she couldn't help thinking that he was beautiful in his own way, too. Whatever he did in the past, he would always have this moment when he walked a mile in the rain to save a friendship he didn't need. And Delilah felt that *this* is what should matter. Not who they were. Not where they'd been. This. Now.

Turning suddenly, she hurried back through the vestibule and into her apartment. She crossed to dig in her shoulder bag that she dropped by the sofa. Pulling out her poetry anthology, she flipped the pages until she found the passage:

Ships that pass in the night, and speak each other in passing,
Only a signal shown and a distant voice in the darkness;
So on the ocean of life we pass and speak one another,
Only a look and a voice, then darkness again, and a silence.

She read over the familiar lines a few times. No matter how many times she read this book, she could find something that spoke to her. Today, it was Longfellow. She and Cameron came from very different places and, soon enough, they would head into very different futures. But, for now, they would "*speak each other in passing.*"

5
Things Are as They Are

'Twas clever, handsome woman then,
and I their rising star;
I could not see they worshipped me,
because I saw too far.
'Tis well for one or two, I think,
that things are as they are.

—From "And What Have You to Say?" by Henry Lawson

The following Saturday, Cameron sat on his couch sipping red wine and listening to Mara chat with their longtime friends James and Moira. He promised them a dinner during his extended stay at home and Mara made sure it happened. He had to admit, he was glad. Talking with people with whom he attended secondary school was another welcome change from the past year or so. They knew him well enough not to judge but didn't hold him in impossible esteem or pester him like Mara's coworkers.

Moira and James, who were Scandinavian in their ancestry, had a few acres of land just outside of town. They kept sheep and goats, and otherwise lived off the money from the sale of the real estate company they ran for thirty years. It wasn't Cameron's choice of retirement, but it was what they always wanted. Overall, they looked like two people who were satisfied with their life.

As Cameron sipped his wine, Mara explained to their friends, "Cameron is staying until April. Except for the required press events, he's taking an actual break from fame."

Moira asked, "Really?"

"Yes. I promised Mara. I promised myself. I've made seventeen films in ten years. I think I deserve a few months away," Cameron replied.

"I would say so," Moira agreed wholeheartedly.

Cameron raised his glass in a casual toast, and they continued to chat for several more minutes. It was nice to listen to normal people talk about their jobs and their normal troubles. He felt like he'd returned from a journey to some alien planet where people lived on vegan smoothies and worried about the thread count of their pajamas.

Just as they were close to finishing a bottle of wine, Cameron felt his phone vibrate. He pulled it out, intending to ignore it, but he recognized his agent's number.

"Please excuse me," he said as he left the lounge to take the call in his bedroom upstairs.

"Charlie?" He answered.

"Cameron!" The voice boomed at him through the earpiece. Charlie Friedman had a distinct, south London drawl and a particular affinity for talking far too loudly. In an arrangement they found mutually beneficial, Charlie acted as both agent and manager, and Cameron trusted him. After almost thirteen years together, it was accurate to say they had each other's best interests at heart, and often their meetings devolved into the two of them drinking in a pub like old school mates.

"Everything all right in the city?" Cameron asked somewhat rhetorically.

"Smashing. I think I'm still a bit pissed from New Year's. You?"

Cameron chuckled. "It's quieter here. But it's a nice change."

"Well, rest up, because I have something for you to look at, for after *Taivas*," Charlie offered suggestively.

"Already? What is it?" Cameron was genuinely surprised.

"Schuster is looking to green-light one more installment in the *Fyrelords* series. Cyrus Whitkey rides again," Charlie explained.

Cameron was slightly taken aback. "We wrapped that nine years ago."

"Exactly. It's the right time to capitalize on the nostalgia and grab a whole new audience. And you know Schuster. If he can milk that franchise for a few million more pounds, he's ready to do so."

Cameron sighed and rubbed his eyes. *Fyrelords,* another book-series-turned-film-series, was the franchise that rebooted his career after many years of chasing the success he had in the early days. In the trilogy, he played the role of Cyrus Whitkey, a stallion-riding rebel who despised authority. The story was set in a post-apocalyptic society of humans ruled by humanoid aliens. In the story, Cyrus and several other key characters live in the "wilds," refusing to be governed by the alien rulers. Cameron thought it to be redundant and somewhat stereotypical when he first read the novels, but the films were incredibly successful. Cyrus Whitkey became one of the most recognizable characters in the world. Cameron knew the role of Cyrus, along with his riding skills, helped land him the part of Marcus Eperra in *Heir of Taivas.* Still, he was imagining twelve or more weeks of filming on horseback in Texas or Arizona, and it wasn't exactly the next project he was hoping for. And he was starting to feel typecast.

Landing on another issue, he asked, "Has Schuster approached any of the other cast?"

Charlie answered, "Chad's nipping at the idea already. You know he hasn't had much luck these last few years."

"And…Naomi?" Cameron pressed.

"Maybe as a cameo," Charlie retorted, "but she's much too old for the female lead. Schuster wants Tara Ford. She's all the rage in the States."

Cameron laughed harshly. "Naomi's too old? Then what about me? And isn't this Tara about twenty-five?"

Charlie laughed easily. "She's twenty-nine. But everyone knows, with women, younger sells. You could be eighty and women will still swoon, but Naomi is playing mothers and politicians now. I'm sure they'll offer her a cameo, for the fans. But Cyrus needs a beautiful girl to fall in love with him."

Growing more and more frustrated, Cameron asked, "All right, but didn't Cyrus and Elianna get married after the last one? It was very much implied. How do you rewrite that?"

"Who knows. They'll sort it somehow. If we have you and Chad, and if they get Chesney back, it will be a hit," Charlie explained with excitement.

Cameron rubbed his eyes and sat down on the bed. "So, it doesn't matter if the story is utter shit as long as we can sell it on the coattails of success from ten years ago?"

Not missing a beat, Charlie answered, "That's how this works, Cameron. Sometimes, artistry is great. Most of the time, it's all about making money. You know that."

Cameron wasn't sure there was enough money in the world to make him want to work with Naomi again.

Charlie continued, "Just think about it. And if seeing Naomi is an issue, we'll make sure you don't shoot together."

Cameron sighed. "I'll consider it."

"It would be a great one to go out on," Charlie added carelessly.

"Go out?" Cameron snapped back. "Are you assuming I'll drop dead soon?"

"No one lives forever, Cameron. This could be big. Just think about it. You could fuck Tara Ford. You know how many people want to do that before they die?"

"You're a filthy tosser, Charlie. You know that?" Cameron threw out.

"I know," Charlie agreed, "but I also know *you*. And I know you loved this part. This trilogy made us both filthy fucking rich. So think about it."

Cameron stood up from the bed. "I will. Just give me some time. We've not even wrapped *Heir of Taivas* yet."

"Time is money and all that shit," Charlie threw back, "but you know that. Enjoy your holiday, or whatever you're calling it. And don't forget that you have dubbing and press shots next month."

"I know." Cameron rolled his eyes. "I have done this before."

"Sod off," Charlie said through laughter.

"Same to you," Cameron shot back before hanging up the phone. Charlie was absolutely foul sometimes, but it was just his brand of friendship.

Cameron stared at his phone, considering the proposition. Then he filed it away in his mind. Mara, James, and Moira would be wondering what became of him.

The following Monday marked seven straight days of rain. Delilah usually didn't mind it, but it made the walk to the pub far less pleasant. She spent the weekend inside reading by the fire, so the idea of going outside today was not appealing. But she wanted to talk about the books. Cameron was the only person with whom she could talk about the story in which she was immersed. She hated to admit it, but she missed him.

Delilah walked slowly, which was easier on her body but worse on her hair and clothes. By the time she got to The Quill and Fiddle, she was covered in a fine mist that clung to her auburn curls. Once inside, she was glad for the familiarity of the big fireplace and Flora's genuine smile. Crossing to the usual booth, Delilah found Cameron was already there. He had tea in front of him and his phone in his hand. He was so engrossed in it that he didn't realize she was there until she took off her hat and coat and sat across from him.

"Delilah." He acknowledged her and set the phone down.

"Cameron," she greeted him in return.

"It's been almost a week."

Delilah shrugged. "It's been rainy. I like rain. I don't like being wet."

Cameron smiled. "That…is confusing."

Delilah shrugged again.

"So, are you still reading?"

"Yes." Delilah hesitated. "But first, I have a confession."

He arched one eyebrow perfectly.

"I Googled you. Again."

Cameron gave her a confused look.

"I looked you up on the internet. I mean, I did it once before, but that was just because I had no idea who you played in the movies. This time, I read everything I could find."

Cameron put his elbows on the table and rested his chin on his hands. "And?"

"And, I'm sorry I did it. I was angry."

He sat back and folded his arms over his chest. "And what do you think of me, after your search?"

Delilah was taken aback. She hadn't expected that question. She assumed he wouldn't want to talk about the specifics of his past or that he would deny it as all being tabloid rubbish. Pursing her lips, Delilah thought about it. She considered her answer very carefully before speaking:

"I grew up in West Virginia, in a little place called Branton. My father teaches English at the local high school. My mother was a classically trained opera singer. She grew up on Long Island, but she ran off with my dad when he graduated from NYU. I've trained in a variety of circus arts, as well as dance, and I have performed as an aerialist all over the US. I did the Cirque show you saw the pictures from and a few others, as well as performing with The Big Apple Circus, Disney, and a few Broadway shows. I've never been married. Never had a long-term relationship. I was always more of a 'love the one you're with' type of person. I've lived a bit of a selfish life, if I'm totally honest."

Delilah fell silent, hoping Cameron would understand why she suddenly shared so much.

"You keep surprising me, Delilah MacClare."

She could tell that he meant it in a good way.

He blindsided her by asking bluntly, "How old are you?"

"Really?" She chastised him with one word.

Cameron smiled. "Oh, come now. You know *you're* wondering the same thing about me."

She couldn't deny it. "I'll be forty in March."

"Will you?" He looked genuinely surprised.

"I'm going to hope you thought I was younger," she shot back.

Cameron chuckled. "Yes."

She cocked her head to the side. "And you?"

"I'm sixty-one. And four months."

"That's…specific."

Cameron shrugged. "When you're my age, knowing exactly how old you are helps you remember exactly how old you are *not*."

Delilah laughed, unable to argue.

Cameron's expression turned serious again. "Delilah…what would you call…this? What are we?"

Delilah tried to keep smiling, but it didn't reach her eyes. She struggled with labels because she found relationships were easier when they remained ambiguous. She preferred for her and Cameron to be Schrödinger's cat—existing in multiple states without having to choose.

Ships that pass in the night, she thought once again.

Delilah took a deep breath. "I think…we're friends. I think there are twenty years and enough baggage between the two of us that we should stay…friends."

Cameron listened, his eyes darkened by the low lighting. His lips curved into a slight smile. "All right. If you insist. I wasn't sure that I liked you that much. But…friends."

The next time Cameron saw Delilah, it looked as if she hadn't moved in two days. He assumed she had gone home and that her clothes were different, although her wardrobe was hard to differentiate. Standing just inside the door of the pub, he wondered if she continued to wear drab, oversized clothes for all of summer, or if, at some point, when it became warm enough, she started to look like a woman rather than a homeless doll. He also wondered if she would still be around in the summer for him to find out.

You'll be gone by then, he realized.

Shaking off that fact before it could bother him, he crossed to Flora, who was wiping off tables on the far side of the room, and asked, "Has she been here since Monday?"

Flora glanced over at Delilah, who was holding a book open and staring into the mirror again. Flora laughed. "Yes and no. She read most o' both days. She goes home in t' late afternoon if you're not 'ere."

"I thought so. I couldn't come yesterday. I had a collection of tedious things to tend to," Cameron explained his absence.

Flora continued wiping tables. "Was she expectin' you in t' last coupl've days?"

"Not specifically."

"Did she ever tell you 'er story? Not tha' you 'ave to share it wit' me, but, after New Year's…is she all right?"

Cameron almost forgot that Delilah's panic attack took place in the pub in front of several people. Flora's concern was genuine, though, so he said, "I think she's fine."

Flora stopped cleaning and stood up straight. "I 'ope that's true. She just seems like such a sad 'un. Stares at t' wall or 'as 'er nose in a book. Dun't talk to anyone 'cept you."

Cameron wondered if he should take that as a compliment.

Flora continued, "I'm glad yer stayed in town this time, Cameron. I'd like t' think it's good for ye."

"*You're* good for me. You keep me humble." He flashed her a charming grin and ambled across the room to where Delilah sat. With his hands in the pockets of his black coat, he asked, "Is the mirror telling you something about the book that I don't know?"

Delilah turned away from the old, chipped mirror on the worn, paneled wall. She slowly registered that he was standing there and smiled.

"Can I join you?"

"You're asking?"

Cameron smiled broadly, pulled off his coat, and sat down.

"I've almost finished this one," she offered before he could ask her.

He noted the copy of *Seven Summits* in front of her. "More thoughts?"

Delilah's eyes were distant. "Maybe. I'm not sure."

"Are you upset?"

Delilah looked back at the wall. "I'm...I'm letting it settle."

His brow furrowed as he tried to decide what to ask. He wondered if she did something more than read the book, if something else happened

After a lengthy silence, she explained, "I just need to think for a bit. Can I just sit here?"

Her eyes were pleading, and Cameron couldn't argue with her. "Of course."

Delilah fell back into her thoughts, and she didn't speak for a long time. She sipped her coffee and stared into the distance or occasionally flipped through her book. Cameron pulled out his phone and proceeded to waste time. He was endlessly amazed at how many hours he could squander scrolling through his phone. Eventually, he ran out of messages to check and posts to read, so he checked the weather. It might as well have said, "You live in England." Setting the phone down, he watched Delilah as she stared into space. She took off her knit hat and he fixated on her hair. Her hat had flattened it somewhat on top, but it tumbled around her shoulders and down her back in a flow of waves and curls. It was completely unkempt and uncontrolled, but it shone like embers in places.

He blurted out, "Is that your natural hair?"

It took Delilah a moment to register what he said. When she did, she smiled demurely and pushed her hair back with her hands. "Unfortunately, yes."

"It's beautiful."

She dropped her hands and looked at him, her eyes begging questions.

Suddenly, Cameron imagined kissing her. He saw himself with his hands in her hair and his lips discovering hers. Abruptly, he cut off the thought. Making an excuse about having an appointment, he grabbed his coat and left the pub quickly, forcing himself not to look back.

6
And So Hold On

If you can make one heap of all your winnings
and risk it on one turn of pitch-and-toss,
and lose, and start again at your beginnings
and never breathe a word about your loss;
If you can force your heart and nerve and sinew
to serve your turn long after they are gone,
and so hold on when there is nothing in you
except the Will which says to them: "Hold on."

—From "If" by Rudyard Kipling

Over the next two weeks, Cameron had to turn his attention back toward work. As much as he was determined to make this a legitimate hiatus, he wasn't retired. He had to keep things going, and Charlie had a list of things that needed sorting. Amelia, his publicist, also needed his attention. By taking two trips to London and making several phone calls, Cameron worked through some of the less glamorous parts of being an actor. Details had to be confirmed for several appearances and photo shoots, the least of which was the *Heir of Taivas* premiere in July. It seemed simultaneously both far off and very, very close. He also had two scripts and a potential guest television role to consider. And Charlie continued to wheedle him about the offer to make another installment of the *Fyrelords* franchise.

In addition to his work, Cameron made a trip to the cemetery with Mara to visit their parents. He hated standing in the frosty grass, surrounded by death and trying to say the right thing to his sister. He loved his parents, but they were gone, and he would rather remember them from afar. Mara, however, brought lots of flowers and talked to them like they were standing next to her. She obviously needed this, so he endured his discomfort for her.

Before it seemed plausible, January was coming to a close. The weather, however, continued to deliver cold, damp, and gray days. As much as Cameron loved home, it was beginning to wear on him. He liked the privacy Chatfield provided, but he preferred the excitement and activity of London or New York. The endless dining and entertainment options in the city made winter more bearable. However, Delilah made winter in Chatfield more bearable.

On the final Friday of the month, Cameron returned to The Quill and Fiddle. He ordered tea from Flora and dropped into his booth. Pulling off his coat, he checked his phone for messages. He was still waiting on some interview dates and an email with the television script. When his tea came, he gave his attention to adding just the right amount of milk.

Suddenly, a book slapped on the table in front of him. Cameron startled, but before he could register what was happening, he was gifted with a solid strike to his left arm. He turned, shocked and ready to be angry at the culprit. Delilah stood there wearing her usual drab layers and looking both angry and devastated. The book she'd dropped on the table was her copy of *Seven Summits*.

Slapping his arm again, she said, "Jermias? Really? Jermias is the bad guy? *The whole time?*"

Cameron just stared at her, not exactly sure how to take her outburst. Tilting his head, he offered, "Yes, and…I'm sorry?"

Delilah threw herself down in the seat across from him and crossed her arms. She stared him down, but he did not produce any better explanation.

After a tense silence, he asked, "You do know I didn't *write* the story, don't you?"

She still stared.

He tried again, "You also know I can't un-write the story…"

She waved her hand dismissively. "Yes. I mostly just needed someone to punch."

"I'm glad I can be your punching bag," he grumbled.

"I'm sorry. I probably don't know you well enough to hit you."

Cameron watched her carefully. "Do you get this upset about everything you read?"

She met his eyes. "Um...I don't know. I think I used to. My father had me read all the classics before the school required them. I remember getting really angry about *Pride and Prejudice* and *The Scarlet Letter*. Oh and Shakespeare. I used to cry and rant over Shakespeare."

He pressed, "But not anymore?"

She looked away. "Lately, I've read a lot of fluffy romance. There's not a lot to get upset about in that."

"No, I suppose not," Cameron agreed softly. "So, your father, he was a literature teacher?"

"Yes. He still is. He refuses to retire until they kick him out. He has a doctorate in English and American Literature."

Cameron couldn't hide his shock. "Yet he teaches secondary school?"

Delilah nodded. "Yep. In West Virginia, in the Allegheny mountains."

"Why?" Cameron was still baffled.

Delilah smiled. "Because he loves it. He loves working with teenagers. And he has more students go to college after leaving his class than any other teacher in the four counties near where we live."

"Impressive," Cameron conceded.

"He loves what he does. He's happy." Delilah shrugged. "What else matters?"

"Good point," Cameron agreed. "And what about your mother?"

She looked at him as though deciding whether to answer. Then she stated, "She died when I was in high school. Leukemia."

Cameron's expression softened. He wondered if he was finally tapping the reason behind her panic attacks and her solitary nature.

She went on, "It's all right. You don't have to say anything special. She was sick my entire life. My father knew when he married her that their future was uncertain. But he didn't care. They had a great love story. Like something out of Brontë or Austin."

To Cameron, Delilah seemed okay with the whole situation. The expression on her face was more of sweet nostalgia than pain. If this was her great secret, she was giving it up rather easily.

"Her family hated all of it, though." Delilah went on, "They couldn't forgive her for moving to Nowhere, West Virginia and marrying a mountain man. They couldn't see him as anything else. She was a beautiful singer, classically trained, and she could've done a lot of things. She had job offers from major opera companies. But she kept getting sick and she hated the competition. She couldn't handle the stress. Some people have a lot of talent, but they just can't take the spotlight."

Cameron cocked his head. "I can certainly understand that."

"I only met her family once, because they mostly disowned her when she left New York. She came from a huge, Italian family. Her name was Francesca Maria Giavonno-MacClare, but everyone called her Kitty. She had lots of brothers and sisters. I was very young the one time I met them. I think her mother, my grandmother, asked to see us just to find out if I was going to have the singing career my mother gave up."

"And, were you?"

"No," Delilah shook her head. "I could never sing like that. And I haven't seen them since."

"So," Cameron asked carefully, "is that why you're so upset over all the characters losing their parents?"

"Maybe a little, but I accepted what happened to my mom a long time ago."

"Okay," he conceded, not entirely convinced.

She stared at him as though choosing her question carefully. "And what about your parents?"

He smirked. "You didn't read about them on Wikipedia?"

Delilah became defensive. "I told you. I don't believe everything I read on the internet."

Cameron explained, "They're both gone now. It's one of the reasons Mara wants me to come back more often—to visit them at the cemetery. My father was a coal miner, which sounds like the beginning of an American country song. My mother eventually worked for the library in Rugby. She was just about running the place when she retired. She was like your father, always had this hunger for the written word."

"No actors in your family?"

"No." He shook his head. "But I have a cousin who's a theater director and a great-niece who sorely wants to get into the business. Although, she's four, so she also wants to be a unicorn."

Delilah laughed. "I think the acting bug comes from your mother. Having an appreciation for great stories lends itself to producing actors."

Cameron couldn't argue with her.

"Did you go to college?" She asked next.

He confirmed, "I took off at eighteen for drama school. I knew what I wanted. What about you?"

"I went to circus school."

"Circus school?" He scoffed.

"It's a real thing!"

"It sounds brilliant."

"It was!" Her voice started to sound far away. "I studied Trapeze and Lyra and Acro, or Acrobatics. I got to travel, in the US at least. My body was one big, bruised callus for years, but I loved it. The silks, what you saw in those pictures you found, came later, but they were my favorite. The silks are…magnificent."

Cameron held her in his gaze, trying to decide whether to ask his next question. Eventually, he chose to risk it. "Why did you give it up?"

Delilah looked down at her hands. She examined her fingers then wound them together, and he was sure she wasn't going to answer. As he was about to change the subject, she finally spoke.

"I have some health issues. Sometimes, it's hard to breathe."

She gave no more explanation, and Cameron tried to find the connection between what happened on New Year's and her "health issues," if there was one. He wondered if her mental health struggles affected her more physically than she was willing to admit. He had so many questions he didn't dare ask. He had promised not to push or pry. Looking at her tightly clasped hands, he could also see she was trembling. Not wanting her to go through what she went through on New Year's, he reached out and gently put his hands over hers. She was instantly present again at his touch.

"Delilah?" He asked carefully.

She took several long, slow breaths. She closed her eyes for a minute, continuing to breathe deeply. When she opened her eyes, she looked much calmer. She gave a little smile. It was the first time he touched her. He felt a rush of pride that his touch was enough to calm her down. It fed the part of him that loved to play hero, that loved to be loved. But, unlike in films, she pulled her hands back and gave him nothing more.

The next day, Delilah was deep in her copy of *Heir of Taivas: Retribution* when her phone rang. Morning had quickly become noon, and she saw it was her father calling.

She answered, "Hey Dad."

"Morning Lilah. How are things across the pond today?"

She smiled. "Cold. Lots of rain. But I've got some excellent books to keep me company."

"More adventures of what's her name? Mohara?"

"Yes," Delilah snapped back, "and I still think you should read them."

Stephen laughed. "You'll be happy to know that I bought the first one. I used the gift card you sent for Christmas, so I'll call it a gift from you."

"Well, I'm proud to have given it to you."

"Anything for you, Lilah," Stephen's tone softened.

"Cameron's asked me to watch the movies with him, once I finish the last book," Delilah stated.

"Well, if I was in all those movies, I would want to show everyone, too."

It was Delilah's turn to laugh. "I bet you would. You would make everyone write essays about it, though." She paused. "I think it's nice that Cameron loves the story. I always wondered if actors really get invested in the material like they say they do. And he's been a good friend. You would like him."

"Maybe I'll get to meet him if you go back over there this summer. I could visit you," Stephen suggested.

"He's going back to London in the spring," Delilah stated.

There was a long, comfortable moment.

Delilah broke the silence. "Do you think I'm stupid for thinking this is a real friendship?"

Stephen answered, "I think it's hard to define 'real friendship.' Might it be temporary? Maybe. But does that make it less real?"

"I guess not," Delilah conceded.

There was another stretch of quiet before her father went on, "Lilah, I know we've had our differences over the years about how you live your life, but you know how much I love you. And this is not going to sound like my usual advice."

"Okay?"

"You left home so you could live again. You need to remember the world is still spinning, and people are still laughing and working and loving. You need to feel *something*. You need to *live*."

Delilah chewed her lip then quoted, *"There is only one way to live, and that is with the past at your back, the present in your hand, and the future in your sight."*

"Exactly," her father agreed. "And that is from?"

"It's *Heir of Taivas*, Dad. I keep telling you they're brilliant. All great works of literature were once new and not fully appreciated."

Stephen returned, "I will agree with that."

"Read them all. You will want to teach with them after you do, I promise."

"I don't know about that," he laughed again, "but I'll start the first one immediately, for you."

"Thank you."

"How's the suitcase holding up?"

"Still closed."

"Good." He added gently, "I miss her, too."

Taking a deep breath, Delilah replied, "I know."

Later, after they hung up with each other, she walked over to the window in front of the sofa. Kneeling in front of a weathered suitcase in faded, Tiffany blue, she ran her hands over the smooth leather and rusted metal clasps. She sat there for several minutes, staring at it. Suddenly, she pulled herself to her feet as an idea struck her. Going to the kitchen, she dug through her drawer full of miscellaneous household items. Pulling out a fat, black marker, she went back to the window. She sat there for another minute, considering. Then, with careful penmanship, she tipped the case and scrawled across the front:

There is only one way to live, and that is with the past at your back, the present in your hand, and the future in your sight.

The following Monday, the last day of January, Cameron made it to the pub at midday just as fat, wet snowflakes began to fall. The day promised to deliver several inches of snow, so he wondered if Delilah would venture outside. He had learned enough about her to know bitter cold tended to keep her in her flat by her own fire. Thus, he was pleasantly surprised to see her in their booth. She stared into the old mirror above the table again, looking distant.

Crossing the space, he sat down in front of her. She didn't move. After a long silence, he asked, "Delilah?"

She turned her head and her eyes slowly focused on him. Cameron noticed she looked especially disheveled today. She wore a ratty, dark green jumper and gray tracksuit bottoms. Her hair, which looked especially dull and ignored, was flattened by a gray hat, and her face was pale.

When she still didn't speak, Cameron asked, "Are you all right?"

Emotion suddenly flooded into her face and Delilah stated coldly, "I can't read any more."

"Okay..." He didn't understand.

"I mean," she struggled, "this is why I haven't...this is why I stick with fluffy romance novels. I can't..."

Cameron watched her intense struggle, afraid of saying the wrong thing.

She calmed down a little. "I'm sorry. I shouldn't be unloading this on you. You've already had to witness enough of my crazy. I just had to tell you that I can't finish the books. And I can't watch any of it. I'm sorry."

Studying her, Cameron chose his question carefully. "How far into it did you get?"

She took a deep breath. "Almost to the end of *Retribution*. When Amy...when she...when Jermias kills her."

"I see..."

Suddenly, she went on, "I just don't understand why it had to be *her*."

Cameron thought it over, trying to come up with a decent answer, then said, "Because, he has no mercy."

"But why?" Delilah slammed her fists down on the table. "Why Amy? Of all the characters, why Alex's sister? Her *twin* sister?"

Cameron elaborated, "Jermias has already killed several others, including his own brother. The characters are starting a war, and death is the inevitable consequence of war."

"But," Delilah pushed herself out of the booth as though her emotions were running too high to stay seated, "Warwick could have written it any other way. He could have chosen *anyone* else. That was the cruelest choice!"

Cameron tried to understand. "Why?"

She didn't answer, but stood with her arms crossed.

"The sprites he killed were children, and the other Eperra had a family. What about them?"

Delilah was trembling now. He hadn't meant to push her, but he never knew when a conversation was going to trigger her. Sometimes, she could argue him into the ground without a hint of emotion. Other times, it was as though one push would send her over the edge. This was obviously one of those times.

Carefully, Cameron said, "I think Warwick was just trying to show us the cruelty of war and the devastation wrought by hate. He *wants* us to mourn these characters."

Delilah's hands were now shaking and her eyes full of turmoil. She looked like she wanted to scream at him, but she couldn't find the words. Suddenly, she seized one of the saltshakers from a nearby table and hurled it across the table in front of him. Cameron pushed himself out of the booth as it struck the mirror hanging over the table, shattering the glass into ugly shards. Flora gasped from across the room and the other patrons looked over, surprised and concerned. Delilah dropped onto the edge of the booth and, for the first time since he met her, she cried. Her whole body shook and tears flowed.

Cameron froze. There was no script for this. The last woman to genuinely break down and sob in front of him was his wife, and that was thirty years ago. Since then, he made a conscious effort not to stay with anyone long enough for them to cry in front of him because he had no idea what to do. Thankfully, Flora came over and relieved him of the decision.

"What on Earth is goin' on, luv?" She pulled up a chair and put her arms around Delilah.

"I'm sorry," Delilah mumbled. "I'll pay for it."

Flora waved her hand. "It's all right. We'll sort tha' later. What's wrong?"

Delilah looked up, wiping her face as she did, and glanced at Cameron. She looked over at the mirror then settled on looking at her lap. She took a deep breath, as though deciding whether silence or talking would be worse. Cameron wasn't sure what he was hoping for either, information or blissful ignorance.

Finally, Delilah spoke, "My sister died. My twin. My identical twin."

Flora sat back, her shoulders settling into a grim acceptance of the situation. "How long ago did she die?" She asked gently, her hand on Delilah's knee.

"Almost ten years ago," Delilah answered, her voice shaking. She took a heavy breath and said almost inaudibly, "She died on September eleventh."

Cameron sat back down in the booth as the confession hit him like a cold splash of water. Even with the little information he had, a picture was starting to form. His mind pulled up memories of airplanes and explosions and masses of terrified people. In his head, the casualties were numbers and the repercussions were political. It was a significant international event that had collective meaning for society as a whole. But here, in front of him, was the tragedy made personal. Here was one life irrevocably changed. Suddenly, a massive, undefined disaster became a singularity. The words Cameron spoke only minutes before now carried far more weight. *This* was the cost of war. Yet, for the victims of September 11, none had the chance to choose to enter the battle. They were not a collective loss, but three thousand graves, three thousand pictures on walls or names scrawled in baby books. They were three thousand mothers, fathers, brothers, sisters, and children. And somewhere, another Delilah was grieving for each and every person. Not for the event or the place or the size of the tragedy, but the *person*. The realization hit Cameron hard, and he had no words.

After a long time, when Delilah stopped crying and reached for napkins to wipe her face, Flora asked carefully, "What was 'er name?"

Delilah looked into the distance for a minute then answered, "Anna. Her name was Anna."

7

Griefs Unspeakable

A heavier task could not have been impos'd
than I to speak my griefs unspeakable.

—From The Comedy of Errors by *William Shakespeare*

Later that afternoon, with snow falling in earnest outside, Cameron sat at Mara's kitchen table with his feet propped up on the chair across from him. His phone was on the table, for once ignored. He swirled mediocre whisky in a tumbler in his left hand. Blue Label Scotch was his drink of choice, second only to a good red wine, but Mara didn't keep decent liquor in the house. She had no use for it. He usually didn't notice, but, today, he yearned for his well-stocked drinks cabinet back in London. He kicked off his shoes and knew he looked disheveled. It was no wonder Delilah couldn't see him as a famous film star and that she was confiding in him like they were childhood mates.

No wonder she cried in front of you.

That thought brought him back to the elephant in the room, to the reason he was drinking in the afternoon. Alone.

Cameron bolted from the pub as quickly as he could after Delilah's breakdown. He said something about having a meeting and left her with Flora. He told himself she was in better hands, and that Flora, being a woman, would likely provide far more comfort than he could. And in a way, he was right. Fundamentally, Flora was a better nurturer. However, Cameron knew, deep down, that he acted like an absolute git. *He* was the one who sat opposite Delilah for months, talking to her, getting to know her, and calling her his friend. He was the one who gave her his mobile number, walked her home, and even once imagined kissing her. He suspected all along that she had a dark secret. He knew she was troubled and that she was probably in Chatfield to escape something. Still, the truth was uglier than he could bear.

You should talk to her. It doesn't matter how you feel.

Again, Cameron accepted the factual nature of his thoughts but couldn't make himself commit to act on them. So many excuses for not doing the right thing ran through his head: He was not in a position to help someone with such deep wounds. He was leaving in a couple of months and getting more involved would only hurt Delilah. He was fundamentally terrible at being empathetic. Cameron was a selfish person, which he believed was one of the necessary traits for working in the film industry but not typically helpful in relationships. There were so many reasons to back slowly out of Delilah's life. Yet, at sixty-one years old, his conscience finally decided to make an appearance.

Cameron threw back the last swig of Scotch just as Mara came through the front door, bringing with her a flurry of snowflakes. He assumed she'd been at the market. Dropping her bags and shedding her coat, she meandered into the kitchen while looking at the day's post. Cameron poured another glass of liquor and the sound of clinking glass caused Mara to look up.

Taking in her brother's condition, she dropped the envelopes on the kitchen table and asked, "Rough day?"

Cameron quirked his eyebrows up and nodded his head in confirmation.

"We had a child come in last evening who lost an arm in a farming accident a few miles north. He barely survived," Mara threw out.

Cameron sighed heavily. "Does everything have to be a competition?"

Mara's expression softened a bit. "No. I'm sorry. It was just one of those cases that puts things in perspective."

"Well, believe it or not," Cameron fired back, "I got a little dose of *perspective* today, as well."

"Really?" Mara looked more interested.

Cameron took another sip of Scotch. "Delilah's twin sister died on September eleventh. In the US attacks. And I gave her a series of books where one of the main plot points is the death of a twin—the cruel and unnecessary murder of a twin."

Mara's face softened into compassion. "You didn't know. And, how very terrible for her."

"It *is* terrible," Cameron agreed.

"Was it the book that made her tell you?" Mara guessed.

"Yes."

"Is she all right, after talking about it?"

He took another drink. "I think so. She was talking to Flora when I left."

Mara's expression hardened again. "Good God, Cameron! Could you not even stay around long enough to let her talk it out? Especially after all this discussion of how she's your friend! Do you not have even a rudimentary understanding of how friendship works?"

"Mara," he snapped at her, "I'm not in the mood for this."

"You're never in the mood for the truth!"

Meeting her eyes, he snapped back, "I didn't know what to say to her. I think we can agree there was little I *could* say!"

Pressing her lips together, Mara came back with, "I've told you before, Cameron. Sometimes, you just need to *be there*." She stared at him, her eyes filled with unspoken things.

Cameron knew exactly what she was thinking about. Again.

"Mara, I am not going to apologize to you for Marianne anymore. I understand that nothing will ever redeem me for what happened between us, but I'm done apologizing."

Mara sighed. "There is something that would redeem you, Cameron."

"What?" He demanded, downing the last of the Scotch.

"Be around for more than just the good times. For once in your life, step up when things are hard. For God's sake, you didn't come home when either mum or dad passed away! You barely made it to their funerals! I saw you *once* when I lost and buried my husband!"

"I am aware of all the ways I've hurt you," he cut in, "but it is frustrating to come home to someone who only wants to fight with me!"

Mara stared at him, and he could tell he made a point.

Cameron went on, "I can only apologize so many times, Mara. I can't make up for all my wrongs."

She heaved a sigh. "Maybe you can't, but you could start by not making the same mistakes over and over again. Stop running from everyone you start to care about."

"I don't intend to run from her," Cameron shot back tightly.

"Prove it," Mara challenged.

Then she walked away to get ready for work, leaving Cameron to decide for himself how to proceed.

———————————

Cameron avoided the pub for the next few days. He kept checking his phone, wondering if Delilah might text him, but she remained silent. She was either upset with him for running out on her, or she regretted breaking down in front of him. He wasn't sure which one he hoped for. Either way, he knew he was only making it worse by staying away. He also knew he would have to do something, eventually. The town was too small for him to simply avoid her altogether. He would have to pack up and head back to London to completely cut off the friendship. He considered pushing her toward Flora in a sort of transfer of friendship. He managed to do that once before when one of his castmates suddenly wanted to have lunch every day and talk about her dying mother. They had a rather flirtatious rapport until then, so he used his charm to pawn her off on one of the extras who was practically begging for friendship. It worked nicely, and he was freed from having to sympathize. Cameron supposed he could do the same with Delilah and she would probably be better off. Flora would have better answers. Or perhaps Mara was the better choice. He considered letting his sister do what she did best: take over. She would love to "rescue" Delilah from him, passive-aggressively admonishing him in the process.

He let his options marinate while he answered emails and read over scripts. For three days, he intentionally stayed away from the pub. He even went so far as to simply stay home and watch television. He was successful in avoiding Delilah, but he couldn't avoid his conscience.

Cameron was pondering calling up Charlie and asking him to book something, anything for him to do, when Mara entered. She had shuffled out of her room mid-afternoon on Thursday wearing a dressing gown, having slept since returning home from her overnight shift.

Sitting down on the chair opposite him in the lounge, she asked, "Have you talked to her?"

Cameron shook his head, avoiding her gaze.

This time, Mara's tone was softer as she pushed, "You need to."

Cameron rubbed his eyes and conceded, "I know."

Taking a calming breath, Mara went on, "You let her into your life, and this is what real friendship is. The good and the bad. You take them both."

Finally meeting his sister's eyes, Cameron snapped, "I do have friends, Mara. I know what friendship is."

"No," she corrected, "you have colleagues. You have people who take you to lunch. You have admirers and you have people who remember you fondly from boyhood. You have business partners. There is a difference."

Cameron wanted to argue with her, but he knew she was right. He simply couldn't see why it mattered so much. He had people he could call if he wanted to have a good time, even if he was no longer interested in getting pissed every night. He knew how to work a room full of people. Granted, Cameron wasn't the one anyone would call if they wanted to have a long, cathartic cry, but there were plenty of other people on the planet who were good at that. He wasn't sure what was to be gained by trying to become one of those people now.

"Cameron," Mara filled the silence, "just talk to her. At least tell her you don't know what to say. Be honest with her."

As usual, she had talked him out of all his arguments.

So he set his mind on finding Delilah first thing in the morning. However, later that night his phone beeped with a message:

> Hey. Please don't feel like you have to stay away from me. I know I'm a mess, but it's my mess and not yours. I don't expect you to have answers. But I think you're better at listening than you realize.
>
> Delilah

Cameron read over her words, surprised at how well she seemed to be able to read his thoughts. Before he could respond, she added:

> I haven't finished the books. I may not. But I think I'm ready to talk about it. If I haven't scared you away.

He couldn't help smiling to himself. Her self-awareness was almost frightening. Yet, it was also refreshing. In spite of himself and all his ideas about handing her off to Flora, he wrote back:

> I thought you might need some space. Sorry for disappearing. Tomorrow?

I'll be there at eleven.

Cameron stared at her last message for some time, trying to sort out how he managed to find someone who both recognized his emotionally stunted behavior and yet, inexplicably, still wanted him around.

The next day, Delilah made her way to the pub, shuffling through the snow-turned-slush. The sun was pushing through the clouds, casting the street in hazy light. The cold air was dry, finally. Coughing into the sleeve of her patchwork coat, she pulled open the heavy door of The Quill and Fiddle. She was early, but she wanted to sit down and collect herself before Cameron arrived. She struggled for days with what to say to him and whether she would be able to get it out when the time came. Up until four days ago, she wasn't sure she would ever tell him, or anyone else, her story. She was taking this journey one day at a time, just like she promised her father. However, now the story was out. She could either face her fear and talk about it, or she could lock herself in her apartment. The latter would be a repeat of precisely why she left West Virginia in the first place. She needed to face this. It was time. It took her usual morning stretching, an hour of meditation, two Xanax, and checking twice to make sure she had the pills with her to get out of the house. She was also coughing, which was both irksome and ominous. She got the cough every winter for the last few years—so it was almost routine—but it still caused fear to settle in the pit of her stomach.

Situating herself in the usual booth, Delilah noted that the mirror was gone. In its place was a print of an English countryside. She understood it was meant to be a safe choice. Most people don't lose their shit over fields with sheep.

Unless, of course, you've been mauled by sheep in a sunny field.

Delilah laughed to herself. She ordered coffee from Flora, who gave her a compassionate look and returned quickly with the mug.

Delilah worked on filling it with milk and sugar, again focusing on the mundane. Sugar crystals into black coffee. Milk that swirled and turned the liquid from black to pale caramel. She watched the clock, horribly uncomfortable with how present she felt in this moment. She wanted to pull out a book and fall into a story, but it seemed that books brought her full circle. They brought her back to her reality.

Cameron arrived at exactly eleven o'clock. He wore a striped scarf with his heavy, black coat, which he pulled off to reveal well-loved jeans and a soft sweater. His expression was guarded, but something in his eyes hinted at deep concern. Delilah looked away from him—his intensity was a bit much this morning.

Once he settled, Cameron stated, "Lunch is my treat. And don't argue because I saw you eat at Christmas and I know you love the food this side of the pond."

Delilah smiled in spite of herself, and she felt her anxiety abate slightly as he signaled for Flora and ordered food. She asked for water to try to ease her nagging cough. By the time their lunch arrived, they'd covered the fact that neither one of them had been up to much the past few days and that Delilah's cough started on Tuesday.

"It's probably from the snow. At some point, when it gets cold enough to snow, I start coughing. It happens every year," she explained, trying to sound casual.

Cameron had ordered fish and chips again, as well as braised cabbage and cottage pie. Delilah unashamedly helped herself to all of it. She also unapologetically dredged the chips in ketchup, because she couldn't resist the urge to combine the taste of home with all the new foods. Cameron took a sampling of everything as well. Flora brought tea, and he praised her cooking.

Once Flora walked away again, Cameron offered, "Delilah, I owe you an apology."

She chewed slowly, looking at her hands.

"I shouldn't have run out so quickly the other day."

Delilah looked up. "I don't blame you. I wish I could run out on the whole thing. In a way, I did for a while."

"I don't know how you do that."

"Do what?" She asked, confused.

"Always find the right words. And never say what I expect you to say."

Delilah chuckled. "I have no idea. I was a dancer, not an actor."

"That you were," he murmured.

Delilah sipped her water as she chose her next words. After a minute, she decided to be direct. There was no reason to avoid it now.

"I've had a lot of people ask me for my story over the years," she started. "All the families from nine-eleven have stories, but mine is particularly interesting to the media because Anna and I were twins. I could've done a few interviews, maybe written a book, but I won't. I wish I could say it was because I don't want to profit from tragedy. And I don't. I really don't. But, more than that, I've never been able to talk about her. Not with people who didn't know her. I could never do her justice."

Cameron asked, "She was your identical twin?"

"Yes. And we loved it. Some twins resent it. They hate being mistaken for each other. They crave individualism. Not us. I mean, we didn't go around pretending to be each other, *Parent Trap* style. It wasn't the outward part of being twins that mattered. It was the bond. It's not a guaranteed thing. Some twins grow apart. But if you nurture that bond, it's a powerful thing."

"Were you very much alike, other than in looks?" Cameron asked carefully.

Delilah took a shaky breath. "In some ways. We both loved music. Our mother sang it. I danced to it. But Anna played it. She played more instruments than I can tell you. She and her husband had a band that had quite a following in the city. She was also a professional violinist. She played. She composed. Anna," her voice broke, "was my music."

Delilah took a few more deep breaths, trying to stave off tears. She didn't want to break down again. Giving Cameron an apologetic look, she pulled out her pills and tried to discreetly take one.

"I don't talk about her. I can talk about my own issues and problems. It's easier for me to talk about what happened to me than it is to talk about *her.*"

Leaning back in the booth, Cameron said softly, "Then tell me about what happened to you."

Delilah ate another bite. After some thought, she went on, "We had an apartment about six blocks from the towers. In Tribeca, between West Broadway and Church Street. Anna's husband, Preston, sublet it right after he started a new job in the financial district, and they were kind enough to let me live with them for the run of a show I was doing. Preston had decided to put his education to use, since playing in a band isn't lucrative, and they were talking about starting a family. He had just started working in the North Tower, somewhere above the fiftieth floor. That morning, Anna went down to the concourse level underneath the towers. There was a bakery she loved down there. She told me she was going to take something up to Preston. Anna was so proud of his new office, tiny as it was."

Delilah closed her eyes. Willing away the pain of the memory, she went on, "Preston made it out. She didn't. I don't know how far Anna got or where she ended up. After she left home that morning, I never talked to her again. I heard the first plane hit the North Tower, and I went tearing out of the apartment. I had no cell phone service. I was on Church Street when the other plane hit. I took shelter in a bookstore. After that, the memories are specific, yet disjointed. I tried to get up to Preston's office or down to the concourse, but firemen were evacuating the whole area. At one point I caught a glimpse of the plaza, this beautiful, open space between the towers. And the things I saw…no one should ever have to see. I've never been to war, but I saw the horrors of war that day. It was a sea of carnage. It was…something that cannot be erased from memory."

She struggled before continuing, "For me, that morning was more about the people than the towers. From a distance, it was two burning buildings. But up close, it was people fighting for their lives, some quite literally hanging by their fingertips. It was people making unimaginable choices. People who just went to work one morning…and died for it."

Delilah looked out across the pub for a moment.

"The next thing I remember was running. I remember people screaming and running with me. I had no idea at the time what was happening—that a skyscraper was coming down behind me. I just remember the sound…this awful, incredible, roaring sound that was bigger than any noise I've ever heard. It was the sound thousands of people heard just before they died."

She hesitated.

"I've wondered…if Anna heard it. But I like to think…she was already gone." Delilah took a breath. "After the second tower came down, there was nothing but silence and people covered in dust, people who all had the same look of blank horror on their faces. After all that noise, the world was gray and eerie quiet. Everything just…stopped. It felt like my world…stopped."

Cameron sipped his tea slowly. "The fireworks, they remind you of that day?"

"Fireworks. Any explosion. Smoke. Fog. Fire. Crowds. I have a long list of triggers." She eventually added, "I don't know why I'm telling you all this."

Cameron admitted, "I don't know either."

Delilah went on, "I've had therapists tell me the story would eventually come out. The PTSD is buried deep, more subconscious. It may never change or be totally gone. But talking about all of it…they agreed that it would come out eventually. But it never came out during a session, no matter how hard I tried to find the strength to tell the story. One of many therapists said, 'You'll pick the person, and you'll talk when you're ready.' I suppose I should apologize for somehow picking you. I know you didn't sign on for this."

Cameron sighed. "Well, I did stir it all up for you, by giving you the books."

"Yes, you did. No one else in my life would've had the balls. Bollocks, over here?"

"Bollocks is one way to put it." Cameron self-deprecated, "I would say I'm just a self-involved prick."

"You didn't know how it would affect me."

"Still, I apologize," he insisted.

"Don't," Delilah snapped back. Then she broke into a coughing fit.

Cameron watched her with concern as she sipped water and got herself under control. She drew on the courage from what she'd already revealed and decided to continue. The next part, after all, she had shared before. Most of it, anyway.

Taking yet another deep breath, Delilah continued, "I tried to volunteer at the site, still hoping they would find Anna. I was willing to do anything, but there was little for someone without rescue or construction experience to do. So I would just go and sit as close as they would let me. The windows in our apartment were blown out, and it was covered in dust. We weren't allowed back in, so my dad came up and rented us a hotel room until I could find a friend to stay with. I heard him and Preston talking one day, saying Anna might've been in one of the elevators. I didn't want to know what that meant. I just wanted to find her. The pile, as they called the massive amount of debris, became my life.

At first, I begged Anna to hang on. I thought, 'In the next couple hours, they'll find her.' Then, I started figuring how long she could make it without water, without food. I read stories of people who survived for weeks trapped in collapsed buildings. I knew, I just *knew*, that underneath the next piece of mangled steel, they would find her. The months went on, and I started praying for her body. I did a lot of bargaining with God—a lot of begging and ranting and raving. As other victims were identified, I thought that the next day, surely, they would find something of Anna. When the initial search was done, I still waited.

The first anniversary came and went, and I was convinced, every day, that I would get a call, like so many others, telling me they had identified *something*. That I could bury a piece of her. But she was just *gone*. Gone like dandelion seeds into the wind, too small and too hard to find."

Cameron stared at her, his face etched with heavy emotion. Eventually he said, "That's beautiful. The bit about the flowers."

"*None* of it was beautiful," she snapped.

"There can be beauty in the telling."

Delilah couldn't disagree entirely. "I still remember the smell from all those days I sat there. I will never, ever forget that smell. It was thick and constant. It was the smell of fires devouring concrete and steel and people. It was the smell of burnt plastic and shoes and computers. The smell of death covered in dust. And the dust was constant. Everyone carried it home. I can remember washing it out of my hair in the shower one night and realizing that the people who died were all in that dust. It was made of them." She paused. "And the dust…is why I cough. It's the reason I stopped dancing, because it destroyed my lungs."

Cameron looked across at her, and she saw sadness in his eyes. Not pity or patronization, but sadness. Sadness for what he couldn't change. Sadness he couldn't articulate. He didn't voice it, but she could see it in him. Delilah hated that she made him feel this way. She was grateful that he was still listening to her, but she hated the way her story incited such heaviness. And she hated knowing that, right now, he was trying to find the right words, because there weren't any. The search for the right response, like her search for her sister, was futile.

"You don't have to say anything," Delilah voiced her thoughts.

Hesitantly, Cameron replied, "But I suppose it's human nature to *want* to say something, though."

"You listened. That's something."

"So it is," he answered softly.

Delilah looked at him, trying to decide where to go from here. It felt good for him to know her story. But she didn't want this to hang over them. Their careless banter was what she really wanted. Now, even more than before, she wanted to talk about everyday things, because it would be the first interaction she had where someone knew her story and life simply went on. Right now, Cameron's job, his fame, and his past didn't matter. She needed his friendship. She needed him to reach across the table and take her hands, the way he had once before, and calm her shaking.

Delilah shook herself out of her thoughts. She attributed it to anxiety and her raw vulnerability, but she sensed a change in their dynamic. In revealing so much, the level of intimacy had shifted. It was ever so slight, but it happened.

Still staring at him, she asked, "What are we, Cameron?"

His eyes were uncertain. "What do you mean?"

"You asked me that once before," she went on, "but, after you leave Chatfield, are we still friends? Are we just acquaintances? Are we two random people who met in a booth? Are we the world's smallest book club? Are we an actor and his fan? What are we, after you leave here and go back to your life?"

Cameron leaned back, and she could see the uncertainty in his eyes. Delilah felt like that was her answer. Their relationship was one for the moment. They found something in each other that would help them move on. And move on, they would. It was right, but it caused a sudden pang in Delilah that she wasn't prepared for. It was as though the breath was knocked from her, and she coughed involuntarily. Suddenly overwhelmed by the past hour of confession, she slid from the booth.

"I need a minute," she said apologetically. "I just need some air for a minute."

Before Cameron could respond, she hurried across the pub and out the door. Once outside, she leaned up against the wood and stone façade of the pub and took several deep breaths. She closed her eyes, willing herself not to lose control. A few minutes before, she was so calm, so relieved to have told her story. Now, she felt like she gave away a piece of herself she would never get back. She opened her eyes and looked at the sky, frustrated with how quickly her feelings could spiral out of control.

Cameron came out of the door and stood a few paces away, watching her. Finally, he questioned, "Delilah?"

He stared at her, and she could tell he didn't have any more answers than she did. So she was quiet. The light was different outside, and Delilah knew it aged them both. Her color was never great, because of her struggle to breathe, but she looked paler in the cloudy light. He was different as well. His hair wasn't as black. His eyes were darker. The creases around his eyes were deeper. They spent so much time sitting that she was always surprised at his height, or her slightness. They stared at each other long enough for Delilah to register how cold it was outside.

In a movie, Cameron would have the perfect thing to say. With a script, he would ease her mind and speak to her pain. He would make it right, or at least make it feel that way, and she would smile. Perhaps, in a movie, they would fall in love. All would be made well with a swell of the soundtrack and a carefully choreographed embrace. This, however, was not a film starring Cameron Burke. This was a cold Thursday with two uncertain people standing outside a pub in the dirty snow. The midday light was harsh, and they were surrounded by silence. Both were sorely out of their element for vastly different reasons. But Delilah stayed. She didn't want to walk away from him, and he seemed unwilling to leave her outside.

Finally, he came to stand next to her and leaned on the wall as well, so that their arms were just touching. He said nothing, but he clearly wasn't going anywhere. Acting on her most basic feelings, Delilah slowly leaned in and rested her head on his arm. He was warm, and he smelled like crisp soap with a faint hint of some sort of woodsy cologne. The street was quiet, and she could feel his breath on her forehead. She closed her eyes and focused on calming herself.

She concentrated on the beating of her heart, gradually forcing it to slow. The heart, she realized, keeps beating, even if it's broken. It's steady, like the march of a soldier, despite the war around it.

After a few minutes, Cameron softly said, "It's really quite cold out here."

Delilah let a faint smile play at her lips, and she followed him back inside.

8
The Unconquered Mind

She bore in silence, but when passion
surged in her soul with ceaseless foam,
the storm at last brought desolation,
and drove her exiled from her home.

And silent still, she straight assembled
the wrecks of strength her soul retained;
For though the wasted body trembled,
the unconquered mind, to quail, disdained.

She crossed the sea, now lone she wanders
by Seine's, or Rhine's, or Arno's flow;
Fain would I know if distance renders
relief or comfort to her woe.

—From "Mementos" by Charlotte Brontë

The following Monday, Delilah was still coughing. She went to the doctor the Friday before and was grateful her father helped set up a temporary physician for her before she left for Chatfield. She liked Dr. Merton. He was cautious without making her anxious. At her appointment, he upped the dose of her inhaler and insisted she do a round of prednisone. Delilah hated the oral steroids. Her stateside doctor decided the inhaled steroids were better for her, chronically. But when her lungs flared up, oral prednisone was unavoidable. This time, the doctor felt confident she was fighting the same bronchitis she got every year. However, he was insistent she would go straight to the specialist in Birmingham at the first sign of anything worse. Delilah knew pneumonia would put her in the hospital and could make her critically ill. She survived a pneumonia infection a few years ago, so she knew that early intervention was essential in her case. Still, she hated the fuss of it all. She resented feeling like an eighty-year-old grandmother rather than the aerialist she once was.

Mid-morning, as Delilah lay on the couch reading, her phone buzzed. Picking it up, she read:

Feeling up for lunch today?

With a twinge of regret, Delilah sent back:

> **I can't. I still have the cough. Lying on the couch is required.**

That certainly sounds dull.

> **Well, it isn't as though my life is all that eventful, anyway. I read and talk to some actor in a pub. :-)**

You're right. That doesn't sound very interesting.

> **I should be better in a few days.**

Then I suppose I'll have to work today.

> **You work?**

Very funny. Feel better. Soon.

Still smiling to herself, Delilah went back to her reading. She decided, after much debate, to finish the *Heir of Taivas* books. Perhaps it was the relief of finally confessing her inner struggles, or her own stubbornness, but she rallied and picked them up again. After finishing the last bit of *Retribution,* she started *The Reaping Stone.* She was engrossed in the book when the door buzzer sounded. Curious, she crossed the room with a blanket around her shoulders, coughing all the way. At the main door to the house, she looked out the front window and saw Cameron standing there. She opened the heavy front door and let him in.

Wearing an apologetic expression, he stated, "I know. It's terribly rude of me to keep showing up uninvited, but," he held up a brown bag, "I brought food."

Delilah broke into a wide smile. She would never have asked him to come, but some part of her hoped he would. And she was grateful. Coughing more, she stepped back and ushered him down the hall and into her apartment. As she closed the door, the space suddenly seemed exponentially smaller with him in it. She felt like a hobbit who invited a tall, rakish lord into her humble hovel. Quickly taking handfuls of Kleenex to the trash, she made the sofa decent.

"If I'd known you were coming, I would've cleaned up and maybe put on something other than my sweater-pants," she apologized.

"Sweater-pants?" Cameron echoed.

Delilah indicated her attire. "They're actually knit dance warm-up pants. Most comfortable thing you'll ever wear."

Cameron laughed. "I actually wouldn't expect any different from you."

She gave him a withering look then went on, indicating the small sofa, "I'm also sorry there's nowhere else to sit. I don't know what this room used to be when this was all one house, but I sometimes think it was a closet with a fireplace in it."

Cameron explained, "It was probably the maid's quarters, with the back staircase and kitchen. It's very English. We invented 'quaint'. You're just used to gigantic, American spaces."

Delilah crossed her arms indignantly. "Yes, well, we invented Starbucks. And Google. And obesity. And the first two are awesome."

Cameron chuckled. "If you say so."

"I do," she laughed, "but my argument is weak and I'm hungry."

Cameron gave her a smug look, as though he'd won a more important battle, and started pulling out food. Delilah realized Flora must have made stew. And bread. The bread smelled like heaven. Going to the kitchen, she returned with two mismatched bowls and spoons. Cameron dished portions and they sat back, silent in their appreciation of good food.

After a few minutes, Delilah stated, "This is amazing."

The stew was warm and thick, easing her cough enough to make it bearable.

"I don't know how Flora does it." She went on, "She practically runs that place. And she cooks? All the time?"

Cameron confirmed, "Yes she does. Her family moved here from Leeds when she was in secondary school. Her parents bought the pub. She had just started working there, for her mum and dad, when I went off to university. Now it's hers. Her brothers were...less than interested. Flora's the best apple that fell out of that tree."

"I don't know the family, but I'm inclined to agree." Delilah took another spoonful of stew. "This is so good."

Cameron nodded in agreement. Then, he carefully asked, "Have you finished the last book yet?"

Delilah glanced to where it lay on her small, kitchen counter and shook her head.

"Will you?" Cameron pressed.

"I want to, but I think...I'm afraid of where it's going."

"I understand. Although, I believe in seeing every story to the end, regardless of how difficult the journey."

Delilah stared at him, wondering if he meant to be so allegorical.

When she said nothing for some time, Cameron went on, "Would you let me read it to you?"

Delilah was surprised at the question, so she couldn't immediately form an answer. She felt a wave of uncertainty, but before she could start coming up with excuses she threw out, "Okay."

"Really?" Cameron looked surprised.

"Yes," Delilah agreed shakily. "The story goes on. I know that too well. I guess I should know how it ends."

Before he could say anything else, she got up and cleared the dishes away. Coughing all the while, she retrieved the book from the counter and returned to the sofa. She sat down and put it in his hands.

"Where were you?" He asked gently.

"Marcus and Mohara have gathered the Acclans in Taivas, along with the Citizens. Alex wants to fight Jermias herself, for Amy. I think the next chapter is the battle."

Cameron flipped the pages until he found the right place.

Delilah leaned back on the worn cushions, closed her eyes, and said, "Read."

She could sense the smile on Cameron's face as he smoothed the paper. In a voice well trained at lifting words from pages, he began, "Chapter thirty-three."

Delilah rested with her head on the worn sofa cushions and absorbed the story as it flowed from Cameron's lips. Marcus and Mohara, just before the battle began, consummated their love affair. From being at each other's throats to making love in an abandoned cabin in the woods, their relationship peaked.

Cameron read aloud Marcus' vow as the characters prepared for battle:

> *"Mohara, I love you blindly, not knowing what will come. I love you boldly, not caring what the world thinks. And I love you without bounds, because there is no amount of time or distance that can cut it off or contain it. I will follow you, and I will fight with you, till my last breath."*

Cameron looked up over the top of the book. Delilah was now staring in rapt attention.

He went on to read Mohara's words as she echoed, "*Blindly, boldly, and without bounds.*"

"You're right," Delilah whispered. "I need to finish the story. That is just…beautiful."

"I wish they were my words," Cameron sighed. "But, alas, they are the words of a magnificent storyteller."

"Well, you read them well."

"Shall we continue?" He asked hesitantly.

"Yes."

For the next two hours, Cameron took her through the end of the story. She forgot how wonderful it was to have someone read to her. Now, Delilah closed her eyes and let the words wash over her. As the story unfolded, the battle in Taivas raged. The Acclans and their army were just managing to hold back the forces of Jermias, keeping him from invading Earth and attacking mankind, as was his plan. Delilah held her breath as the action played out. Finally, Alex managed to trap Jermias and, with the help of the Reaping Stone, harness his own power to kill him. Delilah had just breathed a sigh of relief when Cameron read the last of the chapter:

> *Amid the rubble, Mohara found Marcus. Throwing off her cloak and dropping beside him, she realized she couldn't free him. Wailing for help, she looked into his eyes.*
>
> *He spoke, "You are the Heir of Taivas, Mohara. Now go, and live. You have been given a voice, so use it. Use it for good. And don't forget me. I love you, Mohara." As she held his hand, Marcus took his last breath, and Mohara sobbed for him.*

He stopped reading. Silent tears slid down Delilah's cheeks, and she brushed them away. "Marcus dies?"

Cameron nodded slowly.

With resolve, Delilah said, "Keep going." She closed her eyes again.

Cameron kept reading. The words painted a picture of Mohara's grief and her struggle to take on the leadership role that was thrust upon her. After nearly giving in to her heartache, Mohara took the throne amidst the Arches-Asterion. Sending the Acclans back to Earth to prepare mankind not for an invasion, but for a reunion, Mohara led the way forward. Cameron read her closing words:

"We go on, not because we are strong, but because we carry those who are gone with us. We are the guardians of their memory and the propagators of their legacy. So we must live, and we must live fully, but we will never forget them. They will be part of every moment of joy, and we will hear them in every cry of new life. We will carve something new out of this blood-soaked rock and we will stand, unafraid. We will strive to be better, to be kinder, and to show full measures of compassion. And even though the price of love may be loss, we will pay. No matter the cost, we will love blindly, boldly, and without bounds."

With the story complete, he closed the book.

Delilah sat there, letting it sink in. When she opened her eyes, Cameron was staring at her, obviously unsure of her reaction.

She said gently, "Thank you for doing this. I would never have made it through alone."

He set the book on the table. "I only meant to bring you lunch." After a moment, he asked, "Do you want to talk about it?"

Delilah shook her head. "No. I think the book said enough. And I've said enough for now."

"Delilah, can I ask you something? You don't have to answer, if you'd rather not."

She swallowed hard but didn't refuse.

Glancing over at the suitcase with the *Heir of Taivas* quote, he asked, "What's in the case?"

Delilah took a long, deep breath that sent her into a coughing fit. She took a sip of water to get herself back under control, and she could tell Cameron regretted the question. He already looked apologetic.

Before he could let her off the hook, however, she said, "It's…Anna. It's pictures of us and some of our things from home. I couldn't make myself come without it."

Softly, Cameron said, "I see."

"When I realized I couldn't perform anymore, about four years ago, I moved back into our room in our old house. My dad was glad to have me home, but he thought it was temporary. He's always had so much more wisdom than me. He was devastated when our mom died, and heartbroken when Anna…" she struggled. "But he always picked himself up and went on. He could see life after the grief, and I just…can't. Or I haven't been able to. I would just sit in our room and talk to Anna. It reached a point where I wasn't talking to anyone but her. My therapist said I was on the edge of…dissociating."

Leaning in toward her, Cameron asked, "Is that the reason for this trip? For coming to Chatfield?"

Delilah nodded. "I had to get out of Branton. I needed to be somewhere where no one knew me, or Anna. I needed to do something new, and I needed new friends. It was either curl up there and die, or leave and try to live."

"I'm glad you chose to live."

She couldn't agree with him just yet. Instead, she said, "I had to bring something of Anna with me. But I told myself I would stop talking to her so much…and try to talk to other people." Delilah broke into another coughing fit. She took another sip of water. "Sorry about the coughing. It's something else I live with, like the panic attacks and the nightmares."

Cameron just stared at her, his eyes full of unspoken things.

Deciding to plow ahead with the revelations, Delilah pulled the sleeve of her large, unshapely sweatshirt down to reveal her right shoulder. Cameron's eyes left her face and focused on her bare skin.

She watched him take in the scar that diagonally circumscribed her upper right arm.

Running her left hand over it, she explained, "This happened at some point...that morning. In all the chaos and running I fell. I don't even know what I fell into. I didn't realize I was hurt until both buildings had come down and someone noticed I was covered in blood. It took thirty stitches to close it, but it could have been worse. Still, it's another scar..."

Cameron didn't say anything. He didn't contradict her or placate her. Instead, he reached out and took her hand. Gently, he turned her arm over and leaned in to look at her scar. She caught the scent of him again and his fingers were soft on her skin. Her heart fluttered. When he let her go, he raised his head to meet her eyes. He was very close, and Delilah felt a sudden urge to lean into him. Perhaps it was the intimacy of what she was sharing or the fact that, in the book, she just witnessed his death, but she wanted to touch him. It would be so easy to kiss him, and she felt fairly certain he wouldn't object. Just as quickly, however, she was struck by how bad an idea it was. She could see no scenario where the outcome was good. She was too broken, too volatile, and too naturally bad at relationships for it not to be a disaster. Yet it took everything in her to pull away from him, pull her sweatshirt up, and retreat into her shell of safety.

Cameron sat back, as well, and cleared his throat. "I'll be gone for a few days, starting tomorrow. I have a few meetings and other things to take care of in London. But soon, we can watch the films together."

Delilah was both disappointed and grateful for the sudden change of subject. Forcing her mouth into a smile, she agreed.

Over the next few weeks, the weather warmed slightly, and the sun made a welcome appearance. The days began to lengthen, and the snow melted to reveal the evergreen grass. With the change in the weather, Delilah's cough mercifully abated, and Cameron was immensely relieved. He still didn't completely understand her condition, but he didn't want her to end up in hospital. He wasn't sure whether that was more out of concern for her health, or because visiting would feel compulsory.

It was late February before they were able to carve out time to start watching the *Heir of Taivas* films together. Cameron's work was calling him back to London more often than not, but he was determined to make good on his word and watch them with Delilah.

On the eve of the 27th, as they sat in his home watching *Heir of Taivas: The Acclans,* he concentrated on the ease of their friendship and the way she made him laugh. Cameron focused on how ready he felt to get back to work and how watching himself on-screen renewed his drive to make more films. He turned his attention to anything other than how near Delilah was to him on the sofa. He fixed his thoughts on any subject other than how close he was to kissing her a few weeks ago and how strong that desire still burned. And when the film was over, he was grateful to Mara for coming home just then so he wouldn't have to fill the silence with banalities to keep from touching Delilah.

Shutting the front door behind herself, Mara took in the scene in front of her. "Did I miss out on film night?"

Delilah gave an apologetic smile and held up the DVD case.

Mara chuckled dryly. "My brother never misses an opportunity to watch himself on a screen."

Delilah looked taken aback, and Cameron wanted to slap his sister. He didn't want Delilah to think he was watching these films out of narcissism.

Giving Mara a hard look, he helped Delilah gather her bag and head for the door. She was yawning, and he didn't want to argue with his sister in front of her. As usual, Delilah insisted on walking home alone. And, as usual, he walked with her anyway, making sure she was safely inside her flat. Then he turned around and walked back home, glancing up periodically at the stars in the abnormally cloudless sky.

Delilah.

Lately, it felt like she haunted every moment of his life. Whether he was taking phone calls from Charlie, booking interviews, or confirming dates for photo shoots, he was thinking about her. Delilah had become as much a part of his life as breathing, and he was trying to decide when things took this turn. Everywhere he went he saw things that reminded him of her. He saw books she would love or heard stories that would make her laugh. Since he made the choice to talk to her about her sister, Delilah was consuming him, and he had no idea what to do about it. Normally, by the time he was this caught up with someone the relationship was halfway over. All the heat came first. Then the getting to know the person inevitably began. This time, however, he was captivated by someone with whom he had the most platonic relationship of his life. Delilah was genuinely a friend and he realized, as he approached home again, that he didn't want to destroy that. As much as he wanted to kiss her wildly, perhaps make love to her, he was already in too deep. There was too much at stake. It was a terrible, terrible idea to risk their friendship for a few nights of sex. As reckless as he was in relationships to this point, he would not hurt Delilah. Intentionally or not, he simply wouldn't.

When he walked back through his front door, Mara was waiting for him. She was leaning against the wall separating the lounge from the kitchen, and Cameron knew he wasn't going to be able to put her off.

"Is she home?" His sister demanded.

"Yes, mother," he snapped back.

"I suppose she's forgiven you by now? For leaving her crying in the pub?"

He nodded.

After a long pause, Mara added, "I'm glad you talked to her. It was the right thing to do. Now, be careful with her."

With a heavy sigh, he said, "I am, Mara."

She shook her head. "I don't want to end up picking up the pieces of someone else's heart…"

Cameron cringed. "And we're back to Marianne. *Again*."

"I told you I wouldn't end my friendship with her after your divorce, Cameron. Marianne was and is my friend. And what you did to her is unforgivable."

"Marianne and I had a lot of problems."

With flashing eyes, Mara retorted, "I remember *you* had one very specific *problem*. I believe it's called, 'I Like to Shag Other Women!'"

Cameron felt his anger flare up, but he held his tongue. This time, he would not engage in the argument. Drawing on all his self-control, he admitted, "Don't you think I know what I did was wrong?"

Mara's tongue was stilled by surprise. She eyed her brother suspiciously for a moment, then she said, "I'm glad you have a friend. I just don't think she wants to find herself on the cover of the tabs. Please don't drag her into all that."

Crossing to the television, Cameron switched it off, still trying to maintain his calm. He retrieved the DVD and put it away. Finally, he turned back to Mara. "Talk to Delilah. Get to know her. Ask her what she thinks of me. And stop hating me for something that happened thirty years ago. Maybe give me some credit for the fact that Delilah is one of the most beautiful people I have ever met, and I do not mean just physically, and I haven't so much as hugged her. She's the one holding the cards, Mara." He struggled, "She's got a hold of me in a way that fucking terrifies me. So please…back off."

Refusing to meet her eyes, he left for his bedroom. He didn't see the shock on his sister's face.

The next day—a misty, Monday morning—Delilah picked up her phone to call her father. It was mid-morning her time, which meant she should be able to catch him before he left for work in the States. After a few rings, Stephen MacClare answered his daughter's call.

"Hey," she said with a smile.

"You sound happy."

"It's been a good couple of weeks," she explained. "The sun is starting to come back. And of course, there's Cameron..."

"The friendship is going strong?"

"Yes."

"Well, good for you," Stephen encouraged. Delilah could hear the hope in his voice.

She considered carefully what she wanted to say next. Hesitantly, she admitted, "I also think, if I let it happen, it could turn into more than friendship."

Stephen waited.

"But I keep telling myself it's a horrible idea."

Carefully, her father said, "Lilah, part of me is so glad to hear you say you're interested in any kind of relationship that I could cry. I think even considering it says a lot about how good this trip has been for you. But...is that really the best thing?"

Delilah flatly replied, "I know. There's twenty-one years between us. And he lives in London and New York, or LA. It makes no sense. But I needed to tell someone how I feel. I needed it...out."

Stephen lightened the mood by saying, "Well, who can blame you. Who wouldn't fall for a movie star?"

She laughed. "I know. Such a cliché thing to do. But, it's more than that. He listens, which is something I didn't even know I needed until recently. He doesn't try to fix anything or make anything better. He just listens. And he has this strange way of not letting me wallow in things. He sort of forces the normal out of me."

"Have you told him about Anna?" Her father asked.

"Yes. At first, I think it freaked him out. But he came around."

"Well, that sounds pretty typical, for us men," her father chided.

"True," she agreed with a smile, "but I think the most bizarre thing is that he seems to be attracted to *me*. So that either means he's just attracted to all women, or...I don't really know what the alternative is."

"Lilah, he'd be crazy not to be attracted to you. Take it as a compliment."

"But I shouldn't let it go any further, right?" She pressed.

"I think…that you know what I think."

"Yeah," she softly agreed, "I know. It's a bad idea. There's no chance of a future, and to have a fling with a celebrity…is just stupid."

Stephen asked, "Have I ever told you how smart I think you are?"

"Since I first wrote my own name," she teased.

"Well, I still stand by my assessment. But I have to go. Students are arriving."

"All right. Bye for now."

"Oh," he suddenly added, "I'm almost done with the first *Heir of Taivas* book. It is not without literary merit."

Delilah laughed. "You're so complimentary."

"I'm a literature snob. You've said it yourself."

"Goodbye, Dad."

"Goodbye, Lilah."

Delilah smiled as she set down her phone.

A few hours later, when he must have been on his lunch break, Stephen sent his daughter a text message. She picked up the phone to read what he'd written:

> I'd like to amend my answer from this morning to include this…

> Your mother was terrified of life, and she was gone before she really lived. Your sister had her life stolen. There's a whole world out there, and a friendship with a movie star is only the beginning. So go and live, Lilah.

Delilah stared at his message for a long time, trying to decide what it meant for her to live.

9
Fast Falling

O happy that night,
when sunk on your breast,
your kisses fast falling,
and drunken with love,
my troth I did plight.

— "He Comes" by Yahuda HaLevi

Over the next two weeks, as the days grew longer and the snow disappeared, Delilah found herself alone in the pub more often than not. Cameron spent much of his time in London, sometimes staying overnight. Delilah felt like, were it not for her, he would pack up and go back to the city for good. His work was calling, and he seemed to want to be back in the thick of it. Yet he was committed to finishing the journey they started by watching the last movie.

As for Delilah, she thought hard about what her father said and decided it was time to venture out of Chatfield. She concluded some distance might help her to decide how she really felt about Cameron, and that seeing more of this beautiful country was her first step toward living intentionally. So, on the days when Cameron was gone, she took the train to Sheffield or even further north into Yorkshire. Delilah was fascinated with how the scenery changed with every mile the train covered. In West Virginia, the curving mountain roads were often carved between forests of tall, brilliant trees. This land, however, was vast, open, and eternally green. On her trips, she sought out old abbeys and country homes, and she explored the myriad of little towns and villages that dotted the lush landscape. On one trip she went as far as the moors just north of Scarborough, marveling at the wild, rolling land dotted with sheep. Delilah had no particular plan and oftentimes no specific destination. She just went and watched and appreciated what was around her. One afternoon, she went into Coventry to a bookstore she found online and bought a stack of new books. She purposely picked things written in the last few years that she had never read. At night, she worked her way through them, a quintessential bookworm.

On the eleventh of March, however, she made her way across the little town of Chatfield to Cameron's home once again. He invited her by phone that morning to finally watch *Seven Summits*. The walk was familiar now, and Delilah wondered if she could ever stroll up to whatever palatial apartment he had in the city and ask to watch an old movie. She wondered if he would be the same there.

Her lungs felt better. She was as breathless as ever, but at least she wasn't coughing. She strolled up the stone path to Cameron's house, climbed the steps, and knocked on the door.

Mara answered and looked her over carefully. "Cameron's not home just yet. The train was late. He should be here shortly." She opened the door and ushered Delilah inside.

Delilah hadn't seen Mara for weeks, and she sensed Cameron's sister was not entirely thrilled with their relationship. He promised to bring dinner tonight, and Delilah was already nervous because the evening sounded much more like a date than any of their previous meetings. Now, Mara was making her nerves worse. Setting her shoulder bag down, Delilah pulled off her patchwork coat and her hat. Sitting on the sofa, she glanced at Mara, who was staring her down. Much like Cameron, it was hard to know what she was thinking.

Crossing to sit on the chair, Mara asked, "I don't think you've ever mentioned what brought you to Chatfield?"

"No, I don't think I have," Delilah replied softly.

Dressed in hospital scrubs with her hair in a tight bun, Mara looked quite severe as she pressed, "Do you plan to live here permanently?"

Delilah shook her head. "No. I'm just visiting."

Mara looked as though she were working on the wording of her next question.

Delilah headed her off. "Mara, is there something wrong? Have I offended you?"

Mara's face softened as she sighed. "No. And I'm sorry for interrogating you. I'm not angry with you. I'm worried for you."

Delilah cocked her head. "Why?"

Mara fixed Delilah with a stern look. "I'm worried about my brother hurting you."

Furrowing her brow, Delilah pushed for answers, "How do you think he's going to hurt me?"

"When Cameron was a boy, nothing held his attention long. He went through toys in mere hours, exhausting the aspects that made him want them in the first place, then moving on to something else. Our parents couldn't buy him enough things to keep him occupied, which was good, because it made him read. He tore through books and acted out scenes from them in the garden. His interest in complicated characters and good stories has served him well. But in everything else, I'm afraid he hasn't changed much. He loves whatever catches his attention, then quickly moves on to something else. After this many years, I can't imagine he's going to change. I'd like to think he'll be different with you, but I'm not optimistic."

Delilah asked rhetorically, "You care about him very much, don't you?"

Mara's lips twitched into a tiny smile. "Yes. It's hard to admit, but I do. But I also care about the people he has hurt."

"It's wonderful that you're concerned, but you can't fix Cameron's mistakes or decide which new ones he will make."

"I know. But I'm fond of you and I don't want you to be one of them."

"I have no expectations beyond the next thirty days," Delilah replied, "and no matter what happens, nothing about this trip will have been a mistake."

Mara looked lost for words, as though she hadn't anticipated the conversation taking this turn. "You're a smart woman, Delilah. If anyone can hold their own against my brother, I'd say you can."

Delilah smiled. "I've resisted his charm for four months now."

Mara tried to smile in return. "You very well may have. But has *he* resisted *yours?*"

When Mara got up and headed into the kitchen, Delilah decided to take that as an obscure kind of compliment. She appreciated how much Mara cared, but she didn't need someone else hovering and worrying about her emotional well-being. She had plenty of that over the last five years. And she wasn't afraid of Cameron's flaws. It made him human, and that made Delilah feel less broken.

About thirty minutes later, Cameron came through the door. He was dressed in dark jeans and a pinstriped, deep green, button-down shirt. He set down his bags by the door and tossed his coat at one of the hooks on the wall. Running a hand through his disheveled hair, he offered an apologetic smile and reached for one of the bags he set down.

"I brought food," he tossed over his shoulder as he strode into the kitchen.

Delilah got up and joined him, following the wonderful smells coming from whatever he brought. She discovered it was handmade pasta and Caprese salad from what had to be an expensive, London restaurant. Cameron set about carefully warming the pasta in the oven, since the food made the trip with him.

"I picked this up right before I got on the train. It won't be as good as it is on the patio at Marcello's, but it will do. I figure you've had enough pub food by now," Cameron explained.

Delilah smiled broadly. "I have to admit, you're right. I love Flora. I adore fish and chips. But I've been craving something different."

Cameron smiled, held up a bottle of red wine and added, "I also brought this."

Delilah took the bottle and examined the label. It had been a long time since she bought wine, but she knew enough to recognize this was no mediocre offering. From what she remembered, this one bottle was well over two hundred dollars. Looking at it suddenly brought back memories of sitting in dark, chic little wine bars and sipping glasses of whatever was the best bottle she and her friends could afford that night. She saw herself holding a glass with manicured fingers, her hair tamed and her face painstakingly made-up. She remembered the weight of her jewelry, her favorite black dress, and the stiletto Louboutins she saved forever to buy. They were echoes of another lifetime.

Still looking at the blue and gold label, she said, "Sassicaia. I've heard good things."

Cameron looked surprised. "Really?"

"Yes, really. My life used to include more than sweatpants and small towns."

He looked as if he wanted to ask more questions, and she considered telling him more, but decided against it. He knew enough, for now. She didn't want to turn this dinner into a night of more self-exploration.

So she changed the subject by asking, "Red wine with such light food?"

Cameron shrugged. "I break the rules."

Delilah laughed. "Good to know."

Cameron took the bottle back from her and worked on plating the food. At some point, Mara said her goodbyes and left for her overnight shift at the hospital. By then, Delilah and Cameron were at the kitchen table savoring handmade fettuccine in vodka sauce. It was so wonderful that, for a long time, Delilah had no words. After they devoured the food, they took their glasses of wine into the living room and settled on the sofa to watch the movie. Cameron put his feet on the coffee table and Delilah followed suit. Then they lost themselves in Mohara's ever-darkening story for the next two and a half hours.

When the credits rolled, she looked up at him and said, "It's still hard to believe Jermias is the villain. That's like finding out…Gandalf is the villain."

Cameron laughed heartily. "That is true."

"So, other than making sure I saw all these movies, do you watch yourself often? I mean, like Mara said, do you *like* watching yourself?"

He chuckled gruffly. "Mara exaggerates."

"Still…do you?"

He considered her question before speaking. "Some of the films are unavoidable. I see them just by turning on the television at the right time of day. I don't *plan* to watch myself, but I also don't think it hurts to review yourself, to know what was good and what wasn't."

"I see. Like, to decide if they got you at a good angle?" She teased with a smile.

Cameron rolled his eyes. "There aren't as many good angles as there used to be."

Before she could filter herself, Delilah stated, "I think you'll always have a good angle."

Cameron turned suddenly, and she felt her stomach flutter. He broke the tension with, "I suppose you'll have to wait until July for the next film."

"Well, I can always read the books again if I miss it."

The space between them hung heavy with unspoken words.

Delilah yawned and stretched. "I suppose I should go."

"You don't have to," Cameron threw out. "We could watch some television."

Delilah hesitated. "I haven't watched actual television in a long time. I wouldn't know what to watch."

"I know," Cameron agreed. "Maybe I'm just looking for a reason for you to stay."

Delilah felt a white-hot shot of adrenaline run through her. She was suddenly very aware of how close he was. How silent the room was. How the color of his shirt brought out the green in his eyes. Finally, she said, "Well, maybe I don't want to go."

Cameron gave her a slight smile, clearly glad they agreed.

To diffuse the heaviness that was still in the air, Delilah stood up and stated, "Since I'm walking home, I think I can have more wine. And it's too good not to finish it."

Cameron followed her back into the kitchen where she divided the rest of the bottle between their two glasses. Then they went back to the sofa.

Once comfortable, Delilah asked, "What's worth watching at the late hour of…eleven o'clock?"

"Not much, but I'll find us something."

Cameron flipped through the channels, settled on a talk show, and they watched for some time. As the wine continued to smooth their edges, Delilah leaned back and sank deeper into the cushions. Cameron crossed one arm behind his head, and their feet sat side by side on the coffee table. The silence between them stretched.

After almost an hour, Delilah stretched languidly and rose from the sofa. Setting her glass on the coffee table, she ambled over to the shelves next to the television and looked at the framed photographs there. She giggled at the black and white photos of Mara and Cameron as children, posing in starched clothes at Easter and Christmas. They were both small and gangly, but their eyes gave them away. Delilah noted the couple in the picture must be their parents. Mrs. Burke was surprisingly fair in contrast to her dark-haired husband and children. The shelf also held a few photos of Mara and her husband and a boy who must be their son. The most recent snapshots showed Mara alone with her son's family. They all looked so normal to be related to someone like Cameron.

He stood and joined her at the shelf. "That one is Mara's son, William. She calls him Billy. That's his wife, Susan, and their daughter, Delia. She's four."

Delilah smiled. "The aspiring actress?"

"Of course."

Moving on from the pictures, a stack of CDs caught Delilah's attention. Scanning through the titles, she noted they were all from the eighties, the decade of excess, and most of them were American. There were pop singles, hair bands, and rock albums. The cases were worn and chipped, indicating they must have been purchased years ago. She picked up a couple and said, "Your sister has good taste in music."

Cameron corrected, "Actually, her son had good taste in music twenty years ago. Billy had a habit of leaving his CDs at Grandmother's house. I don't know that Mara has ever bought a CD."

Laughing, Delilah picked up one selection and gasped. "I love this! I had it on cassette and played it until it wore out. This is the music I love."

Cameron looked at her with an amused twinkle in his eyes. She studied the CD case while he studied her.

When Delilah looked up again, she wasn't sure what to say. She was stalling, trying to avoid leaving by looking at old pictures and making small talk about CDs. Eventually, she asked, "Do you have a favorite kind of music?"

He shrugged. "Not especially. I've always been too caught up in my work to become a connoisseur of music."

Delilah exhaled heavily. "Ah yes...work." She carefully asked, "Do you have to go back to London soon? I mean, permanently?"

He crossed back to the coffee table and took another sip of wine. "Yes. I'm afraid I really should be back there already. It's an hour and a half trip by train, and sometimes the train is tedious for me. In my sunglasses and pullover, people assume I'm either famous, and therefore trying to be discrete, or I'm going to attack them and nick their wallets. I should have packed up and gone back to the city last week, but..."

She knew what he wasn't saying. He kept coming back because of her. So she decided to let him off the hook. "I have to leave by the end of April. That's as much time as I get here, legally."

He looked surprised, as though he never considered that her days in Chatfield were numbered as well. Clearing his throat, he said, "Well, I'm glad I was able to introduce you to Mohara. I know that you didn't come here to watch films, but I hope the trip has been…good."

Delilah felt a twinge of unease as she realized this might be goodbye. Tonight could be the last time they saw each other, or at least spent time together in this way. It might be the final curtain on this strange friendship. Delilah took a deep breath, because the idea of never seeing him again caused her chest to ache.

Since she didn't respond to his previous statement, Cameron asked, "Do you have plans for tomorrow?"

Delilah's emotions flip-flopped again as she realized he wasn't ready for this to end either. But the end was inevitable, and she wondered if it was better to let this night be her last memory of him. She didn't want to keep pulling him from his work just because he felt sorry for her. She needed to let him go, so she answered, "I think I have to call my dad tomorrow."

Sensing she was putting him off, he asked directly, "Is this goodbye, Delilah?"

"I think it has to be."

Not backing down, he challenged, "Why?"

She sighed and put the CD she was holding back on the shelf. "I'm not saying we should never speak again. Maybe we text or meet for lunch if we're ever in the same city. But we live different lives, Cameron. Yours is in London, or wherever you're filming. Mine is in West Virginia. I can't overstay my time here and you can't quit working. I think whatever we are has run its course."

He looked at her earnestly. "What if I said this hasn't been enough?"

Delilah considered him, trying to get to the root of his meaning. Softened by wine and plied by his calming presence, she wanted more as well. But she was afraid of more, and she was sure he wasn't thinking about the long-term reality. Carefully, she said, "Cameron, you don't need the mess that is me in your life. Even just as a fling. You have a very public life. And I am poorly equipped at handling spectacle right now. I don't think it would be good for either one of us. We would only resent each other. I can't do it, Cameron. I can't do...you."

He looked slightly taken aback. Then his face softened, and he asked, "Do you want to do...me?"

Delilah flushed. "I didn't mean it that way."

Holding her gaze, he asked, "When was the last time you did something just because you wanted to? Without thinking about the future, or the past?"

She crossed back over to the sofa and sat down. She picked up her glass, drained the last of the wine, and answered, "I *have* to go, Cameron."

But she didn't make a move.

Picking up the CD she had set down on the shelf, Cameron looked it over. Without a word, he turned on the old player and inserted the disk. Selecting a song, he turned up the volume. Delilah felt instant nostalgia as the song filled the air.

Take my breath away...

Cameron held out his hand. "Dance with me."

To cover the gnawing uncertainty in her gut, she quipped, "You dance, too?"

He smirked. "Just tango, waltz, and a little salsa. Things you learn for a role. But I don't think we need anything that posh. We are in my sister's lounge, after all."

Disarmed by his wit, she let him pull her to her feet. He took one of her hands and placed the other lightly on her waist. She was stiff, at first, and he teased her further by leading her in a formal waltz around the small space. She laughed, relaxed, and moved her hands to his shoulders. He sobered, as that movement brought them closer. This was the nearest they had ever been. His scent and his warmth, along with the music, slowly unwound her. She melted into him, letting her head rest on his chest. She closed her eyes, listening to his heartbeat. By the end of the song, she pressed close to him in the most intimate embrace she had shared with another person in years. She looked up into his eyes and tried to guess at his feelings, at what he thought of her right now and what he wanted. She tried to ascertain what *she* wanted.

When the next song started, Cameron disentangled himself from her and crossed the room to turn off the stereo. Delilah took a deep breath, deciding the separation was good. They were playing near the edge of a cliff right now. When Cameron turned back to her, however, she had no chance to voice reason. In two long strides he crashed into her. His hands combed through her hair, and he captured her lips with his. He took her breath, and it was good. It was so good. Delilah wrapped her arms fiercely around his neck, responding with fervor she didn't know she had. She kissed him back as though he was light and air and sustenance. She pulled herself to her toes to reach him and he held her fast and tight. When she finally pulled back, she kept her eyes closed. Her heart pounded in her ears.

When she could speak, she opened her eyes and said, "I bet all the women you've been with were much, much more beautiful than me."

With undisguised desire, he shook his head. "I bet the men you've been with were much, much younger than me."

Delilah didn't argue, but she kissed him softly as though trying to modulate the heat between them.

Pulling away to murmur into her hair, Cameron asked, "What are we, Delilah?"

She pulled herself up to whisper in his ear. "I think, tonight, we are lovers."

Her words were the permission he needed. He picked her up easily and carried her upstairs to his bedroom. Kicking the door partially closed, he set her back on her feet and kissed her long and slowly, crushing her to him. Delilah could tell it took all his will to pull back and say, "I'm afraid I'm not at all prepared for this..."

She looked up at him, read his meaning, and whispered, "It's ok. Just trust me."

He searched her eyes then kissed her again as they discarded their clothes. Cameron threw back the quilts and pulled her with him onto the soft sheets. For Delilah, there was no need for words. It had been a long time, but lovemaking was instinctive and carnal. Her body took over, and, for the moment, all that mattered was the warmth of his touch on her bare skin.

In his bedroom, Cameron was as deliberate as he was in conversation. Delilah let her head fall back as his lips and her skin began an exchange that left her wondering if there was going to be enough air. She took deep breaths, remembering that, for her, this breathlessness was not just a sign of a good lover. She ran her hands over his back, letting her fingers find the ridges of his spine and, eventually, the hairs at the base of his neck. He kissed her tingling lips and perused her body in the dark. Delilah knew she was no model. She was tiny and she wasn't blessed with curves, but he seemed to appreciate that she was lithe and comfortable in her skin. Too quickly, his eyes found the scar on her right arm once again.

Pulling him closer to her, she whispered next to his ear, "Don't look at it tonight."

Cameron said nothing but kept his eyes on her face. He grazed his lips over her neck, and there was no time to reconsider or to change her mind. He was part of her, holding her and moving against her. And it was good. He was weathered and far from young, but the effects of age were lost to the dark. Delilah felt only warmth and breath and fullness. Cameron held her tight, kissing her wanting lips and driving her on toward release. She wound herself around him as though no amount of contact was enough.

As the rhythm between them increased, she looked up at him. His face was furrowed in concentration and his muscles were tense with the effort. She reached up and pushed his hair back, watching how his face contorted in pleasure. He met her eyes and kissed her softly, his chest brushing hers. Delilah just went with him. She held him and moved with him as the sweat and the heat built toward something she hadn't felt in more years than she could recall. She was surprised at her body's capacity to remember, to respond after such neglect. But it did.

As their lovemaking became more urgent, Cameron whispered throatily in her ear, "Delilah…"

Her name was a low rumble off his lips. The timbre of his voice and the intonation of her name made her clutch at him and gasp. She was gone, and he went with her. He tucked his face in her neck and clutched her tightly as he lost control. It was odd to see him so undone. Delilah felt the purr of a moan in her ear as he panted and shuddered. He lost his poise and snarky indifference in her arms. Climax hit him hard, and he couldn't disguise it.

As Delilah held him, skin-to-skin, she wondered how long it had been for him. She wondered how many women had seen his face like this and heard his sultry baritone in their ears. Then he captured her lips to kiss her again, and she didn't care. She kissed him back, feeling the heat and sweat between them and remembering that sex is a messy business. Delilah clutched him, determined to have him until dawn, when the light would reveal them as old and scarred. The light would decide whether they could look each other in the eyes again and would bring them back to their own, respective truths. So she kissed him in the dark, and he whispered her name again.

10
I Am Alone

I am alone, in spite of love,
in spite of all I take and give—
In spite of all your tenderness,
sometimes I am not glad to live.

I am alone, as though I stood
on the highest peak of the tired gray world,
about me only swirling snow,
above me, endless space unfurled;

With earth hidden and heaven hidden,
and only my own spirit's pride
to keep me from the peace of those
who are not lonely, having died.

—"Alone" by Sara Teasdale

When Delilah woke the next morning, she sensed something was off. The sheets were too smooth beneath her. Her skin was bare. She wasn't wrapped up in one of her oversized t-shirts. The light was different beyond her eyelids. As the last tendrils of sleep released their grip, she slowly opened her eyes. Recognition washed over her.

Cameron's house. Cameron's bedroom.

Delilah took several long, deep breaths. Then she slowly sat up, forcing herself to continue to breathe deeply. Her head spun a little and she waited it out, just as she did every morning. She pulled the heavy quilt around herself and, when her head felt clear, she looked around. The light was still pale, not yet revealing the colors of true daylight. The furniture took shape around her, old and dark. The house was drafty, and her arms prickled with goose bumps. She pushed her hair back, knowing it badly needed attention.

You don't have all your medicine.

The realization hit her suddenly. It had been so long since she slept anywhere that wasn't home, she couldn't have properly prepared if she tried. She felt a wave of relief that no nightmares had ripped her from sleep the previous night. She thanked all the wine for that. However, relief gave way to anxiety as Delilah realized she was without anything she needed. She would have to go home, she decided, as soon as it was officially morning. But she didn't move yet. Her eyes finally settled on Cameron.

He was asleep on his side with his back to her. His breathing was heavy and even, and she watched the rise and fall of his shoulders. There was obvious strength in his arms and the line of his back, but there was the softness of age, as well. He had a smattering of freckles across his shoulders. From where she sat in the bed, she studied the lines on his face, the furrow of his brow, and the way he slept with his mouth slightly open. His hair was mussed, as was hers. Sharing a bed was humbling. It was hard to maintain perfection in sleep. Still, she liked him this way. Somehow, knowing that one of *Final Cut Magazine's* 100 Sexiest Men had flaws made her feel better about herself. Suddenly, Delilah was struck with how much she wanted to curl up next to him. She wanted to feel the warmth of his skin against hers and wrap her arms around his chest. She wanted to run her fingers through his disheveled hair and wake him up by kissing his neck. She wanted to wrap herself around him and stay in the warm cocoon of his bed. But she hesitated.

Her emotions were wildly mixed. Cameron had done what no one else had been able to do. He brought her out of the safe, metaphorical cave she'd been living in. He made her feel. No. He made her *want* to feel, again. The night before was perfect. She didn't want to talk about it or explain it. She would never regret it, but in the daylight, Delilah was certain they could go no further. As soon as the media discovered their relationship, their privacy would vanish. She would be tormented with questions about her past. Delilah understood that her personal tragedy was part of a much bigger, public tragedy, but she wasn't ready to talk about Anna with a horde of reporters. And starting a relationship with Camera would most likely include a horde of reporters.

She slid herself gracefully out of the bed and started collecting her clothes. It had been years since she had to search for her clothes on someone else's floor. Moving noiselessly, she slipped into the bathroom and made herself decent. Then she crept, cat-like, down to the living room.

Sitting on the couch, she found her shoulder bag and shuffled through it, looking for her phone. The battery was almost dead, but it was working. She had no messages. She considered leaving Cameron a note and heading home, but that just seemed juvenile. She wasn't going to run from him, but she wasn't looking forward to talking about this. She also didn't want to wake him up. Looking around the room, she saw the CDs lying on the shelf again. Crossing to it, Delilah selected one and put it into the stereo. Turning the volume down low, she selected a song. She hoped Cameron, or Mara for that matter, didn't mind her using their things. She sat down on the floor and listened.

It was a strange sensation, because her world had been silent for a very long time. Music was part of another lifetime. Anna *was* music for Delilah. Without her, everything had faded to white noise, like a film with no soundtrack.

When Delilah did morning stretches at home, she usually did so in silence. Today, however, she let the notes wash over her.

Just call me angel of the morning…

She had picked another eighties ballad, and as the chords echoed, she sat down on the rug and arched her torso over her extended legs. It wasn't dancing. That type of expression still wouldn't come. But as she went through her usual stretches, she found herself moving to the rhythm of a song for the first time in almost four years.

The same morning, Cameron struggled awake when the sun forced its way through the curtains across the room. Rarely did he wake to the piercing sun, so he rubbed his face and turned away. Finally focusing, he stared at the expanse of empty bed beside him. It was rumpled, like he'd been fighting with the sheets all night. It looked like...

He remembered.

Cameron sat up and looked around, noting that he was entirely naked. He rubbed his face again, trying to remember the last time he was in this situation. Too quickly, he remembered.

About four months ago. After the premiere party. He was with Meg, an old friend who occasionally became more than a friend for the night.

Shaking off the memory and sitting up, he immediately wondered why Delilah would leave. He seized his pajama bottoms and headed to the bathroom, both to look for her and freshen up. When she obviously wasn't there, he slowly padded downstairs to the lounge. It was too early for Mara to be home from her overnight shift, so he didn't bother getting dressed further. He stopped just inside the room.

Delilah was stretched out on the floor, her legs in a perfect split. Her toes were pointed, her chest was flush with the floor, and she laid her head on her folded arms as if in sleep, appearing perfectly comfortable. Just the idea of that position made Cameron wince in pain. As she sat up, he started to speak but noticed the soft music playing in the background. Her eyes were closed, so he leaned against the wall and watched her. She moved with grace and absolute control. She pulled her legs together and folded herself over them. Then she rolled to her stomach and arched her back, touching the back of her head with her toes. She moved like no forty-year-old woman he'd ever seen. She pulled herself to her knees then to her feet, yet she kept her hands hooked under her toes. Her nose touched her knees. Cameron couldn't look away.

When she stood up, Delilah saw him. Startled, she gave a tiny smile.

"Morning," she whispered.

"Likewise."

Reaching to stop the music, she said, "I'm sorry if I woke you." She checked the time on her phone. "I need to get home. I have to take my medicine."

He had never asked her specifically what she took, but he assumed it was for her anxiety and to help her breathe.

"I'll take you home when Mara gets here," he offered.

Delilah shook her head. "No. I can walk."

"Delilah, it's seven in the morning. And it's cold."

"I know." She looked away. "But I like to walk."

"It can't be good for you to…"

"I'm not an invalid!" She cut him off. "I won't be."

Taken aback, he replied, "I don't think you are, but…" He hesitated. "I can't just send you out into the cold."

"You're not." She sat down on the couch. "It's my decision."

Moving to sit on the chair across from her, Cameron said, "You don't have to go."

"I have to get my medicine."

"What happens if you put it off a couple of hours?"

Delilah sighed. "Nothing terrible. But, I need to go."

"Why?"

Meeting his eyes, she struggled for a minute before explaining herself. "Do you really think it's a good idea to keep going in this direction? And please know, I'm not upset about last night. It was perfect, and I wouldn't trade it for anything. But, do you really want to do this?"

"Delilah—" he started to argue, but she stopped him again.

"Cameron, think past today. What happens when you leave here? What happens when your work life starts up again? Do you really want to explain me to *Studio Zone*? Or whoever has a gossip show here? Is this worth the chaos and the distraction, for you?"

Yes.

It was his first, most immediate response, but he didn't voice it. He thought more about what she said, and she had a point. They were in an artificial environment in Chatfield. The world he usually inhabited would devour this kind of gossip. Just knowing he had a relationship with Delilah would set them off, but if they found out her story as well, it would be everywhere. He understood why she wouldn't want that. He knew the idea of being asked about her sister made her reach for her pills. They might be able to have a secret affair for a couple months, but even in Chatfield they risked someone realizing they were sleeping together. As nice as people were, a photo of her leaving his home in the morning would fetch more money than most people could resist. Delilah was right. The night before had not changed their reality.

Delilah interrupted his thoughts. "I think we both know ourselves pretty well, and I don't think either one of us is good at this, long-term. I can't deal with the publicity, and I don't want them to vilify you for breaking up with a poor girl who lost her sister on nine-eleven. Let's not push our luck and risk resenting each other."

Cameron leaned back in the chair. She was right. He wanted to argue with her and take her back to bed, but she was right. How many times had he followed an impulse, only to have it publicly implode? There was too much at stake this time. If Delilah opened her heart to someone, she deserved to know that person would stay around, and Cameron didn't trust himself. So he did the first unselfish thing he could remember doing in a long while. He fought the urge to cover the space between them and kiss her madly. He forced himself not to act on what he wanted in the moment, and he didn't argue with her.

After a long silence he said, "You're right. If we stop now, we save our friendship."

Delilah looked relieved. She added, "Let's not talk about last night. That way, it stays a good memory."

Cameron nodded.

She gathered up her bag and went to pull on her coat. She wrapped herself in her winter wear and he watched her, still fighting the urge to make her stay.

When she was ready to leave, he stood and asked again, "Can't I take you home?"

She shook her head. "No. I want to walk alone."

Defeated, he didn't argue.

Before she could open the door, however, he called out to her, "Before we never talk about it again, I want to ask…will you ever tell anyone about this?"

She smiled. "No. Would I be the envy of a million women? Yes. But that would cheapen it. This might be where we part ways, Cameron, but that doesn't mean you weren't exactly what I needed. That we weren't what each other needed."

Before he could reply, she was gone. The door shut behind her and Cameron sat back down on the chair, immobile. For the first time, he didn't follow her home. He was still staring at the empty sofa when the door opened and Mara came through. She hung her bags by the door and shed her coat before noticing her brother was in the room.

Startled, she said, "Cameron! What on Earth? You're never up and about this early. And when did shirts become optional in March?"

He stood up and wrapped a throw blanket around himself. He gave her an apologetic look and started back upstairs to his room. But before he reached the stairs, she asked, "Is someone else here, Cameron?"

He shook his head. "No. I'm going back to bed."

"Cameron?" She stopped him again. "Did someone just leave?"

He thought of several plausible stories, but he couldn't lie to his sister. Even at his age she could make him feel like her "little" brother.

Mara took a deep breath. "Was it her?"

"You don't have to worry, Mara," Cameron sidestepped the question. "She's way ahead of me. I tried to tell you that before. It seems I'm to be the one who's left behind this time."

Mara said no more as he retreated to bed.

"Penny?"

A voice broke through Cameron's heavy thoughts a few hours later. He sat in the pub, trying to convince himself that he wasn't hoping Delilah would show up.

Glancing up, he focused on Flora's face. "Pardon?"

"Penny for yer thoughts?" She smiled at him.

Cameron sighed and leaned back in the booth. "I wouldn't know where to begin."

Flora slid into the booth across from him. She dropped the cleaning cloth she was holding on the table and raked her eyes over him. Eventually, she said, "I know you're 'ome and yer dun't 'ave to play film star 'ere, but yer look like death warmed up."

Cameron looked at the old trousers and shirt he'd pulled on and ran his hand through his uncombed hair.

She looked him over again and asked, "Is it her?"

He heaved another sigh, not sure what to say. Flora just continued to stare at him, refusing to back down.

Finally, she said, "I 'ave seen ye come 'ome several times in't past twenty years. Maybe fewer times than yer should've, but I understand better than Mara. I know whar' it is to be different from t' rest of yer family. I've seen ye go from being a lanky boy who flirted wit' me to a man wit' more money than sense sometimes. I've seen yer stroll in 'ere in suits that cost more'n I make in a month. But ye never stay. When yer showed up four months ago, I was certain yer would find some excuse t' be gone again in a matter of weeks. But, this time, yer stayed. And I know it weren't for Mara. So…"

She left the sentence open-ended, giving him the chance to explain. Cameron thought about it for a minute before saying, "I think you know what's happened."

"Is she in love with ye?"

Cameron huffed his disagreement. "No."

"Do yer want her t'be?"

He rubbed his eyes, trying to figure out how much to reveal about the night before. Finally, he threw in the metaphorical towel and explained, "When she left this morning, she essentially thanked me for a memorable night and headed home to pack for the States."

"Well," Flora smiled. "Ye are memorable."

Cameron chuckled. Flora was one of few people who could get away with goading him so candidly. He shook his head. "That was forty years ago."

Flora shrugged. "It's a good memory. A memory of another time. Maybe that's all Delilah wanted. Maybe she needed a good memory."

Cameron thought it over. "That's what she said. And I should be grateful for it. Grateful she's not calling incessantly and making plans to move in with me, because nothing about the two of us makes sense. I mean, this is what I always hope for. A pleasant goodbye."

Flora gave him a long look. "Is she dying?"

Cameron was taken aback. "What? No. Her lungs are damaged. She can't breathe sometimes, and she has panic attacks. But she's not dying."

"Then y' ve no reason t' feel guilty," Flora stated.

He looked away and muttered, "I'm not sure what I feel is guilt…"

Leaning forward, she added, "Some things are better left as they are. Maybe yer both needed this time, this place. Maybe that's enough."

"Again, that's what she said, but I know Mara thinks I've committed a horrible crime against humanity. Again."

Flora crossed her arms over her chest. "This is where Mara and I 'ave always been different. I couldn't 'ave settled down like she did. Not that young. And wha' did she call me t' morning I first met her? A red headed cow?'"

Cameron rolled his eyes. "Something of the like, I'm sure."

Flora took a beat before going on, "I'm happy 'ere, working half t' night most o' the time and living in sin, as they say, above my pub. Mara's happy with 'er family and 'er memories o' John. And I assume you're 'appy with your own life. That's what matters." She paused. "Yer can't fix Delilah by tryin' to love her, if yer don't. Yer can't fix her even if yer *do* love her. Every story doesn't end wi' two people 'olding 'ands in't sunset. But that doesn't mean it weren't a good story."

Cameron raised an eyebrow. "Is this supposed to be making me feel better?"

She shrugged. "I'm just sharin' my thoughts. I'm no psychologist. Although I've seen quite a few people lose the plot entirely in 'ere."

Cameron laughed wryly. "I believe that."

Flora slid herself out of the booth, dusted off her trousers and her well-worn button-down shirt. She picked up the towel she had dropped and started toward the bar. Then she threw back, "Yer sister were right on one score, though. I think yer do 'ave a thing for redheads."

Cameron was saved from having to answer that by the ringing of his phone. He glanced around, decided he wouldn't be disturbing anyone, and answered the call in the booth.

After his greeting, a familiar voice asked, "Are you in that dreadful little village again?"

Cameron shook his head. It was Charlie.

"Well?" The man on the other end of the line pressed.

"Yes," Cameron admitted, "but I'll be on my way back to London soon. I've pretty well wrapped things up here."

"That's one way of putting it." Charlie laughed. "I'm sure she was lovely and I'm sure you *wrapped her up* nicely. But Janine says you have a pile of shit that needs to be signed. And that girl from the States sent you naked photos of herself. Again. I also told Amelia I would ring you since you haven't answered her lately."

Janine and Amelia, Charlie's secretary and Cameron's publicist respectively, were part of the team that kept his career going. Ignoring the last of what Charlie said, Cameron asked warily, "Why are you assuming there's a 'she?'"

"Of course there's a *she*." Charlie continued to tease, "What else would keep you in that Godforsaken place this long? And there's a photo of you two in the back of this week's *Snapshot*. It's on the website, too."

Shit.

It was the only word that came to Cameron's mind.

"Don't worry. It's dreadful quality. But now they all know where you are, so I would get your arse back to the city."

Cameron sighed heavily. "I'll be back tonight."

He hung up with Charlie and composed a text to Delilah. Before he could overthink it, he pressed send and headed home to gather his things to officially move back to London.

That same afternoon, Delilah was curled up on her sofa, buried in a book. She had taken all her medicines and was considering taking a shower, but talked herself out of it. She told herself it was because she was out of breath from walking home and needed to rest, rather than because *his* scent was on her skin and she wanted to hang onto it. To drown out her thoughts, she devoured the same book for hours. It was a modern mystery novel written by an author she'd become particularly fond of over the past month. She was close to finding out who was stealing babies and selling them overseas when her phone chimed. Lazily picking it up, she saw a text message from Cameron. It read:

> Thought it would be best coming from me. Check the website for *Snapshot* today. Bottom of the home page. I think you were right. We should call this a good memory and move on. But if you're ever in London...

Delilah scanned the message twice then opened her laptop. She found the website for the tabloid *Snapshot*. Scrolling down, she spotted what Cameron referred to. There was a grainy picture of the two of them standing outside the pub. It must have been taken the day she told him about Anna, because she was leaning against him, her face partially hidden by her hair. She wondered how many days this person sat outside the pub waiting to catch them in the street together. The caption under the snapshot read:

> *The mystery of Cameron Burke's absence from social media has been solved. He was spotted in his hometown of Chatfield with a mystery girl. Who is she? The next notch in his headboard? Or a childhood sweetheart? Leave your guesses in the comments section.*

Delilah closed the browser before she could succumb to the comments. She felt a stab of panic as she imagined the next picture and the next. In a matter of minutes her mind followed the same path she and Cameron discussed that morning. Her heart pounded as she imagined checking the site tomorrow to see that they knew who she was. They would seek her out and follow her. And they would ask about Anna. Over and over again, they would ask about her sister and print stories with photographs of the worst day of her life. They would dig up details and print wrong information. Delilah was already trembling before she could remind herself that it was only one grainy photograph. Unless they got it out of Flora, no one knew

Delilah's last name. She took a few deep breaths, forcing herself back to the present.

After another minute, she opened the message from Cameron again. Staring at it, she tried to decide on the right response. Eventually, she replied:

> Agreed. Thank you for making England memorable, but we were ships in the night. Maybe someday we'll "speak each other in passing" again.

She held her phone in her hands, staring at what they both wrote. It was an odd goodbye after one of the strangest relationships she'd ever had. It felt like closure, like confirmation of the right decision, and like her heart was breaking all at the same time. She stared at the phone for several minutes before dropping it on the sofa. Determined not to think about it any longer, she picked up her book.

Over the next two weeks, Delilah plowed through three more books and began making plans to move back home. She went through the motions of talking to her father and making flight reservations. She saw the doctor, made sure she had enough medication for the trip, and cleaned the apartment even though she knew her father would have someone take care of it after she left. Delilah went on, day by day, until the twenty-eighth of March.

It was a Monday, and it was her birthday. *Their* birthday. On this day, she was forty. Anna should be forty. As sisters, they should be bemoaning their aging bodies and looking for gray hairs. They should be laughing together while making plans for the next ten years, and she should be holding the babies she was sure Anna would have had by now. They should be blowing out candles at the horrendously cheesy birthday dinner their father would have pulled together for them. There were so many should-haves that it took Delilah's already stolen breath. Still, she held herself together long enough to call her father. She thanked him for the card he sent, and they shared some good memories. They delicately talked about Anna. He updated her on school and how spring was coming along nicely in West Virginia. Delilah compared it to the cool, wet days England was delivering, and she held it together.

However, when she hung up the phone, the tears started and she cried for most of the day. She cried out of pity for herself, out of anger, then out of pure, aching sadness for what could not be recovered. Delilah cried until her face was raw and her head throbbed. She went through a box of tissues and wondered why some days she felt as though a new life was just within her reach, but on other days the wound was raw and the pain felt fresh again. She wondered if there would ever come a day when she felt whole, or if this half-life was simply her designated journey now.

Delilah was still crying when she heard the postal carrier in the vestibule. If only for something to do, she shuffled out her door and retrieved an envelope from her box. Back on her sofa, she noted the slanting, angular penmanship before tearing it open. It was a birthday card. It was dry in its humor, and Delilah couldn't help but smile through her tears. On the inside was scrawled:

> *Enjoy today. Someday, you will be as old as me. And tell Flora it's your birthday. I know she keeps cake for special occasions. Cameron.*

Delilah read it a few times, trying to keep the smile on her face. She wasn't sure whether he had any idea how hard this day was for her. He most likely didn't think about it also being Anna's birthday. He simply remembered her, and she was glad. She didn't even remember telling him her birthdate.

Without realizing it, she stopped crying and was present again. Delilah's moods swung as fast as a wrecking ball sometimes. She furiously wiped the tears from her face, suddenly determined not to wallow in her grief for one more second. Getting up from the sofa, she decided to take Cameron's suggestion. She pulled on a light sweater and headed toward the pub.

Outside, it was hazy, and the sun tried to break through the clouds. The grass along the narrow streets was filling in and sprouting wildflowers, making the foliage even more vibrantly green. Occasionally, the damp breeze whispered the coming of spring. The world was waking up again, following the cycle of growing new from the remnants of the old. Time had a funny way of marching on like that. Spring and summer didn't care that Delilah lived in eternal winter. She kept moving forward because there was no going back, literally or metaphorically.

Inside The Quill and Fiddle, she found Flora sitting at a table and sharing a round of beers with several other people. It occurred to Delilah that she rarely saw Flora in her element, when the pub was busy. She remembered New Year's Eve and how Flora thrived making the rounds of the place, keeping drinks full while checking on her staff in the kitchen. Today, however, she was leaning against her common law husband Peter, her ample bosom shaking with laughter and her blue eyes bright.

When she saw Delilah in the doorway, Flora smiled brightly and called out, "Come through, luv! We've tak'n a bit of a late lunch break. Pull up a chair an' join us."

Delilah ambled over and sat down at the end of the table.

Flora spoke up again, "I 'aven't seen yer in at least two weeks. Thought ye might've gone 'ome. What brings yer out today?"

Delilah answered shakily, "It's my birthday."

With another wide smile, Flora stood up and stated, "Well, I think I've got some sponge cake that's still decent."

Cameron was right, she thought to herself.

When Flora returned, she set cake and plates on the table. Nodding at each person, she made introductions, "This is Liam, Robert, and Paul. All retired football players. They played wit' Peter several centuries ago at university." The men laughed and agreed with her exaggeration. To the men, she said, "And this is Delilah."

Liam, a tall, rugged man who appeared to have been blonde once, questioned, "Delilah, eh? Where're ya from?"

"The States," she answered carefully. "West Virginia, specifically."

The short, stocky Robert swigged his beer and pressed, "You've been in 'ere with Cameron, 'aven't you? Sittin' in t'back?"

Delilah nodded, and they all looked her over more thoroughly.

"Are yer an actress?" Robert pushed further.

She shook her head as Flora passed out sponge cake.

"Then 'ow do yer know Cameron Burke?" Paul asked in a thick, Scottish brogue.

Delilah felt a twist in her gut. This was just a taste of what she envisioned happening if people found out about her and Cameron.

Flora interjected, "They know each other from right 'ere, and there's n'owt more t' tell."

Robert continued to stare at Delilah as though she harbored something of great value beneath her façade. When he eventually relented, they all went back to laughing, drinking, and telling football stories. After a bit, Flora excused herself to check on the pies she had baking for the dinner crowd. Delilah picked at her cake, half listening to the conversation around her.

When Flora returned, she asked, "How old are ye today, Delilah?"

In nearly a whisper, she answered, "Forty."

"Really?" Flora looked shocked. "There must be something else yer want to be doin' today? Some better way of celebrating?"

With that question, the dam broke again. Fat tears traced Delilah's cheeks and she felt her hands tremble. Seeing her distress, Flora expertly shooed the men, including Peter, from the pub.

"Come back for dinner," she called after them. "Pies'll be ready about six!" Returning to the table, she sat down and handed Delilah a clean cloth. "Do yer want t' talk about it?"

Delilah wiped her eyes. "There's not much to say. It's my birthday. So, it's *her* birthday, too."

Realization washed over Flora's face. "Ah. I see, luv."

"I'm sorry," Delilah furiously wiped her tears again. "It seems like every other conversation we have involves me bawling in front of you."

Flora shrugged. "I run a pub. Lots o' folks go off t' rails in front o' me. Some of 'em come 'ere just for that reason."

Delilah couldn't help laughing.

The older woman sighed. "Wha' can I do to make it better?"

Delilah thought it over. "Do you have any decent wine?"

Flora headed behind the bar to search. Returning a minute later, she had a bottle in her hand. Uncorking it, she poured it into mugs. Delilah carefully tasted it and was pleased. It was a good chardonnay. The crispness of it stood in sharp contrast to the heady red wine Cameron shared with her. She thought back to that night, now two weeks prior, and remembered.

"Finally found somethin' good t' dwell on?" Flora broke the reverie when she saw Delilah's slight smile.

Delilah decided to be honest. "I'm thinking about Cameron."

Flora took a sip from her mug. "Now there's a phrase that's probably been uttered a few 'undred times by a good number o' women."

Delilah cocked her head. "I didn't come to Chatfield to meet someone, you know. I came here to find myself again, as cliché as that sounds. I came here to get away from my demons, and also to face them."

"That's a brave goal."

"I wouldn't call it brave," Delilah argued. "It was more about holding onto the last threads of my sanity. And I mean that seriously."

Flora adjusted the clip that held back her russet hair and asked rhetorically, "And sleeping wit' a film star weren't part o't plan?"

Delilah's eyes widened and she felt another stab of panic. Flora *knew*.

"Dun't worry luv." Flora leaned forward on the table. "I wouldn't tell if they offered me a million quid."

Delilah relaxed slightly, grateful. "Did Cameron tell you about us?"

Flora shook her head. "No. I guessed."

Delilah sighed. "I keep going back and forth between feeling like it was an incredibly stupid thing to do, and feeling like it was exactly the right thing."

"Maybe...it were both?"

Delilah let that idea sink in. "I just want things to stay good between us, and I know we would screw it up if we kept on. We both have too much baggage."

"That's probably true," Flora stated. "Did Cameron ever tell yer he was married?"

Delilah sipped her wine. "Sort of. I read about it."

"Did he tell yer about me?"

Taken aback, Delilah answered, "No."

Flora smiled and shook her head. "I'm not surprised. Did he tell yer he 'as a son?"

Delilah's stomach churned. She shook her head while taking another swig of wine. She was more certain than ever that Cameron had another, entirely separate life into which she would never fit.

When there was silence, Flora went on, "His name is Andrew. They 'aven't seen each other in years. The media lost interest long ago because no one will talk abou' it, and only a few of us know he's Cameron's. Andrew works in finance somewhere in't States."

Delilah was quiet for a long time. She took another sip from her mug before speaking. "Well, I think we made the right choice then."

"Which was?"

"Not to see each other again, romantically."

Flora nodded. "Have yer never bin married? Never wanted t'ave kids?"

Delilah shook her head. "No. And no. My life has always been about me, I guess. I never wanted kids. But my sister wanted to be a mom. Now, sometimes, I think I should have left that option open. For my father."

"That's a terrible reason to reproduce, luv."

Delilah sighed heavily. "I know. But sometimes I think if my father had grandchildren, if we had family holiday gatherings and such, our lives wouldn't feel so…broken."

Flora offered, "Someone much smarter than me once said tha' anything that dun't kill ye, makes ye stronger."

"Did you hear it from a wise person or see it on a motivational poster?" Delilah snarked.

Flora shrugged. "In this pub, it could've been a pissed miner quotin' a motivational poster."

Delilah chuckled. "I recognize it, actually. It's Friedrich Nietzsche."

"Either way," Flora held her gaze, "it's a good point."

Delilah looked away.

"I'm also sure," Flora added, "tha' wise people dun't 'ave kids t' make their fathers 'appy."

Delilah couldn't argue with that.

———————————

A little more than a week later, Delilah boarded a train for London. She had arranged to spend her last week in England seeing the city before flying home to the States. She also wanted to be closer to the airport in case her flight plans changed unexpectedly. Delilah knew that international travel could be tricky.

Her belongings fit into a large case and a couple duffel bags. She also had with her the vintage suitcase from the apartment in Chatfield. She was proud of herself, because she hadn't opened it once in six months. Now, Delilah guarded it with her life. She stowed it between her ankles on the train and held it in her lap in the cab from Euston Station to her hotel a couple of blocks south.

The hotel room was a bit of a splurge, but she was within walking distance of attractions to occupy her. Over the next several days, Delilah explored the area, including The British Museum and Regent's Park. Stumbling across the open-air theatre located there, she felt a tug of longing at seeing the stage. She could almost smell the musty dressing rooms, the cases full of makeup, and worn leather dance shoes. She took pictures of Big Ben and Westminster Abbey from afar because she didn't want to risk getting caught in throngs of people. On her second-to-last day in the city, Delilah called it a night early. She was curled up under the thick duvet on her hotel bed, watching television, when an advertisement for a morning program caught her attention.

"Tomorrow," the perky blonde anchor said, "we'll be talking with Cameron Burke, who is currently filming a guest role on the hot new dramedy *Lost the Plot*. We'll dish about his juicy role, as well as the release of the much anticipated fourth installment in the *Heir of Taivas* series, in theaters this summer."

The blonde went on to encourage viewers to watch live the next morning. Delilah felt her stomach flip. She knew enough about the station to know their morning show was filmed in London. Googling on her phone, she located the studio about a mile away. Another search showed pictures of fans waiting outside for autographs with morning show interviewees. For the first time in a month, Delilah knew where Cameron would be. She was standing by her decision not to get involved with him further, but a part of her wanted to see him one last time. She wanted to see him at work, as if to prove to herself that the man who kept her company in a little pub, the man who watched movies with her and walked her home in the snow was, in fact, the same man in those movies. She needed to see Cameron-the-Actor for the first time.

The next morning, Delilah stood outside the television studio. Not surprisingly, there was already a group of people gathered. Delilah set about waiting at the back of the crowd. She had braided her hair down her back and pulled one of her knitted hats down over her ears. She kept her plain, leather jacket wrapped tightly around herself, and she wore sunglasses.

Shortly after ten, Cameron made his appearance. To much cheering and screaming, he walked, accompanied by security, out of the studio door and toward the crowd. He was dressed smartly in dark trousers and expensive shoes. He wore his dark gray shirt open at the collar under a well-tailored sport coat. His hair was rakishly disheveled in the way that took a few hours at the salon rather than tossed by the wind of the English countryside. He smiled at the crowd and his eyes were gray-green in the morning light. He was Cameron, but different. As he began to make his way through the crowd, signing anything he was given, Delilah came to a startling conclusion: It was as though Cameron himself had a twin. This man looked and sounded like the man she knew, but he was also entirely different. *This* was Cameron-the-Actor.

Suddenly, he saw her. With a slight flicker in his eyes, he recognized her. Delilah didn't move. Either smiling at him or running away would draw attention to her. So she stood still. Cameron kept talking and signing. To the rest of the crowd, nothing had happened, but Delilah felt her heart pound. He knew she'd come. He knew she'd sought him out and there was no playing this off as an accidental meeting.

Part of her wanted to wait for him, to let the rest of the people filter away and run to him. Yet she held back, because it made no sense that he would want that. Maybe he enjoyed their unexpected, interim friendship and their one night together, but she meant it when she said she would not ask for more. Delilah didn't want his world. She didn't want to smile a big, fake smile while the media discussed her sister and carelessly showed images of planes hitting buildings. She told herself to be grateful for what Cameron already gave her. He made her want to live again, and that was enough. So she chose to walk away.

With purpose, but not too quickly, she turned and walked down the street. Taking deep, calming breaths, she slowly made her way back to the tube station and on to her hotel. Once she was safely in her room again, she began to pack her things, if only to take her mind off seeing Cameron again. However, she wasn't surprised when, a couple of hours later, her phone chimed that she had a message. Picking it up, she read:

> Saw you this morning. Why didn't you mention you were in the city?

Delilah took a deep breath and answered:

> I knew you were busy. I know this is a crazy time for you.

> That it is. Still, we could meet for tea later. I have an hour.

> I can't. I have a red-eye flight home tonight.

> I understand. But the offer always stands.

She felt a pang in her chest and fought the urge to change her mind. Eventually, she typed:

> I know. Maybe someday. For now, good luck with the television show. And the premiere this summer. I'll be watching.

Delilah left it at that.

Later that night, the lights of London-Heathrow disappeared beneath her as she was lifted skyward. Her ears were plugged to block out the whine of the jet engines. Her mind was medicated to numb memories of airplane parts scattered across city blocks. Her eyes were closed to discourage conversation, and the suitcase with all her memories of Anna was stowed between her feet. Delilah was going home, and the story of her and Cameron was over, whether or not she liked the ending.

11
Deep Vault of Blue

Go, sit upon a mountain steep,
and view the prospect round;
The hills and vales, the valley's sweep,
the far horizon bound.

Then view the wide sky overhead,
the still, deep vault of blue,
the sun which golden light doth shed,
the clouds of pearly hue.

—From "Pleasure" by Charlotte Brontë

Your lungs sound good, for you. No change on the scans, either.

Delilah thought over the words her longtime physician, Dr. Sadler, said as she left her most recent appointment since returning to the states.

They took pretty good care of you across the pond, he quipped, his eyes crinkling with laughter.

Delilah was grateful to have found the mostly bald, gangly doctor who monitored her health problems carefully without taking himself too seriously. She was also grateful for the results of her checkup. She was in a holding pattern, her doctor said, with her normal oxygen saturation staying between eighty-nine and ninety-two percent. For anyone else, that would mean hospital admission. For Delilah, it was her normal.

Dr. Sadler's office was about forty-five minutes from her hometown of Branton, West Virginia. Today, the drive gave Delilah and her father a chance to catch up.

"You haven't told me what you managed to see while you were over there," Stephen MacClare mentioned once they were on the highway heading home.

It was Thursday morning, and Delilah had been back for two days. She spent much of it sleeping off her jet lag. Stephen was on spring break from teaching, so he was able to take her to the appointment. Delilah hadn't driven herself anywhere in the past eight months.

Glancing at her father, Delilah answered, "An odd assortment of things. I spent some time exploring the countryside near Chatfield, and north of it. There are lots of old castles and country houses that aren't big tourist attractions. And just by riding the trains, you can see a lot of beautiful scenery. The last week in London I went to the Palace and the parks and those types of things."

"It sounds lovely."

Delilah nodded in agreement.

Stephen drove cautiously, ever the rule keeper, as they rode in his old pickup truck that recently reached two hundred thousand miles. As he drove, Stephen raked his sandy-gray hair back to try and tame the unruly curls. Even short, it tried to curl in the spring heat. His eyes were greener than Delilah's, but she had his straight nose and thin lips. Today, he had clad his slightly taller than average frame in his usual denim and flannel, making him look more like a rugged mountain man than someone with a doctorate.

Delilah broke the silence. "Did you finish the first *Heir of Taivas* book?"

"I did. And the second one. They're not exactly Orwell, but they're compelling."

"And they get better," Delilah retorted.

"I concede, I may have judged them too quickly," her father teased with a smile.

There was a comfortable silence as the miles passed beneath them on the winding, undulating West Virginia highway. Delilah remembered a teacher saying once that if you ironed West Virginia out, it would be as big as Texas. She was inclined to believe it. Now, they were entering the outskirts of Branton, which sat a few miles over the border with Virginia. Nestled in the mountains, one two-lane highway cut through the center of town. Dark green mountains formed a backdrop on either side. To the west were the Alleghenies, and to the east were the Blue Ridge Mountains, including the Shenandoah National Forest. The closest city was Harrisonburg, Virginia, some fifteen miles east and where Delilah's doctor practiced.

The town of Branton was made up of clapboard houses and log cabins, one gas station, a collection of locally owned restaurants and shops, and an elementary school. Delilah traveled some ten miles through the mountains by bus for middle and high school, and her father still made the same trek now for work. The houses here were surrounded by scrubby grass and sprawling black oak or cottonwood trees. This morning, ribbons of white clouds were streaked across a hazy, blue sky. The air was dry and scented with pine and the promise of new maple leaves.

Staring out the truck window, Delilah couldn't help but draw parallels between Branton and Chatfield. She always imagined England to be a strange, foreign place, but having lived there, the similarities outnumbered the differences. Essentially created as mining communities, both towns had a population of locals who kept the small businesses alive. The rows of terraced houses on narrow streets in England were mirrored by the rows of tiny cabins lining dirt roads in West Virginia. The miners in Chatfield came home to meat pies and tea. In Branton, coal darkened hands devoured corn bread and gripped mugs of black coffee. There were differences, but in the ways that mattered they were much the same. Delilah smiled at the realization.

After driving another half-mile, Stephen ventured, "Have you talked to Cameron since you left?"

Delilah shook her head.

"Do you think you will again?"

"I don't think so. At least, not soon."

"So it was a temporary friendship?"

Delilah sighed. "I think so. We might text each other occasionally. But it's dangerous to do more."

"Dangerous?"

"His life is too public," she clarified. "There would be too many questions."

Her father pushed further, "So…it was just friendship?"

She knew what he was asking.

"Yes, mostly. We just talked about books and watched a few movies. There wasn't much else to do there. We had dinner once and…we spent one night together," she finished weakly.

"I thought so," Stephen said softly.

"I promised not to talk about it."

"I'm not asking you to."

"But you don't think it was right?"

Stephen sighed. "You know what I think. I believe in marriage and commitment. I don't think sex should be a recreational activity."

Delilah looked away, not wanting to have this conversation again.

"However," Stephen went on, "I see something different in you. You seem present. And I'm glad for that."

Mulling over his comment as the road passed beneath them, she stated, "He's twenty years older than me."

Her father said nothing.

"Do you think I have some sort of bizarre, Electra Complex?" Delilah asked with concern in her voice. "Was I trying to date my father?"

"I surely hope not. I hope I haven't messed you up that badly."

Not amused, she argued, "It wasn't *you* that messed me up."

Stephen sensed her change in mood. "Delilah, I know that you aren't your sister. I may not have always agreed with your choices, but I never expected you to get married at twenty-three and have lots of children. That isn't you, Lilah. That was Anna, and I don't expect you to become her. You can't. You cannot replace her. Not for me, and not for you, just like she could not replace your mother. It hurts like hell every day that they're gone, but it's time we talked about it."

She glanced over at him. "I really have put you through a lot, haven't I?"

Stephen tipped his head to the side. "Well, it's not every father's wish that his daughter will sleep with someone his age."

Delilah looked away again, not wanting to continue this vein of conversation. "I was referring to moving back into your house four years ago, then proceeding to nearly go crazy."

Watching the road, Stephen said, "We all handle things differently, Lilah."

"Still, I'm sorry. And you're right. It is time to talk about it."

Over the next several weeks, Delilah slipped back into a familiar routine. She unpacked her things and put the Tiffany blue suitcase back under her bed. She settled into her room—the same room she and her sister shared growing up.

Delilah's childhood home in Branton was a modest, one-story cabin her parents picked out when she and Anna were about three. It sat on a few acres of land on the edge of town. It had a comfortable family room at the rear of the house and a formal living room at the front that was used as a dance studio, a music studio, a playroom, and as many other things over the years. The kitchen, off the family room, was still sporting chipped Formica and appliances from circa 1983. The four bedrooms down the hall also changed little in twenty-five years.

Delilah knew it was probably unhealthy to live in her old room like she was in high school again, but she didn't care. She was safe here, so she slept in her familiar twin bed at night and read books during the day. She ate meals with her father and worked up the nerve to drive. A few weeks in, she decided to read the books Cameron gave her again. She denied it was because she missed him and told herself instead that she needed a good story to occupy her mind. She also thought she might appreciate them more the second time around.

On a sunny Wednesday in mid-May, Delilah decided to take a walk through the forest behind her house toward the first ridge of the mountains. She grew up climbing these trees and learning the trails so well she could find her way back at night. She taught herself not to fear heights here, and she read many books nestled in the branches of an old cottonwood. Later, when she came home between gigs, she hung her aerial silk from the branches of a spreading oak so she could practice daily. Now, however, she could barely walk a half-mile without stopping to catch her breath. Frustrated with her lungs, she turned back toward home.

Delilah absolutely hated not being able to breathe. She kicked at pinecones as she watched the sun slip behind the mountains. Today was a beautiful day, with thick, white clouds dotting the sky. Fireflies would prick the twilight soon. Spring was lovely, but Delilah used to be partial to fall. In the fall, the air was dry and cool, and the days were so bright and cloudless it seemed the sky couldn't be real. It was a pure, unbroken blue she took for granted as a child.

See that sky, Lilah? So blue it's hard to look at? It means fall is here and the leaves will change soon. It's September blue, and it means winter is coming soon.

Delilah let the memory wash over her, remembering Anna's words from their childhood. It was that same blue sky that killed her sister. Had the skies been overcast or rainy on September 11, it would have been difficult to navigate a Boeing 767 into the Twin Towers, or any building. The terrorists were flying by sight at that point, navigating the island of Manhattan by what they could see. Poor visibility could've thwarted the entire plan, or sent the planes into other, unintended targets. Delilah wished desperately that there had been clouds, or rain, or hail.

It was also on one of those clear days when Stephen first suggested Delilah go to England. Eight months ago, on September 20, Delilah had a debilitating panic attack in the parking lot of the grocery store. She was there to get corn and tomatoes for dinner, because her whole family was visiting, and Aunt Polly was cooking. A stranger casually commented, as he passed Delilah in the parking lot, on how beautiful the sky was. The comment triggered an attack that was so bad Delilah couldn't remember coming home. She understood the store manager called her father, and he picked her up from the gravel parking lot while concerned or voyeuristic shoppers looked on.

The morning after the attack, Delilah felt like a child who couldn't be trusted to leave the house alone. She walked the forest trails out of frustration until she couldn't breathe. She was fast approaching middle age, yet instead of buying a new car or getting a boob job, she was losing her shit in parking lots. It made her want to scream. It made her want to die, and her father knew it. So he encouraged her to go away. Stephen felt like being away from home and all the things reminding her of Anna would allow Delilah to get some perspective, or at least separation. She knew he took a gamble on whether putting some distance between her and her tragedy would ground her or send her over the precipice of suicide. Ultimately, Stephen was right about the trip being good for her. What he hadn't anticipated was her meeting Cameron Burke.

When she returned to her house on this May evening, she took her laptop out onto the back patio and randomly searched Cameron's name. Since their relationship was over, she saw no harm in Googling him again. His earliest photos were from his first Hollywood movie, which launched his career. He was just thirty when *Red, Red Rose* was released. It had all the action and romance of a late-seventies blockbuster. Cameron starred as a young executive who was quickly swept up into the criminal life of the woman he loved. From what

Delilah could tell, this film was also where he met Marianne. They made two more films together, with great success, but Marianne disappeared from Hollywood shortly thereafter.

Delilah opened and read Cameron's filmography again. She noticed that after his initial success, there was about a ten-year span when most of his work was on lesser-known films and television shows. She wondered if that lull had anything to do with his breakup with Marianne. She couldn't find all the details, but she gathered the divorce wasn't amicable. This dip in his fame also helped explain why Delilah hadn't recognized him. She was too young for his first films, and his next major success came from his role as Cyrus Whitkey in the *Fyrelords* trilogy. The first film was released at the height of her career, and she had little time for, or interest in, anything other than theater. The second two films came after September 11, when the world around her ceased to matter. After *Fyrelords,* things clearly picked up for Cameron, because she at least recognized the titles of most of his films. He was also nominated for several awards, taking home a few of them, including an Academy Award.

He must have quite a trophy case somewhere, she thought to herself.

Moving on from his filmography, Delilah looked at his array of photos again. In many of them, he had a woman on his arm. Marianne had dark, curly hair and wide, striking brown eyes. Naomi Ruiz-Sosa was caramel-skinned with silky black hair. Catherine Beckworth had shiny, flame red hair and bright blue eyes. They were all incredibly beautiful and Delilah felt certain she was no match for them.

Searching on YouTube, she watched Cameron in interviews, in autograph lines, and on red carpets. He was silver-tongued and charismatic, and he always entered events to an underscore of squealing women and hearty applause. The comments section on each clip of him was filled with everything from simple praise to graphic innuendo. She also found candid pictures of him on the streets, in restaurants, and getting into cars. Delilah could only imagine what it would be like to have a camera always trained on you.

He seemed to bask in it, but she imagined it must be draining. She assumed that was why he was in a pub in Chatfield hoping for solitude.

After an hour of watching videos, Delilah realized she wasn't paying attention to the specifics of what Cameron was saying. She was simply watching him, listening to his voice and recognizing his mannerisms. She let herself pretend he was talking to her. The sound of the patio door opening behind her made her jump, and she snapped the laptop shut.

Delilah spent the next two weeks watching Cameron's movies and trying to ignore how much she was starting to feel like a creepy fan. She started with the earliest ones and worked her way through all that she could either rent or stream online. With each film she watched, she felt like she was seeing a different facet of Cameron-the-Actor. Some of the movies contained scenes that she chose to fast forward because of the cinematic violence, but Delilah otherwise made her way through them.

In *Whom the Sword Devours,* a modern retelling of the Biblical story of David and Bathsheba set during World War II, Cameron starred as Sir Benjamin Frederick, Field Marshal of the British Army. Catherine Beckworth co-starred as Josephine Trent, his "Bathsheba." His role as Captain Edward Moore in *Absolution of Men,* in which he portrayed a slave ship captain who gave up his lavish lifestyle to work for the abolition movement, won him the Academy Award. Delilah's favorite film, however, was the one she watched last. It was an English film titled *Cadence is Calling* that received only a limited release in the US. Delilah was sure only Cameron's die-hard fans saw it. In the story, Cadence is dying of cancer, and her brother, Michael, is called from his corporate job to care for her when she discontinues treatment. Resentful at first, Michael reconnects with his sister and finds unexpected love with Sarah, a quirky neighbor. It was a simple story, probably one that had been told before, but Delilah appreciated it. Cameron's portrayal of Michael was down to earth, and she wondered if that's why she liked it so much. The man on the screen, although thirteen years younger, was more like the man she remembered than any other character he played.

About an hour into the movie, Michael and Sarah end up in bed together. As she watched Cameron's body move, as the camera focused on his mussed hair and his face in the act of lovemaking, she was overcome by memories of him with *her*. Delilah's body tingled as she recalled his weight on her and his skin against hers. She remembered his contours, his mouth, his hands, the texture of his hair, and her name on his lips. It was an overwhelming sensory experience, and she was suddenly wildly jealous of the fictional woman on the screen.

As soon as the movie ended, Delilah turned it off. She missed him, and she couldn't deny it. She missed waking up in the morning with somewhere to go. She missed their bantering, the way he pushed her, and the way he asked hard questions. Shaking off the feeling, she got up and straightened the sofa. It was time, Delilah decided, to stop the Cameron Burke Film Festival. The school year was days from being complete, and her father would be home in the mornings. This new obsession was no better for her than locking herself in her room and staring at pictures of her sister. It was time to act on what she said to Cameron and move on.

Three days later, on the fourth of June, Delilah took her father's truck and headed across the state line to Harrisonburg to pick up refills of her medications. Stephen offered to get them earlier in the week, but she wanted to go herself. She was ready to start driving again. After she picked up her medicine, she was examining the feminine products display at the pharmacy when a voice behind her asked, "Delilah?"

She turned around to find a tall, slender woman. Her glossy, black hair was razor cut into a stylish bob and her dark brown eyes lit up as she smiled. She was wearing gray leggings and two layers of tank tops. The woman held herself with a practiced grace even though two children were talking over each other to get her attention. They were girls with bows in their almost-black hair. They both looked older than five, but Delilah was terrible at guessing the ages of children. Their mother was Jenna Dabrezil, now Jenna Lassiter. She and Delilah danced for the same studio throughout most of their childhood. Delilah vividly remembered sharing long bus rides to competitions and helping each other sew elastic onto their ballet shoes. It had been years since they last saw each other. The last Delilah heard from Jenna, she was getting married, but Delilah was unable to attend. Age and children had softened Jenna, but she otherwise appeared much the same.

"Delilah MacClare?" Jenna asked again. "For real?"

Delilah nodded, not sure what to say. They stood in front of the Kotex display, sizing each other up.

Jenna broke the silence by saying, "I see some things never change. We're destined to meet in awkward situations." She reached out and selected a box of tampons.

Delilah laughed, remembering the night they spent searching hotel bathrooms for a feminine supply dispenser. That was the night they really became friends. They were thirteen at the time.

"It's been a long time," Delilah said softly.

"Long enough for me to produce three little monsters," Jenna quipped as her girls hid behind her.

"They don't look like monsters," Delilah noted.

Jenna laughed. "Maybe not these two. But I have a son. He's twelve. His current hobbies are eating and not changing his socks."

Delilah laughed, but she was humbly reminded of how much time had passed without her attention

"How long have you been back home?" Jenna asked, still smiling.

"It's been about two months," Delilah replied, not wanting to mention that she'd been home for four years before her trip to England.

"Are you still performing?"

"No. I…it's been…" Delilah struggled, her smile slipping.

Then it happened. That moment when the person she was talking to remembered exactly what happened to her family. That change in expression when the person went from being glad for the chance meeting to wishing they hadn't said hello. No one ever knew what to say. They usually offered some platitudes about Anna or just looked at her with pity. Jenna did the latter. However, her expression quickly changed.

Working up another smile, she said, "Doesn't matter. It's been too long since talked."

Feeling sudden relief, Delilah agreed, "It has."

Before either could walk away, Jenna added, "We're heading to a movie. I promised the girls they could see that musical movie for kids. You know, high school girl tries to make it on Broadway. Can't wait."

"That sounds…mind numbing," Delilah joked.

Laughing, Jenna offered, "You should come. I could use adult company. We could catch up."

Delilah started to refuse. She didn't want to intrude on a mother's time with her children, and she wasn't sure that catching up was the best idea. Something stopped her from immediately declining, though. It might have been her father's constant insistence over the past few weeks that she go out and do something, or it might have been the fact that Jenna didn't acknowledge the elephant in the room, the elephant in Delilah's life. She banished it, or at least rendered it into something to be brought up at Delilah's choosing. Jenna was being so…normal.

Before she could think on it further, Delilah answered, "Sure. I drove all the way out here. Why not see an implausible kids' movie?"

Jenna laughed, and they took their purchases to the counter. After paying, they headed to the movie theater a couple of blocks over. It was the only theater nearby, and it was bustling with the Saturday crowd. Delilah took a few minutes to calm herself before getting out of the truck.

It's a children's movie, she told herself after looking it up on her phone. *Just singing and barely a plot.*

Holding her head high, she followed Jenna into the theater. While they waited for the movie to begin, they reminisced. Jenna's family moved to West Virginia from New York when she was twelve. Jenna's father was a Haitian immigrant and her mother's family came from Puerto Rico. The girls connected in tap class one day when Delilah mentioned her mother was also from Long Island.

However, they were opposites in dance. Jenna was tall and long-limbed, with beautiful feet that were perfect for pointe work. Delilah, on the other hand, preferred acrobatics and lifts, even before she discovered the silks. The two girls were fast friends for years, and Delilah regretted letting that friendship slip away.

Now, Jenna updated Delilah on her life. She and her husband Jason lived with their three children, Isaac, Klarita, and Sunny in Harrisonburg, Virginia. She had been teaching dance for ten years at the studio where they met as children. Jenna's life clearly revolved around her family, and she reveled in it. She was happy, and Delilah was glad to know that.

Delilah shared a little about her years as an aerialist. She talked about her shows in Las Vegas, and she raved about the time she spent working for Disney in Florida. As for the last four years, however, she said nothing. And Jenna didn't ask. Before they could share any more, the lights dimmed and the previews began. Delilah marveled at all the movies she knew nothing about. Everything seemed so much bigger and louder than the last time she was in a theater. And maybe it really was.

The third preview began with lightning flashes and low narration, and Delilah quickly realized what she was watching. It was the preview for *Heir of Taivas: Retribution.* Her breath hitched as she watched the ominous images of ragged Citizens cowering with fear in the green mountains of Taivas. The preview was a barrage of suspenseful music and otherworldly characters being forced into servitude. There were scenes of Mohara rallying the Acclans of Earth. Finally, there were several clips of Marcus Eperra astride a black stallion, wielding a sword with his cloak swirling. When it was over, Delilah realized she'd been holding her breath. She let it out slowly. The older girl sitting beside Jenna looked on in awe, however. She gasped in delight and whispered to her mother something about being so excited.

Jenna leaned over and said, "Klari wants to see that movie. So far, I've told her she's not old enough."

Delilah glanced down. "How old is she?"

"Ten," Jenna whispered back.

Delilah silently admonished herself for being more nervous during a preview than a ten-year-old was about an entire movie.

Ninety minutes later, they exited the theater. The girls were full of candy and happily singing the fluffy songs from the movie. On the way out, they passed a row of large posters advertising upcoming releases. There were three for *Retribution* placed around the lobby, each featuring different characters. Delilah stopped in front of the one nearest the door. It was of Marcus looking rugged and fierce in his tunic, black leathers, and with long, black hair wild around his face. Delilah stared at the poster, finding Cameron behind the character. It reminded her of seeing her friends on Playbills or on show posters. It was him, but not.

She stood there a second too long, because Jenna turned back and said, "Isaac can't wait for that movie, either. I gave in and let him read the books. I guess I should be grateful that in between stuffing dirty clothes under his bed and eating all the chips, he loves to read."

"He sounds like a perfectly normal boy," Delilah mused.

"I guess so." Jenna smiled. "He loves Marcus, for sure. Marcus Eperra has made my son love a book series with a female protagonist. But I'll admit to loving him too, and Cameron Burke is a silver fox, for sure."

Delilah felt her stomach flip. Turning to smile at her friend, she said, "That he is." Then she looked back at the poster and added, "You know, I met him once."

Jenna's eyes widened. "Really?"

"Yeah. On a trip I took."

"Did you talk to him?"

"A little."

"What was he like?" Jenna pressed.

Choosing her words carefully, Delilah answered, "He was…intense."

Jenna returned with longing, "Stuff like that, meeting amazing people, makes me wish I kept dancing longer. But I suppose I fell in love."

"To each, his own," Delilah quipped softly, because Jenna certainly seemed happy.

Before they parted ways, Jenna added, "We should exchange numbers. Or maybe I can add you on Facebook?"

Feeling a little ridiculous, Delilah replied, "I don't have Facebook."

Jenna looked at her as though she admitted to thinking the earth was flat.

"I do have a phone."

Jenna recovered. "Good enough."

They exchanged numbers and said their goodbyes. Delilah watched as her friend corralled her giggling girls across the parking lot, then she headed back to the truck. An hour later, when she was home, Delilah opened her laptop. Taking a deep breath, she decided to start a Facebook account.

Two weeks later, on a hot June night, Jenna invited Delilah over for dinner. They had been texting since they reconnected, and Jenna was currently one of Delilah's five Facebook friends. The others were her father, her cousin Mandy, Jenna's son Isaac, and her Aunt Polly, who posted lots of pictures of her dogs.

Delilah accepted the dinner invitation after spending a restless day trying to read *The Great Gatsby* again. It was a great story, but she wasn't focused. For the first time in a long time, Delilah realized she was lonely, or at least aware of her isolation. And bored. So, that night, she headed to Jenna's house.

Between bites of spaghetti and a colorful salad, they enjoyed each other's company, and Jenna's girls plead their case for going to the waterpark at Massanutten the next day. The more time Delilah spent with Jenna, the more the years fell away. They told old dance competition stories and bemoaned their injuries. Jason was amenable. Fit, with thinning blonde hair and gray eyes, he had inspired Jenna to take up running. Delilah listened as they talked about their last half marathon.

After dinner, the kids begged for a movie. The girls produced a handful of sparkly-encased titles that made their brother roll his eyes. Isaac, with sharp focus, scanned the shelf and pulled out his selection.

Jenna took it from him, held it up and said, "I told you he was obsessed. I'm trying to talk him down from going to see *Retribution* at midnight in a few weeks. Mostly because I have to go with him."

Delilah smiled. Her friend was holding up *Heir of Taivas: The Seven Summits*.

"You can't get away from it right now," Jason inserted. "Everywhere you go, every time you turn on the TV, it's Mohara and Marcus all the time."

"Can we watch it?" Isaac pleaded softly.

Jenna's son was on his way to being tall and slender, like her, but with soft, hazel eyes and light brown hair.

With an apologetic look, Jenna said, "It's Isaac's turn to pick, so it looks like we're watching it again. This is about the fifth time.

You're welcome to stay if you want. Although I'm sure you're sick of it, too."

Delilah didn't immediately respond. She vividly remembered the last time she watched this movie. Memories of good wine and slow dancing filled her mind. It felt almost wrong to watch it without Cameron. But she couldn't explain all of that to Jenna and her family.

Instead, she shrugged and smiled. "I'll stay. I've only seen it once."

Jason made some popcorn and they crowded into the Lassiter family room. The movie ran more than two hours, and Delilah was glad that the violent magic was at a minimum in this one. Seeing Jermias, the wise ruler of Taivas, reveal himself as the villain at the end was still shocking. As the credits rolled, they all listened to Isaac exalt his favorite parts of the movie. Then Delilah said her goodbyes, and Jenna walked her out onto the porch.

Before Delilah could leave, Jenna spoke, "I'm glad you came. And I'm glad we reconnected. We should've kept in touch."

Delilah agreed, "We should've. But I was busy focusing on myself."

Jenna shrugged. "You made your career happen. And that's awesome."

"Maybe," Delilah reluctantly agreed, "but I'm back now, so…"

Her friend smiled. "I hope we see more of each other."

"Me too," Delilah agreed, starting down the porch stairs.

"Delilah?" Jenna called after her. "I haven't forgotten about her. About Anna."

Delilah swallowed hard and turned around.

"But I won't make you talk about her. I won't even ask." Jenna went on, "I just want you to know that a lot of people loved her. And you. We've missed you."

Delilah smiled, grateful.

The next morning, Delilah lay in bed for a long time staring at the ceiling. The day was already warm, but the humidity made it easier for her to breathe. She eventually sat up and got her bearings, waiting for the dizziness to pass as her lungs struggled to get oxygen to her brain. Reaching for her phone, she checked the time. It was ten-thirty. Thinking back to the night before, she remembered what Jenna said. The next installment of *Heir of Taivas* was due out in less than a month. She wondered if her friend would give in and take Isaac to see it at midnight. Delilah considered whether she should join them. She wanted to see it, but not alone.

Chewing her lip, she wondered when Cameron would see it, and she wondered what festivities were planned for the release. Tapping the browser on her phone, she did a search. Quickly, she had a flood of information. The London premiere was in about three weeks and looked like it would be a huge event. Four days after that would be the US premiere in New York City. Delilah read over the media coverage and assumed Cameron must be incredibly busy. Not that she expected him to keep in touch. She effectively told him they were done. Still, she was curious. She wondered if he found someone else to keep him company, yet.

She navigated Facebook, then tried to figure out Twitter, looking for Cameron's accounts. She hadn't considered following him on either until now. She supposed her hesitation stemmed from their unspoken promise not to see each other as the rest of the world did. She also had no idea how to use Twitter. She found Cameron's Facebook fan page and 'liked' it before she scrolled through it. It was hard to say if all the posts were his, but she felt like they were. He would want to control something like this, she decided.

Switching to Twitter, Delilah managed to make an account. Then she looked up Cameron again. Finding the account that was verified as his, she followed @TheCameronBurke. She hoped her name, @Waterfall_Angel, would get lost among all the others who followed him. Scrolling through his tweets, she perused what he said recently. They included:

Cameron Burke @TheCameronBurke

Tune in on July 7 for live coverage of the Retribution premiere. #HeirOfTaivas

Cameron Burke @TheCameronBurke

@TaivasFan60: In reality, I do not wield a sword. I wield an iPhone. #AsYoungAsMyPhone

Cameron Burke @TheCameronBurke

Say no to outtakes. Magical battles are not as interesting without the special effects. #Don'tRuinTheMagic

Delilah smiled as she read through several more tweets. Cameron was just as snarky online as he was in real life. He commented on everything, from his own work to other actors and the weather. She went back a little further, scanning the tweets from just after he left Chatfield.

Cameron Burke @TheCameronBurke

Much needed holiday with my beautiful sister, but glad to be back in London. #NoPlaceLikeHome

He included a few pictures of Chatfield and of him and Mara. Delilah noticed there was absolutely no mention of her. She was both relieved and slightly sad. It was as though they never met. What transpired existed only between them.

Out of some deep-seated need to remind herself what they had was real, she picked up her phone and pulled up Cameron's contact info. Before she could second-guess herself, she typed:

> I know it's been a while, but I wanted to wish you luck with all the premieres and such.
>
> Delilah

A few minutes passed before she received a reply:

Thank you, stranger. Are you
still at home?

> Yes.

Have you been well?

> I have. At least for me. I
> found an old friend and
> we've been hanging out
> some.

Good. I'm glad you have
someone else to argue with.

> She's a good friend. But I do
> miss fish and chips. And
> Flora.

And what about me?

> I suppose I also miss having
> lunch with a moody actor. ;-)

You do so much for my ego.

> I think your ego is fine. But I
> did watch Seven Summits
> again. And a few of your
> other movies. I got curious.

I hope you weren't
disappointed.

> Of course not. They were
> excellent. It's always odd to
> see you like that, though.

And I was hoping you'd think
I look better on film. They
hide the wrinkles and the
lack of exercise better on
camera.

> Haha. I prefer the real you.
> But I am going to see

Retribution. Probably with
Jenna. My friend.

Good for you. Have a lovely
time with your friend.

Absolutely. I'll think about
you, though.

And I'll miss watching it with
you.

Same here.

Maybe we'll catch up in the
States sometime?

Maybe. Until then…keep
making beautiful movies.

I'll give it my best.

Delilah set down the phone and forced herself out of bed, but
the smile remained on her face.

On the evening of July 7, Delilah scanned the web on her laptop,
looking for pictures and videos of the *Retribution* premiere in London.
Finding plenty, she marveled at the sheer size of the crowd and the
length of time people waited to be close to the red carpet. She saw
Cameron signing autographs and found pictures of him with other
cast members. She couldn't help noticing there was no woman on his
arm, although she wasn't sure that meant anything.

The next day, Delilah found more clips from the night before,
including some from the after-party. She noticed, however, that
Cameron was absent from the party. Shutting her computer, she
decided she had spent enough time staring at the screen.

Instead, she vacuumed the house for her father—which took
forever because the chore made her breathless—then she made
dinner. Helping around the house was a contribution she tried to

make in exchange for living, jobless, in her father's house. Delilah wanted to be useful and to abate his worries. So she made chicken salad for sandwiches and cut up fresh fruit.

That evening they ate on the front porch, and Stephen talked about the students he was tutoring over the summer. Delilah listened, enjoying the stories. It was a beautiful, warm evening, with fireflies dancing against the backdrop of a rose-streaked sky. The stars were starting to appear when she gathered their plates and carried them inside. Stephen stayed behind to check the raspberry bushes that grew along the side of the house. They were once wild, but he was trying to tame them this year.

Delilah smiled to herself as she rinsed the plates. It had been a good week. In fact, it had been a good month. She was proud of herself, because the pull of people and things outside of the house was stronger than her internal struggle. Since she returned from England, she had no serious panic attacks and few nightmares. She was given a good report from her doctor. She felt…better.

"Lilah?" Her father was calling her from outside.

The kitchen window was open and, although she couldn't see the front of the house, she could hear and answer him.

"Yes?" She called back.

"There's someone out here for you," Stephen called back.

Delilah rinsed her hands and headed back toward the front door. She thought it might be Jenna. Her friend knew this house from when they were kids, and she might've stopped by on her way to visit her parents in Franklin. Delilah came out the door wiping her hands on her old warm-up shorts that said "dancer" on the butt. Her t-shirt was damp from rinsing dishes. Her hair was both limp and frizzy from the heat and tied back carelessly with an elastic. She looked like a mess who was too old to be such a mess.

And Cameron Burke stood in her driveway.

12
To Love What Death Has Touched

'Tis a fearful thing
to love what death can touch.
A fearful thing
to love, to hope, to dream, to be —
to be,
And oh, to lose.
A thing for fools, this,
And a holy thing,
a holy thing
to love.
For your life has lived in me,
your laugh once lifted me,
your word was gift to me.
To remember this brings painful joy.
'Tis a human thing, love,
a holy thing, to love
what death has touched.

—"'Tis a Fearful Thing" by Yahuda HaLevi

Cameron leaned on a car that looked like it cost more money than Delilah made in her entire life. Dressed in casual trousers and a basic button-down shirt, with finger-tossed hair and his hands in his pockets, he looked like the man she remembered. Only the car was a new addition to his image.

He held her gaze and offered, "Hello."

The way his voice turned that one word into a sonnet made her stomach knot. She was both glad to see him and uneasy. This, after all, was her home, her safe place. This was sacred ground for her, and he had brazenly entered her territory. She wasn't sure what to do, or what to say.

When she didn't speak, her father approached Cameron, offered his hand, and said, "I'm Stephen MacClare."

"Cameron Burke."

"I figured as much," Stephen offered with a smile.

The two men sized each other up. Stephen had about four years on Cameron, and he was almost as tall. Stephen was sporting his lawn-working coveralls and his hair was curling in the heat. His hands were dirty, and the lines on his face were more pronounced from the sweat. Cameron, on the other hand, masked his age with polish. He pushed his dark hair back and smiled.

"I'm so sorry to just turn up like this. And I'm sorry to intrude on your evening," he apologized. "But I was on my way to New York and," he turned and met Delilah's eyes, "I wanted to see you."

She couldn't help but laugh. "On your way to New York? Even the most geographically challenged person knows that Branton, West Virginia is not on the way to New York City."

Cameron shrugged. "This is a stop I wanted to make."

When Delilah didn't move, her father dusted his hands on his coveralls and offered, "Why don't you come inside? We're not fancy, but we have a sofa."

"All right," Cameron agreed, still looking at Delilah.

She pulled open the screened door behind her, and Stephen led the way inside. As Cameron passed her, Delilah caught the familiar scent of his cologne. As she stepped inside, she closed her eyes and let the men disappear into the living room. She wasn't ready for this. This was the absolute last thing she expected to happen. Delilah was used to calling the shots, pulling the punches, and a hundred other metaphors for being in control. Taking a deep breath, she followed them into the living room.

Her father was sitting in his usual worn recliner on the far side of the room. Cameron was sitting on the sofa to her left. He looked up at her as she entered, and Delilah stopped. She leaned on the rocking chair just inside the door. The chair was her mother's. She rocked both Anna and Delilah to sleep in it. The desk across the room to her right was her grandfather's, but Stephen used it for work and bill paying now. Delilah's grandmother made the curtains framing the sliding doors that led to the backyard. Amidst all these familiar, comforting things sat the world-traveling, Academy Award-winning, spotlight-stealing Cameron Burke. Delilah felt the progression of their relationship was surprising in Chatfield. Here, his presence was downright ridiculous.

Delilah looked from Cameron to her father and back again. She had no idea what to say. Her father knew too much for her to pretend she had no idea why Cameron would seek her out. And Cameron knew her too well for her to act like this wasn't making her anxious. She looked back and forth between two men who both had a profound impact on her life, who were the antithesis of one another, and who both had reason to be wary of the other. After a solid two minutes, Delilah had still said nothing.

Finally, she choked out, "How did you find me?"

Cameron smiled. "You're the only MacClare family listed as living in Branton."

"Oh," she whispered. "And you drove here?"

Cameron nodded. "I flew into D.C. this morning, had my assistant meet me with my car, and drove from there."

"Why?" She asked softly.

"Because I wanted to see you," he stated again.

Delilah's eyes flicked to her father. He was watching her. Then he glanced back at Cameron.

Clearing his throat, Stephen spoke up, "I'll just go change. Give the two of you a chance to talk."

As he walked from the room, her father gave her a long look before disappearing down the hallway. Delilah sat down in the rocking chair and wound her fingers together.

Turning on the couch to face her, Cameron asked, "Why do I get the feeling you're not delighted to see me?"

Delilah tried to smile. "I'm just surprised. We don't have many visitors." She rubbed her face. "You know how I feel doesn't always make sense. You know me that well at least."

His face softened into compassion.

She sighed and went on, "If the media or the paparazzi…if they found you…here…"

Cameron sat up straighter. "I made sure they didn't follow me. There are some places they're not interested in going. I'm famous, Delilah, but I'm not royalty. I do manage to find places where I can be alone. I was in Chatfield for quite a while before they figured out where I'd gone."

"But if they do figure it out…"

He held her gaze. "Do you want me to go?"

She considered the question before responding. "No. Yes. I don't know."

"You sought me out in London, and you texted me two weeks ago. You seemed like you wanted to see me, too."

Glancing away, Delilah admitted, "You're right. I've missed your company. But I think we made the right decision. I still don't think we make any sense together, Cameron."

"Who says I want more than friendship?" He countered.

She looked at him intently but couldn't find an argument.

He leaned back on the sofa. "If I was someone else, just an average bloke you met on holiday, would you be so concerned?"

"Maybe not," she conceded, "but anyone who drives three hours out of their way to see me probably has expectations that I can't meet."

"Just two and a half hours," Cameron corrected with a hint of a grin. "What were your expectations when you came to see me outside of the television studio?"

She thought it over. "I wanted to see the other side of you."

"My thoughts were the same about driving out here."

"There's a difference between traveling a few blocks and hours of driving to find someone!"

"That's true," he agreed. "I suppose I really, *really* wanted to see you."

"I can't be one of your women, Cameron. I don't want to be on the list. Not because I'm too good or any better than the others, but because I'm too much of a realist. I stand by what I said before. If we keep our distance, we can stay friends."

Leaning toward her again, he said, "Then I'm here as your friend. And as a friend, I'd love to see you do something besides hide here."

Delilah started to argue, but her father came back into the room. He was dressed in jeans and a clean t-shirt, and he'd made an effort to comb his hair.

Standing in front of them, he asked, "Have you had dinner, Cameron?"

"I picked up some takeaway on the way in."

"And no one recognized you?" Delilah scoffed.

Cameron smiled. "Most people, even if they think I look familiar, assume it could never be the real me. And if someone did take photos, good luck to them selling photos of me at a takeout window."

Stephen chuckled. "Where are you staying tonight?"

"I suppose I'll find a hotel," Cameron shrugged.

Delilah laughed out loud at the absurdity of that idea.

"There isn't a decent hotel for miles," Stephen explained. "You're more than welcome to stay here. I'm sure it's nothing like you're used to, but we have a decent guest room. Has its own bathroom."

Delilah smiled tightly, knowing her father would offer hospitality to anyone, regardless of his personal feelings. She was also certain there was no way that Cameron Burke would stay in her house.

Cameron looked at them. "I don't seem to have any other options, do I? But it wasn't my intention to impose like this, so I'll leave it up to Delilah."

He looked at her, and Delilah knew he wanted her permission.

Unable to send him away, she said, "Stay."

Cameron smiled.

Delilah got up and hurried down the hallway to her bedroom. She needed to be alone.

The next morning, Delilah woke up to the muffled sounds of talking. Stretching to sit up in bed, she remembered.

Cameron is here.

She sat there, trying to decide what to do. She felt badly for being so cold to him the night before. The more she thought about it, driving hours out of the way to see her was *exactly* the kind of thing Cameron would do. It went along with buying expensive books for someone he just met or drinking a two-hundred-dollar bottle of wine while at home watching *Heir of Taivas*. He was a self-declared rule breaker and Mara warned her about his impulsiveness. Now, she had to decide whether she wanted to indulge him or ask him to leave.

Dragging herself out of the bed, Delilah grabbed some clothes and went to the bathroom between her bedroom and her father's study. Years ago, her parents tried to move her into the adjoining room, when she and Anna were school age. Before it became a study, it was meant to be her bedroom, but Delilah refused to sleep in a room without her sister. So her parents conceded and let her and Anna stay together in the biggest bedroom. Even when they became teenagers with their own interests, they stayed in the same room, often talking to each other in the dark before sleep.

After taking a shower and clipping back her damp hair, Delilah pulled on some short leggings and a baggy t-shirt. As she closed the door to the closet she used, she glanced over at the other one on the opposite side of the bathroom door. Their house was built in the early seventies, when small closets and bi-fold doors were all the rage. After Anna died, Delilah became protective of her sister's closet. In it were all her sister's things she managed to rescue from their Manhattan apartment, along with what Anna didn't take when she left for college. The room itself had changed little since then. Their posters were still on the walls and their *Sweet Valley High* books still filled the shelves. Their contrasting collections of cassette tapes were under the beds, and their stereo, circa 1990, was still on the dresser. Shortly before Anna passed away, the twins talked about redecorating and making it into another guest room. After September 11, Delilah swore never to change it. It was a shrine, and Delilah knew it. She knew it was strange to not only keep it this way, but to sleep in here. But she didn't care. She needed this place.

Crossing to the other closet, she opened it gingerly. To the far left hung some of Anna's clothes. In the middle was a collection of ridiculous things they both wore in high school. To the right were Delilah's clothes from their apartment in the city. She ran her hands over the expensive fabrics. Most of the clothes were out of style now, because the pre-nine-eleven Delilah MacClare spent all her extra money on designer clothes. She bought them secondhand from uppity consignment stories or saved for pieces she really wanted. On the shelf above were her Coach and Louis Vuitton purses. In boxes on the floor were her shoes, a collection of Louboutins, Jimmy Choos, and Manolo Blahniks. There were less expensive pieces mixed in here and there, but Delilah's old wardrobe was all about flash. On the floor of the closet, in a basket beside the shoes, was her old dancewear. In the back, in a place where she couldn't—or wouldn't— have to see it, hid her sister's violin, tucked safely in its worn case.

Taking a deep breath, Delilah ran her hands over the hanging clothes, stopping on a black dress. Pulling it out, she looked at the crisscrossing straps and the asymmetric hem. It was Versace, and by far the most expensive thing she owned. She remembered how good it made her feel. She also remembered how Anna spent her money buying coats for homeless children.

I was a frivolous brat, Delilah chastised herself.

"Wow. That's an expensive collection."

Delilah whipped around to see Cameron staring into the closet from behind her. He was dressed casually again. Recovering, she returned, "And now you're in my bedroom?"

Cameron shrugged and with a spark of mischief in his eyes said, "You were in *my* bedroom."

She swallowed hard, unable to deny that.

He looked at the dress in her hand. "And I thought you might not have anything to wear."

"What?" She asked, putting the dress back and closing the doors.

"I want you to come with me to the premiere."

She stared at him.

"On Monday," he explained, "I want you to come with me to the *Retribution* premiere."

Delilah stood there, mouth open, as though she'd lost the ability to speak. Eventually, after she found her voice again, she said, "No."

He cocked his head. "Why?"

She gave him a long look. "I think you know why."

"I know it's a big ask. I know there will be crowds and cameras, but I'll be with you. The entire time."

Shaking her head, Delilah insisted, "No."

"Is it more than all the cameras?"

She looked him in the eyes. "It's the city…"

His face registered understanding.

Delilah turned and walked out of the room. She headed down the hall to the kitchen with Cameron following behind. She was saved from talking about it further by her father, who was frying bacon.

Stephen looked up and said, "I wasn't sure what people eat in England. My parents didn't talk about it much. But my father did like bacon."

"We mostly eat, well...food," Cameron deadpanned. "And we do have bacon in England."

Delilah smiled. "English bacon is different."

"That it is," Cameron agreed.

Delilah set about making some eggs and toast, trying to ignore the absurdity of the entire situation. Her father kept to himself, getting out plates and saying little. When they sat down to eat, Delilah busied herself with pouring cream and sugar into her coffee. She realized Cameron was watching her as she stirred it.

"You know," Stephen cut into the silence, "you should take a drive through the Shenandoah valley today. It's not fall, but it's still a beautiful drive."

Delilah looked at her father like he'd lost his mind. He was acting like they had movie stars for breakfast every day. She had grown used to being around Cameron, but she expected her father to be more ill at ease. Instead, he was suggesting they go for a drive as though they were hosting her incredibly dull cousins for the weekend. She wondered if, inside, he was just as uncomfortable as she was and wanted them out of the house.

"That sounds lovely," Cameron answered, smiling at Delilah.

She sat there with her coffee cup in her hand trying to figure out what to say. She finally choked out, "Ummmm…"

Her father gave her a pointed look. "You haven't driven up there in a while. It would be a nice change, don't you think?"

Delilah held his gaze, certain he was talking about more than a change of scenery. "All right…yes."

After breakfast, Delilah took her time brushing her teeth and finding her shoes. She could hear her father talking with Cameron and wondered what they could possibly find in common to talk about. She assumed the topic was her, but she hoped her father was rambling on about books instead.

By late morning, Delilah led Cameron outside. She had her keys in her bag, but he sauntered over to his own car. In the daylight, she could see that it was a deep gray, Bentley convertible. She'd been out of the loop for a while, but she could guess at the price tag.

"Bentley Continental GT. In gunmetal," he answered her unspoken question while pulling out a fancy key that wasn't a key.

"Is it yours?"

He smiled. "Yes. I had my assistant meet me at the airport with it. I have another one in London."

"Well," she quipped, "if you're going to own a car, why not spend a couple hundred thousand on one? Or better yet, get two."

He stopped short of opening the door. "It's fascinating, the unexpected things that you know."

She slid into the car after he opened her door. He folded himself into the driver's seat and took a minute to put down the top of the car. She watched as it smoothly disappeared into the trunk area and marveled at what money could buy. Cameron put the car into gear and followed her winding driveway to the two-lane road that ran through Branton. Once they were out of town, Delilah couldn't help feeling a thrill in her chest as he dropped the car down a couple of gears and the acceleration pushed her back into her seat. The engine roared as he opened it up on the mountain highway.

"The speed limit's thirty-five through the park," she goaded him.

Cameron laughed. "We're not there yet, are we?"

"How does it feel to be driving on the *right* side of the road?" She fired back.

"I can drive *anywhere*."

Delilah smiled and sat back in her seat. Like this, things felt right between them. This was the way they were in Chatfield, alone in their secret place in the world. Delilah relaxed and let the familiar scenery pass. She gave Cameron directions to Skyline Parkway, which ran the length of Shenandoah National Park. Like so many places, she hadn't been this way in years. The parkway was about a three-hour drive from end to end through the northern Blue Ridge Mountains. The Alleghenies were off to the west, creating rolling beauty from horizon to horizon. The scenery wasn't as colorful as in the fall, but everything was lush and green, with gray outcroppings of rock hinting at the mountains beneath the foliage. With the top down, they had a panoramic view. Delilah marveled at the richness of what she often took for granted. Showing it to Cameron made her look around again. He made her see and appreciate the world she'd been shutting out.

Toward the end of the drive, they stopped at an overlook point. Delilah picked one where only a few people were stopped. It was Saturday, however, so it was impossible to avoid everyone. Glancing at Cameron, she said, "We don't have to get out."

Cameron shook his head. "I didn't drive all this way just to see it from the car."

Delilah looked around. "How are you going to keep them from recognizing you?"

"I have sunglasses," he stated, pulling them out and putting them on.

"Really?" She scoffed. "Now you look like…you. In sunglasses."

Reaching into a bag behind her seat, he pulled out an old ball cap. Pulling it down over his head, he asked, "Do I look American enough, now?"

Delilah laughed, because he did look different. Cameron killed the engine and got out of the car. She grew suddenly serious and followed him. He walked to the far end of the overlook and sat down on an old bench. Delilah joined him, noting that no one looked in their direction.

She asked, "How often can you do this? Go out and have no one recognize you?"

Cameron shrugged. "It greatly depends on where I am. In London or Los Angeles? Nowhere. Almost nowhere in New York. I can usually manage some time at home before they find me, as you saw. But no one would expect me to be *here*."

Delilah glanced over at some teenagers pointing at the valley with their parents on the other side of the parking area. She imagined what they might do if they realized that Cameron Burke or, to them,

Marcus Eperra, was sitting just across the way. She smiled, because it was a fun secret.

After a few minutes, Cameron asked, "Why are you so afraid of having me here?"

Delilah swallowed. "You know why."

"Do you think I intend to exploit you?"

"No. But I don't think you can control what will happen if they find you here. Or if I go anywhere else with you."

"Which is why you won't come to the premiere?"

"Yes," she confirmed softly.

Without looking at her, he said, "They can write what they want. They can say what they want. But they can only get to you if you let them."

Delilah looked away, not sure how to make him understand. "This isn't just about hurting my feelings, Cameron. I have diagnosed PTSD. One of my triggers is large crowds, and you're asking me to put myself in a situation with masses of people. I don't think you understand that I don't *control* the panic attacks."

He softened. "You're right. I don't completely understand. I can't."

She was grateful he admitted as much. They sat in silence for another few minutes as the sun slipped in the sky, turning the mountains into silhouettes. The air was warm and heavy with the promise of mid-summer storms. Cameron was just a few inches from her, but she kept her focus forward. It was as though they reset themselves, reverting to the unspoken agreement not to touch one another. It would be simple just to let it all fade and be this way— side by side. Occasional friends. Secret friends. Delilah didn't think he would ever talk about her in public if she didn't concede to it. She didn't think he wanted her as some sort of trophy, because she wasn't one.

"Cameron," she asked again, "why did you want to see me? Why did you come all the way out here?"

He was silent for a minute.

She studied the reflection of the mountains in his sunglasses as he said, "Because I can't stop thinking about you."

"Cliché," Delilah returned.

He tried again, "You make me think about something other than myself."

She took a breath. "I'm not a charity case, Cameron. I'm not a project. I can't be the thing you use to fix your image."

"I know," he said softly.

They didn't say much else, even as they got back in the car and made the drive back to Branton. They put the top of the car back up and the sun slowly melted behind the trees as they drove. They stopped on the way home and picked up fast food, with Delilah making the purchase so Cameron could stay out of sight. At Delilah's home, they ate and made small talk with Stephen. Then, exhausted from being out all day with lungs that had to work twice as hard, Delilah fell into bed.

The next day, Delilah found it less odd that Cameron was in her house. He spent most of the morning on the phone doing what sounded like making arrangements for the premiere. She watched an old movie on television and worked her way through half a box of cereal. Sometime close to noon, Cameron joined her in the living room.

He sat in the chair across from her. "My apologies. My publicist is a bit out of sorts because I made this detour."

"I would imagine so."

Cameron leaned in and asked again, "Come with me tomorrow. Please? Just for the day. Let me give you one amazing evening."

She shook her head. "No."

He didn't argue. He watched the movie with her for several minutes before asking, "Where's your father?"

"At church," Delilah returned. "He promised my mother he would always go."

"They must have loved each other very much."

Delilah nodded. "He's always had great faith. He sees beyond this life in a way I can't, or that I haven't been able to since…"

The silence was heavy with what she didn't say.

Cameron took a deep breath. "Delilah…can you show me your sister? Maybe some of the pictures you had in Chatfield?"

She caught her breath, because she hadn't expected the question. And she wasn't sure how she wanted to answer. Of course he was curious, because there were no photos of the twins on display in the house. Delilah put them all away years ago in one of her bouts of grief-induced insanity. Deciding there was no reason to hide this last piece of herself from him, she got up and motioned for him to follow. Leading the way to her bedroom, she turned on the overhead light. Reaching under her bed, she pulled out a long, wooden box. Sitting cross-legged on the floor, Delilah pulled out the first of several photo albums. Cameron crossed the room to sit on the bed near her. Opening the album, she let him look at the photos.

"These are from when we were children," she explained as he flipped the pages.

She watched his face color with understanding as he looked at pictures of her and Anna in matching dresses and smiling with missing teeth. It was hard to know who was who in the early pictures. Delilah picked up another album and rose to sit on the bed next to him.

"These are from high school." She turned the pages of the book in her lap.

In these, the differences were more obvious. Anna's pictures featured her playing her violin or some other instrument, her face blissful. Delilah was always posing, whether behind their birthday cake or in her dance recital photos.

"My father took a lot of pictures." She explained, "He made all these albums for us when we went to college. Or when Anna went to college. I went to circus school."

"What did she study?"

"Music education," Delilah answered. "She played professionally for years after college, but she was working on her master's degree in music therapy when she died. She wanted to help children who'd been through trauma, and she was ready to give up performing and work with kids full-time. She also wanted a family of her own."

Cameron smiled wryly. "So, we both have sisters who deserve sainthood, while we each feed our external locus of self-esteem."

Delilah cocked her head. "Is that your clinical diagnosis of us?"

He shrugged, still smiling.

She suddenly realized he was right. She *did* understand what it was like to have someone like Mara as a sister. Anna wasn't as forward as Mara, but she always pushed Delilah to focus, to look toward the future. As she thought more about it, Delilah felt her attraction to Cameron begin to make a little more sense. They were more similar than she realized. They had common ground, rather than just an ambiguous attraction.

Looking at the pictures in her lap, she said, "Anna was always the conscientious one. She was cautious. She was content to play her violin or the piano all afternoon. She always fed the pets I begged for, and she recycled *everything*. She saved up her allowance and sponsored a child overseas. I spent all of my money on clothes and music." She paused. "I used to say that our parents named us perfectly. Anna was named after a Biblical prophetess who blessed infant Jesus. I was named after a Biblical whore. Of course, it was funnier then."

Cameron looked her over. "I'm sure you were different, but I think 'Biblical whore' is a little extreme."

Delilah laughed. "Maybe, but 'selfish' and 'vain' are not. Anna wanted babies, and she would've been a great mom. Me, on the other hand, I had surgery to make sure I would never have to deal with kids."

His face fell into understanding.

"Sometimes," she added softly, "I wish I could undo it. I wish I could give my father the grandkids she didn't. I wish I could be…"

She stopped, not sure how to finish. Instead, she handed Cameron the album in her lap and showed him a picture of her and Anna dressed for homecoming one year. Delilah had on a miniskirt and a denim jacket with knock-off designer pumps. Her hair was blown out and crimped. Anna was wearing a long skirt and sandals with her hair in careless braids. She also wore a patchwork coat.

Cameron looked from the picture to Delilah. "That's her coat. The one you were always wearing."

Delilah nodded. She recognized that the Delilah he knew looked more like Anna than the Delilah in these pictures. She allowed herself to disappear, and she was trying to keep Anna alive through what she saw in the mirror.

Softly, she said, "They were her sweaters, too. The ones I wore all winter. I just…I needed to be able to see her, somehow."

"Tell me more about her," Cameron asked gently.

Delilah set the photo album aside. Pulling out some of the smaller albums, she flipped through to show him pictures from their life in New York.

"Anna went to NYU, like our dad," she explained. "We lived together while I went to circus school and performed with Big Apple. But then I started performing in other cities and Anna got married. We were apart more than we'd ever been in our lives. I know not all twins are like us, and I don't fault them for it. But she was my landing place. I always knew I could fall back on her in between jobs or if something didn't work out." She struggled. "I took her for granted. I know I did."

Delilah took a minute to gather her thoughts.

"Anna married her boyfriend, Preston, when she was twenty-three. They were both professional musicians, and they had a band that did several big gigs a year. I used to tease her that someday she would be playing for a show I was dancing in, just like in high school. Years later, when they got the apartment in Tribeca, they let me move in. Preston was a genius in both music and math, and math is much more lucrative than music. He was working at One World

Trade, and I was performing in *Pippen* at a theater in New Jersey when…" She shook off the heaviness. "I loved the city: the constant activity, the restaurants, and the shows."

She handed Cameron a picture of her and her friends dressed for a night out. She looked like another person with her hair shiny and straightened and her face perfectly made up. He smiled at the person captured in the photo.

Delilah added carefully, "Once, I went to see this brand-new company of dancers that was touring when I was maybe twenty-six. They were very innovative. They did a piece completely without music. It was intentional, and the idea was to make the audience *miss* the music. It was called *Stolen*, and the dancers were quite literally trying to find their music. It made you realize how much of an equal player the music is. Lyrics, dance, they are all driven by it." She added very quietly, "Anna was that…for me. She was my music."

Cameron was now staring at her, and Delilah decided to move on and spare him having to keep searching for words.

"These," she changed the subject by offering him a slim portfolio, "are my résumé pictures."

He took the portfolio from her and flipped it open. Each page had a glossy photo of her from a different show. There were several shots of her on the lyra and a few from her shows in Florida with Disney. There were the ones he saw, and more, from the music video she did. Finally, there were her Cirque photos. He stopped at those, studying the lines of her body in a black silk.

She leaned over and explained each pose, saying, "This is called 'sail.' And this one is 'crucifix'."

Suddenly, she realized how close they were. Her hair was tumbling over his arm, and she was almost in his lap. He was silent, and she knew he was using every ounce of control not to touch her. She pulled back, not wanting to lead him on.

He said carefully, "I wish there was something I could say that would be helpful. But there are no words for a loss like this, no words for the way she died or for what you lost."

The words threw a switch within her. Before she could stop them, tears rolled down her face.

"I'm sorry," Cameron apologized. "I shouldn't have asked you to do this."

She shook her head and quickly wiped her cheeks. "No. I'm not going to cry today. I'm not."

He gave her a tiny smile. "But...you are."

She laughed in spite of herself, then let a few more tears fall before she truly tried to stem the flow. She stood up to retrieve some tissue from the bathroom while he continued to look at pictures. When she returned, he'd traded them for a worn notebook from the back of the box.

"What are these?" He asked curiously.

"Those are Anna's journals. It was something we both did. Hers are full of composed music and lyrics," Delilah explained softly. "There's another box under the bed full of her original music on tapes and CDs." Crossing to the bookshelf at the foot of her bed, she touched a row of spiral-bound notebooks and said, "These are mine. Instead of music, I wrote bad poems and copied down song lyrics. I cut things out of magazines and pasted them in there. Sometimes I just copied poetry. I occasionally wrote free verse. Mom gave me a book of poetry for my last birthday before she died. She gave Anna her professional violin and encouraged us to make the journals. I think they were supposed to help us work through losing her. I'm not sure why I still keep them. I keep a lot of things I probably shouldn't."

Cameron offered, "Mara keeps our parents' things in a trunk at the end of her bed."

Delilah wiped her eyes with the tissue again. "My father thinks I should pack the room up and change it. He doesn't say it, but I know he does. I think it hurts him to see it. We're opposites when it comes to grief. And he's probably right. He was right about England, after all. It was good for me to get out of here for a while."

Turning toward her, Cameron seized the opportunity. "Come with me tomorrow. Please."

She sighed. "Why do you want me there so badly?"

"Because I want you in my life. And this is what my life is. This series of films is one of the biggest things I've ever done, and I cannot think of anyone else I want to share it with."

Delilah was struck by his open sincerity. Taking a deep breath, she said, "I'll think about it."

After they returned the wooden box to its sanctuary, she showed him a few more lighthearted things: yearbooks and prom photos and her collection of 80's power ballads on cassette. When her father returned home, they ordered pizza.

"It's the only thing you can order here," Stephen teased, "because it's the only restaurant that delivers."

They opened some wine with dinner and Cameron answered Stephen's questions about filmmaking. Then Delilah and her father cleaned up while Cameron took another phone call.

Cameron's phone call turned into three, and Delilah decided to take a bath. She leisurely soaked her body, keeping her hair clipped up to keep it out of the water. When she emerged from the tub, she dried herself and dressed in a long nightshirt. She sat on her bed, thinking over the past two days. She considered Cameron's invitation and warred with it. Finally, she went to the medicine cabinet for a Xanax before slowly making her way back to the living room. She didn't find Cameron there, so she walked back down the hall.

Delilah knocked on the guest room door and heard him softly bid her entry. Turning the doorknob, she slipped inside. She shut it behind her and looked at him. He sat on the edge of the bed in black pajama pants and a white t-shirt, checking his phone.

Delilah straightened her nightshirt, wondering why she hadn't thought to put on a robe or something. Or at least pants. She still wasn't used to having anyone else in the house.

Crossing her arms over her chest, she stated, "I thought a little more about what you asked."

"And?" Cameron looked expectant.

"I'll go, but only to the premiere. And I won't go downtown."

He smiled broadly. "I'm so glad. I want you to be there. I want you to see the film and have a wonderful time."

"I will certainly try."

"You deserve to be happy."

"No," she scoffed, "my *sister* deserved to be happy."

Standing up, he came around the bed to where she was standing and insisted, "So do you."

"And a movie premiere is going to make me happy?" She countered.

He stepped closer. "It's a start."

They stood there for a long time, not speaking. Delilah felt the tension between them. It was thick and almost palpable, but she had a feeling he wouldn't touch her again, possibly ever, unless she gave him permission. She'd pushed him away too many times, and he had too much pride to be rejected outright. He did take another step forward, however, so that she could feel his warmth. She could smell the crisp, pine scent of soap on him.

The weight of the decision to go to the city with him pressed on Delilah, and her desire for distraction overrode the conviction to keep her distance. In one bold move, she stepped forward and placed her hands on his chest. She felt his surprise. Pushing up onto her toes, she kissed him softly on the mouth, and that was all he needed.

Cameron wrapped one hand around her head and kissed her urgently. Delilah squeaked in surprise but did not pull back. He backed her against the door and pressed into her. She snaked one arm around his back and the other up around his neck. Her body flushed as their kiss intensified. When he pulled away, she pulled him back in. For the next few minutes, Delilah let one breathless kiss follow another as she drew him tighter against her. She couldn't deny that she wanted this, but it was about more than sex. She wanted to be touched. Delilah realized over the past few months how much she missed human contact.

Finally, she pulled back to catch her breath. Her chest rose and fell heavily as she tried to take in enough air.

"Are you okay?" Cameron asked softly.

She nodded and kissed him softly again. He kissed her hair and pulled her against him. She could feel the contours of him, remembering the one night they spent together. He ran one hand up and down her spine and she told herself she should pull away. Delilah could feel his arousal stirring through the thin layers they wore. Her father was down the hall. She had never had sex in this house. It felt like a sin. But she was no saint.

"Delilah?" He whispered in her ear, and all arguments were rendered null.

Pulling back just enough, she kissed him hard on the mouth again. She put her hands on his chest and pushed him back toward the bed.

When they reached the side of it, he whispered into her mouth, "What are you doing?"

"I think we established…that we are lovers," she answered hoarsely.

Cameron didn't argue. Suddenly, their languid exploration of each other became fervent again. She pushed him back onto the bed and fell on top of him. Delilah pulled his t-shirt off and kissed her way over his body. She remembered the way he felt in the dark, but now she appreciated the lines of his body in the soft light. He pulled her t-shirt over her head and tossed it away. Their kisses grew deeper and more desperate as he rolled her to her back. His pajama bottoms and her panties joined the pile on the floor, and Cameron kissed her from neck to navel, grasping her hips in his hands before claiming her mouth again.

There was no waiting tonight. Delilah could tell he had been fighting desire for two days, perhaps for two months. Now, he drove inside of her. She wrapped her legs around his back and prayed her father wouldn't hear the complaints of the old bed as Cameron thoroughly shagged her.

Delilah bit her lip to keep from crying out as her body climaxed. She thought she caught a whisper of profanity as Cameron buried his face in her neck and went with her. His breathing was ragged, and she held him close, appreciating the heaviness of him on top of her. She ran her hands over his back, tracing the lines of his shoulders. She entwined her legs with his, not ready to let him go. Pushing his hair back from his forehead, she combed her fingers through it a few times. He met her eyes, and his post-coital gaze became curious.

She kissed his lips. "You're beautiful like this. So messy. So…expressive."

He looked at her as though he wasn't exactly sure what she meant.

"I mean," she went on, "some men hold back. They try to be stoic. Or they put on a ridiculous show. But you are completely undone."

"Thank you?"

She released the grip with her legs so he could shift some of his weight off her, but she continued to run her hands through his hair. She kissed him tenderly and asked, "Is it wrong that all I want is to see you like this again and again?"

Cameron drew a deep breath and kissed her forehead. "God, you do undo me. I'm supposed to be the one with all the good lines."

"I think I win this round," she teased as she pulled away from him. She slid out of the bed and searched for her shirt.

"Leaving so soon?" He almost seemed desperate.

"My father is a light sleeper."

"Stay," he argued. "You're an adult. If you give me a little while, you can undo me again."

Delilah laughed softly. "No. I need some sleep and I have to pack if I'm going with you. Sleep is good for my anxiety. And you have to drive tomorrow."

Cameron returned, "I'll take care of you. I promise."

Delilah nodded as she pulled on her shirt. Cameron sat up and pulled his pants back on, eyes still on her. She crossed back to kiss him gently once more before quietly slipping from the room.

13
I Went Back

I went back to the clanging city,
I went back where my old loves stayed,
But my heart was full of my new love's glory,
My eyes were laughing and unafraid.

I met one who had loved me madly
And told his love for all to hear,
But we talked of a thousand things together,
The past was buried too deep to fear.

—From "The Ghost" by Sara Teasdale

Cameron woke the next morning with the ghost of Delilah's hands on his skin. He kept his eyes closed for a few minutes, remembering how she felt beneath him, how her kisses drove him to madness. He remembered her face, with her lips parted and her eyes closed, her eyelashes splayed over her delicate cheeks. He let himself remember burying his face in her hair as climax rocked him. He wanted to burn the memory into his brain in case she ran from him again. If she decided, once again, that they should part ways, he wanted to have the night before so deeply marked in his memory that no amount of age or time could take it from him.

Stretching his joints, he wondered if she was awake. It was four-thirty in the morning, and he wanted to be asleep. However, he promised both Amelia and Charlie that he would be in New York by midday. Amelia spent the weekend making excuses to the press for the events he missed. Charlie called several times to fuss about him

206

disappearing into West Virginia. Cameron apologized and promised to make up an interview today. He really didn't want to, now that Delilah was coming with him, but he still had a job to do.

Rolling out of bed, he stumbled to the shower to wake himself up. As he stood under the steaming water, he wished Delilah was with him. He imagined her hair wet from the water and her glossy eyes looking up at him. He thought of all the ways she could undo him, starting in the shower.

Is it wrong that all I want is to see you like that again and again?

He took a deep breath as her words from the night before washed over him. He wished he was twenty years younger. He imagined if she ever really opened herself up to him, he would never be able to keep up with her. Delilah had a fire inside her. He was sure of that now. Anyone who could hang some thirty feet in the air by just one ankle was no delicate flower. She had once blazed through life with raw hunger. Cameron was also sure that, ten years ago, she wouldn't have looked twice at him. He would've been too old for her, and she would've been too independent for him. Somehow, they met in the middle. Her life had aged her more than her physical years and time had made him less snobbish. He didn't care how she dressed. He didn't care that she could best him in any argument. Cameron just wanted her with him—in the shower, in the bed, in front of a fire...

For God's sake, Mara's right, he chastised himself, *you make everything about sex.*

He turned the shower water to cold before his thoughts could go any further. He would be damned if he would let his sister be right for more than a moment. After the shower, he dressed quickly, choosing tailored denims and a deep blue, Burberry button-down. He pulled on his best casual socks and shoes, certain he would be photographed today. As much as he hated it, the paparazzi would be out in full force, even more so when they saw Delilah. He could at least give them nothing new to discuss as far as his appearance went.

After combing his hair and packing his things, he exited the room. The door to Delilah's room was open, so he set his bag down and softly crossed to her doorway. Before he could knock or enter, he heard soft voices from inside.

Fearfully, Delilah said, "I don't think I can do this."

Cameron heard her father reply, "I don't think there's anything in this world you can't do."

She sighed. "Don't be trite, Dad."

Stephen took a minute to answer. "I don't mean it carelessly. I know what you've already been through, Lilah. I know what you've seen and heard, and I know how hard it's been to face the world, rather than hide from it. But you have. I didn't make you go to England. *You* did that. I didn't make you talk about your sister. You did it. And I believe you can do *this*, if this is what you want."

As Cameron listened, he was grateful for Stephen MacClare. He would never have known what to say. He would have thought the same thing, but it never would have come out that way. He knocked lightly on the door, not wanting to eavesdrop any longer.

"Come in," Delilah bade softly.

Cameron leaned on the doorframe and smiled at her. She was standing by the closet, dressed in leggings and a t-shirt again. Her hair was pulled back in a careless ponytail. In her hands she had the Versace dress he'd seen two days before. Stephen kissed his daughter on the forehead then headed out of the room through the bathroom that led to his study.

Looking at the dress in Delilah's hand, Cameron softly said, "Bring it. Wear it."

She clutched the hanger and whispered, "It shows a lot of skin."

"Then wear whatever makes you comfortable."

She looked the dress over again. With a huff of determination, she zipped it into a garment bag. Picking it up, along with another bag, she slipped out the door past him. Cameron picked up his own things and followed her. Leaving their bags in the family room, they went into the kitchen. She set about pouring herself coffee, filling it with things, then sealing it in a travel cup.

"Coffee?" She offered.

"I despise coffee."

It was her turn to be shocked that he didn't share her vice.

"I'll pick up something down the road," he added.

She headed through the family room toward the front door. He stopped her by saying, "Delilah?"

She turned around.

"Are we going to talk about last night?"

She stared at him.

"I don't want to complicate this day any more for you, but I need to know what you want from me. At least, for today, what are we?"

Setting down her cup on the counter, she crossed to him. Delilah reached up and touched his face. Then she ran her fingers through his hair like she did the night before. Then she kissed him gently.

Then she whispered, "We are...this, today."

Cameron wasn't sure if that was an answer, but it was enough for him. Just then, he realized Stephen was standing in the entryway to the room. Cameron stepped back, clearing his throat. As positive as Stephen had been, he wasn't sure how Delilah's father would react to seeing his daughter kissing a man who was nearly his age.

Stephen looked them over for a moment without speaking. Finally, he gave a slight nod and headed into the kitchen.

"Thanks for making coffee, Dad," Delilah offered.

Stephen smiled at her and reached for a mug for himself. Delilah suddenly traversed the space and gave her father a hug.

"I'll be back soon," she whispered into his shoulder.

With that, she picked up her travel cup and her bags, and headed down the front hall and out the door. Cameron followed more slowly, picking up his suitcase as Stephen tailed behind. When they reached the front door, Cameron turned and faced Delilah's father.

Clearing his throat, Cameron struggled with what to say. He managed, "Thank you for your hospitality."

Stephen gave a slight smile. "Take care of my daughter."

For the first time, Cameron felt the gravity of what he was doing. He looked into Stephen's eyes and saw a man who wanted to say a lot of things, but who recognized that his daughter was fully an adult. Cameron realized, no matter what happened, he could not run from Delilah. Whatever their future, he was going to have to face it. Age was irrelevant. If he botched this up, he was going to have to explain himself to Stephen MacClare.

After a firm handshake, Cameron headed out the door. He found Delilah waiting at the car. Tossing their bags in the back, he opened the door for her. She waved once more to her father before climbing inside. Cameron joined her and they were off.

For the first couple of hours, Delilah curled up in the seat beside him and slept. Her breathing was even and heavy as he focused on the winding roads that led them out of the mountains. The sun rose ahead of them, painting the sky with brilliant pinks and oranges. Just as the sun broke dawn into true morning, Delilah woke. She stretched and dug a pair of sunglasses out of her shoulder bag. Cameron followed suit with his own pair.

Yawning, Delilah said, "England is beautiful, but you can't beat the summer in Virginia."

"You haven't seen the sky over the lochs in Scotland," he returned.

"True," Delilah conceded softly.

"I could take you there," he added gently.

She didn't answer, as though she was determined not to give him more than today.

They stopped just over the border with Maryland for breakfast. Delilah got takeaway from a little café, and they parked at an empty rest area to avoid being seen. They ate in the car, trying not to spill food on the leather interior. When they got back on the road, Cameron put the top of the car down and opened up the engine again. Free of the mountains with their hairpin turns, he gave the car a chance to show what it could do. He loved to drive, and he often took trips to Germany or Switzerland just to be able to push whatever car he currently fancied to its limit. This car and the one in London were his most recent gifts to himself. He was cautious of the American speed limits, however, because he didn't need his picture taken while getting citations today.

Delilah turned up the radio and flipped the stations until she found music she liked. She turned it up loud and sang along, her hair whipping in the wind and her fingers drumming along to the rhythm. Cameron could see the itch in her to dance. He could see it in the slight sway of her body and the lift of her chin. No matter how long it had been, that fire had not been snuffed out. It lingered, like embers buried but ready to burst into flame if given fuel.

When they reached the edge of a more populated area, having traversed much of Pennsylvania's farmland, Cameron stopped and put the top of the car back up. He checked himself in the mirror before continuing the drive, because he was about to become his public self again. He adjusted his sunglasses, knowing it was time to start smiling for the cameras. Delilah, on the other hand, became more withdrawn. She tried to corral her flyaway hair into the elastic again. Then she sat quietly, and Cameron understood that every mile that brought them closer to the city brought her more anxiety. When the skyline of Manhattan came into view, she looked away and dug her medicine out of her bag. After taking some, she sat back in the seat and closed her eyes. Cameron shifted the car back into its automatic mode, not wanting to deal with shifting gears in the city. Before he could take the wheel with both hands again, Delilah reached over and laced her fingers through his.

She didn't let go until they made their way through the Lincoln Tunnel, through the Manhattan traffic, and Cameron pulled the car into the private entrance, off West 61st Street, of the soaring, limestone building he called home when he was in the city. He bought the flat several years ago, when he became weary of hotels.

He decided that, at least when he was in London or New York, he should have a place of his own. He was turned off of living in LA after his divorce from Marianne.

The Art Deco building at the lower west end of Central Park was only three years old, but it mimicked the architecture of the 1920s. It was a coveted, expensive address. If you had an extra ten million dollars, it was well worth it. Looking out the window, Cameron saw his assistant, Adam, waiting at the entrance to the building.

Sitting in the driver's seat, Cameron turned and looked at Delilah. She still had a tight grip on his hand, and she was studying the building and the doormen waiting to serve their purpose. He had spied a few photographers across the street, beyond the private drive. They tended to stalk the entrance to the building because the flats were owned by the wealthy and famous. They were also aware that Cameron would be in the city today.

Squeezing Delilah's hand, he said, "This is it."

"You live here?" She asked incredulously.

"When I'm in New York."

He could see her processing the scale of his wealth. The bottle of wine had impressed her. The car had thrilled her. This was making her hesitate—this and the city around it. Cameron glanced at Adam again. He knew the young man wouldn't approach until Cameron opened the car door.

Still looking at Delilah's profile, he went on, "It's just a few steps from the car to the door. All we have to do is get inside the door, and I don't think anyone can see us."

She took a deep breath and let go of his hand.

He added, "Adam will make sure the bags come up."

Delilah adjusted her sunglasses. Cameron exited the car and quickly came around to open her door. He helped Delilah out as Adam met him on the pavement. Cameron dropped the key to the car in his hand.

"I'll need the car again later this week," he stated. Cameron had no desire to drive in the city, but he would need to get Delilah back home.

Adam raked his blonde hair back from his face and walked with them toward the door, saying, "I emailed you the schedule. The first thing you have is the interview with *Final Cut*. Then photos for that. They'll have lunch for you at the shoot. Melanie will meet you here this afternoon at three and your clothes are in the apartment. Red carpet starts at four."

Cameron nodded. He was used to the rundown.

"I'll meet you upstairs in half an hour," Adam threw out as they reached the entrance. Then he turned around and let Cameron and Delilah continue through the door.

Once they were inside the building, Cameron slowed down. He let go of Delilah's arm and pulled another set of keys out of his shoulder bag. She looked around, taking in the huge, marble columns and the polished floor. Her eyes raked over the rich embellishments of the neoclassical décor. Cameron led her directly to the elevator and up to the twentieth floor. Opening the door to his flat, he let Delilah enter first.

She took a few steps inside, then slowed. Moving out of the short entryway, she took in the living space. The floor-to-ceiling windows just ahead gave an expansive view of the park below. The floors were polished stone and the furniture was sleek and modern. The kitchen to the right was finished with granite and glass tile. There were two bedrooms, one on either side of the living area. Delilah looked in each one, taking in the bedding and all the electronic gadgets he had collected in the city. Cameron knew the place was a bit sterile. Most of his most personal possessions were in his flat back in London, but he spent time with a designer making this place appealing to him. And he had to admit, he liked the impressiveness of it.

Delilah set her bag on the kitchen counter and crossed to the windows. She looked out at the park, taking in the scene far below.

He watched her from behind as she folded her arms over her chest. He knew what she was thinking. She wasn't impressed with the view. She was familiar with the view. Perhaps not from this perspective, but she was no doe-eyed country mouse. She was remembering.

Coming to stand behind her, Cameron put his hands on her shoulders. She reached up and covered his right hand with hers. Then she turned and walked away from the window as though the sight was too much. She made her way to the kitchen and busied herself by studying all the appliances.

Cameron cleared his throat. "I'm sorry I have so much to do today. I would say you could go out, maybe go shopping, but…"

She gave him a half-smile. "I know the city, Cameron. I'd rather just stay here."

Cameron relaxed a little. "Well, there's the television. You can stream whatever you want. And, if Adam did his job, there should be food."

"He seems nice," Delilah mused.

"He's my personal assistant," Cameron explained, "and he'll do."

They were making small talk again, and he felt completely out of his element in his own home. Of all the women he brought here, he never stumbled with any of them. He might have argued with them or been entirely ready for them to leave, but Cameron was never so unsure of himself.

He broke the silence with, "You're welcome to either bedroom, although I usually take the one to the left."

She cocked her head and smiled. "I thought I would stay with you."

Just that quickly, the uncertainty disappeared. He strode quickly across the space and gathered her in his arms. She met him halfway in a fierce kiss.

After a minute, she whispered in his ear, "You know, we are finally alone, in a place that no one else calls home."

He captured her lips again and a rapid succession of thoughts flooded his brain. He calculated that there were sixteen minutes until

Adam would show up. Cameron wondered what the fallout would be if he told the interviewer from *Final Cut Magazine* to sod off. He questioned whether he really needed to do another interview, then imagined the absolute bliss of simply staying in the flat with Delilah all day. Finally, he pulled away from her long enough to see there were now fourteen minutes until they would be interrupted. Twenty years ago, he would already have divested her of her clothes. Now, however, he wasn't forty anymore, but he kept kissing her. He savored the moment, lifting her up onto the countertop. He let the heat simmer, to brew below the surface as a promise for things to come when they had more time.

What seemed like a minute later, there was a strong knock on the door. Cameron reluctantly pulled away from Delilah. She pushed her hair back and he gave her a half-smile. She hopped down from the countertop, and he went to open the door. Adam entered, leather bag over his shoulder, tablet and phone in hand. He motioned for the porter to leave the luggage in the front hall.

"Did you get the schedule?" Adam asked as the porter exited.

Cameron pulled out his phone and checked his email messages. True to his word, Adam had sent a comprehensive schedule.

Holding up a few sheets of freshly printed paper, Adam added, "Here are the questions from *Final Cut*. Sophie is doing the interview."

Cameron glanced at Delilah. She was watching with interest. Adam's phone rang and he took the call, so Cameron excused himself to go freshen up before leaving. When he returned to the lounge, Adam was still on his phone and Delilah was still watching him.

When Adam ended the call, Cameron offered, "Adam, this is Delilah. Delilah…Adam."

The two of them shook hands, and he could tell that Adam was curious. Cameron offered no explanation, however. Realizing it was time to leave, he put his phone in his pocket. Crossing back to where Delilah stood against the kitchen counter, he leaned in and kissed her gently. Then he headed toward the front door. Adam followed, and Cameron could see he wanted to ask questions. Adam had been trained well, however, and he wouldn't say a word until Cameron offered more information.

On the elevator ride downstairs, Cameron stated, "Delilah will be staying with me. She is off-limits. No questions, no interviews, and no pictures we can avoid."

Adam nodded and asked nothing further.

A half-hour later, Cameron was sitting in a posh café with Sophie, a veteran writer for *Final Cut Magazine.* He met her years ago, when she was younger and more annoying. She was a brunette then. Now she was a streaked blonde with a too-short skirt. However, she was now tolerable to talk to. She asked decent questions and she knew what to avoid, so he only vetoed a couple of the questions from her list. Her current piece was a promo of the *Heir of Taivas* franchise, with an interview on his experience making the films. Cameron was intentionally vague when answering her questions about his upcoming projects, although she had to realize he couldn't comment on things that were in negotiation. Still, she always tried.

At the end of her hour, she pulled out her phone and held it out. "Lastly, would you like to comment on the woman in this picture?"

Cameron glanced at the phone and saw a photo of him and Delilah from not two hours ago, getting out of his car.

Shit.

He was continually shocked at how fast gossip could travel.

"I've been instructed to ask," Sophie threw up her hands as though she wouldn't have pried on her own.

Cameron shook his head. "No, I would not like to comment."

She looked back at him, her keen eyes searching for a way to get at his secret. She opened her mouth to try again.

Cameron stood up and walked away. He knew what an interview with him was worth, and he knew he had enough clout to leave her sitting there for overstepping his limits. Let her be angry. He could call her a twat and her editor would still print the story, because he was Cameron Burke. He met Adam at the door to the restaurant, rolled his eyes toward Sophie, and let his lanky, blonde assistant lead him on to the next appointment.

After hair, makeup, and a short photo shoot at a studio for shots to accompany his interview, he was able to eat lunch. Someone from *Final Cut* made sure there was food at the studio, and Cameron tried to pick something decent from a table with too many items containing kale. It seemed that LA had finally forced itself on New York and another city was now terrified of gluten and meat. He knew wraps and salads were probably better for him, but he was raised on Sunday roasts and meat pies. Still, he had to eat. So he smiled graciously and found a decent vegan wrap.

While he ate, he texted Delilah:

Are you bored yet?

She replied:

No. There's a *Lord of the Rings* marathon on television.

Traitor.

Don't worry. I'll be watching you tonight.

For tonight…I can have Melanie do hair and makeup for you.

That's a good idea. Tell her to bring power tools for this hair.

Consider it done. Be there soon.

Suddenly, he wanted to be home. He finished his lunch, gathered up his things, and told Adam to call for the car. Thirty minutes later, he was in the elevator of his building again with Adam at his side.

Breaking the silence, Cameron said, "Once we're on the way to the premiere, you can have the night off. I'll text you if anything comes up."

Adam nodded.

Back in the flat, Cameron found Delilah curled up on the sofa, now watching *Seven Summits* again.

He smirked. "I suppose I should take this as some sort of compliment?"

Delilah fired back without looking, "I'm not watching it because of you. It's a review for tonight."

He saw Adam try to hide a smile as she quite effectively took him down a peg.

"Melanie will be here in fifteen minutes," Cameron threw out before heading to the shower.

The next little while was a blur of preparation, and he was starting to feel the effects of being awake since four-thirty in the morning. After showering, Cameron dressed carefully, checking every inch of the black, Armani suit for imperfections. He wore a dark blue shirt, open collar, and black, Armani Bluchers. He liked dark when it came to clothing. Melanie came when he called and worked magic on his hair. There was less to work with nowadays, but she kept him looking age-appropriately stylish. Once he was satisfied, he put his necessities in his pockets. Phone. Door keys. Mints. He had been standing in the lounge for a minute when Delilah came out of the other bedroom. Melanie had taken her there so they could spread out makeup and accessories. Now, looking at Delilah, Cameron might as well be having a stroke.

Tamed into soft waves, her hair shone with brilliant streaks of rust and garnet. Some of it was pulled up and piled in loose curls on her head with crystal pins holding it in place. The rest tumbled down her back. Cameron had never seen Delilah in makeup, except in pictures. It never occurred to him that she needed it. Melanie had been subtle with her brushes and colors, but the effect was breathtaking. Delilah's eyes were dark-rimmed, accenting their wide, impossibly brown-green depths. The Versace dress fit her well. It had an uneven, angle-cut hem and crisscrossing straps over an otherwise open back. She had on gold sandals that he suspected were Jimmy Choo. Her dress showed off her fit, if not curvy, body. But he was drawn back to her eyes. He suspected it from the beginning, but now he was sure—her eyes could melt him.

Adam, who was working on his laptop, and Melanie, who followed Delilah out of the bedroom, watched the two of them silently. Cameron realized they were both a far cry from the two disheveled people who met in a pub. As Cameron looked at her, he wished they were alone. He wanted to appreciate her this way before the world intruded.

Delilah sensed his inability to find words and said, "The dress still fits."

It so much more than fits, was his immediate thought.

He cleared his throat. "Melanie, you have outdone yourself."

She smiled and accepted his gracious tip before clearing out her things.

Once she was gone, Cameron looked at his assistant pointedly. "Adam? A minute."

Understanding, Adam gathered his things and indicated he would be waiting at the elevator.

Now that they were alone, Cameron crossed to Delilah. "You are the reason men write songs, and give up kingdoms, and squander fortunes."

Delilah tipped her head to the side. "Thank you?"

He noticed she subconsciously placed her left hand over the scar marring her right bicep. Stepping closer, he said, "No one will notice. And if they do, they will not *know*."

She looked up at him and slightly nodded her acceptance.

He kissed her again, long and slow. Once again, his mind did calculations. How long would Adam wait before worrying? How late was too late for the red carpet? Could he get this suit off without wrinkling it? Then he chastised himself.

Stop it. You're acting like a lad on his first night on the pull. Get yourself, and your prick, under control.

"Cameron?" Delilah pulled back and looked up at him. "I think we have to go."

He took a deep breath and wondered if she understood how much control she had over him. He wondered if she knew how bad it was for his narcissism that she could so easily pull away. She reached for her purse to check the contents. She fixed her lipstick and made sure she had her medication. Then he led the way out the door.

Their car for the evening was a limo, and they made it inside without much incident. Cameron assumed the whole of the entertainment and media community was waiting at Lincoln Center.

Delilah was quiet as they rode. She glanced out the window a couple of times and then curled into him. Their destination was close, but progress was slow because of all the road closures and the sheer number of people converging on one place. She ran her hand over his chest, fingering his shirt buttons. She touched his face, then began to kiss behind his ear with feather-light pressure. Cameron inhaled sharply, not sure what she was doing. She continued to pepper him with light kisses while running her hand over his chest. He kissed her back, not opposed to snogging in the back of a car. It wouldn't be the first time. After another few minutes, she looked up, pulled his face to hers, and kissed him harder. He went with it, relishing their time together. At the same moment she nipped at his ear, she ran her hand up his leg to the apex of his thighs. Cameron shifted suddenly and groaned into her hair.

Fuck.

The duality of the word was not lost on him.

Sensing the intensity of his reaction, Delilah pulled her hand away.

Cameron disentangled himself. "I'm afraid there are a lot of people waiting to see me and I think I need to be in a...different frame of mind."

Delilah pulled away and he adjusted his trousers. Somehow, in the past three days, they'd gone from never touching one another to acting like randy adolescents. Cameron wasn't going to complain, but he was a little unsure of the suddenness of it all.

Shifting away from him, Delilah straightened her dress and her hair. Then she glanced up at him and said, "I'm sorry. I'm just trying to distract myself from...everything. It's an old habit of mine, using sex to keep from talking, or dealing with things. Old habits never die, I suppose."

Putting his arm around her shoulders, he said, "I understand more than I want to admit to you."

She laced her fingers through his and kept her head on his shoulder the rest of the way to the theater.

When they arrived at Lincoln Center, Cameron could feel Delilah tense. He watched her take her medication and wondered how he ever convinced her to do this. He also realized she probably wasn't doing it for him. When the car stopped, he squeezed her hand tightly.

"Are you ready?"

"Some things," she returned, "you are never ready for."

The driver opened the door. To the roar of screaming and applause, Cameron stepped from the car. The crowd was surreal. He looked around at the people, from teens to older adults, some holding signs and all waving from the barriers. The red carpet was already full of reporters, photographers, and other actors and actresses. Cameron took it in. Then he reached back into the car for Delilah's hand. She took it and pulled herself to her feet. He watched her take in the sight in front of her with something between disbelief and fear. Putting his arm around her again, he led her away from the car.

Cameron could hear the reactions of the crowd. Some couldn't care less who was with him. Some were too young for it to matter. But to others, the question of Delilah was immediate gossip. He watched the photographers turn and find him. He felt Delilah tense as they aimed their cameras and started shooting. Walking into the fray, Cameron stopped periodically and flashed his confident smile. He knew how to stand and how to hold himself. It was instinctive, now. He took the barrage of sights and sounds in stride. Delilah, however, held his hand and smiled demurely. She stood just behind him as he worked his way down the lines of fans. He signed all sorts of things that were thrust his way. Then the inevitable questions started.

Reporters from almost every news and entertainment source were covering the red carpet. Watching them vie for everyone's attention, while simultaneously trying to hold one person's attention, was comedic to Cameron. The first person to flag him down asked a series of rapid-fire questions about the choice to take on the role of Marcus Eperra, and he did his best to answer. Before he could completely escape, another reporter stepped in his path. She flashed a bright smile and asked more banal questions.

Eventually, she demanded, "And who is your special guest tonight?"

Cameron glanced at Delilah, not sure what she wanted him to say. They really should have discussed this.

Raising her chin, she answered evenly, "I'm Delilah. And it's lovely to be here."

Cameron felt a rush of respect for her. She was grace under fire right now.

They made their way slowly down the red carpet, stopping for pictures and for Cameron to answer more questions. Selfishly, he loved the attention, and the clicking and flashing of the cameras was incessant. The roar of the crowd made it hard to speak over them. It was a rush like no other. By the time they reached the theater, he sensed Delilah was at the end of how much she could handle. He led her into the hall with a final wave to the crowd. Once inside, he slowed down. He watched Delilah take in the soaring, multi-story windows and the modern gold and white finishings. He was greeted by several other cast members now that they could drop their smiles and be a little more real with one another. Each of them also greeted Delilah but asked no further questions.

When they found their seats in the center orchestra, Delilah leaned back and closed her eyes. Cameron reached under the seats and pulled out bags of treats and bottles of water.

"Perks," he said with a smile.

Delilah opened her eyes and smiled back. She took one of the bags and looked through it, nodding her approval. After an indeterminate amount of time, the director and several others took the stage and talked a bit about this latest film and its process. Cameron was glad to see Joe Warwick and wondered what it must have been like to have this entire story bouncing around in his brain. Cameron was proud to have contributed, but he knew such a narrative was beyond the scope of his creativity. After much talking and congratulating, the film began.

The story played out much like the book, and Cameron knew this one would be hard for Delilah. This film began with the four lead characters estranged from each other as they tried to make sense of Jermias turning on all of them. He was painted, through the first three books, as wise and strong, with a hardness that he would surely use for good. Instead, he wanted to invade the human world and conquer it, revealing himself as thirsty for blood and power. As the lead characters gradually made their way back to one another, this film laid the groundwork for the action of the final film. Jermias' turn toward villainy made it all the more heart-wrenching when it was he, in the end, who killed Amy. Seeing her fall, lifeless, on a huge screen made the parallels that Delilah drew to her own life so much more obvious. Like Mohara, Amy was dark-haired and of Himalayan descent, but when Alex wept for her sister, Cameron knew Delilah was seeing Anna. He remembered clearly the look on her face in The

Quill and Fiddle when she explained the connection and shattered the mirror. Now, she leaned in and rested her head on his shoulder. Cameron kissed the top of her head, and she closed her eyes, taking deep breaths.

By the time the film was over, Delilah's face was streaked with tears. She pulled tissues from her purse and cleaned up her face. She didn't get up but stared at the blank screen. Cameron watched her dig through her purse, pull out her medication, and use the bottle of water she was given to take more. He had no idea if there was some sort of limit on how much was safe, but he assumed she'd been dealing with this for enough years to know.

He asked, "Delilah…are you all right?"

She pulled out a mirror to check her face and lightened the mood by saying, "It's good that this makeup is waterproof."

As they made their way back out of the theater, several other people stopped Cameron to talk. Some were colleagues and others were fans who won tickets to the event. He took a few pictures and signed more things. Delilah followed along, holding tightly to his hand. Cameron noticed the glances and outright stares from others were becoming more and more curious as the night wore on, especially from those who knew him. He said nothing and kept moving.

Once they were back outside and waiting for the car, Cameron turned to Delilah and said, "There's an after-party I should make an appearance at. I would love for you to come, if you like."

"Where?"

"Some posh club in the theater district. There will be drinks and probably dancing," he explained. "We can go straight there in the car."

Delilah worried her lip as she thought about it. Then she raised her chin and said, "Okay."

Cameron was genuinely surprised that she agreed. When the car came, they slipped inside and he gave the driver the address. He watched Delilah reach into her purse and nervously hold her medicine bottle as they drove. Thirty minutes later, they were walking into the club.

Delilah looked around, taking in the long bar and the lacquered tables. It was a rather large space, and across the room there was a dance floor with colored lights. A live band was playing covers of popular music. Cameron found them a table off to the side that offered a little privacy. Given the volume of the music, there would be no deep conversation, but they could stay out of the fray of activity. Delilah took a seat and Cameron offered to get drinks. She asked for wine, and he brought her back the best bottle he could get. Pouring glasses for each of them, he asked permission to make a round of the room. She nodded, sipping from her glass and smiling her approval. He wondered again, watching her drink, how much medication she'd taken. She was being amenable to things she normally would decline. When she smiled up at him, however, he decided she was all right. He kissed her quickly before walking away.

Cameron took his glass and headed into the crowd. He made small talk with several people and watched others take to the dance floor. The cell phone cameras were flashing as most of the younger cast members were eager to post pictures of their ridiculously expensive clothing. Some were on their second or third outfit of the night.

Suddenly, a voice from behind him said, "Cameron Burke. You've been difficult to catch tonight."

He turned and smiled. It was Meg Abbott. She played Synesi, the one female member of the Arches-Asterion in *Heir of Taivas* and the one peer of Jermias in opposition to him. She was also one of only two relationships Cameron had ended amicably. Years ago, when they split, they both decided they were better as friends. Now, they kept it platonic—most of the time. Tonight, she was dressed in a silver Ralph Lauren that skimmed the floor. Her dirty-blonde hair fell in loose waves just past her shoulders. Only the lines around her eyes belied that she was fast approaching sixty.

"Meg," Cameron greeted her with a kiss on each cheek.

"Congratulations," she purred in her highbrow, West London accent. "Another successful film and, based on the age of the fans, a whole new generation of girls who wouldn't mind being *on the job* with you."

Cameron rolled his eyes. "There is such a thing as *too* young."

"I only wish it worked in the other direction," she threw back. "I surely won't have hordes of young men chasing me down."

Cameron smirked. "Would you really want them to?"

Meg shrugged, sipped her drink, and asked, "Who's the redhead?"

Cameron savored his wine and didn't answer.

"Oh come on, Cameron." She nudged him with her shoulder. "You know I won't tell. I hate gossip. Is she new talent? Did she make some Indie film the Canadians raved about?"

Cameron couldn't help laughing. There was a reason he liked Meg. She was the closest thing to a real friend he had in this business. Glancing over at Delilah, who was sipping wine and watching the dance floor, he answered, "No. She's not an actor. Her name is Delilah."

"And?" Meg pressed.

"And she's with me," he hedged.

She looked up at him with bright blue eyes and said, "Such mystery! I didn't think anyone without an award, or a title, or a *Cosmo* cover could get your prick up."

He shook his head. "Stop, really."

She curved her lips mischievously and leaned in to say, "And what a fine prick it is."

Cameron inhaled sharply and looked over at Delilah. This teasing was typical between them, but he wasn't taking the bait. "Not tonight, Meg."

She waved her hand dismissively. "I'm just taking the piss out of you."

He took another swig of wine and continued to watch Delilah. He hadn't thought about the extreme probability of running into the women of his past while with her, and Meg was the least of his worries. Some of his partners would keep their distance, but others liked to remind him of what he gave up or snark at him. He wondered if it would bother Delilah. She seemed to have a realistic understanding of who he was, or had been. She was also candid about being no blushing virgin herself, but he didn't want the teasing to hurt her if she heard it.

Meg, who had been staring at him for a solid minute now, stated, "Wow. Whoever she is, she's got you more distracted than I've seen in a long time."

Cameron was unable to argue.

Meg mused, "If I remember correctly, didn't Delilah completely wreck Samson?"

He tipped his head and answered, "Maybe she did. But maybe he needed it."

With that, he excused himself and walked away.

Returning to their table, Cameron leaned in and kissed Delilah on the cheek. Then he held out his hand. "Come. I promised you an unforgettable night. I want you to meet the cast properly."

Delilah looked like she was going to argue, but Cameron could tell the wine and medication had mellowed her. Taking his hand, she stood up. He refilled both of their glasses before leading her from the corner. For the next hour, he introduced her to all the people she'd seen on-screen over the past six months. She shared a little about herself and appeared to enjoy stories from the set. As they moved through the room, she posed for a few more pictures with Cameron. They finished the wine and Cameron noticed her swaying to the music. He could see her glance longingly at the dance floor.

Returning their glasses to the table, he leaned in and murmured in her ear, "You should dance."

She shook her head.

"They're playing your music," he pushed.

The band was doing a cover of Whitney Houston, and Cameron saw her eyes flick in their direction. After another minute, the song changed. The bodies on the dance floor slowed as the music thrummed a familiar melody. Cameron met Delilah's eyes. It was the same song he played the night they first slept together.

Take my breath away...

He could see the longing in her eyes. Focusing on only her, he led her to the dance floor. Then he pulled her into his arms like he did in his sister's tiny lounge and moved them to the music. Her fear numbed, Delilah wound her arms around Cameron's neck and kept her eyes on him. Her body, however, couldn't resist moving in rhythm with the song. Cameron swayed with her, running his hands over her exposed skin. He glanced over at Meg, who was watching them with intense curiosity.

As the song played, Delilah came further out of herself. She let him spin her out slowly then pull her back in to his chest. It was barely dancing, but it was more than he expected of her. He wondered again how much Xanax she took before the wine. Or with the wine. As the song wound down, he kissed her then let her go, expecting her to retreat to the corner. Instead, as the music changed, she pulled him back in. The next song was a cover of an old Patti Smith song. The rhythm was faster, but with a sultry drive. Delilah closed her eyes and let the lyrics wash over her.

Because the night...

When she opened her eyes, he saw an unexpected light in them. Standing on her toes, she asked near his ear, "Did you say you know how to tango?"

He nodded, hoping he remembered.

She took his hand and pulled him further onto the dance floor.

Cameron asked uncertainly, "Are you sure?"

Delilah looked him squarely in the eyes. "Shut up and dance with me."

Cameron almost forgot to lead as they moved together. Their tango was slow and deliberate so her struggling lungs could keep up. However, Delilah's dance training showed. She could promenade without breaking eye contact. She twined her legs with his and turned with precision. Cameron knew people were staring. He knew the cameras were flashing, but he didn't give a damn. He spun her out and back in. She stopped flush against his chest, hiked one leg around his waist and dipped backward effortlessly. He held his hand lightly around her waist, and her head nearly touched the back of her knees.

When the song ended, Delilah put her hands on his chest. She was breathing heavily, so Cameron put his hands on her arms to try to steady her. Those around them clapped for their impromptu dance. Meg, he noticed, was still watching. After a minute, once Delilah caught her breath, she captured his mouth in a kiss.

Moving to his ear, she asked, "Can we leave now?"

Cameron was trying to act like he had a rational thought left, but he didn't. This was beyond his expectations for the night. He looked in her eyes, wondering again how medicated she was. He recognized her behavior was probably a result of her admitted need to distract herself from the city and its memories. If he hadn't already slept with her, he would have had a serious battle with his conscience over whether he should take her home. However, since they already crossed that boundary, and she told him earlier she intended to share his bed, he had no restraint. He led her back across the club and asked security to bring around the car.

When they were in the limo again, Cameron pulled open another button on his shirt. He shrugged off his jacket and Delilah kicked off her shoes. She slid closer to him, and he noticed her hair was wonderfully mussed. Her makeup was a little smudged as well, but it was worth it to have danced with her.

As the car pulled away from the curb, he watched her breathe as she looked out the tinted windows. Noticing how quickly her chest rose and fell, he asked, "Are you okay?"

She looked up at him, her eyes heavy. "Yes. It's just a little harder for me. You know."

He put his left arm around her. "You just need some sleep."

Looking up at him again, she replied, "I'm fine." Then she said, "You danced with me."

He shook his head. "No. *You* danced with me."

Her eyes were searching as she said, "I had no idea how much I wanted to dance with you, until tonight."

He leaned down and kissed her forehead. She reached up with her hand and trailed her fingers over his neck, then down to where he opened his collar. She traced his collarbone, and the desire that had been brewing all day burned between his legs.

"Hopefully this will be a short trip," he whispered suggestively in her ear.

She looked back up at him. "Or maybe it won't be."

Before he could register her meaning, she pulled another couple of buttons on his shirt undone and ran her fingers over his chest. She reached up and pulled his face down to hers so she could kiss him thoroughly. He started to say something between kisses, but she wasn't interested in talking. She sat up straighter, turning so she could thread her fingers into his hair. Just as she did earlier, she trailed her warm lips over his neck and nipped at his ear. Again, she ran her hand up his thigh. He moaned into her mouth. When she pulled back, he thought she was going to let them both calm down, like before. Instead, she pulled herself up onto the seat and straddled him. Cameron gasped at the sudden weight and Delilah pressed hot kisses from his ears to his neck, then back to his wanting mouth. Deciding he was a fool to stop her, he ran his hands up her thighs and kissed her wildly in return.

When she pulled back, he was *sure* that, this time, she intended to allow them both to straighten up before the short trip was over. However, she made quick work of his trousers and before he could make a good argument, she hiked up her dress and sank down onto him. Cameron moaned and glanced up to make sure the privacy screen was closed. He was unable to believe this was happening. At sixty-one, he was shagging in the back of a limo. He thought his days of this kind of carelessness were over.

You never appreciated it, back then.

He also knew that, back then, it would have been over in about a minute. Now, however, he slid his arms up the back of Delilah's dress and kissed the bare skin of her shoulder. Cameron let his head fall back as she shagged him senseless. He opened his eyes and looked at her, watching her give and find pleasure. She took his breath away when it should have been the other way around. When she threw her head back in release, he went with her. Cameron closed his eyes and hoped the privacy screen was soundproof as he couldn't hold back a cry of ecstasy.

As they came back to the world, Cameron whispered throatily in her ear, "I love you, Delilah MacClare."

There was no time for her to respond. The limo slowed to a stop, and they hurried to put themselves back together. They stumbled from the car a few minutes later rather rumpled and poorly assembled. He was carrying his jacket and Delilah had her shoes in her hand. Cameron knew their clothes were wrinkled and their hair askew, but he couldn't make himself care. Before they went into the building, he pulled her in to kiss her again. Then they hurried into the privacy of Cameron's home.

14
Within Your Skin

I think of you in terms
of highlights and shadows,
lights and darks,
chalk and charcoal.
I paint you with my fingertips
and draw you with my touch.
You are line and shape
in an intimate space.
I observe the firmness of form
beneath my hands,
within your skin.
I study the anatomy of you—
of movement,
of breath,
of life,
of eros and of agape—
as you become part of me.
And I realize
for possibly the first time
why artwork exists
why human beings create.

— "Advanced Life Drawing and Anatomy" by Julie Ann Cook

When Delilah opened her eyes the next morning, it took her a minute to be certain where she was. First, she expected to be surrounded by the apartment in Chatfield. Then she wondered why her bedroom at home was so bright. Finally, she registered that she was in Manhattan. The cityscape came into focus through the floor-to-ceiling windows. It was a sight she honestly thought she would never wake up to again. She lay still, studying the geometric silhouette of the buildings and piecing together the day before. Most of it quickly came back, but the evening was foggier. She remembered getting ready and going to the premiere. She remembered seeing Cameron on the huge screen and crying. And she remembered alternating pills with drinks. There were no gaps in her recollection. The whole evening was there, including having seduced and made love to Cameron in the back of a limo, but it was like seeing it through the wrong end of a telescope. Taking a deep breath, she knew she wouldn't have been so bold if she was sober.

Rolling to her right, she looked at Cameron. He was sleeping beside her for the second time since they met. He was shirtless and wearing just underwear beneath the tangled sheets. Delilah remembered him carrying her to bed and she remembered him helping her undress and put on a t-shirt. Her hair was a mess, and she reached up and realized she had hair pins everywhere. She passed out once they reached the bed last night. Cameron must've undressed and crawled in with her. Now, she watched his even breathing, her eyes following the trail of salt and pepper hair to his navel. His hair was disheveled, much like hers. They were both a mess. And, judging by the light outside, it had to be late morning already.

Delilah wasn't running out this time. There was a part of her that was still afraid of sharing a bed with Cameron, knowing how she occasionally woke up with nightmares, but her desire to be with him was outweighing the fear. Like she wanted to do four months ago, she pulled herself closer to him to feel his warmth. She rested her head on the pillow beside him and put her hand on his chest. Gently, she made circles with her fingers. She ran her hand over his skin and down across the plane of his stomach. She traced the line of his thigh like she'd done the night before. At her touch, he stirred. With his eyes closed, he shifted and gave a little sigh. Delilah shifted her weight across him so she could slide her left hand into his hair. She lightly kissed her way from his ear to his neck, then down his chest. He slowly wound his arms around her and pulled her closer.

As she went back to kissing his neck, he murmured, "Good morning."

"The day has potential," she snarked softly.

Snuggling herself beside him so that her head rested on his shoulder, she hooked her left leg over his hip so that they were touching from head to toe.

Looking up at him, she said, "Last night was…incredible."

He pushed her hair back. "Do you remember all of it?"

She gave him a long look. "Yes. It's fuzzy, but yes."

He returned, "You are a brilliant dancer."

"And you are…you are Cameron Burke."

"Oh good." He feigned great relief. "You do know my name."

She swatted him playfully. "I just mean, it's an intimidating thing to see them screaming for you like that. It's bizarre to meet the kind of people you know. Even knowing all about it, to be in the middle of it is…crazy. You are bigger than I ever imagined."

He seized the innuendo. "And here I thought I was slightly above average, at best."

She swatted him again. "You are terrible. Do you have any other thoughts?"

Running a hand over her shoulder he answered, "I have a beautiful woman almost on top of me. What should I be thinking about?"

Delilah pulled herself onto him. He drew a quick breath and she leaned down and kissed the spot behind his ear that she was learning drove him crazy. He tensed beneath her, but she pulled back.

Sliding off the bed, she looked down at him. "I'm a mess. I think a shower is necessary."

She was aware that he had an unobstructed view of her nearly naked backside as she walked away. The bathroom door was just across from his side of the bed, and Delilah felt him watching her as she turned on the shower. She intentionally left the door open as she pulled out all the hairpins and ran her fingers through her tangled hair. Leaving the bathroom once, she retrieved her shampoo and other toiletries from her bag. Checking the water temperature in the shower, she smiled and stepped out of view to brush her teeth. Making sure Cameron was still watching her, she crossed to the shower, pulled the t-shirt over her head and dropped it behind her. She saw him shift in the bed. Shaking out her hair, she gave him a full view of her body. Then she turned around, showing him her backside again, and stripped off her undergarments. She was intentionally teasing him and enjoying it. Before stepping into the shower, she pulled her left leg up into passé and slowly lifted it until her toes pointed toward the ceiling. She wrapped her left hand around her calf and pulled her shin to her nose, so she was standing in a vertical split. Then she lowered her leg and stepped into the shower.

As she did, she heard him breathe, "Good god, woman."

Delilah let the hot water run over her with a satisfied smile. Although it had been a long time, she was good at this part of a relationship, and she knew it. She was no uncertain innocent waiting for the sexy movie star to teach her about passion. Dance was physically demanding, and Delilah was always happy to extend that energy and intensity into the bedroom. It was easier to seduce someone than to talk to them. Since most of her past relationships were with men she wouldn't see again after the run of a show, she was better at seduction than commitment. Since she had no idea how long this affair with Cameron could last, she decided to focus on the present. As the water soaked and warmed her, she suddenly remembered the last thing he said to her the night before:

I love you, Delilah MacClare.

He certainly couldn't have been serious. He said it immediately post-orgasm. He most likely didn't remember saying it. She'd heard men say all kinds of ridiculous things in that moment. Delilah decided to file it away. She wasn't going to ruin this with discussions of love and a future neither of them could predict. So she lathered her hair and let the soap cover her body.

A minute later, as expected, Cameron padded into the bathroom. She heard the sink running, then watched his blurry movements through the steamy glass. She saw him shed his underwear and approach her. She tipped her head back into the water as he opened the shower door. When it clicked shut behind him, she felt his much larger presence as she rinsed out her long hair. It hung nearly to her waist when it was wet and straight. When she opened her eyes, he was staring at her. Delilah raked her eyes over him, appreciating his long-limbed frame. Ten years ago, she never would have imagined a sixty-one-year-old man could be attractive. She preferred young, muscled dancers, and straight ones were hard to find. So she pounced every chance she got. Now, she realized that age was not necessarily bad. Cameron's body might not be rippling with muscles, but with age came experience and patience. Whereas most of Delilah's previous flings had consisted of short bursts of passion and a lot of television reruns, Cameron didn't pounce. Even when there was urgency, he watched her, read her, and exercised deliberation. Whether it was because of experience or necessity, she didn't care.

Now, he covered them both in lather and kissed her wet mouth. He pressed close, and Delilah savored having every warm, slick inch of his body against hers. She kept her arms around him as he washed his hair. As he rinsed the soap away, she watched the way the water streamed over his shoulders and down his torso. He kissed her slowly, thoroughly, and did things with his hands that made her gasp and shudder. When he pulled her from the shower, they barely managed to dry themselves before tumbling onto the bed.

With her laid out in the bright sunlight before him, Cameron made it his mission to kiss every inch of her skin. Delilah pulled her damp hair behind her head and let him. Cameron took full advantage of not having to worry about time or intrusions. She wove her fingers into his hair as he made love to her with intense focus. He wound her up slowly, working his mouth over her neck as his skin slid over her breasts. Delilah savored the feel of him and the way he looked into her eyes as if to make sure she was with him. Not one to be passive for long, she let her hands slide down his torso. They came to rest on his buttocks.

Nuzzling her face into his neck, she whispered into his ear, "I won't break."

She could feel him smile against her ear as he said, "Patience."

Finally, he drove more forcefully against her. Delilah arched her back, letting a whisper of profanity escape her lips. That seemed to spur him. Delilah wasn't sure how long their coupling lasted, but she recognized that sweat broke out across her chest. At some point she reached up and took hold of the mattress edge behind her. Cameron had built the tension so slowly that she was wound impossibly tight. The friction reached a tipping point, and she fell hard. She clutched his shoulders so tightly she knew she would leave marks. The feeling of his climax tipped her body over the edge again. When she opened her eyes, he looked completely at the mercy of the moment. Delilah slid her hands back down to his buttocks and pulled him hard against her.

"Oh…fuck," he choked out, and she watched him tense through a last, unexpected rush of pleasure.

They were still for some time, both breathing hard and fast. Delilah felt the sweat on his brow as she pushed Cameron's damp hair back. He kissed her mouth long and slowly, then nuzzled his nose in her neck again. She wrapped her arms around him, holding him. He seemed very affected, and she wasn't sure what to say. Eventually, he shifted his weight to lay beside her, but he kept their legs entangled. As she slowed her breathing, Delilah realized they were as exposed as they would ever be. They were naked in the blazing, noontime sun, touching from hair to toes. Every line and wrinkle and scar were on display. They smelled of soap and sweat and sex. There was nothing left to reveal. Except one thing.

I love you, Delilah MacClare.

She thought about his words again. Delilah was afraid to ask directly if he meant it. She wasn't sure which answer she wanted.

She asked instead, "How many women have you slept with?"

Cameron pulled back enough to look her in the eyes. "I could ask you the same thing."

She laughed. "I have not slept with any women."

"Very funny," he returned. "Do you really want to know?"

She gave him a half-smile. "I'll show you mine if you show me yours."

Cameron looked her over appreciatively. "I think we've done that."

"I'm teasing. But I do want to know."

He hesitated. "I've lost count."

Delilah reconsidered. "How many that you had a relationship with, long or short-term?"

He looked away from her for a minute before saying, "About twenty. But there's been so many others that, I hate to admit, I can't remember."

She ran her hand up and down his arm, thinking.

He returned, "And you?"

She took a deep breath. "Thirty-two."

Delilah felt him tense as the truth soaked in.

"I'm no one's virgin bride," she self-deprecated.

He pulled her close again, kissed her forehead and asked, "How long had it been, before…?"

"Before you?" She admitted, "Almost nine years."

He chuckled. "I'm glad I didn't know *that* back in March."

"Me too," she agreed. "Who was your first?"

Delilah was starting to think he wouldn't answer when he said, "It was Flora."

Pulling back, she looked up at him in surprise. "Really?"

Cameron explained, "I was eighteen. It was the summer before I left for university, and I was quite out of sorts. I was both excited and terrified about school. Flora and I had been flirting for weeks. She was just as forward back then, maybe more so. One night she decided I shouldn't go off to school as a virgin. Maybe she thought it would calm me down. I don't know. I just remember her dragging me upstairs at the pub. By the time I realized what she was doing we were in her bed, and I'm sure it was dreadful for her. We had a bit of a fling that summer. There was one fairly memorable night, and Mara caught me sneaking Flora out of the house the next morning. I think that was the beginning of my sister's intense disapproval of me. And of Flora. They haven't gotten on since. By the time I returned the next summer, Flora had found someone else, but we've stayed friends."

Delilah put her hands on his chest and smiled. "I'm glad you didn't tell me *that* back in March."

Cameron laughed. "Your turn."

She looked away briefly. "I was sixteen. It was at a cast party after a high school show. His name was Ben."

"Not a boyfriend?"

Delilah shook her head. "No. Just a friend."

"Well. We have that in common."

She didn't argue. Running her fingers over his hip, she asked, "Who is your biggest regret?"

Cameron drew a long breath and looked away for some time. He twined her hair in his hand as he answered, "I don't know her name. It was a long time ago. She was at the premiere of the third major film I made. She was in the crowd waiting for my autograph and she had this look on her face, like she was undressing me with her eyes. She wasn't screaming or talking. She was so still, and I just knew she was imagining fucking me. So, I wrote the room number and my hotel on the picture she had me sign. It was an incredibly reckless thing to do. By the time I got back she was there, waiting. We never really spoke. I gave her what she wanted, or what she seemed to want. Then I asked her to leave. And I never saw her again."

"And you regret it?" Delilah asked.

"Yes. For several reasons. The most important being that I was married at the time."

"She never told anyone?"

Cameron shrugged. "I don't know. This was long before smart phones and the internet. It would have been much harder to tell a lot of people back then, or to prove it."

"That makes sense."

He added, "It was the first and last time I ever slept with a fan."

She nodded.

Leaning on his elbow, Cameron stated, "Your turn. Biggest regret."

Delilah suddenly wished the conversation had taken a different turn. She picked at the bed sheet below her, not wanting to answer.

Sensing her change in mood, he said, "You don't have to tell me."

But she did. He was honest with her. It was only fair, and he could never hate her worse than she hated herself.

Taking a deep breath, she said, "It was my sister's husband, Preston. Nine years ago."

Cameron's brow furrowed.

Delilah plowed on, "It was about one year after…that day. The first anniversary was a nightmare. I was still hoping to find something of Anna, and it was looking bleak at that point. I tried to go to the ceremony, but I broke down and couldn't. I was in our apartment a few days later, cleaning it out and crying like a child, when Preston showed up to help. The place was a mess that neither of us wanted to touch until then. We were both devastated and struggling, and I've mentioned my tendency to use sex as a distraction. So, I kissed him, and I think he let himself pretend I was Anna. It was wrong on both our parts. There was never, *ever* anything between us before that. We might have stayed friends, were it not for that day. Afterward, we couldn't be around each other. My father never completely understood why he stopped talking to us. He eventually decided it was because Preston was able to get out and Anna didn't. But it was really because of me, and I regret that my father lost that connection to Anna."

Silence stretched as neither said anything. Cameron held her wordlessly.

"I told you. Biblical whore."

His brow furrowed again. "I'm sure there was more to her story. I'm sure Delilah was more than one choice she made."

She read his meaning. "Maybe…"

He kissed her softly.

Trying to lighten the mood, Delilah asked, "Any other partners I should know about?"

Cameron considered the question. "There are some that I'm sure you've read about. Those are all true. Oh, and Meg, from the party last night. Meg and I parted ways romantically some time ago, amicably, but we've always had a…complicated friendship."

Seeing him struggle to explain, she helped him by offering, "Friends with benefits?"

He laughed uncertainly. "I suppose. But not anymore."

Glancing away, Delilah worked up her courage then asked, "Cameron…do you have a son?"

"Yes."

"But you don't see each other?"

"No." He explained, "I'm afraid he prefers it that way."

"Who is his mother?"

"Marianne. My ex-wife."

Delilah gave a little nod, but she didn't push further. It felt like they both shared enough for this morning.

To keep Cameron from having to comment further, she changed the subject. "Your phone is making sounds."

He glanced at the bedside table where his phone had been vibrating on and off since they woke up. "That it is. Someone always wants something."

"Are you supposed to be somewhere?"

"No. Not today."

Reluctantly disentangling himself, Cameron rolled over and reached for the phone. Pulling himself up against the pillows, he started checking messages. Delilah pulled herself to her knees and hugged a pillow to her chest. She watched him, feeling another sudden surge of realization at the improbable nature of her situation. She asked herself how it was possible that she was sitting here with Cameron Burke while he casually checked his phone in all his long-legged, naked glory.

After a few minutes, Cameron looked up at her. "I think you should know that the rest of the world is having a shit storm right now."

"What?"

"Come here," he motioned for her.

Delilah curled herself beside him so she could see his phone. Cameron pulled up his text messages, which consisted of Adam and someone named Amelia sending him messages and links to things he needed to see. As he clicked on them one by one, Delilah felt her gut churn. Every tabloid and entertainment site printed photos of them. There were many shots of her and Cameron arm in arm on the red carpet. It was odd to see herself like that, but Delilah expected those. There was also complete video coverage of the event, including Cameron's interviews. A video of their impromptu tango was already uploaded to YouTube and commented on:

> *Who is the girl with Cameron Burke?*
>
> *OMG! That should be me!*
>
> *Did she win a contest or something?*
>
> *Cameron Burke is so endlessly hot I can't stand it.*
>
> *Like fine wine, baby. Like fine wine.*
>
> *But who is SHE?*
>
> *I did win a contest, and I was there. Her name is Delilah and that's all I know.*

Delilah felt like she was having some sort of bizarre, out of body experience as she watched and read about herself. Cameron played the video of their dance, and she watched herself move, critiquing every line and step in her mind. He lightly nuzzled her hair as he watched, and she knew he saw something very different. He was not critiquing.

"We do look good," she joked.

He smiled in agreement then clicked another link. Every site had its own take on the two of them. The headlines read:

Who Is Cameron Burke's Redheaded Flame?

Has Marcus forsaken Mohara?

Delilah groaned. "Those are terrible. Really terrible. Who comes up with this stuff?"

"People who like bad metaphors. But they make a lot of money doing it."

As they searched through the onslaught of privacy invasion, Delilah felt her worry ease somewhat. There were a lot of pictures of her out there, but no one seemed to know who she was. None of them even had her last name. So far, she was simply the mystery redhead. She wondered, if she stayed uninteresting, if that's all she would be.

Sliding out of bed, she pulled on underwear and a clean t-shirt from her bag. Rummaging through her purse, she pulled out her phone. Cameron pulled on pants while Delilah scrolled through her own messages. Her father had called once. And Jenna had called four times. Delilah also had several text messages. Her father's were expected. He mentioned seeing her in pictures and asked her to call when she was ready. Jenna, however, had sent a copy of one of the red-carpet photos and asked:

> OMG, is this you? Call me.
> Just, call me.

Delilah laughed to herself.

Cameron heard her and asked, "What's funny?"

She held up her phone. "My friend, Jenna. My only friend right now. The one I was supposed to go watch the movie with this Friday. She has found our pictures online."

"I see," Cameron smiled.

Delilah stared at her phone, trying to decide what she should say.

"You would think there are more important things in the world for people to read about than us, but I'm afraid me walking a red carpet with someone new is a ridiculously big deal."

Delilah still had no idea what to do.

Cameron went on, "I think we need to decide how we're handling this. Adam is getting calls from Amelia. Amelia, my publicist, is getting phone calls from the press. All the nosy bastards want to know something."

"Can we say nothing?"

Cameron tipped his head thoughtfully. "We can. But I have learned that things usually go more smoothly if you are ahead of their assumptions. If something is going to come out anyway, it's better if it comes from you."

Delilah nodded, thinking.

Cameron asked gently, "What are you most worried about them knowing?"

"Anna," she snapped. "I don't want to be asked about her on the street or to have her pictures everywhere. Our pictures. I'm not afraid of fame, Cameron. I've spent most of my life onstage. I've had my own fans. It's not recognition or gossip that bothers me. It's having the worst parts of my life plastered all over the media."

Cameron suggested, "Perhaps we make them focus on us? If we give them a little of what they want, then the story is about you and me, or you *with* me, rather than who you are. I've also learned that if you talk enough and appear open enough, they think there's nothing else to tell. At least, for a little while."

It was Delilah's turn to nod.

"Come here," he said again.

She curled beside him. He put his left hand in her hair and pulled her close, so they were nose to nose. She instinctively moved her hand to his jaw line. She closed her eyes, and just before he kissed her, he snapped a picture with his free hand. Then he finished the kiss.

When he pulled back, she said, "That was sneaky."

He smiled. "Perhaps."

Cameron manipulated the picture on his phone then showed it to her. The attraction between them was undeniable. Their eyes were closed, their lips almost meeting. Her hair tumbled over her shoulder, bare because her shirt was too big. The photo was cropped too close to tell that they were in bed. Cameron enhanced the light and shadow to hide any flaws and put the focus on their profiles. It was a beautiful picture, and Delilah knew he was asking permission to put it out into the world. She looked at it for a long time, trying to make peace with a decision. Suddenly, she remembered something from years before.

Her father took her and her sister on a weekend trip to Manhattan at the end of their senior year of high school. While there, she was able to take a few circus classes. One evening, in their hotel room, Delilah described to her sister her fear of letting go of the trapeze. She was *capable* of performing a throw from one trapeze to the other, but fear was stopping her on every try. Delilah knew that right past the terror was a rush of adrenaline-fed joy. Still, she couldn't make herself do it. After listening, Anna said:

Tomorrow, Lilah. Just let go. Just go for it. You said it's only scary for a moment. Let go and trust yourself.

The next day, Delilah did just that and nailed her first trapeze trick.

Now, taking a deep breath, Delilah said, "Post it. That will be our statement. We're in this now, come what may."

Cameron fiddled with his phone for another few minutes. Then he smiled when hers chimed. Delilah looked down. She had a Twitter notification. She opened the app and read his post:

Cameron Burke @TheCameronBurke

"When she dances, the world stops to watch,
and I shudder that she is mine."
#WhomTheSwordDevours @Waterfall_Angel

He included a link to the picture they just took together.

"You've known that handle was me? All this time?"

He pretended to be offended. "You didn't see that I followed you back?"

She huffed, "I don't really know how it all works."

Cameron laughed lightly.

Delilah added, "That's a beautiful quote, though."

He returned, "I wish I could say it was original. But it's from one of my films."

"It's the intention that matters," she stated. "Send me the picture."

Using her phone, Delilah posted the same photo, along with:

Delilah MacClare @Waterfall_Angel

"Though she be but little, she is fierce."
#MidsummerNight'sDream @TheCameronBurke

Cameron read her tweet, smirked, and posted:

Cameron Burke @TheCameronBurke

"It would be an excellent match, for he was rich
and she was handsome." #SenseAndSensibility
@Waterfall_Angel

Delilah, realizing it was now a contest, tweeted:

Delilah MacClare @Waterfall_Angel

"My very soul demands you: it will be satisfied,
or it will take deadly vengeance on its frame."
#JaneEyre @TheCameronBurke

Delilah pulled a couple of still shots from their dance the night before and posted them to her Facebook page. Then she changed her profile picture on both Facebook and Twitter to the one Cameron had just taken. She only had five friends and followers at this point, but she still posted a link to the video from the night before and changed her status to:

In case anyone wondered, I can still tango.

Finally, she sent a quick reply text that said:

Yes, Jenna, that is me. We'll
talk soon.

Cameron, after reading her last tweet, snaked his arm around her again. "That should keep everyone occupied for a bit."

Delilah dropped her phone in agreement.

"So...you demand me?" He teased.

"Until I'm satisfied," she returned with a sly smile.

He captured her mouth with great intention.

Later that evening, as the sun set behind the city, Delilah decided she needed to call her father. Curled up on the sofa in her t-shirt and yoga pants, she dialed his number.

He answered quickly. "Lilah?"

"Yep. It's me."

"You looked absolutely beautiful last night. I saw pictures," Stephen complimented her.

"Thanks. I'd forgotten how much I love dressing up."

"You looked like *you* last night, Lilah."

She knew exactly what he meant.

"Where are you staying?" Her father changed the subject.

"With Cameron. He has an apartment on the west side, near Washington Circle."

The line was silent.

"That sounds expensive," her father finally said.

"Very. And beautiful. It has these tall windows, and you can see most of the park and a bit of the river through them."

"How long will you stay?"

"Cameron is in the States until Sunday. Then he has to go back to London."

"Do you think you'll go with him?"

Delilah hesitated, not ready for the question. "No. At least, not on Sunday."

They both struggled with how they felt about the situation.

Finally, Stephen changed the subject. "Tell me more about the premiere."

Delilah filled her father in on the details of the night before. She didn't mention all the wine and pills. She felt, on some level, he knew. Stephen could appreciate how significant it was that she went out in the city at all.

After saying goodbye, Delilah smiled to herself. Her father was a good man, the best man she knew. She wished, more than anything, that she could give him what he wanted. She wished she could settle down and be happy—deeply, lastingly happy. As she watched the sky fade to twilight, she wondered if that was possible. She glanced over at Cameron, who was in the kitchen making drinks with top shelf liquor and sandwiches with basic ingredients. He smiled at her, and she smiled back.

One day at a time, she said to herself. *One day at a time.*

15
Lost

I am not yours, not lost in you,
not lost, although I long to be
lost as a candle lit at noon,
lost as a snowflake in the sea.

You love me, and I find you still
a spirit beautiful and bright,
Yet I am I, who long to be
lost as a light is lost in light.

Oh plunge me deep in love—put out
my senses, leave me deaf and blind,
swept by the tempest of your love,
a taper in a rushing wind.

—"I Am Not Yours" by Sara Teasdale

Two days later, on Thursday, Cameron woke to Delilah's hair splayed across his hips. He let out a low groan before slowly opening his eyes. She flicked her eyes up and met his, and he could see she enjoyed having him at her mercy. And she did, in more ways than this. He was hooked on her like a potent drug. This was the closest thing Cameron ever had to a real honeymoon. Even his actual honeymoon with Marianne was nothing like this. This total isolation, this complete fixation on each other without regard for what the world thought, was foreign to him. When it came to relationships, he was used to juggling sex with showing off one another. This week, however, he forced himself out of the flat only to meet obligations Amelia set up for him. Each day, he dragged himself from Delilah, then rushed back to her. The paparazzi photographed him and shouted questions. The interviewers asked, on camera, about Delilah, and he answered the way they agreed:

Delilah is a part of my life. We met in my hometown, and her family is Scottish.

He pointed them in the direction of Britain to keep them from her real past. Cameron's goal was to convince them, for as long as he could, that there was nothing else to tell. He wanted Delilah to stay with him, and he was afraid she would run as soon as the press mentioned her sister. Cameron was also afraid she wouldn't be able to handle it. He felt fiercely protective of her and not just because she was currently making him see stars with her mouth. He was invested in her. Her happiness had somehow become wound up in his own. Cameron couldn't imagine his life without Delilah MacClare. It was unsettling.

But, he said to himself, *that's what the beginning always feels like, doesn't it?*

Closing his eyes, he let her work her magic. There was something about the fact that she didn't even pretend to be innocent that sent a rush of desire through him. Delilah knew who she was, and who she was not. Like a great sky bird that was struck down, he wanted her to fly again. However, he was also afraid, if she did, she would realize how many other, younger men were out there, and she would be gone.

Delilah pulled away from him, and he opened his eyes to watch her climb, cat-like, over his body. She took him to the hilt inside of her, then worked her mouth over his neck, covering him in her soft, lilac-scented hair. She hadn't yet said a word to him this morning. She just moved against him, sitting up and closing her eyes. Delilah put her hands on his chest and shook her hair back so that he could see the spray of freckles across her breasts. He lost himself in her, both literally and metaphorically. He felt her nails lightly digging into his skin as she focused on her own pleasure. Delilah knew her body, and she knew what she liked. Just being Cameron Burke wasn't enough to make her scream. However, he was learning what would, and he put his hands on her hips. When she tipped herself forward to nip his ear again, he drove against her. She cried out in release, and he helplessly went with her.

Then she laid herself across his chest, and Cameron stroked her tangled hair, appreciating her warmth. She lay there for a long time, and her chest rose and fell deeply.

Eventually, he asked, "Are you all right?"

Shifting her weight to lie next to him, she smiled. "Oh…yes."

When she said nothing else, Cameron wondered if she fell back to sleep.

Suddenly, she pushed herself up on one arm, looked up at him, and said, "I hope you don't mind that I woke you."

He stared at her, not sure how she could think any man would not want to be woken up the way she woke him.

"And," she went on, "I'm sorry if I'm a bit…insatiable. But it's been nine years. Nine years and…it's nice to be touched."

Cameron stared in shock before laughing heartily. She was apologizing for shagging him, after apologizing for waking him up with her mouth on his prick. She was truly unprecedented, so he kissed her long and hard.

When he pulled back, she put her arms around his chest and pulled even closer to him. After another minute, he asked, "Can I take you out once more while we're here? To dinner and a show? Straight there and back, nowhere else."

Delilah ran her fingers lightly over his chest. Cameron was certain she was trying to find a way to say no.

Taking a deep breath, he tried again, "I'll take care of you, Delilah. But I don't want you to do it for me. Well, selfishly, I do. I don't want you to hide yourself in here forever. You deserve…more."

She continued to trail her fingers over his skin. Before she could answer, her phone started ringing across the room. Cameron immediately missed her warmth as she slid away. She rooted through her bag on the floor and emerged with her phone.

Looking down at it, she said, "It's Jenna again."

Cameron sat up. "If she's your friend, answer her."

Delilah stared at the phone for a minute until it stopped ringing. Pulling on a shirt, she said, "Not yet."

Pulling back on the pajama bottoms she removed that morning, he returned, "Is she asking about me?"

"I'm sure she wants to."

"I don't mind if you tell her."

She glanced over at him. "I know you don't. But it's not about you. Just like me not going out isn't about *you*." She hesitated. "Tell me, if I never go out in the city again, is that wrong?"

Cameron considered it. "Do you *want* to go back out there? Ever?"

She looked at the floor. "I don't know."

"I really wish you would try."

Delilah looked up at him. "It's not about you Cameron. I'm sorry, but it just isn't."

Later that afternoon, Delilah was curled up in a chair by the window. Cameron was out filming an interview for a late-night program. Looking north across the park, she considered the phone in her hand. After some deliberation, she took a deep breath and called Jenna. She put her friend off for days and she knew that was no way to treat someone who just came back into her life and offered such genuine friendship.

Jenna picked up immediately. "Delilah? Tell me it's really you, finally calling me!"

Delilah cleared her throat. "Yep, it's me."

"Oh my god! Why didn't you tell me you had tickets to the premiere? And how in the hell did you manage to dance with Cameron Burke?"

Delilah swallowed hard. Jenna had no reason to think she had any real connection with Cameron before the previous Monday, except for a brief meeting. Her friend also knew nothing about Chatfield. Delilah considered not saying any more. However, she was quickly overcome by a need to talk about the whole thing with another woman, especially one who knew her during adolescence and who was there for her first real kiss.

"I met him in England, Jen."

There was a pause on the line. "England? The trip you just came back from?"

"I came back in April," Delilah corrected.

"How, in the entire country of England, did you manage to meet Cameron Burke?"

Delilah explained, "He came into the pub where I was reading. I had no idea it was his hometown. I had no idea who he was."

Incredulously, Jenna demanded, "Didn't you see *Absolution of Men?* and *Fyrelords?*"

"No. Not before last month. Other things were going on."

"I see…" Jenna had no other answer.

Delilah took a deep breath. "Jen…there's more."

"Obviously," her friend returned. "He invited you to a movie premiere. Or at least remembered you."

"He invited me," Delilah clarified. "He came to see me at home, in Branton, and asked me to go."

"He came here?" Jenna nearly squealed.

Unable to avoid smiling, Delilah said, "You sound like a fangirl."

Jenna laughed. "I *am* a fangirl."

"A forty-year-old fangirl with a husband and children," Delilah teased.

Jenna sighed. "Give it a minute before you ruin it."

Sobering, Delilah said, "He came to Branton because...we got close in England. We spent a lot of time together."

"Really?" Jenna also grew more serious.

"Yeah," Delilah confirmed. "I read *Heir of Taivas* for the first time. And we watched it together. I hadn't read or seen any of it because...because of..."

Jenna interjected, "I understand."

"And...we slept together. In England."

There was a long silence before Jenna demanded, "What?"

Delilah started to go on, but Jenna cut her off.

"Wait, you're telling me you slept with Cameron Burke? *The* Cameron Burke? Cyrus Whitkey? Marcus Eperra? Are you *serious?*"

"I'm definitely serious."

"Oh my god. What was that like?" Jenna asked in amazement.

"Ummmm," Delilah wasn't sure what to say.

"I'm sorry," Jenna continued, "that's rude and I sound like we're teenagers again. But, oh my god!"

Delilah considered what else to share.

Jenna plowed on, "Does he live up to all the hype, though?"

"He's just a man, Jen."

"No," Jenna argued, "someone who was on the list of sexiest men alive isn't *just a man.*"

Letting that one go, Delilah said, "Because of what happened in England, he came to see me at home and asked me to come with him to the city, and to go to the premiere."

Jenna waited a beat. "Wait...where are you right now?"

Delilah swallowed hard. "In his apartment."

"Oh my god! You're staying with him? You're sleeping with Cameron Burke? Like, regularly? How could you not tell me about this?"

"I'm out of the habit of telling people things. And I haven't had anything to tell for a very long time."

"Still," Jenna insisted, "you have to tell me *something.*"

Delilah gave in, unable to resist sharing secrets with her friend. "Well...Cameron knows what he's doing."

"I bet he does!" Jenna threw back with obvious innuendo.

"Truth? We have a lot in common. He's intense, and he has a look that makes me putty. He says I undo him, and I believe he's correct."

"Oh. My. God."

"You've said that a few times."

"I have no other words."

Delilah continued, "He's a good kisser. Every time he kisses me, I'm just...gone." She paused. "He also makes me think. He talks to me like no one else will. He pulls me out of myself, which I sometimes hate. But I think...he's making me better."

There was a hesitation before Jenna asked, "Delilah...are you in love with him?"

Delilah was taken aback. Quickly, she said, "That would be ridiculous."

"But everything up to this point has been perfectly reasonable?" Jenna shot back.

"Neither one of us are 'falling in love' kind of people," Delilah replied.

"Well, I'm happy for you. Truly."

"Thanks," Delilah replied softly.

Jenna changed the subject. "I also called because I thought you might still be in the city. Jason and I are coming up tomorrow."

"What for?"

"A much-needed child-free weekend. After I take Isaac to see *Retribution* tonight at midnight."

"I see," Delilah stated.

Jenna continued, "I was hoping we could go see a show tomorrow? Maybe get dinner?"

Delilah swallowed hard. Unlike Cameron, Jenna had no idea what she was asking. She knew the general story about Anna, but she didn't understand how the city itself affected Delilah. She started to decline but thought about what Cameron said that morning. He asked a good question, whether or not he realized it. Did she ever want to go back out there? Was it a goal that mattered to her?

Suddenly, Delilah remembered a conversation she had with her sister about a month before Anna died. At the time, Anna was interning with a therapist in her field of study. She told Delilah about a little girl who was mauled by a dog. Long after her injuries healed, she remained terrified, to the point of fainting, of all animals. The therapist was working with the little girl to help her gradually overcome that fear.

After observing one day, Anna said, *Can you imagine never knowing how loving animals can be and what a joy it is to love them back? That's why I want to help her, and others. Because she* wants *to love them. She doesn't* want *to live with this fear. If someone wants to overcome something, they should be given every chance.*

Delilah felt something twist inside of her. She hated fear. Becoming an aerialist was all about overcoming fear. She now realized that what she wanted, more than anything, was not to be afraid.

Taking a shaking breath, she told Jenna, "I'll be here tomorrow, and Cameron mentioned going out one more time. Can I ask him and text you?"

The heaviness was dispelled when Jenna replied, "You want to bring Cameron Burke to dinner?"

Delilah laughed. "I would like to bring the man in my life to dinner, yes."

Jenna laughed as well. "I'll try to see him that way. Just let me know."

"I will."

The following evening, Cameron and Delilah rode in the back of another, more practical, car. Cameron wasn't keen on taking a limo everywhere he went. If he wasn't driving, he would rather be inconspicuous. Upon Delilah's request, he got them into a little place in Midtown that specialized in Spanish tapas and good wine. He also secured them tickets to a show, using no small measure of his celebrity influence to get the tickets. He wasn't sure how Delilah's friends would feel about him effectively taking them all out for the night, but he wanted to do it for her. He was thrilled Delilah agreed to go out and making the arrangements himself was the best way to make sure they could all go and have a measure of privacy.

When they arrived at the restaurant, Jenna and Jason were waiting at the entrance. Cameron saw Jenna's eyes widen when he and Delilah emerged from the car. Jenna was the opposite of Delilah—tall with cropped black hair and dark eyes. She wore a short, deep red cocktail dress and low heels. Jason seemed friendly but out of his element. He looked like the type who dusted off the sport coat a few times a year at the insistence of his wife. Cameron wore Armani again, open collar and sans tie. Delilah had pulled another dress out of her bags, this time in deep green. It was cap-sleeved and expertly tailored. Cameron wasn't sure if it was designer, but it looked made for her. Crossing the pavement to Jenna, he watched as she and Delilah exchanged hugs and greetings.

Delilah turned back to him and said to her friend, "This is Cameron. Cameron, Jenna and Jason."

He shook hands with Jason then turned to Jenna, who stared at him in awe. She offered her hand and looked amazed when he touched her.

When he pulled back, Jenna said, "I can't...I mean, I have no idea what to say. It's...Cameron-freaking-Burke!"

She grasped Jason's arm and tried to suppress a squeal. Jason responded by looking at her like she'd gone mad. He deadpanned, "Ouch."

Jenna lightly swatted him. "I don't mean to be ridiculous, but it's Cameron Burke!"

Cameron teased with a wry smile, "Now that everyone on the street knows who I am, shall we go inside?"

Jenna looked even more in awe of hearing him speak. Cameron glanced at Delilah, who rolled her eyes and grabbed her friend by the arm. She effectively pulled Jenna into the restaurant with the men trailing behind. They were ushered to a table in the far corner, allowing them some privacy. Cameron selected a couple of good bottles of wine, and they all picked several dishes to try. Once the wine was poured, Cameron glanced around, wondering when someone would speak. He found it both amusing and tiring that people often couldn't form a coherent sentence around him. And Jenna was still staring.

She finally exclaimed, "It's so bizarre to be sitting this close to you."

Jason smirked. "And your husband is right here."

Jenna rolled her eyes. "You know I love you. This is just…surreal."

Cameron turned to Delilah. "Now, this is what I expected when I sat down across from *you* the first time. Just a little bit of mindless adoration."

Delilah gave him a withering look. "If you're looking for 'mindless,' I can find you some girls who fit the bill."

He grimaced, then lightly kissed her temple. "Too late. You've ruined me for everyone else."

Delilah looked up at him, and he could tell his words affected her.

They worked their way through the first bottle of wine before the food came, and Jenna calmed down. She answered questions about herself and managed to converse in an almost normal way. Jason was less star-struck and more interested in asking questions for the sake of his son. He also showed a genuine interest in the workings of the film industry. With the arrival of the food, they opened another bottle of wine. Cameron could see Delilah relaxing as the alcohol muted her anxiety. He decided he liked her a little tipsy. It caused her hands to wander.

As Delilah laughed at one of Jenna's stories, she leaned in and rested her head on Cameron's shoulder. Then she laced her fingers through his under the table. Jenna watched the two of them, and her face was a mixture of amazement at what she was seeing and happiness for her friend.

After dinner, they walked about a block and a half to the theater. Cameron made sure to select a restaurant close enough to the show to minimize the time Delilah spent in the street. They managed to make the journey with only a few curious glances. Cameron also made sure they arrived early enough to be in their seats before the bulk of the crowd arrived. He found that it usually made for less of a fuss. With Adam's help, he managed to procure last minute tickets to a revival of *Anything Goes*. The four of them were seated near the front of the orchestra, and they had only been sitting for a few minutes when the taking of photos began. People tried to be discreet, but Cameron knew everyone was snapping away with their phones.

For the next three hours, they all lost themselves in the show. Cameron was thrilled that Delilah not only agreed to come, but appeared to be enjoying herself. She kept her eyes on him most of the time they were outside, but she relaxed once they were in the theater. Now, as the show drew to a close, she snuggled close to him, tracing his fingers with hers and smiling. Occasionally, Jenna would look over and smile as well. For all her squealing, she seemed to be a good friend to Delilah.

When the show was over, Cameron led the way out of the theater. Their car waited just around the corner so he and Delilah could make a quick exit. He tipped an usher generously to help them get out of the building. Once the crowd realized who he was, it was hard to get past them as they stopped to take pictures and shout their praises. It was flattering, but also intrusive. Cameron put his arm tightly around Delilah and followed the usher quickly through the crowd. Jason and Jenna followed behind.

When they emerged onto the street, there was another crush of people on the sidewalk. Cameron noticed Delilah had her hands over her face, so he led her quickly to the edge of the crowd. There, she backed against the stone wall of the building. Her breathing was fast and hard, and she looked as though she might faint. Cameron put his arms around her and held on tight.

"You're all right. It's only people at a show. You're all right."

After a minute or so, she looked up at him. She was shaking, but she looked more stable.

Her voice shook. "It's the crowd…and the street…"

"Just keep your eyes on me."

She obeyed, and Cameron quickly led her to the car and helped her inside.

Turning back to Jenna, he said, "I'll have her ring you."

Jenna agreed with a look of concern.

Late that night, for the first time since they started their affair, Delilah woke up trembling from a nightmare. Cameron held her close, without asking questions, until she fell asleep.

Two days later, back at home in West Virginia, Delilah invited Jenna and her family over for dinner. In the same way Cameron wanted to include her in his life, Delilah also wanted Cameron in *her* life. He obliged by agreeing to meet Jenna's children. In his presence, Klari turned suddenly shy, and Isaac stared openly. Sunny just looked confused. After a solid hour, Isaac worked up the nerve to ask Cameron a question, which led to another and another. Delilah felt a rush of admiration for Cameron as he patiently answered things she was sure he'd been asked a thousand times. Jenna gave Delilah a long look, and she knew what her friend wasn't saying:

He cares about you. He's talking to my son. I like him. And not just as a fangirl.

After dinner, the kids played outside. Delilah and Cameron walked together through the trees behind the house, and Delilah wasn't sure what to say. Tomorrow, thousands of miles would come between them for the second time. The past week was a blur of sex, sleep, and reading while Cameron worked. They knew everything about each other, physically. Now, it would seem, it was time to talk again, to decide their future. But neither was willing.

They walked a bit longer before Delilah said, "This is the tree I used to climb to hide from everyone when I wanted to be dramatic."

Cameron looked up at the spreading oak.

"It's bigger, now." She went on, "And this is the one where I used to hang my silk."

She pointed to another soaring tree a few yards away. Some of the lower branches were cut away, and one thick, arching branch stretched outward some twenty feet overhead. There was a makeshift ladder nailed to the tree and leading to that branch.

Cameron stared up at it. "How did you ever get up there the first time?"

"I used a climbing harness."

Cameron shook his head in disbelief. "When I was sixteen, I could barely climb a rope at school."

Delilah cocked her head and looked him over.

"I was blessed with height, but I was what you might've called…gangly."

Delilah laughed, trying to imagine him young and wiry and wearing gym shorts. She wasn't sure if that was a thing in England, but it was a fun image.

Stopping to lean on the tree, she said, "This is where I would come when I needed to work through stuff when life got complicated. This is my 'spot in the pub', if you know what I mean."

Cameron nodded.

She looked up at him. "What happens when you get back to London? What will you do?"

He looked away. "I have to meet with my agent. I must attend a film festival in Switzerland, and I have to film two more episodes of *Lost the Plot*. I'm doing a few interviews. Then, in October, I start filming *Heir of Taivas* again."

She felt a sudden hollowness in her chest. There was certainly no room for her in a schedule like that.

Sensing her feelings, he said, "I would love for you to come with me, to travel with me."

Delilah looked down at her hands. "I would have to renew my passport. You know, do some paperwork."

He stepped toward her, and she could see the turmoil in him. She knew he wanted to ask her to do the paperwork, to do whatever it took to come with him, but he couldn't say it any more than she could. Delilah knew he would never beg her to come, just as she would never beg him to stay. Their mutual failures at relationships had created a stalemate. So, Cameron did what came naturally. Closing the distance between them, he cupped her face and kissed her. When he pulled away, Delilah still had no words. Without pushing further, he took her hand and led the way back to the house.

Back inside, they discovered that Stephen agreed to let the children watch a movie. Dark clouds brewed in the distance, and no one wanted to drive the mountain roads during a thunderstorm. After the children agreed on a movie and sprawled on the living room floor, the adults took their seats. Jenna and Jason managed to squeeze themselves into the recliner together, eliciting eye rolls from their children. Stephen took the rocking chair with a newspaper in his hands, so Cameron and Delilah took the sofa. It was old and soft, and they sank into it. Cameron kicked off his shoes and stretched his long legs under the coffee table. Delilah shed her flip flops and curled into him. After a while, she snaked one arm around him. He pulled her closer, and she hooked her legs across his lap. They stayed that way, clinging to one another, as the movie played. The others glanced over periodically, and Delilah knew they were in awe that Cameron Burke was watching an old movie with them. To Delilah, however, he was simply Cameron, and he was leaving her in the morning.

Later that night, Cameron made love to Delilah with a slow tenderness that was different than the energy of the past week. He held her tightly as they moved together. Afterward, she pulled herself up on the pillows so his head rested on her chest. She absently ran her fingers through his hair as he traced the line of her hip with his hand.

Eventually, she said, "I'm going to miss you."

His breath was warm on her chest. "And I will miss you."

The words felt inadequate, but Delilah was too afraid to say more.

The next morning, after Cameron kissed her goodbye and drove away, Delilah curled back up in the guest bed that still smelled like him. She wrapped herself in the afghan and browsed through the pictures on her phone. She had a lot of shots of her and Cameron. Most of them were taken in his apartment, and she wouldn't show them to anyone else. They weren't intentionally explicit, but in many of them they were curled in his bed. She also had several photos from the night they went out. Delilah stopped to study one Jenna took of them at the restaurant table. Delilah was smiling at the camera, but Cameron was looking at her, his face full of more emotion than she usually saw in him. She stared at the picture for a long time, then sent it to him.

A few minutes later, her phone chimed with a message. Pulling it up, she read the text Cameron sent:

> Please do the paperwork.
> Call me ridiculous or
> completely mad, but I don't
> want to do any of this
> without you.

Something in her broke, and she felt tears prick her eyes. This was exactly what she was afraid of. She didn't know how to be without him now. He stirred her heart, which she swore never to leave exposed again. For the first time in years, this house wasn't a haven. It felt hollow and empty, and Delilah didn't want to be alone here. The ghost of her sister wasn't enough. She wanted to chase

Cameron down and tell him there was a good chance she loved him, but she was scared. Two days ago, she had a panic attack just from the crowd outside a theater. Wiping her eyes, she felt her sadness become anger. Before September 11, 2001, she saw fear as a challenge to be overcome. Delilah scoffed at fear, to a fault. The old Delilah would already be on the plane with Cameron. Tragedy, however, paralyzed her. She now lived in a state of terror.

Terror.

She understood, in an intellectual sense, what the word meant. What was done to her sister, to nearly three thousand victims, and to the citizens of her country, was labeled an act of terrorism. Delilah both accepted and endorsed that conclusion. Until this moment, however, she never considered the intentions of terrorists as it applied to her individual life. In her mind, terrorists acted to terrorize nations and individuals were the collateral damage. Now, for the first time, she realized that she, as an individual, had been terrorized. She followed the natural chain of words:

Terrorist. Terrorize. Terror. Terrified.

It was not just Anna's voice that was silenced.

Delilah felt a fresh wave of anger at all the things beyond her control that brought her to this place. Picking up her phone, she typed out a message to Cameron:

I'll do the paperwork.

Then, she hoisted herself off the bed and stormed down the hall to her father's study. In one jerk, she pulled down the door to the attic. Climbing up the ancient ladder, she was met with a blast of warm air. Crawling through all the boxes, she found one large, plastic tote. She opened it and pulled out a thick chain of braided turquoise fabric. Pulling it into her lap, Delilah cradled its weight and breathed in its scent. A million images flashed through her mind. Folding it back into the tote, Delilah dragged it down the ladder. She pulled the tote to the back door. Hoisting the fabric into her arms, she ignored the complaint of her lungs as she carried her silk outside to its familiar place high in the oak trees.

16
To Bind the Wind

It is enough for me by day
to walk the same bright earth with him;
Enough that over us by night
the same great roof of stars is dim.

I do not hope to bind the wind
or set a fetter on the sea,
It is enough to feel his love,
blow by like music over me.

— *"Enough" by Sara Teasdale*

One week later, Delilah hung from her silk in the tree behind her house. Her lungs burned as she held herself precariously ten feet off the ground. A sheen of sweat from the summer heat covered her. The trees were in full, verdant splendor with leaves heavy from a summer storm. The grass below was lush and cut through with moss. Delilah, barefoot, wore only leggings and a sports bra. She held on as long as she could before unwinding herself and dropping to the ground. Inhaling long pulls of heavy, humid air, she was proud to have finally stayed up for a whole minute.

"Lilah?"

She opened her eyes to find her father staring down at her. Stephen was fixing the lawn mower, so his jeans were smudged with grease.

"Jenna's here." He went on, "She was hoping to see you."

Delilah smiled and stood up slowly. Stephen gave her a worried glance, but she waved him off. "I'm fine."

Crossing through the trees, Delilah followed Stephen back to the house. She found Jenna in the family room sitting on the couch drinking diet soda. Delilah joined her, and they spent the next few minutes catching up on the past week. Jenna and her family just returned from Virginia Beach.

After they were caught up, Jenna changed the subject carefully, "So, how are things…without him?"

Delilah hesitated. "I miss him, Jen. I miss him terribly. And I told him I would renew my passport so I can go back overseas."

"To live?" Jenna questioned.

"To be with him wherever he's working," Delilah explained. "He wants me to travel with him."

"Can you do that?"

"I'm not sure, but I'm trying to figure it out."

"You know," Jenna offered, "all fangirl feelings aside, he looks at you like you're his world. It's crazy intense."

"Well, he said he loved me, once. But it was…in a heated moment."

"Ah," Jenna smiled. "The mid-sex profession of love."

Delilah laughed. "Is that an official thing?"

"Of course it is."

"Do you think he meant it?"

Jenna thought it over. "I don't know. He does have a…history. And he can't deny it. It's been all over magazines and such."

"He does," Delilah agreed, "but then, so do I."

Jenna cocked her head in curiosity.

"Come on. You remember me in high school. More and more, I'm realizing Cameron and I have a common history. We're like tempests, or something else poetic."

"Maybe you make sense for each other?" Jenna suggested.

"Or maybe this will end in a public disaster. And I really don't think I can handle that."

"But look at how much you've already handled," Jenna pointed out.

Delilah couldn't argue.

Jenna held her gaze. "At what point did he stop being famous to you? When did he become just…Cameron?"

Delilah immediately answered, "He's always been 'just Cameron.' I don't know him any other way. Every now and then I get this glimpse of the way everyone else sees him, but the rest of the time he's just the man that I…"

"That you what?" Jenna pushed.

Delilah heaved a sigh and leaned back onto the couch. "I don't know. He's the man that I…that I don't know how to live without right now."

Jenna started to respond, but Stephen came in from the yard just then. Smiling at them, he asked, "Can I watch the last of the news?"

"Sure," Delilah agreed, putting her feet up on the coffee table.

Stephen turned the television on low volume in the background and went to get himself a drink. He returned and sat across from them in the recliner. Delilah changed the subject. She and Jenna talked about the upcoming school year for Jenna's children, as well as a new year of teaching dance. After about twenty minutes, Jenna stopped mid-sentence and focused on the television.

Following her friend's gaze, Delilah asked, "What?"

"Can you turn that up?" Jenna requested.

Stephen, who was now reading the newspaper, turned up the volume. Delilah focused on what caught her friend's attention. The celebrity news show *Studio Zone* came on after the news and the reporters, none of whom Delilah could name, were tossing around various items of gossip. It only took Delilah a second to hear what Jenna heard.

"I want to go back to Cameron Burke for a minute," a bleach-blonde woman stated. "We all know him…silver fox Cameron Burke who makes us all want to ride *like* him or…well I'll leave it at that. He was just in New York for *Heir of Taivas* premiere week. He did the talk shows and such, per usual. He hasn't been linked with anyone since Selena Bingham nearly two years ago, but we've all seen the video of him dancing with a redhead at the premiere after-party."

"And these pictures were taken at the Stephen Sondheim Theater on the night of the fifteenth—Cameron and the same redhead leaving the show together. And this is the two of them leaving his building the next morning," added a brunette with purple streaks in her hair.

"So he's found some new girl. Not surprising," threw out a dark-haired young man.

"But...who is she?" Asked Purple-Streaks.

"Probably an intern or an extra. Or a wannabe actress," replied Dark-Hair.

"No, Cameron Burke usually goes for A-list, or higher-ups in the industry, to the dismay of every fangirl out there," argued another young man with trendy glasses.

"Well," piped up Blondie again, "so far all we've had on her is a Twitter handle and a Facebook page, but this week some new photos have emerged."

The images Cameron found months before of Delilah in the silks flashed onto the screen. She stared at them, finding she wasn't surprised. She knew this was coming because so much of her work had been professional and public.

"Apparently, Delilah is some sort of circus performer," Blondie explained.

"Or was," Glasses interjected. "There's no record of her working after about two thousand-seven."

"So, she has no connection to film at all?" Asked Purple-Streaks.

Blondie shook her head, "It doesn't seem so. And all her work was in the US."

"Then, how does she end up with Cameron Burke?" Mused Glasses.

Dark-Hair piped up, "Cameron was MIA for several months this winter, saying he was 'on holiday' after working nonstop for several years. He makes no mention of her until July, but there's one photo that was published last March…"

They showed the grainy image of Cameron and Delilah standing outside the pub.

Jenna piped up, "Is it as bizarre as I think it is that they have this much information about you?"

"Bizarre is not a strong enough word," Delilah replied.

The host spoke up, "Cameron Burke hooking up with another woman isn't really surprising. But why her? He usually picks women he works with. Cameron isn't one to, pardon the expression, 'bang the groupies.'"

"I don't know," said Purple-Streaks, "but today he tweeted:"

Cameron Burke @TheCameronBurke

"She wants to tame me. I fear she is succeeding." @Waterfall_Angel

"It's an *Heir of Taivas* quote," Glasses stated.

"So, what do you think," the host asked, "is she a fling, or worth watching?"

The others chimed in with their votes.

Blondie added, "Whoever she is, she got to spend a week shacked up with Cameron Burke. We know that much. And who cares about his reasons? Who would say no?"

"He's going on sixty-two," said Glasses, who appeared to be in his early twenties. "How much 'shacking' can he still be doing?"

Blondie threw back, "I have heard on good authority that Cameron Burke has no trouble…"

Delilah seized the remote and turned the television off. No matter how morbidly curious she might be, she drew the line at watching her sex life be discussed in front of her father. Stephen gave her a look that was hard to read then headed back outside.

Carefully, Jenna asked, "Did he really tweet that today?"

Checking her phone, Delilah said, "I don't know. I don't check it as often as I should. I don't know why anyone follows me. I hardly tweet anything."

Pulling up her account, she found that Cameron had sent the tweet in question that morning. She smiled when she read it again. Even if the rest of the world saw it, it was meant for her.

Sensing Delilah's love life had been discussed enough, Jenna asked, "So, you're climbing the silks again?"

Delilah met her gaze. "Yep."

"I would love to take some aerial classes. It would be a great thing to add the studio." Jenna went on, "I'm glad you're going back to it. I thought about coming to see you perform a few times years ago, but I was busy having babies. Maybe now I'll be able to."

"I'm going back to it as much as I can," Delilah clarified gently.

Jenna's brow furrowed in confusion, and Delilah realized there was so much her friend still didn't know.

Delilah took a deep breath. "I have trouble breathing. It's a side effect of…being at the pile. From the dust. It makes it hard to climb, and to dance."

Jenna looked as though she might break out some words of pity, but she picked up on exactly how much Delilah did not need that. Instead, she smiled and said, "I'm hungry. Want to get dinner in Harrisonburg?"

With a wave of relief, Delilah replied, "Absolutely."

Two days later, *USA Now* broke the story of Anna and Delilah. Jenna texted her a picture of it on the grocery store rack, and Delilah pulled up the magazine's website to look more closely. There was a side panel picture of her on the cover, and the interior spread was posted online almost exactly as it was printed. There were pictures Delilah expected, the same ones of her and Cameron that kept circulating. There was one from Cirque, another of her in *Pippen,* and both hers and Anna's yearbook photos. Finally, there was one photo showing the immediate aftermath of September 11 in order to capitalize on the emotionally charged imagery. With heaviness in her gut, Delilah set out to read the article.

At least it isn't wildly inaccurate, she thought afterward.

The authors managed to dig out most of the facts. They also included a few snippets about Anna's career as a musician, specifically about her time playing for shows in Manhattan. As Delilah expected, they played to the drama of it all, emphasizing Anna's complete disappearance and speculating how that might have affected Delilah. In order to get all the information, they must have found someone from Branton who was willing to talk for money. The idea of that made her cringe. She imagined the overdone sadness with which they talked about her. The only solace she found was in the fact that they at least told something close to the truth.

Delilah was lost in thought, chewing the inside of her cheek, when her phone startled her. Retrieving it from the table beside the bed, she answered when she saw it was Cameron.

"Hey," she said softly.

"Hello yourself."

Before he could ask, she said, "I just read the article."

She could hear Cameron sigh. "I was waiting until I was sure you were awake before I called."

At five hours ahead, the whole of the United Kingdom must have already read her story, Delilah realized.

"I'm debating whether to look for more articles or just turn off my phone," Delilah returned.

"I suppose that depends on whether you want to know everything they know, or if you just don't want to see it," Cameron advised.

"I guess I should at least give them points for accuracy," Delilah conceded. "They don't have the whole story, but they haven't fabricated anything. But then, they don't have to when there's that much truth to print."

"You make a good point."

They both considered the situation.

"Are you all right?" Cameron asked gently.

"It's not as bad as I thought it would be."

"They're going to want to talk to you," Cameron explained. "They're already calling my publicist."

Delilah snapped, "Why are they so interested?"

"Because, they are. It's human curiosity, however inappropriate."

"I guess that's true..."

"What do you want me to say? Publicly?" He asked carefully.

Delilah struggled, not sure what she wanted. "I don't want you to deny any of it."

Cameron stated, "I'll confirm the general story, and I'll ask them to leave you alone. Kindly. No need for them to follow this up with a sidebar about me being an arse."

Delilah tried to laugh.

"How is West Virginia?" He changed the subject.

"Hot," she replied. "It's been so long since I've spent time outside, I forgot how humid it gets here."

"So, you're spending time outside?"

Delilah hesitated. "I've been climbing."

"Climbing trees?"

"No. Climbing my silk."

"Really?"

"Yes."

Delilah could hear him smile as he said, "Brilliant."

"Cameron?"

"Yes?"

"I miss you."

"And I miss you," he answered throatily.

"I'm working on the paperwork," she added.

"I'm so glad."

She hesitated. "Do you really want me to come?"

"Of course I do."

"I suppose I'm trying to give you every opportunity to tell me this was just a fling," Delilah stated.

There was a brief silence before Cameron replied, "Delilah, I'm not great at coming up with beautiful things to say. I leave that to the scriptwriters. But I know that I have missed you every day since I left. I've never been so aware of being alone before."

Delilah felt warmth flood her. "That was a beautiful thing to say."

"Perhaps."

"So, how is London?" She changed the subject before her heart could really begin to ache for him.

He laughed. "The same. It's been a bit muggy here. I would go to the coast if they wouldn't print pictures of me in swim trunks."

"Well, every now and then you've got to give the fangirls something to cut out and tape to their bedroom walls."

"Don't be crass," he threw back, but she could tell he was teasing. "Besides, I've come to believe I'm merely riding on my youthful charisma at this point. One day they will all wake up and realize I'm an old man who likes wine more than exercise."

Delilah laughed. "Lucky for you, I didn't fall in love with your youthful charisma. Or your body-by-red-wine."

As soon as it came out, Delilah realized what she said. It wasn't intentional. She wasn't trying to sneak in a confession of love.

Cameron asked carefully, "And *did* you fall in love?"

Delilah struggled. "I don't think we should discuss it on the phone."

"Fair enough," he agreed.

They talked for another few minutes, and he explained he would be in Switzerland the following week so calls might be less frequent. Delilah assured him she was doing more than sitting around alone. They said goodbye, and Delilah sat on the guest bed running her fingers over the afghan that no longer smelled like him. She had taken to sleeping in the guest room since she came back from the city. Something about sleeping in her old room felt strange now. It was hard to be content with ignoring the outside world when the man she might love was out in that world. Still, Delilah struggled. She was holding out on admitting her feelings for Cameron because it would mean finally leaving her sister behind.

A soft knock on the door pulled her from her thoughts. She looked up to see her father in the doorway. She smiled at him, and he entered slowly. Sitting on the edge of the bed, he handed her a magazine.

Before she could question him, he said, "I suppose this is what you and Cameron were discussing?"

Delilah looked down and saw it was the same magazine she was reading online. Pulling it toward herself, she glanced at the cover then flipped it open to the article. Somehow, seeing it in glossy print struck her harder than seeing it on her phone. She ran her fingers over the images of her sister and realized she wasn't as okay as she thought. Stephen sensed her pain and pulled her close as she broke down and cried.

Eventually, Stephen softly said, "It's never going to make sense, Lilah. I'll never understand why this had to happen to her. It'll never stop hurting. But I would go through it all again for the chance to be her father. The price of real love is sometimes loss. But it's worth it."

"How can you be so strong?" Delilah wiped away her tears.

Stephen squeezed her tightly. "For you, Lilah. For you."

Over the next couple weeks, the effects of the article manifested themselves in Delilah's life. She now had thousands of Twitter followers and hundreds of Facebook requests from people she never met. She had to set her Facebook account to private and only accept those people she knew personally, because she wanted at least one place to share things privately. Otherwise, she kept away from all media. The only thing she watched online was an interview with Cameron from Switzerland. He was, of course, asked about her, and he responded with perfect English reserve:

"Delilah is part of my life," he said. "She has a story, like all of us do, and it's her decision if and when she wants to talk about it."

She was more than grateful for his words.

Delilah's father was fielding phone calls from people wanting to interview him and his daughter. They also received several requests for interviews by mail. Neither Stephen nor Delilah ever made their address private, because there was never a reason to. Delilah made sure her cell number was unlisted, but their home number was public information. They dealt with all this on a smaller scale ten years before, but those calls quickly stopped when everyone realized they were not going to talk about September 11. Now, the interest was renewed. Delilah ignored them because, as Cameron said, she would choose to tell her story if and when she was ready.

Delilah was also dealing with people she'd known her whole life staring at her as though she was a celebrity. Some whispered and turned away. Others smiled. Teenagers who she assumed were her father's students smirked and gossiped. At the supermarket, an older woman whom Delilah recognized from her father's church came over and gave her an unsolicited hug.

While getting dinner in town one night, a former classmate approached Delilah and said, "If you ever get tired of him, you can pass him on to me."

Delilah smiled awkwardly and walked away. She wasn't sure if she would ever get used to that type of blatant innuendo. To balance the stress of it all, she spent hours a day in her silk. She could only do short climbs, but the exercise felt good. Sometimes, she simply sat in the fabric like a swing, staring through the trees at the sky.

On a particularly warm day in mid-August, Delilah sat on the back patio of her house watching the clouds try to cover the sun. It was too hot to climb today, and her silk glinted turquoise in the distance. She was proud of what she did physically over the past month. Her lungs limited her stamina, but she could do more than she expected. Delilah was surprised at how good she felt. She was so focused on what she *couldn't* do for so long that she failed to consider what she *could* do.

Her father came through the sliding glass door, breaking her reverie. He sat down on the chair beside her and watched the sky.

Eventually, he said, "I've got a letter. They've invited us to the anniversary ceremony on September the eleventh. In the city."

Delilah felt a twinge of panic shoot through her. "It's been ten years…"

"It has."

Delilah was quiet, not sure what to say.

Her father drew a long breath. "Lilah, I'd like to go."

She turned to look at him, and there was vulnerability in his face she wasn't used to.

He went on, "I'm not asking you to go. But, I'd like to go there and remember her, and to see the memorial. To visit the last place that she…"

Stephen couldn't go on, and Delilah heard his voice catch. She stared at him, surprised to see her father openly cry. For the first time, she realized how much he must have kept from her all these years.

Studying his profile, Delilah said, "Then you should go."

He added, "I would love for you to come with me, if you decide you want to."

Delilah did not immediately refuse.

Three days later, as a late afternoon storm lashed the trees, Delilah picked up her phone and called Cameron.

He answered on the second ring. "Hello to you."

She smiled. "And to you."

"We didn't make the cover of any tabloids this week."

"Thank God."

"We're almost a normal couple."

"I think 'normal' will always be a stretch for us," Delilah argued playfully.

They chatted, and Cameron filled her in on the process of filming his guest role on *Lost the Plot,* a show she couldn't watch in the States. Then she told him about her continued effort to be able to climb again.

Finally, she seized the moment and asked, "Cameron?"

"Yes?"

"Do you think you could come over for…the anniversary?"

Delilah didn't have to say more for him to know what she meant.

"I think I could," he answered gently.

"We're invited to the service every year. This year, my dad wants to go. And I want to go with him."

"I would be honored," Cameron stated. Then he asked, "Would you consider coming back to England with me, afterward?"

"I'm allowed to go back in October."

"In October, then," he pressed. "And don't worry about the expense. I know you've done a lot of traveling and—"

"Cameron," she cut him off. "It's all right. That's not an issue."

"But I don't mind—"

"I have money," she blurted out. "We have money. They gave it to Preston, for Anna, and he insisted my father have it."

After a hesitation, Cameron replied, "Well, there goes my last reason for why you would choose me. If it's not the money, you must really want to spend time with a snarky old man."

His joke broke the tension.

"So, you'll come?" Delilah asked again.

"Of course."

17
Blue Dust

Blue dust of evening over my city,
over the ocean of roofs and the tall towers
where the window-lights, myriads and myriads,
bloom from the walls like climbing flowers.

—"Evening: New York" by Sara Teasdale

"Are you ready?"

Delilah was staring out a long, slender window at the street below. It was September 11, and she and her father were staying in a modest hotel room in the city. Cameron was unable to fly in until late the night before, so Delilah decided not to meet him until morning. She also didn't want to add to this trip the awkwardness of Stephen having to stay in Cameron's apartment.

Ten years ago on this day, Delilah woke to a morning so bright she had to close the curtains. She remembered climbing back into bed and trying to sleep while a sliver of hazy blue sky was still visible. Her sister opened the bedroom door just after 8 a.m.

Anna tossed a pair of ballet shoes in her sister's direction and said, "Get up. You have class at ten."

Delilah groaned. "Why did I agree to teach that class?"

Anna smiled. "I have no idea, but you said to wake you up."

Delilah rolled back over and set her alarm for ten more minutes.

She heard her sister say, "I'm going down to World Trade. I want to get that book Dad told us about."

Rubbing her eyes, Delilah said, "No you're not. They're not even open yet. You just want bagels."

Laughing, Anna replied, "You caught me. I live for Au Bon Pain. And I'm going to stop by Preston's office. Now get up."

It was the last thing they said to one another. Forty minutes later, at 8:46 a.m., just as Delilah finished getting dressed, the world changed.

Now, ten years later, she was up too early to know if the sky would be clear. She was standing at another window, looking down at a different street. But the memories of that September morning were vivid.

"Delilah?" Her father asked again.

She turned around. He was dressed in the best suit and tie he owned. His sandy-gray hair was combed straight. Stephen looked nothing like his day-to-day self. Delilah felt her breath hitch as she realized what this was. She glanced down at her own, dark gray dress. She chose it because it was long-sleeved, in case the morning was chilly, but part of her must have been thinking the same way as her father. This was the memorial service they never had. It was the first time they would physically acknowledge that Anna had died. The realization settled in Delilah's stomach.

With a nod, she retrieved her purse and coat and followed her father out of the hotel room. When they reached the lobby, she saw a car outside in which Cameron waited. Taking her father's arm, Delilah headed through the doors. There were a few photographers outside, forever in search of a good shot regardless of how inappropriate their presence was. The driver opened the car door quickly. Once they were inside, Delilah reached across the seat and took Cameron's hand. He smiled at her but said nothing.

When they reached the National September 11 Memorial, it took them some time to get through security and enter the area reserved for families. By the time they were in place, the sun had crested the horizon. The morning was clear, much the same as ten years before. While they waited for the ceremony to begin, Delilah looked around at the rest of the crowd. This was the first time she'd ever stood shoulder to shoulder with these people and acknowledged her place among them. She felt guilty for having stayed away so long while many of them made this journey every year and—despite what she knew were emotions similar to hers—honored the memory of whomever they lost. Delilah studied their faces, finding shades of grief or reflection. Many of the families knew each other, and they hugged and spoke softly to one another. Delilah noticed some of them had pictures or posters as a tribute to their loved ones. She had nothing but her sister's patchwork coat clutched tightly in her arms. Scanning the crowd again, she saw that some of them recognized Cameron. She hoped sincerely they didn't think he was here to be seen.

The ceremony began just after 8:30 a.m. with drums, bagpipes, and the presentation of the flag. At the time the first plane struck, there was a moment of silence accompanied by a single ringing of a bell. Delilah felt her heart hammer in her chest as she remembered the sound of the impact that day. She also remembered looking out her window toward the trade center and the sucker punch sensation when she realized where her sister was. Now, she took a deep breath, determined not to panic. After the moment of silence, a few more words were spoken before family members began to take the stage and read the names of the nearly three thousand victims. At 9:03 a.m. there was another moment of silence for the impact of the second plane. Cameron glanced at her with concern in his eyes. She closed her eyes again, remembering the sound of whining jet engines, so terribly close, and the unreal force of the explosion. She was outside by this time, running down Church Street trying to find her sister.

As the ceremony moved on, many family members offered brief, personal tributes after reading several names. The sky grew cloudy and the temperature dipped. It felt fitting, Delilah decided, as though the morning had paid its own tribute to that cloudless, perfect day, but had now moved on to offer weather more fitting of the mood. She found comfort in slipping on her sister's coat.

At 10:28 a.m., a final moment of silence marked the time when the North Tower fell. She reached for Cameron, and he put his arm around her, letting her lean into him. On the other side, she took her father's hand. Delilah closed her eyes one last time and remembered the great, roaring sound the collapsing building made. She would never know exactly what happened to Anna before 10:28 a.m., but by that time, her sister was gone. It was the only certainty she had.

For another hour, the victims' names were read in succession. Finally, at 11:27 a.m., a young man said from the podium, "Lillianna Faith MacClare."

Glancing down at her, Cameron whispered, "Lillianna?"

Delilah whispered, "Her full name. She didn't change it when she married."

Despite her intense effort at control, she felt two tears run down her face. She looked up at the sky, rolling with clouds. She glanced at the sea of humanity around her and felt, as the names kept coming, the vastness of the loss.

Three hours later, Cameron walked with Delilah and Stephen across the newly finished memorial. The sound of water rushing into two, acre-sized pools mixed with the whisper of a fall wind. He pushed his hair back, exhausted from a morning filled with heaviness, and thought about what brought him here. Cameron knew he wasn't the person anyone came to for comfort in times of sorrow. Mara had a list of occasions when he failed to show her any emotional support. The one time he tried to stay in a relationship long enough to deal with the difficult bits, he failed miserably. With Delilah, however, by the time it became clear just how hard supporting her would be, he was already in love with her. And he knew he should tell her. He should confirm that he meant what he said in the back of the limo. He was so in love with her he was standing in a literal valley of the shadow of death because Delilah wanted him here.

The memorial was only open to the victims' families and survivors today, and they milled about, their faces cast in the murky sunlight. It took Delilah and Stephen a little while, but they were able to locate Anna's name on the parapets of the North Pool. Cut into the bronze surface of the memorial, in a simple typeface, was her name:

Lillianna Faith MacClare

Delilah's sister never felt more real to Cameron than in this moment. Until now, she was a ghost Delilah spoke of occasionally, a mythical figure, the heroine whose life was cut too short. But looking down at her name in relief, carved into metal and set in stone, she was real.

Delilah stood for a long time with her hand pressed over her sister's name. She ran her fingers over the letters as though memorizing their contours. Stephen eventually pulled out a piece of paper and used charcoal to make a rubbing of his daughter's name. Cameron saw others doing the same thing. He stood back, giving father and daughter their space. This was their time to grieve. He was a mere observer, the audience to a scene that was not, and could not, be about him. He was old enough, now, to understand that.

After some time had passed, Cameron saw Delilah's strength give way. She gracefully folded to her knees. Crossing her arms on the polished edge of the memorial, she let her tears fall. It was not sobbing or wailing, but just a quiet grief. Stephen knelt beside her, placing one arm around her shoulders and one hand on Anna's name. Cameron stood a couple paces away. He removed his sunglasses in spite of the public setting, out of respect. Clasping his hands behind his back, he stood for as long as they wanted to remain.

Delilah was silent as they made their way back uptown forty-five minutes later. It was after three o'clock, and the sun was starting to dip behind the skyscrapers. The driver from that morning met them just outside the perimeter of the memorial grounds, and Cameron gave him instructions to take them back to the hotel. Delilah said little to him all day, but he couldn't be angry with her. The events of the day trumped any reunion he thought he deserved after two months apart. So he let her be, only following her up to the hotel room because she tugged on his hand and indicated that he should. Manhattan was not known for its spacious, mid-priced hotel rooms, but this one at least had a bedroom separate from a tiny sitting area. Delilah pulled Cameron in for a long embrace once they were in the room.

Finally, she pulled away, stretched up, and kissed him on the cheek. "I want to take a nap."

With that she turned and went into the bedroom. The door clicked shut behind her. Cameron stood there, knowing what she really wanted was to take her medicine and pass out. He couldn't blame her, though.

Stephen broke the silence with, "Care for a drink?"

Cameron chuckled. "From a hotel room mini fridge? I would normally say no, but at this point, what the hell."

Stephen smiled and pulled out a few tiny liquor bottles from the mini fridge in the corner. Using the only glasses available, he poured them each a tumbler of Tennessee bourbon. Passing one to Cameron, he said, "I never learned to drink much else. It's mostly bourbon or beer, where I come from."

Cameron took the glass. "I have no complaints. Although I never could drink beer. A good Scottish ale, perhaps, but never American beer."

Stephen sat down on the tiny sofa, and Cameron took the well-worn chair across the small space. They spent a few minutes lost in their own thoughts.

Eventually, Stephen spoke up, "I never thought we would be here again. I honestly never thought Delilah would come back to the city, let alone do what she did today."

Cameron nodded, understanding.

"Where were you, ten years ago?" Stephen asked slowly.

Taking a drink and leaning back into the lumpy chair, Cameron thought it over. "I just finished a film in Texas. I was supposed to catch a flight out of Dallas, but I ended up watching the television in the airport for hours." He returned, "You?"

Stephen looked away before saying, "It began as a normal school day. Then, someone turned on the television in the main office. When I saw what happened, I left immediately and started trying to call Delilah…"

Cameron listened.

Taking a long draw from his glass, Stephen went on, "The first year after…that day, Delilah refused to come home at all. She had enough friends in the city with whom she could stay. Delilah was never one to sit still or quit. She was absolutely determined to find her sister, one way or another. I usually hold it together most of the time, but I couldn't do what she did. I wouldn't have lasted a day near that pile…"

The clock ticked in the silence.

Eventually, Stephen went on, "Delilah finally did come home, shortly after the first anniversary. She cleaned out their apartment and brought her sister's things home. She stayed for a while, but she was restless."

Cameron smiled. "I think I sensed that about her from the beginning. Perhaps that's part of what drew me to her. She didn't seem the type to be sitting in a pub doing nothing."

Stephen laughed. "That she is not. She went back to performing after a few months at home, but not in the city. After that first year, she wouldn't go back. I think it all caught up with her, and she couldn't bear even looking at pictures of all of it. We both accepted, by then, that there would be no miracle." He paused. "It's strange, how logic is suspended when we desperately want the truth to change. It took more than a year to accept that Anna wasn't going to materialize alive, but we held out hope that they would find something, someday…"

Cameron took another drink, not wanting to interrupt Stephen's thoughts. This was something else he couldn't imagine—having to accept someone's death without a body or a burial, or any physical proof.

Taking a swig himself, Stephen went on, "Delilah might not have been a celebrity, but I believe she could have worked consistently until whenever she chose to retire. I think she would have found a new normal. Delilah thinks Anna was the 'good sister,' but Delilah was always the strong one. We have that in common. Anna was like their mother, kind to a fault, tenderhearted, humble, but easily wounded. Me? I served briefly in Vietnam. I learned early how to see the most horrific things and keep going. Maybe Delilah learned that from me, or maybe it was in her from the beginning. She has this fierceness that can't be snuffed out. But being told she can't dance was almost more than she could handle."

"You mean, because she can't breathe?" Cameron asked.

"Yes. Were it not for that, I think she would have found a new way to live, a catharsis in performing. But being told she couldn't perform anymore, that broke her again. That was when she moved back home and back into her old room. She started wearing her sister's clothes. She eventually stopped going out at all. I would find her in her room talking to Anna. I think she was losing her grip on reality. The panic attacks and the nightmares were taking over her life. She had no reason to live, and that scared me. So, I took a chance and suggested she go to my mother's place in England."

Finishing his drink, Cameron asked, "Did you ever imagine she would find me?"

Stephen smirked and shook his head. "No. I thought she would make some new friends, maybe find a new hobby or a cause she cared about. Mostly, I hoped she would see that there is still a world out there, and that she's part of it."

Cameron got up and poured himself another drink. Sitting back down, he added carefully, "I want you to know, I didn't meet her and decide to pursue her. She was never just someone that I wanted to..."

Stephen waved him off. "I know. Honestly, I was waiting to see how long Delilah would stay interested in *you*."

Cameron's brow raised. "Really?"

Stephen explained, "She's never been one to stay with anyone for too long, but I've never seen her so smitten, so anchored to someone as she is to you. Although, I shouldn't be surprised. With what she's been through and what she's facing, she needs an anchor."

Feeling grateful, Cameron said, "Maybe this could be a new beginning. Maybe she could find a way to do what she loves again."

Nursing his drink, Stephen answered, "Maybe. Pulmonary Fibrosis doesn't like to follow rules."

Feeling a stab in his gut, Cameron asked, "That's what she has? Pulmonary Fibrosis?"

Stephen met his eyes, realizing they were not operating with the same amount of information. "Yes. She was diagnosed in late 2006."

"Is that a name for the damage to her lungs?"

Setting down his glass, Stephen explained, "No, that's what is *happening* to her lungs. It's a progressive destruction of lung tissue. Over time, her lungs lose the ability to exchange oxygen as they should. They are gradually turning into scar tissue."

Swallowing over a sudden lump in his throat, Cameron asked, "Progressive? As in, if it's not treated?"

Stephen shook his head. "There is no treatment other than to slow the progression. The only real treatment is a lung transplant, which she should qualify for soon."

"So…" Cameron's words stuck in his throat.

Sensing Cameron's distress, Stephen asked, "Did she not tell you?"

"No. She always says she has trouble breathing, like the damage is over and done."

Stephen looked away, as though the heaviness of the information he was sharing just caught up to him. When he looked back at Cameron, he said, "I'm sorry you found out like this. I wish I could tell you more, but I can't. No one knows. Some people live for twenty years with this disease. Others barely survive a year. The fact that Delilah is young and healthy is good. It means it's likely she can get a transplant and be well again."

Cameron didn't respond.

Stephen added, "I'm truly sorry she didn't tell you. She hates pity. Always has."

Cameron nodded, but more words wouldn't come. All he heard is that Delilah was dying. This disease was not just a hurdle to overcome, a disability to live with, but something that could take her from him. And she never bothered to tell him. As his emotions rolled and boiled, Cameron swigged the rest of his drink in silence.

"I want to go dancing."

Cameron's thoughts were interrupted by Delilah's demand. He was sitting in the same chair as earlier. Stephen went out for food since they all skipped lunch, and Cameron stayed. He turned to see Delilah standing in the doorway to the bedroom. She was wearing fitted denims and two layers of tank tops. Her hair was piled on her head and her makeup was fixed.

Staring at her, he asked, "Now?"

She glanced at the clock. "Yes."

"Your father went after food."

"After, then."

Cameron stared at her while a maelstrom of emotions swirled in him. He wanted to scream at her and demand to know why she would withhold such important information from him. He wanted to seize her and never let go.

Choosing the more reserved response, he stood and crossed to her. Pulling her close, he kissed her softly. "All right."

She kissed him back, then pulled away to turn on the television.

Two hours later, after eating deli sandwiches in the hotel room and making a quick escape through the back exit, Cameron and Delilah were ushered into a trendy nightclub on the north end of

Tribeca. It was still early, but the lights were flashing and the music was blasting. Cameron immediately got several looks of recognition and other patrons pulled out their phones to take pictures. He was too tired to fight it tonight, so he simply looked away. Delilah appeared not to notice, and Cameron suspected she took a large dose of her medication. He was also certain she was still processing the memorial service and this was her distraction for the night. So he let her dance. Taking a seat at a table in the shadows, he watched her take the floor. At first, she was almost alone, but gradually others joined in. As the music played, she moved her body in perfect rhythm. Delilah possessed a musicality that was unparalleled, and she transitioned from song to song without losing a beat.

At some point, Cameron managed to strike up a conversation with a young bartender.

After bringing him a glass of passable red wine, she said, "Cameron Burke?"

He nodded.

"I'm Erica." She smiled and asked, "No dancing for you tonight?"

Cameron shook his head. "I'm here for her."

She followed his gaze. "Ah. The famous Delilah."

"Famous?"

Erica tipped her head toward the far side of the room. "Famous enough for the cameras to come out."

He saw what she meant. Several phones were aimed at Delilah.

"We get a lot of 'famous' in here," Erica quipped.

"So, I have no effect on you?" Cameron couldn't help flirting.

Pointing at a stunning woman with a wild cloud of black hair on the dance floor, Erica leaned in and said, "That's my girlfriend."

Cameron laughed and raised his drink in a mock toast.

Erica helped another customer, then set to organizing her liquor bottles. Crossing back to him, she said with a nod toward her girlfriend, "You know, she's a professional dancer. I moved here to be with her."

Cameron returned, "So was Delilah."

He felt another pang in his chest. Until today, he would've said she was picking up where she left off. He hoped she might perform again. Now, however, he wondered if all this was making her sicker. Cameron worried she was aggravating her condition, and that scared him. As he watched her, the absolute joy on her face made him ache. How much should one person have to endure?

Later, he helped a tipsy and breathless Delilah back to her hotel room. There wasn't time to arrange a car, so they walked several blocks. Delilah was sweaty and her hair was tumbling from its clip. She was unsteady on her feet, and Cameron supported her with one arm. Just before they reached the hotel, she stopped suddenly and stared down West Broadway.

She stated, "I walked this way a lot to get to the pile to volunteer. They let us bring food and water down for the firemen at first. I remember looking up at night and thinking, 'when the dust clears, it'll be there.' The moonlight made the air sort of gray-blue and hazy. And I would think, 'when it clears, it will be there, with the windows glowing from here to the sky.' I thought, 'the towers, the people...all of it, it's just beyond the blue dust.'"

Cameron stood there with her, not sure what to say. She was echoing the thoughts of thousands of people, but it felt deeply personal. He simply stood with her until she tried to walk again. She wasn't as steady as she sounded, so he carried her the last few yards and up to her hotel room. Stephen answered the door, and let Cameron take her to the bed.

Returning to the tiny sitting area, Cameron said, "I thought she should come back here instead of my flat. Her things are here, and I didn't want you to worry."

"Thank you," Stephen replied.

Before he left, Cameron added, "I'll call her in the morning."

Back in his flat, he sat up for a long time. He stared out at the skyline through the soaring windows. Cameron thought about Delilah and the way she looked tonight, dancing to exhaustion. Then he looked up pulmonary fibrosis on his tablet and read everything he could find. One phrase kept appearing, over and over:

Most patients live approximately three to five years from the onset of symptoms and subsequent diagnosis.

Delilah had a terminal illness, whether she wanted to admit it or not. And she hadn't told him. It was a huge thing to omit, and Cameron was angry. He was frustrated. But more than anything, he was hurt. He hurt in a way that was foreign to him. The wound was sharp and deep and would not be soothed.

In the morning, he sent Delilah a text:

> Must head back to London
> rather unexpectedly. Still
> hope you'll join me. Ring you
> soon. C.

Cameron was supposed to stay in the city for another two days, but instead he booked a flight and left for the airport. Because he had no idea what to say to Delilah.

So, he said nothing and ran thousands of miles away.

18
The Things We Must Not Tell

There's the old love wronged ere the new was won,
*   there's the light of long ago;*
There's the cruel lie that we suffer for,
*   and the public must not know.*
So we go through life with a ghastly mask,
*   and we're doing fairly well,*
While they break our hearts, oh, they kill our hearts!
*   do the things we must not tell.*

—From "The Things We Dare Not Tell" by Henry Lawson

Three weeks later, in mid-October, Delilah arrived in London. Adam picked her up at the airport and drove her straight to the studio where *Heir of Taivas* was filming. Delilah told Cameron she could occupy herself until he was through for the day, but he insisted she visit the set. She felt it was because he wanted her to see him work, and Delilah couldn't deny that she was curious as well.

"Is this Cameron's car?" She asked as Adam drove through London.

"Yes," Adam answered, "but this one is just for driving him around the city. He has another for when he wants to take off on his own."

With a hint of a smile, she asked, "Is it a Bentley convertible?"

Adam replied, "Yep."

Delilah was starting to feel like she knew Cameron. Perhaps that was why she could tell something was wrong. When he left so quickly on September 12, she was certain it wasn't just his work that called him home. Something happened. Over the past few weeks, she racked her brain trying to figure out what it was. Her best guesses were that the whole experience of the memorial service was too heavy for him, or he thought they were moving too fast. Either way, Delilah knew they needed to talk.

Once on the studio lot, Adam flashed his credentials and parked outside one of the massive buildings. Delilah stepped from the car, and he led her inside, down a corridor, and through another doorway. He cleared himself and Delilah with another couple of people with clipboards. Finally, Delilah found herself inside a cavernous studio. It was enormous, with towering set pieces and blue screens stretched to the ceiling. She stood in awe of the incredible detail of it all, recognizing a few sets from the previous movies. Eventually, another woman with a clipboard ushered her to a seat. She stressed the importance of quiet and Delilah nodded compliantly. She turned to focus on Nora Borthwick and Harriett Bristow, who were performing just beyond the cameras. They were dressed as Mohara and Alex, respectively, and were filming the scene in which Mohara decides to wage war against the Arches-Asterion. Delilah watched as Alex did her best to talk Mohara out of it. Then, from the shadows, came Cameron.

Delilah felt her breath hitch, and her worries were temporarily pushed aside when she saw Cameron as Marcus Eperra again. The familiar, black and silver costume made him look like a cross between a rogue knight and Celtic warrior. The cloak that billowed when he walked gave him an air of power and a hint of mystery. When he spoke, the lines rolled off his tongue, and Delilah couldn't take her eyes off him.

As the scene progressed, Marcus and Mohara argued about their future, then became tearful about the uncertainty of it. Delilah watched them get closer and closer until their interaction climaxed in a heated kiss. Although she was watching it without the benefit of music or all the visual effects, Delilah thought it was beautiful. The characters had chemistry and their tragedy-bound love affair was well communicated.

After kissing each other breathless, Marcus pulled away from Mohara and spoke the same words Cameron read to Delilah from *The Reaping Stone* eight months ago.

When he finished, Mohara took his hands and echoed, "Blindly, boldly, and without bounds."

Delilah remembered those words from the books. Watching both actors deliver the lines in character, however, gave them another degree of effect. She wondered if Cameron wanted her to come to the studio because he would be filming this specific scene.

Suddenly, the director yelled "cut" from somewhere to Delilah's right. The sound startled her, and she jumped. Something in the movement must have caught Cameron's attention, because his eyes scanned the room until they fell on her. While the crew made adjustments and fixed Nora's makeup, Cameron crossed to Delilah. She stood up, and he stopped just a few feet from her, as though unsure how to proceed.

Clearing his throat, Cameron said hesitantly, "I hope it's not off-putting," referencing the costume and makeup.

"Not at all," she answered, looking him over. "It's beautiful. I hardly recognize you."

He gave a wry smile. "I hardly recognize myself. But I recognize the character. He's like an extension of me by now."

Delilah felt some of the tension melt away. She stepped forward and touched the heavy cloak, admiring the faint detailing in the rich fabric. Then she reached up and gently touched his face, studying the makeup. It was the first time she touched him in a month. Her fingers were feather light as she brushed strands of the black wig back from his face. His own hair was not quite this dark and certainly not this long.

Stepping back, she stated, "It's funny, but I'm more star-struck at seeing Marcus in person than I was the first time I saw *you* in person."

Cameron smiled, and Delilah's heart ached. She knew they needed to talk, but the physical pull between them was strong. Delilah put her hand on his chest and Cameron seized her wrist. He put his other hand in her hair, and before she could argue, he kissed her. A minute later, when he pulled away, Delilah realized several cast and crew members were openly staring at them. She pursed her tingling lips self-consciously.

From across the set, Nora's accent suddenly changed from Nepalese to thick East London as she said, "Are you going to snog everyone in the room, Cameron? Save something for this scene you bloody prat!"

The others laughed, and Delilah realized she was teasing. Obviously, Nora was an actress not embittered by Cameron's love life.

Cameron shrugged, smiled, and Delilah watched him saunter back onto the set.

Two hours later, Cameron led Delilah into his trailer outside the studio. It was well-appointed, with windows tinted for privacy and a full sofa. He pulled out bottled water from the refrigerator and offered some to her. She declined. Cameron took a swig and they stood, silent.

Logically, he knew they needed to talk. He needed to tell her what Stephen revealed and how he felt, but the words escaped him. The need to talk to Delilah was tempered by the experience of seeing her again and the fact that she didn't seem angry that he left her in New York. Her absence this past month gnawed at him painfully, and now he wanted her like cool water after a day in the scorching, desert sun. He kept still, however, forcing himself to try to find words.

A minute later, after she also said nothing, he asked in a low voice, "Delilah?"

Her eyes met his and, before Cameron could stop her, she threw her arms around his shoulders and kissed him hard on the mouth. His mind told him to stop her so they could talk, but the rest of him ignored reason. Three months of celibacy caught up to them. He fisted his hands in her hair and kissed her back. The heat between them hit Cameron straight between the legs and he reeled at the speed and strength of his reaction. Their kisses were hard and urgent as he picked her up and braced her against the wall. She wrapped her legs around his waist and kissed down his neck, making him stifle a moan. It wasn't until she started trying to get at his skin that Cameron was forced to slow down. Putting her feet back on the ground, Delilah made quick work of his costume belt. With just a few motions, she dropped his trousers to his knees. Cameron looked at her, with her eyes clouded with need and her lips begging for him, and raging desire burned the word "no" from his vocabulary.

He picked her up and pressed her back against the wall. She wrapped her legs around him again. The next few minutes were a blur of fierce, wet kisses and tugging at clothing. Before he could process how stupid this might be, he was up to his hilt inside of her and trying not to make too much noise. She had her hands clasped around his neck, her fingers holding him tightly. The next thing he knew, he was gone, gone so hard his knees buckled and he braced himself against the wall. She had a vice grip with her legs and her mouth was open in silent ecstasy.

It felt like an eternity before Cameron could pull away. They both breathed heavily and neither was able to stand. Leaning against the wall, Cameron readjusted the costume so he was decent. Delilah pulled her leggings back on and collapsed onto the couch, her chest rising and falling heavily.

Softly, Cameron asked, "Are you all right?"

She indicated that she was, but her eyes remained closed.

As his breathing slowed, he asked her carefully, "Was this…was it about me? Or was it the character and the scene?"

Delilah opened her eyes and looked him over. "Of course it's the character and the costume. And the lines. All of it."

He felt deflated.

"Maybe *this* was about the costume, but I know the man beneath it." She added, "Or, I think I do."

———————————

Later that evening, Adam drove them back to Cameron's London flat. He bought this place many years before the one in New York during a rough patch in his career after his divorce from Marianne. For reasons he was sure a therapist would love to explore, neither place felt exactly like home. This flat was in Fulham, just west of Chelsea Harbour, on the River Thames. At five stories, the sandy brick and white stucco building was far less imposing than his place in New York. Cameron's flat was on the top floor and offered several views of the river. He was a fan of windows, favoring flooding light and a view of the city at night over private gardens. The inside was light, with pale wood floors and whitewashed trim work. The furniture was in shades of brown and black, filling three bedrooms. He watched Delilah look around, studying his framed photos and books. Stopping at an open shelf unit in the lounge, she found his awards. She examined each of them, from the Golden Globe to his SAG Awards. She scrutinized the BAFTA statuettes and finally, his Academy Award.

She picked up the Oscar, testing its weight, and said, "It's heavier than I would've thought."

Cameron smiled and shrugged.

Smirking at him, she went on, "Most people go their whole lives and never hold one of these." She put it back on the shelf. "I suppose I can check that off my bucket list."

He knew she was teasing, that she wasn't ticking off items before she died. She smiled at him, but Cameron felt a twist in his gut. The past few weeks had not brought him any more wisdom as to what he should say about her illness. He kissed her, and Delilah melted into him. So he did what was easier and took her to bed. She lay in his arms afterward, twirling her hair around her fingers. She pulled the duvet over herself against the chill in the air.

Suddenly, she said, "Wait, I almost forgot."

Climbing from the bed, she wrapped a throw blanket around herself and left the room. Cameron pulled himself up in the bed, puzzled.

When she returned, she came to his side of the bed, held out a bottle of wine, and said, "Happy birthday."

He couldn't help looking surprised as he took the bottle from her. Two weeks before, on September 22, he turned sixty-two. Cameron hated for anyone to make a fuss, so he generally tried to avoid the subject of birthdays. He so rarely mentioned it he was surprised Delilah remembered at all. Turning the bottle over in his hands, he couldn't help smiling.

"Sassicaia?" He questioned.

Crawling over him to get back into the bed, she said, "Yes. You seem to be a fan. And this might be a bit sentimental, but it reminds me of that first night…"

Cameron wasn't sure what to say. It had been so long since someone bought him a birthday gift with any real thought behind it that he was dumbfounded.

"Plus, what do I buy a man with millions of dollars?" Delilah added lightly.

He smiled. "I…I really am fond of it. Thank you."

She pushed her hair back, and he could see how happy she was with herself.

Before he could overthink it, Cameron pulled her in, kissed her softly, and said, "I really think I love you."

Delilah pulled back and searched his eyes. Then she leaned her forehead against his. "I think I love you, too."

They drank the wine on the terrace, curled under a quilt in a chaise lounge. For the night, Cameron let himself pretend there was nothing beyond the two of them. He let Delilah talk, listening to her describe her rediscovery of her silk. Cameron knew there were other things they should discuss, but he lost the conviction. He didn't want to ruin a perfect night. By the time the bottle was empty, it was late, and they were both foggy from alcohol.

He confessed, "I have to film the sex scene tomorrow. With Nora."

Delilah replied, "I suppose that's the sacrifice in loving an actor. I will always share you."

After a minute, Cameron admitted, "I've never filmed an intimate scene when I was in a relationship with someone else."

She understood his meaning. "Think of me, then."

Cameron looked her over slowly. "I don't know that that's a good idea. The thought of you makes my body react like a much younger man."

Winding her fingers through his, she asked, "Does it now?"

Cameron squeezed her hand. Then he said, "Delilah, there won't be anyone else. Ever. You have my word."

She turned in the chair and leaned in to kiss him. "Don't say 'ever.' The future is never certain. Just say…for now. For now, you are mine."

He held her close.

With a smirk, she added, "And tomorrow, think of the queen."

The following evening, Cameron accepted a dinner invitation for the two of them from Mara. She was in town for a few days visiting her son, William, and his family. They all met at a pub in Covent Garden that had long been a favorite of Cameron's. It was dark, with polished mahogany accents and heavy upholstery. They got a high, private booth and ordered drinks and greasy food. William, who favored his blonde, brown-eyed father, was a beer-and-burgers sort of bloke, raised on Mara's cooking and her extreme aversion to pretension. Mara sipped sherry and ordered stew. Cameron and

Delilah ordered a bottle of wine and shared fish and chips, another nod to their early meetings at The Quill and Fiddle.

Over the next couple of hours, Mara and Cameron caught up on each other's lives. William discussed his practice and his daughter's fifth birthday party. Delilah listened, her face content. Cameron knew Mara was evaluating them both as they talked. She was weighing how long Delilah would continue to stay around and what he might be doing to keep her interested. Cameron found it infuriating. He could genuinely say he did nothing wrong this time. He and Delilah might have some things to discuss, but they would get there. Eventually, he would ask her about what Stephen said in New York.

When the conversation turned to how long Delilah would be staying in London, he said, "I was hoping she might stay indefinitely."

Delilah argued with a smile, "I don't think that's legal."

"It would be if we got married."

Delilah turned and stared at him in shock. Mara and William were speechless as well.

"Are you serious?" Delilah demanded.

Taking a sip of wine, Cameron said, "Absolutely. If we got married in the States, it would be valid here as well. And it would make it easier to travel together. We could stay anywhere we want, as long as we want."

She stared at him in absolute shock. "Cameron, are you asking me to marry you?"

"If you like."

Mara and William were still staring. Neither moved.

Cameron added, "You don't have to answer just now."

And she didn't.

The next day, Delilah took Mara up on her offer of lunch and a tour of the city. Mara asked the night before, partly to change the subject from Cameron's impromptu proposal, and Delilah saw no reason to refuse. They visited the usual tourist sites, including Buckingham Palace and the Thames Path. However, they ended up taking the bus or the tube more often than not to accommodate Delilah's inability to walk long distances. At midday, they got lunch at a little café and sat on a bench in Hyde Park to people-watch. The air was cool and drier than usual, which made for a clear day. Delilah was starting to like Mara, overall. Her countenance was often severe, but she obviously cared deeply for those close to her, including her brother.

As they sat together in the crisp afternoon, Mara filled a silence by asking, "Would you really consider marrying my brother?"

Delilah tipped her head sideways, thinking. What Cameron asked the night before caught her off-guard, but it was entirely like him. She knew him well enough by now to know that Cameron was impetuous. It was just like him to throw out the idea of marriage just to reconcile her travel issues.

After a moment, Delilah said, "Possibly. But I'm not sure he was totally serious."

Mara looked away as though considering her words.

Delilah pressed, "Is there a reason why that bothers you so much?"

Looking back at Delilah, Mara said, "We discussed before that Cameron doesn't have a great history when it comes to commitment."

Delilah squared her shoulders. "Neither do I."

Mara didn't respond.

Delilah took a deep breath. "Why does it matter so much to you? I know he's your brother, but it's his life. It's *my* life. You can't always save people from themselves."

"I know," Mara agreed, "and I know it's not my place to meddle any longer. But I suppose I've never gotten past what happened with Marianne. And I don't know that Cameron has, either. Perhaps I'm not just afraid you will get hurt, but that you'll hurt one another."

Feeling a flutter of anxiety, Delilah asked, "Mara, what happened with Marianne?"

Mara appeared to struggle with her response. She finally stated, "A lot."

Delilah sat back on the bench, indicating she was ready to listen.

Mara went on, "They met on the set of his first major film, *Red, Red Rose*. She played Rose, and Marianne was actually more well-known than him at the time. They were about thirty, and he had only done stage and television work at that point. But Cameron wanted to make films—specifically, American films. My brother wanted to be famous in the Hollywood way. *Red, Red Rose* promised that. And he fell for Marianne. Their relationship played out in magazines and on television. They got married right after filming was complete and right before the premiere of the film. At the time, I was happy for them. Truly."

Delilah could tell she meant it.

"After that, Cameron's career took off. He and Marianne made two more films together and traveled the world. They were a fairy tale couple, but he quickly began to outshine her. The last film they made together earned him several award nominations. Marianne had just started working on her next project, without him, when she became ill." Mara hesitated. "She was diagnosed with stage three breast cancer. She stayed in London for treatment, because she was diagnosed here. We were good friends by then, and I came to the city to help her. It was awful. She had a double mastectomy and reconstructive surgery. There was radiation and chemotherapy. All of it. And Cameron was nowhere to be found. He stayed gone, working, and hardly ever rang her. He always had excuses, but I knew he simply didn't want to deal with a sick person—a less than perfect person. He was the same way with both of our parents. He wasn't there when either of them passed."

Delilah felt a stirring in her gut, the nudging of a truth she had avoided until now.

Mara kept on, "Thankfully, Marianne recovered, but her career did not. She and Cameron tried to reconcile their relationship. And for a couple of months, I thought they might, but then it came out that he was unfaithful to her. While she was going through everything, he was sleeping with his new co-star, and before that one of the assistant directors. And who knows who else. Marianne filed for divorce, and I supported her. I was absolutely devastated at the depth and breadth of my brother's heartlessness."

Delilah felt the knot in her stomach grow.

Mara sighed. "I wish that was the end of it, but a couple of months into their complicated divorce, Marianne revealed that she was pregnant. She was adamant that it was not Cameron's and told everyone she had an affair with an old friend from her school days. She even went so far as to settle for far less money in the divorce agreement than she could've gotten because of her admitted infidelity. I was shocked at all of it. Perhaps I was raised with impossible standards, but I never imagined two people could weave things into such a mess. Marianne and I remained friends, though. We'd been through too much together to part ways, even after the divorce. I saw her more than Cameron, actually. The baby was a boy. She called him Andrew and raised him in London. I went to his birthday parties and she sent pictures as he grew. We moved on. I don't think Marianne ever completely got over Cameron, though. She never remarried. I think she stayed in England just to spite him. When Andrew was eleven, she sent him away to school, a good school, and we lost touch for a bit."

Mara took a deep breath. "When I came to visit next, Andrew was about thirteen. He was right on the cusp of adolescence and he'd changed so much. And as soon as I saw him, I knew. I knew he was Cameron's son. It was harder to tell when he was little. Marianne is also dark-haired and tall. Andrew has her brown eyes. But when he lost the little-boy softness, he was a mirror image of Cameron. He still very much is."

Delilah wasn't sure what to say. She knew about Andrew, and she knew that Cameron now knew as well, so she said, "He knows. Cameron knows Andrew is his."

"I know," Mara stated. "I told him. Marianne was angry with me for quite a while for telling, but I thought Cameron might do the right thing by him. However, he barely said anything at all. He's never met him that I know of. Andrew moved to the States for university, and he works there now. He has a job in finance. Marianne and I patched things up, but we don't talk about it anymore. Cameron is a wound that will never heal, for her. I don't agree with what she did, hiding his child from him, but I know *why* she did it. Because he doesn't care. My brother is like a typhoon that demands a lot of attention, causes a great deal of drama, then leaves a path of destruction. And that is why I worry for you, Delilah."

Delilah looked away, her thoughts swirling. She was unsettled, but she didn't want to discuss it with Mara. Instead, she said, "I've left my share of messes in life as well. I've got some regrets. I didn't get involved with Cameron thinking we would move into a cottage and have babies."

Mara stated, "I would just hate to see you hurt."

Raising her chin, Delilah put on more bravado than she felt. "You can't keep people from hurt, Mara. None of us can. If we never hurt, we never live."

Mara pushed back her silver-streaked hair and said no more.

Over the next three days, Delilah was alone in the flat more often than not. Cameron was working long days, and a persistent rain settled over the city. He invited her to come to the set again, but she didn't want to venture out in the weather. Her lungs were already protesting the cold and the long day she spent with Mara. Delilah also didn't relish the idea of watching Cameron pretend to love another woman. Instead, she spent hours in front of the apartment's windows, watching the river swell and churn. Everything, from the sky to the water, to the stone and steel of the cityscape was now a muted gray. It was amazing how the same city could create such varied backdrops and inspire art of so many varied moods. Three days ago, the sun set behind a watercolor sky—the opening act before a thousand stars gave their brilliant, nightly performance. Now, however, it was just gray—gray and cold and listless. The dreary weather mirrored Delilah's feelings, which shifted drastically since she arrived in London. She wasn't exactly sure how she felt about what Mara told her, but she was troubled. Her worries churned like the river outside.

The opportunity to talk finally came on Tuesday afternoon. Cameron finished on set by mid-afternoon, so he was home just as the gray city outside darkened. It was impossible to track the exact movement of the sun behind the heavy clouds, but Delilah sensed the light fading. After dropping his shoulder bag and shedding his coat and scarf, Cameron greeted Delilah with a kiss. Then he set to making tea—something she had yet to master. Ten minutes later, they sat together at the square kitchen table, Cameron with tea and Delilah with coffee. For a moment, the setting was another reminder of their days sitting in The Quill and Fiddle, each with their own vice and silence between them.

Finally, Delilah asked bluntly, "Cameron, why did you ask me to marry you?"

He was unfazed. "Because it makes sense. It means we can be together all the time."

Tipping her head, she returned, "Most men come up with an elaborate proposal. Something romantic. Most men buy a ring."

Cameron set down his mug. "I thought you might find that...overdone. And it was sort of out before I realized it. Maybe that shows that I meant it?"

"Or that you don't know what you're asking?"

Cameron leaned on his arms. "Are you angry with me?"

Delilah sighed. "Not angry. But I know something's on your mind. There's a reason you left New York so quickly last month. And I want to know what it is."

Cameron turned away. He stood up and crossed to the window, looking out at the misting rain. Then he turned and met her eyes again. "Delilah, why did you not tell me how sick you are?"

"What?"

"Your father told me, quite accidentally, that you have a progressive lung disease."

Anger shot through her. "So, you *were* talking about me that day?"

"Yes." Cameron did not deny it.

Delilah stood up and faced off with him. He never once asked about her condition in detail. Instead, he asked her father, as though she were a child. She threw out, "Is *that* why you asked me to marry you?"

Cameron argued, "Not exactly."

"Not exactly?" Delilah felt her voice rising. Now that it was coming out, she realized she was much more upset than she was willing to admit the past few days. "Well, while we're sharing things, I talked with Mara for a while the other day. She told me a little more about your relationship with Marianne. It seems that sick people tend to make you run pretty fast. Specifically, into the arms of other people."

Cameron's posture shifted, and she could tell she struck a nerve. His eyes flashed, his jaw set, and he said curtly, "I believe that is Mara's version of the events."

"Is it not true?" She demanded, "Did you or did you not abandon your wife while she fought breast cancer? While she lost her breasts and her hair and her whole life, you went on making films and sleeping with other women? Is that not true?"

Working his jaw, Cameron admitted, "Yes, that's essentially true. But you've known about Marianne and I for a long time."

"I knew you divorced! I did *not* know that you cheated on her while she went through cancer treatment! That's a different kind of callous."

"Did Mara mention the bit where she lied to me about my son?"

"Yes!" Delilah shot back. "And who can blame her? What reason did she have to believe you would give a damn about him? And clearly you didn't! How can you never visit your own child, Cameron? Especially now that he's an adult! She can't be keeping him from you anymore. How can none of it matter to you?"

Delilah realized she had been pushing a lot of things under the rug that, collectively, bothered her more than she wanted to admit.

Standing up straighter, Cameron returned, "I told you before. Andrew is the one who prefers I stay away."

"Can you blame him?" Delilah spat.

"What Mara doesn't know," Cameron fired back, "is that I *did* go see him once, when he was seventeen. And he told me to fuck off. So I did. I'm not going to force myself on him. And I don't disagree that he has good reason to hate me."

Delilah felt her anger falter a little. "Is there some sort of better explanation for what you did to Marianne?"

Cameron hesitated. "I was young, Delilah. I had a lot of fame and too much money all at once, and yes, I'll admit, I wasn't ready for everything that happened."

"No one is ever *ready* for cancer, Cameron."

"She *lied* to me," he emphasized. "She hid my child from me until it was too late for him *not* to hate me. She lied. And so did you."

Delilah snapped to attention. "What?"

"You lied too, by omission at least. You never told me that you have a terminal illness! Were you ever going to tell me?"

Delilah squared her shoulders. "So you could run away from me, too? Because it's just too damn difficult for you to deal with the hard things? Well, if you stay around anyone long enough, you're going to have to deal with their worst! Their ugly! Their brokenness! How can you possibly propose marriage without a basic understanding of what *in sickness and in health* means?"

Cameron crossed his arms. "As I recall, you are not exactly the model for fidelity yourself."

Delilah felt her anger flare up again and burn hot, and she shot back, "I have *never* walked out on someone who really needed me! I was *there* when my mother died! Of cancer!"

She saw Cameron flinch before he spoke, "You still could've told me, Delilah."

"Why? So you could estimate how long to stay with me before you run? Before I end up on oxygen and need a wheelchair?"

"I'm willing to marry you, Delilah. Doesn't that count for something?"

"*Willing*? As in, one step down from being forced?"

"Delilah," his voice was choked, "I love you."

"Do you?" She snapped. "Do you really know what that means?"

He looked at her, and Delilah thought she could see a deep, aching sadness in his eyes that couldn't be feigned. For a moment, she wanted to forgive him.

Instead, she said, "I think I should go."

"Delilah…" Cameron began weakly.

But she gathered her things and left before his eyes could change her mind.

19
A Place in His Heart

He shunned all the girls in the camp, and they said he was proof to the dart,
that nothing but whisky and gaming had ever a place in his heart;
He carried a packet about him, well hid, but I saw it at last,
and, well, 'tis a very old story, the story of Cameron's past:
A ring and a sprig o' white heather, a letter or two and a curl,
a bit of a worn silver chain, and the portrait of Cameron's girl.

—From "Cameron's Heart" by Henry Lawson

Delilah spent the next week in a hotel.

Cameron called and left her several messages, but she ignored him. In one text, he indicated he would be leaving soon to film on location in Scotland, but she wasn't ready to talk to him. His words couldn't undo his actions. He would only ply her with his deep-voiced charm, and Delilah knew, if she saw him, she would end up back in his bed. So, the next day, she decided to get out of the city. Bundled against the cold, end-of-October rain, she took the train north to Chatfield by way of Coventry.

Flora was behind the bar when Delilah entered The Quill and Fiddle. She looked up at the sound of the opening door and smiled broadly. "Delilah!"

Delilah crossed the space, and Flora came around the bar to wrap her in a hug. Then Delilah took a seat on one of the bar stools. It was mid-afternoon, and the pub was quiet.

"How are ye?" Flora asked, returning to her post.

"Not bad," Delilah answered with a smile.

"And Cameron?"

Delilah glanced away. "He's busy. Filming."

"Sounds about right," Flora stated. "Wha' brings ye back t' Chatfield?"

Delilah looked down at her hands.

Flora asked instead, "Coffee?"

"Sure," Delilah agreed, then added, "I've missed this place."

"It grows on ye," Flora threw back while banging cups and saucers around at the bar.

Delilah stated, "It was easier when we were here. When we could just be two people with books and drinks between us."

Returning with a cup of coffee, Flora set it down and said, "Life 'as a way of creepin' in and complicatin' things, dun' it luv?"

Delilah nodded and poured milk and sugar in her coffee.

"Wha' really brings ye back, Delilah?"

Delilah stirred her now pale coffee and took a sip. "I needed to get away from him. And I wanted to talk to you."

Flora cocked her head, curious.

Delilah sighed. "Do you know about everything that happened with Marianne?"

Flora drummed her fingers on the bar. "I think I've put together most've it. Had t' drag a lot of it out o' Cameron years ago."

Delilah looked away, not sure what she wanted to say next.

"Wha' bothers ye most abou' it?" Flora asked gently.

Delilah replied, "That he left her when she was sick. *Because* she was sick." Anger rose in her again. "By the way, he asked me to marry him."

"He did?" Flora gave a surprised chortle.

"Yep. He asked me to marry him at dinner with his *sister*. At a pub. And without telling me how he effectively abandoned his first wife and son."

Flora stopped cleaning glasses. "Now, t' one bit o' that story that Mara likes t' leave out is 'ow Marianne kept that boy from 'im. She knew 'e was Cameron's from t' beginning, but she lied for a long time."

"Cameron could've gotten involved once he knew. He could've tried harder."

Flora leaned on the bar. "Maybe 'e could've. Maybe 'e should've. We all have a lot o' those."

Delilah felt her anger fade a touch.

"Are ye angrier about what 'e did, or that 'e never told ye?"

Delilah thought about it. "I don't know. I think I'm mostly angry that he could be that heartless. It's one thing to be careless or fickle; it's another to be heartless. And I'm angry that he thinks marrying me so we can travel together makes sense. It just seems to prove that he has no idea what marriage is about."

"And wha 'tis it abou' then?"

"It's about loving someone for life. It's about being there no matter what. In sickness and health. And never sleeping with anyone else."

"That's true," Flora stated, "but loving someone 'no matter what' means just that. No matter 'ho they *were*. No matter wha' they *become*. It's a bugger."

"Maybe that's the trouble. I don't know that he would love me if I was in a hospital bed," Delilah admitted.

"Ye know..." Flora refilled Delilah's coffee cup. "Cameron 'as never remarried. He never 'ad any more children. If anything, I think 'e might be just as afraid o' makin' t' same mistakes again as ye are of experiencin' them."

Delilah added more sugar and milk to her coffee. She sipped quietly, thinking. Eventually, she said, "He already ran from me once. My father told him...how sick I am. And he ran back to London."

Flora stared at her with concern.

Delilah explained, "I have Pulmonary Fibrosis. My lungs are basically turning into scar tissue."

Flora hesitated. "Is there treatment?"

"A transplant. If I'm lucky."

"And ye kept this from Cameron?"

"Yes. But only because…" She hesitated. "Because I don't want to be treated like I'm dying. I've done that. I'm *not* dying. There's been little change in my condition in the last five years. And it was nice being around someone who never asked, never worried…"

Flora turned away to pour herself a coffee. "It seems like the two of ye need t' talk t' one another."

"We tried. And it didn't go well."

Flora smirked. "About as well as deciding who gets t' booth int' corner?"

Delilah couldn't help smiling. "It was just so much easier here. Who cares if I'm sick, or what the future holds, if we never commit to a future?"

Flora cocked her head. "'Course that's easier. What do ye think Cameron 'as been doin' since Marianne? Exactly that. But there comes a time, for most of us, when easy i'nt enough anymore. There's not much reward in 'easy,' luv."

Delilah stared at her cup for some time, thinking about that. She understood. "You know, my father knew my mother was sick when they met. She was in remission then, but he knew the risk."

"And yet 'e married 'er anyway?"

"He did. But Cameron is not my father."

They both sipped their coffee.

Finally, Delilah asked, "Do you think he regrets what he did to Marianne? And his son?"

Turning to wipe off the counter, Flora said, "I think you should ask him that."

Delilah stayed in Chatfield for two weeks. She returned to the tiny flat where she spent six months unknowingly falling for Cameron. It was the same, but the space felt more claustrophobic, as though she grew and it didn't quite fit anymore. She read books and visited Flora, much as before. She went to see Mara once, feeling it would be rude to be in town and ignore her. They talked for a bit, and Delilah tried to explain her breakup from Cameron without giving away too many details.

On a cold Monday at the beginning of November, when the sky outside threatened icy rain, Delilah received a call from her father. The phone rang just after 5 p.m. local time, which meant it was lunchtime for Stephen back in the States.

After chatting for a few minutes, he said, "Delilah, you got a call yesterday that I think you need to return."

Curious, she asked, "What was it?"

"It was from someone named Cassandra," Stephen explained. "I think she wants to offer you a job."

Delilah felt a stab of shock. "A job?"

"Yes," Stephen confirmed. "She's from a company called Manhattan Aerial Arts, and she said she has an opportunity for you."

Dumbfounded, Delilah said, "I'm not sure what to think about that."

Stephen suggested, "It never hurts to explore the option, Lilah."

She sighed, "I'll call her."

After giving her the contact information, he went on, "I also need to tell you that someone has been persistent in wanting to interview you about Anna. Most of them gave up again a couple of months ago, but this lady won't."

Delilah heaved another sigh. "Maybe we should change our number? I wish we'd thought to make it private before all of this happened with Cameron."

"Maybe we should. But…I think you might want to call this one back."

Feeling defensive, Delilah returned, "I'm not going to make money off her, Dad. I'm not going to let them use our story for ratings."

He responded carefully, "I know how you feel. But this woman didn't offer money. She seems to genuinely want to share our story. She's putting together a documentary. It's just stories."

Delilah shook her head. "I won't share her, Dad. I can't."

He didn't respond for a minute. When he did, Stephen said, "You know I will never talk about her publicly without you. We agreed on that, and I'll never go back on it, but...I've been thinking a lot since the last anniversary." The line was silent for a moment. "I understand wanting to keep her to ourselves. She was my baby, just like you, and her memory is all we have. But if we don't share who she was and how she lived, then she will only be a name engraved on a memorial to a tragedy. A name. She'll die again with us."

Delilah let his words sink in.

Stephen went on, "We have the chance to make sure the world remembers Anna MacClare. And I believe that every time we put a face to this tragedy, every time we humanize it and turn it from a mass of victims to individual faces, there is the smallest chance that someone will see their mother or son or sister in them, rather than a collective enemy, and make a choice against violence. And that is the only good I can make out of losing my baby, Delilah."

Holding the phone tightly, Delilah felt her resolve crack.

On Tuesday, the twenty-ninth of November, Cameron found himself in a tiny pub in an equally tiny town somewhere outside of Edinburgh. He had been filming for ten weeks now, four of those on location, and he had three more to go before Christmas. He felt the strain of long days outdoors on horseback. Part of the appeal of Marcus Eperra was his ability to ride. Since this movie contained the final battle, there was also a lot of swinging around a broadsword. Even with stunt actors for the most difficult bits, it was exhausting. Cameron was tired, and he wasn't prepared for his phone to ring, interrupting his efforts to loosen his sore body with Scotch. Yet, he answered.

"Cameron? It's Charlie!" His voice boomed over the line.

"I know. My phone tells me that much," Cameron grumbled.

"Well, who pissed in your tea?"

"No one," Cameron returned. "I'm fine, really."

"Good, because I have an offer for you."

Cameron sighed, not sure he had the energy to listen.

Charlie plowed on, "Meg Abbott is directing a show in New York. It opened this month, but it's struggling. Her people think it needs a name to sell it, to draw a bigger audience and hopefully get it extended. She asked for you specifically."

Cameron sighed again. "I haven't done theater in years. More years than I care to count."

"It might be a nice change," Charlie suggested, "and it's for Meg. She says she'll give you anything you want. I'd say she'd be more than happy to be back *on the job* with you."

Clearing his throat, Cameron retorted, "Really, Charlie?"

Charlie laughed. "Don't get defensive, as though you two don't shag every time you find yourselves in a dry spell."

Cameron couldn't deny that, and he wasn't in the mood to argue. "How long is the run?"

"Three months. You have the option to renew if the show makes it through that," Charlie explained.

"What is it?"

"Modern drama by Billie Horowitz. Alcoholic father causes a wreck that ends his son's baseball career. Kid loses part of his leg. Father goes into therapy to try and get himself together. There's some smart, dark humor in the AA group scenes. Very self-aware. They have an amputee actor playing the son. It's a good show, but it's not finding its audience. Comes across darker than it is."

"It does sound dark, Charlie."

"It's robust. And it's a good part. Gabrielle Carlisle is the mother, and she's lovely." Charlie name-dropped an A-list Broadway actress as bait—a blonde actress with breasts that defied her age.

Not taking the bait, Cameron asked, "Why do you insist on making every offer with a side of women?"

"Well..." Charlie had no defense.

"Never mind. What's it called?"

"*Anonymous.*"

"I'll give it some thought," Cameron finally agreed.

After he hung up the phone, he stared at it for a long time. His mind rolled over lots of things, from the lines he needed to learn for the next day to whether there was any food in his hotel room. Suddenly, the date on his home screen caught his attention.

November 29.

He scrolled back through his Twitter feed to confirm his suspicion. Today marked exactly one year since he met Delilah. On this day, one year ago, he sat down across from her at The Quill and Fiddle. And tonight, he was alone. Since she stormed out, he tried to ring her so many times, and he left countless messages. Now, Cameron was starting to wonder if this was best. Delilah said often enough that they were destined for heartbreak, that one or both of them would leave eventually. In fact, most of the past year consisted of them taking turns running away.

Cameron absolutely did not know how to support someone who was dying. It wasn't that he didn't care. He never knew what to say, and his feelings never came out correctly. He knew, unequivocally, that he should have been with Marianne through her treatment, but selfishness mixed with panic made him hide. He sought distraction in everything else, and he put his wants ahead of his wife's needs. It was wrong, but he couldn't find atonement now. It had been too long, and it seemed better to leave it all in the past. He loved his work. He loved his lifestyle. Now, he was trying to walk away from Delilah like he had so many other women, but it wasn't working. Like a splinter, she pierced him, and he didn't realize how deeply she was embedded until he tried to extract her.

Still sipping his drink, he found her number in his phone. Though he swore a week ago was the last time he would try to ring her, he dialed again. To his surprise, Delilah answered this time.

"Hello?" Her voice was soft and unsure.

"I'm glad you answered," he returned genuinely.

"I was expecting another call."

Wounded, he explained, "I'm sorry, I was just...I noticed the date. It's been a year since we met."

"So it has."

"Did you not remember?"

"I've had a lot going on."

The response struck him as strange, because a year ago she had so little going on.

"And what has been keeping you busy?"

She hesitated. "I'm home now, in Branton, but I've been offered a job in Manhattan. It's a teaching and choreographing position for an aerial arts school. Jenna recommended me to someone she knows."

"That's brilliant," Cameron replied, feeling both genuinely happy for her and sad that she would be establishing herself three thousand miles away.

She added, "I'm also doing an interview soon. About Anna."

Cameron felt another twist in his gut, realizing how much she changed in a year if she was willing to talk publicly about her sister. It was no wonder she left him behind. He met her at her lowest, when she was vulnerable and needy, but she was neither anymore.

"Who is it with?" He asked.

"Her name is Katie Brooks. She's a survivor herself, and she's doing a documentary about other survivors and families of victims. She has a nonprofit organization with a website where she's archiving stories. It's sort of like our own memorial, told *by* us and *for* all of us. My father and I are doing it together."

Cameron felt the hollowness of not being needed.

Delilah broke the silence, "How's the movie coming?"

"More good days than bad."

"I'm looking forward to it."

"It's a good year away from release."

"I know."

They descended into small talk, like two acquaintances who bumped into each other waiting for takeaway.

Before Delilah could end the conversation, Cameron took a chance and asked, "If I'm in the city, can I see you?"

"I don't think that's a good idea, Cameron," she answered quickly.

Her words hurt, but he refused to say it. Instead, he gently replied, "I was wrong, Delilah. I know what I did was wrong. You weren't the only one with your troubles locked away. We've both opened up some things this past year that we needed to face."

"I suppose it was time," she said obliquely.

"Is there nothing I can say to change your mind?"

The line was quiet. Then she answered, "I think you and I are better off on our own."

"There's nothing wrong with needing someone, Delilah, with being vulnerable."

"Perhaps," she came back, "you should listen to your own advice."

Cameron had no more arguments. After he hung up, he proceeded to drink far more than he should. His 4 a.m. call time would come too early, but tonight he needed the vice.

Three days later, Cameron received a call from Meg. He was on a break from shooting and was expecting a ring from Adam. He answered without paying attention to the caller ID.

"Cameron!" Meg exclaimed, her voice rich and smooth.

"Meg," he returned, off guard.

"I'm glad I caught you. I was starting to think you were avoiding me."

He couldn't completely deny the accusation.

Sensing his reaction, she said, "If you *are* avoiding me, I assume it's because you know what I'm asking?"

"You're wondering about the play," he stated flatly.

"That I am." She laughed. "You are a hard man to pin down, Cameron Burke."

Her tone was infectious, and he couldn't help smiling. "And you are a persistent woman."

"So, what about it?"

"I don't know, Meg. It's a play. I haven't done that in some time."

With a dismissive tone, she said, "No matter. It's your roots. All English actors are born on the stage. I specifically remember your *Antony and Cleopatra.*"

"Good grief, Meg, I was in school then. And I think we had to pay people to fill the seats."

"Perhaps, but you were still good. You have wonderful stage presence. Although, I know plays don't pay out the millions you're used to."

With that, she struck truth. Cameron's career choices were usually made out of hunger for wealth, and he was seeing it now.

Meg said more directly, "I can't pay you millions, Cameron, but this is a good show. It has so much to offer audiences. Billie's work has so many levels. It just needs to be sold, and one way to do that is with a name. It might seem a little whorish, but I need your name. And I also believe you can bring something new to this part."

"That doesn't seem fair to whatever actor you're talking about firing," he returned. Although, he was saying it more as an excuse than out of concern.

"He's a fine actor, but he's too…dark. Emotionally. The role of the father is complex, and there's so much sharp wit in the script. It's almost English, the way the dialogue flows. The father's ability to deprecate himself without it feeling morose is so important. It's a tenuous thing, finding humor in alcoholism and permanent disability. *You* can do that."

"I do find both of those things hilarious," he deadpanned.

"And there it is," she said, "that sharp wit."

Cameron waited a beat. "I don't know that I'm available. This is very short notice."

"I know," Meg conceded. "Put-in rehearsals are mid-February and you'd be up at the end of the month. Through May."

"Charlie will kill me for throwing this in the schedule," Cameron stated, even though he knew Charlie was already working on it. He had a soft spot for Meg as well.

"Just, try. For me?" Meg purred.

Cameron hesitated. "I need you to know, we're not starting things up again between us. If that's what you want, I can't do this."

Meg laughed lightly. "Cameron, haven't you heard? I'm with Nathan now. We're quite serious."

Thinking it over, Cameron realized he was out of the social loop. But he did vaguely remember hearing something about Meg and the acclaimed British film director Nathan Ashworth.

"We're quite smitten," Meg added softly, "and I'm certainly not getting younger. Perhaps it's time to settle down?"

Her words cut a little. Cameron didn't want to be with Meg romantically again, but it was hard to stomach the fact that she was settling down when he managed to mess things up so fantastically with Delilah.

"All right," he conceded. "I'll think about it."

"Good. I need to know by next Tuesday."

"Then I will think quickly."

Meg laughed. "Cheers!"

Despite his reservations, Cameron agreed to do the play. He was unable to deny Meg. He knew how much she wanted her first directorial attempt on The Great White Way to be successful, and he wanted that for her. Regardless of their past, she was wildly talented and a natural leader, and he had to support that. He was also driven by the fact that this was something he should do, and for once *should* outweighed *want*. There was also the fact that, although he tried to pretend it didn't matter, Delilah would be in New York as well.

The last few weeks of filming for the final installment of *Heir of Taivas* were scheduled to take place at the studios in London. However, Cameron had a few days off for Christmas. Since he was heading south anyway, he decided to pay his sister a visit. He was still angry with her for unloading everything she knew about Marianne on Delilah, but he knew he would have to see her eventually. He wasn't so heartless as to ignore her forever.

He arrived on Christmas Eve, and Mara managed to get the evening free. She woke in the early afternoon and joined Cameron in the lounge. He was flipping through the television channels, trying to keep his mind occupied. He had his pages for the next leg of filming as well as the script for *Anonymous* open on the sofa beside him.

Mara sat down on the chair next to the sofa. "You're always so busy."

"It is my work," Cameron returned.

"I'm glad you came home," she changed the subject.

"Are you?" He shot back, unable to resist the jab.

"Of course I am," she said stiffly.

There was an uneasy silence.

"Is the film going well?" Mara finally asked.

"Mostly," he answered. "We've been outdoors in Scotland, so it's been cold."

"Aye," she agreed.

Cameron tried to go back to his pages, but he could sense his sister staring at him. He asked, "What is it Mara?"

She took a breath. "Have you heard from Delilah since you left London?"

Cameron's head snapped up and he stared at her, trying to temper his response. "Only briefly. She went back to New York. She has a job there."

"Well," Mara stated, "good for her."

"Good that she's away from me?"

"I didn't say that."

"You didn't have to."

She sighed. "I hope you haven't come here just to argue. I thought we were past this."

"Why?" He demanded. "Because you offered a half-hearted apology two months ago for spilling every detail about my divorce *and my son* to Delilah?"

Mara leveled her eyes at him. "She asked, Cameron. And you had months to tell her prior to that."

Cameron threw back, "I didn't know you were timing me. I thought, since it's *my life*, I could decide when to talk about it."

Rolling her eyes, Mara spat, "Oh come now, Cameron. If you hadn't managed to talk about something that important in ten months, you were never going to talk about it!"

"That was not for you to decide!"

Giving him a patronizing look, Mara asked, "Are you saying you were actually going to tell her everything yourself?"

"I thought she knew."

Mara laughed darkly. "And you really thought she would marry you, if she knew all the details?"

"I was hoping she would marry me based on who I am *now*, not thirty years ago."

"And are you so different?"

Taking a beat, Cameron said, "I think I am."

Mara looked incredulous. "And how many women have there been since Delilah left you?"

"How do you know she left me?"

"I read the tabs."

Cameron returned, "None, Mara. There have been *none* except for her. For more than a year."

Mara looked at him in disbelief. "You expect me to believe that?"

Cameron stood and walked to the window to try to calm his temper. Then he turned and said, "Yes Mara. Yes I do. I expect you to believe me because, of all the things I have been, I have never been a liar. I admitted my gross failure at fidelity to Marianne. Since then, I've never tried to hide my actions. Quite the opposite. I've been proud of every notch in every bedpost or dressing room or wherever the bloody hell I was! And yes, I regret what I did to Marianne! And to several others! I know I've hurt people. But this time, I met someone who cut away all the fame and the pretense and the posturing. Maybe, to this point, I've had no idea what love is. I've been a selfish prick. But I am certain that I love Delilah MacClare. I need her, but she doesn't need me. She never did. And that makes me love her more!"

Cameron stopped ranting and Mara stood there, stunned.

Taking a deep breath, he crossed back to the sofa and collected his scripts. "This was a mistake. I'm going back to London. You'll be happier without me and I'm used to Christmases alone."

"Cameron!" she called after him, but he wasn't listening.

He slammed his way out of the house. Cameron was grateful he decided to bring his own car for this journey. Throwing his things on the back seat, he was out of Chatfield as quickly as possible, taking his frustration out on the open road.

20
Labor and Love

Earth is one chamber of Heaven,
Death is no grander than birth.
Joy in the life that was given,
Strive for perfection on Earth.
Here, in the turmoil and roar,
Show what it is to be calm;
Show how the spirit can soar
And bring back its healing and balm.

Stand not aloof nor apart,
Plunge in the thick of the fight.
There in the street and the mart,
That is the place to do right.
Not in some cloister or cave,
Not in some kingdom above,
Here, on this side of the grave,
Here, should we labor and love.

—From "Here and Now" by Ella Wheeler Wilcox

Delilah's phone rang as she struggled her way into her studio apartment on a cold, windy January afternoon. She dropped her bags in the tiny space, nearly tripping over a basket of laundry as she tried to find her phone. She rented this place in Turtle Bay on the recommendation of a new friend—the same new friend who was the artistic director for the aerial arts school where she was now working—because it was close to her new job.

Breathlessly answering her phone, Delilah asked, "Hello?"

"Hey. It's Jenna. You sound like you've been running?"

Delilah explained, "Not running. Just walking up two flights of stairs with bags. With jacked up lungs."

Jenna returned, "It's good to hear you have a sense of humor about it."

Delilah sat down on her tiny sofa to catch her breath. "I suppose I have found a certain level of acceptance."

Over the past few months, she and Jenna made up for their years apart. They were now as close, or closer, than they were as teenagers.

"Seriously," Jenna said, "I'm so glad you're teaching. As much as I wish it were here, I know you're amazing."

"I try," Delilah said softly.

"Do you still like it?"

"Absolutely. I didn't get to do much that was new at first because they were in the middle of their Christmas show, but I'm digging in now that it's time to work on spring routines. I'm mostly teaching silks, but I've also got a modern dance class that's a lot of fun."

"It sounds perfect. I hope I can get up there sometime soon," Jenna stated, "but that's not why I called. I was at the store today, because with three kids I go *every* day, and they had one of those year-in-pictures magazines. You're on page fifty-seven."

"Really?" Delilah was surprised.

"Yep. You should check it out," Jenna encouraged. "I have to run. Sunny just poured juice all over the kitchen floor, but I'll send you a pic of the cover so you can find it."

"All right," Delilah laughed and hung up the phone.

A couple hours later, when she went out to get coffee and dinner, Delilah stopped at the newsstand down the street. Comparing the pictures from Jenna to all the new magazines, she found the one her friend referenced. She bought a copy and tucked it under her arm because she was already struggling with her coffee cup and food.

Back in her apartment, she put everything on the counter in the tiny kitchen area. Delilah looked around, realizing once again that she had far too many things in such a small space. Her bed was perpetually unmade, and her dancewear hung from every surface. Even the smallest piece of furniture felt too big in the space. It was a typical New York City studio, and it was growing on her. Delilah hung pictures all over the walls, some in frames and some simply tacked up. A lot of them were her old press shots and show posters, but there were several of her and her sister as well.

A few weeks before, on the day of her interview with Katie Brooks, Delilah presented her with several photos of Anna. She wasn't sure she could do it until she handed them over. As hard as it was, Delilah had to admit, her father was right. As fiercely as she guarded her sister's memory, it now felt better to share it. She felt calmer since the interview. She might be alone, but Delilah no longer felt hollowed by loneliness. She still relied on her anxiety medication, but she hadn't had a full-blown panic attack in weeks. She even considered, once or twice, going back downtown but had yet to act on that impulse.

Taking her Chinese takeout to the sofa, she switched on her appropriately tiny television. Leaving it on a sitcom, she flipped open the magazine she bought. There were quite a few artistic photos of nature as well as some poignant ones of the war in Afghanistan and the Tsunami in Japan. Finally, she turned to page fifty-seven. In an instant she was taken back four months. A photographer captured the moment when she fell to her knees in front of the North Pool at the memorial. Her father was kneeling beside her, one arm around her and the other on the parapet. Cameron stood behind them looking stoic but grieved. Delilah felt a sudden stab of emotion as she re-lived it. Then, she studied Cameron. He wasn't posing. His usual camera-ready expression was missing. He looked troubled, and his jaw was set as though he was warring with himself—like he wanted to run.

But he was there. He could've made an excuse not to come, but he was there the whole time, a tiny voice nagged at her.

She shook it off. Delilah reminded herself that he *had* run back to London the next day. One picture wasn't enough to make her forgive him. One right didn't rectify the other wrongs. She was rebuilding her life, and she didn't need someone in it who might or might not consistently support her. It was easier to be alone.

However, over the next several weeks, Delilah couldn't avoid all the advertising that Cameron would be taking over the lead role in a new play. She knew the theater district like her own backyard. If his intention was to stay away from her, he had done a poor job. She refused to give him her attention, though. She focused on work, where her ability to climb had hit a ceiling at roughly two minutes. The reality was that she would never be able to perform whole songs again, let alone shows, but she was finding her place as a choreographer. Often, Delilah remembered how Anna would get up early and bury herself in pages of composition before Delilah stumbled out of bed for school. She remembered the exhausted elation when the notes came together and her sister played a complete piece, hearing as only a composer could. Delilah's discovery of choreography made her feel that way. It was a tenuous connection between her and Anna—something that reached beyond the grave.

On February 25, Jenna drove into the city to spend a long-awaited weekend with Delilah. The two of them went shopping and had dinner at a tiny Italian place Delilah loved. They walked into Times Square like tourists and reminisced about the trips they took to the city when they were students. They bought wine and stayed up too late talking. Delilah bemoaned her latest round of steroids, prescribed to treat the cough that had been nagging her for several weeks. It wasn't enough to stop her from working, but it stubbornly lingered.

On Sunday, they went to brunch and turned the conversation to jobs and family. Afterward, they decided to hit TKTS and see if they could get tickets to a matinee. Delilah didn't expect much selection since it was only about two hours before curtain time when they got in line. When they reached the window, the only tickets left were for a couple of musicals they had both already seen and a few plays. The agent read the titles, and Delilah looked at her friend for guidance.

"Oh," the agent added, "I do have two for *Anonymous*. Might want to catch it. Sales are really picking up now that Cameron Burke took over the lead."

Delilah looked down and pulled the hat she wore further down over her hair. She sighed. The only thing worse than a bad breakup was breaking up with a celebrity. Posters and digital signs for Cameron's show were plastered all over the city. In certain neighborhoods, there was a chance she might run into him. Magazines printed sidebars about how many times he'd been spotted with Gabrielle Carlisle and speculating about where Delilah went. At the studio, almost everyone over the age of twelve figured out she was "Cameron Burke's Delilah." Some couldn't care less. As for the others, the school manager, Libby, a quick-witted native of Queens, quickly silenced any gossip.

Uncertain, she glanced at Jenna.

"It's up to you, but I did hear that it's good," Jenna said noncommittally.

The ticketing agent looked at them with an impatient expression.

"What the hell? Let's see it. Curiosity was going to get the best of me eventually."

"It's really up to you," Jenna stressed.

"We'll take them," Delilah said to the ticket agent.

Two hours later, from their seats in the mezzanine, Delilah and Jenna watched the show unfold. As she heard, it told the story of David, an alcoholic father of three. His adult son comes back home to live after losing part of his leg in a horrific accident—one caused by his drunken father. The family is splintered at the opening, with each character struggling differently. True to the reviews, the show was exposing for Cameron. He had no wigs or cloaks to hide behind. His character, David, spent the show in jeans and old button-down shirts. His hair was cut through with silver, and Delilah wondered whether it was natural. The scenes featuring David's alcoholic support group were sprinkled with dark humor and punctuated by the realities of addiction.

As Delilah watched Cameron play the scenes with his onstage son, Tyler, she couldn't help but feel the sting of truth. She thought about his real-life estranged child and wondered again about that broken relationship. Toward the end of the show, when David and his wife Diana reconcile, Delilah watched Cameron effectively make out with Gabrielle Carlisle for a solid minute. It was a beautiful reconciliation, but her gut twisted.

Delilah, who was admittedly terrible at recognizing celebrities, *did* know Gabrielle Carlisle. She was in her early fifties and had worked steadily in the theater for thirty-five years. She did mostly plays, because she was a self-admitted mediocre singer. However, she was nominated for the Tony for Best Actress in a Play at least once.

"You know, it's sad," Delilah said to Jenna as they left the theater, "that Gabrielle Carlisle couldn't sell the show on her own. Her reviews are great. But making money means appealing to the masses, I guess."

"Yeah," Jenna agreed, "and Cameron Burke sells anything."

"That he does."

"He was good, though."

"He was." Delilah forced a smile.

"Coffee?" Jenna changed the subject.

"Absolutely."

Cameron had forgotten how exhausting eight shows a week could be. He had only been at it for three weeks, but he was feeling the strain. It was a Friday in early March, and he dreaded the idea of going outside after the show into the clear but frigid night. The wind had been biting cold for the last few days, tearing its way through his heaviest coats. For once, he longed for the English winter, because damp and dreary seemed better than this dry, bitter cold. He wrapped himself in his heavy, black coat and wound a scarf around his neck. He checked his pockets for his personal items and started to head out of the dressing room for the night. He nearly ran into Gabrielle— Gabby—as she came around the doorframe.

Jumping back, she laughed. "I was trying to catch you. Want to grab a late dinner?"

Cameron considered the empty flat waiting for him and answered, "Why not?"

Gabby smiled and led the way.

This was becoming routine, the two of them getting dinner after a show or late lunch between. Sometimes it was just drinks, and sometimes the rest of the cast came along. Whether alone or in a group, Cameron was spending a lot of time with Gabby. At first, it was to get to know her in order to create the kind of chemistry they needed on stage. She was as grounded in theater as he was in film, so she helped him find himself on the stage again. He had to admit, it was a little embarrassing how much he had forgotten about theater. There was a time when it was all he knew. After drama school, he toured with an acting troupe and eventually did a few things in the West End. However, films became his life. Now, Gabby was helping him find his roots.

As they ate at a trendy wine bar that was open late, they shared stories of being young and doe-eyed when it came to acting. They swapped horror stories and reminisced about friendships forged in the crucible of live theater. Gabby was easy to talk to. She was only about eight years his junior and they countered each other well. She was on the short side, with bright, blonde hair, brown eyes, and features that aged well. Her breasts, often the subject of gossip, were perfect, filling out her scoop neck sweater in a tasteful and alluring way.

Glancing around, Cameron realized the other patrons in the restaurant were watching them. The more meals he and Gabby shared, the more people speculated. Cameron believed their friendship was firmly none of the public's business. Still, something tugged at him deep inside. The few times he dared to examine his feelings, he found himself wondering if Delilah saw the pictures of him with Gabby in the tabs. Cameron knew she wasn't far away. It was easy enough to figure out where she was working. She must know he was here and doing the play. Yet she made no effort to contact him. He told himself, if she was moving on, then so was he, and he could have all the dinners with Gabby Carlisle he wanted.

Focusing his attention back on her as they lingered over wine, Cameron suddenly asked, "Would you like to come back to my flat? It's not far, and I have the car waiting."

She looked at him with studious eyes, as though dissecting his meaning. This was the first time he had made such an offer. Gabby was too old to play innocent and fierce enough not to be overly flattered.

After a minute, she said, "All right. Just for a bit. We do have a two-show day tomorrow."

"We do," Cameron agreed, leading the way.

A half-hour later, they were in his flat looking at the view through the tall windows. Gabby voiced her appreciation of it, and they went through the usual pleasantries.

Cameron offered, "Would you like a cup of tea?"

"Tea?" Gabby quirked up an eyebrow.

Cameron explained, "Well, we've already had quite a bit of wine."

Gabby laughed. "Tea it is then."

Taking care to make it just right, Cameron brought the pot over to the coffee table and poured it into two cups. He bought a good tea service when he bought the flat. Now, he was glad to have it. He carefully added milk to his cup and watched as Gabby filled hers with sugar and milk until it was pale.

Just like Delilah, with the coffee, he thought, then quickly shook it off.

They sipped and talked about the next day's shows and the notes they were likely to get from Meg. She was a consummate director, guiding without forcing her way, shaping without discouraging creativity. It was easier for Cameron to appreciate her knowing she was with someone else. Almost finished with the tea, he rolled his shoulders, trying to get rid of the tension from the day.

Noticing, Gabby got up and came around behind the sofa. Before he could say anything, she put her hands on his shoulders, kneading his muscles with her long fingers.

Eventually, she said, "You need to relax. You're so tense. It's not good to go on stage this way."

"It's been a stressful few weeks," he returned.

She continued working with her hands, rubbing the tension from his arms with practiced expertise. Cameron closed his eyes and let her, his body weary and his mind cluttered. Gabby came around the sofa and, before he could speak, she straddled his lap. Grinding herself against him, she kissed him firmly on the mouth, and he let it happen. He had been alone for four months, and he saw little hope in reconciling with Delilah. So he opened his mouth to Gabby and indulged in mindless snogging.

After a few minutes, she pulled him up from the couch and led the way to his bedroom. Pushing him down on the bed, she kissed him harder. She slithered herself down his body, kissing his neck and opening a couple of his shirt buttons. She worked her way down until she was between his legs, pulled open his belt, and started to divest him of his trousers. Before she could get to skin, however, Cameron's eyes snapped open and he stopped her. He realized he was picturing Delilah with her hair splayed over his thighs. She was the last woman who had been in this bed, and the memory aroused him more than any of Gabby's ministrations. Thirty years ago, he would've let Gabby finish him off while thinking of Delilah. Looking at him with her hands still on his trousers, she clearly thought his current state was all her doing. And some of it was. Some of it was merely physical, but the idea of anyone else touching him with this level of intimacy was suddenly vile to him. On a base level, he wanted the release. But if there was even a thread of a chance of Delilah coming back to him, he wouldn't ruin it for this.

So he gently pushed Gabby away and fastened his trousers.

Gabby looked confused. "Did I do something wrong?"

He shook his head. "No. But we can't do this."

She tipped her head and asked, "Why not? You seem ready for it."

Deciding the truth was easiest, he replied, "I was thinking about her."

Sitting beside him, she asked, "Delilah?"

He nodded.

Gabby looked him over and surmised, "You really must be in love with her."

"I must be," he conceded.

As they walked out the rear door of the building to wait for her car, Cameron said, "I hope this won't affect our working relationship. I feel like we have good rapport, onstage."

Gabby smiled at him. "Cameron, I've been in this business a long time. I'm a big girl. And I'll admit, I came home with you because, well, I've heard good things. But you've broken no hearts tonight." She leaned in and kissed him gently right beside his mouth. "We'll be fine."

Her car arrived, and Cameron watched her go. He stood there, grateful she was so gracious after he effectively led her on.

She will be okay, he thought to himself, *but will you?*

Without an answer, Cameron went back inside alone.

After another week of work and walking back and forth in the March winds, Delilah was ready for a weekend off. She was second-guessing everything she was doing for the spring show and her cough was nagging on. So she spent Saturday in bed watching old movies from her teenage years and drinking hot water with honey. She absolutely despised tea, which everyone kept recommending for the cough, so she settled for the water. She had already run through two rounds of steroids and wanted desperately to be done with all of it.

The next day, however, the apartment walls felt like they were starting to close in. She had to do something. Wrapping herself up in a fur lined coat, her favorite boots, and a new knitted hat, she headed out for an early lunch. After savoring warm soup at the deli near her apartment, she got a coffee to go and headed back outside. Walking a few blocks west, she decided to hit TKTS, something she did almost weekly. Going to shows was always one of Delilah's favorite things about living in the city, and she was enjoying catching up. She liked to pick the less popular ones, to give the new writers and directors a chance. So she got in line with only about an hour before most curtains went up. At the window, she found there wasn't much left.

Like an echo of another Sunday weeks ago, the ticket agent said, "I have one for *Anonymous*. We're getting less of them. Great show."

Delilah stared at him, noting his well-groomed hair and flawless smile. He was young, probably an actor working his day job. She started to decline, but something stopped her. There was a pull she couldn't resist. When faced with the choice of sitting in her apartment alone all afternoon or watching Cameron on stage, she chose Cameron. She placated herself by saying there would always be a connection between them, and what was the harm in staring at him from the Mezzanine? Thousands of other fans did it every day. She took the ticket.

Seeing the show a second time, she found nuances she didn't notice before. Gabrielle and Cameron had an easy repartee. He seemed so vulnerable, so exposed and real in the role that Delilah couldn't help remembering all their conversations in the pub. It made her ache a little. That was the Cameron she wanted, not the man with too much money who would cheat on his sick wife.

After the final curtain call, Delilah made her way out of the theater. She twisted her hair up into her hat, and she was glad the afternoon sun was still bright enough to justify her sunglasses. She adjusted her coat. Outside the theater, she watched a group of fans head around to the stage door. Before she could stop herself, she followed them. Although everything in her said this game she and Cameron kept playing—this push and pull—was asinine, and all logic and good sense told her to go home, she followed the crowd to the stage door behind the theater.

A group of mostly women gathered in front of the barricades that kept the door clear. They held phones and playbills and chattered nervously. Delilah stood near the end of the line, unnoticed. After several minutes, Gabrielle came out the door. She had her own following, so she made her way through the line of people, smiling politely and signing playbills. Delilah appreciated her poise, considering she must have to do this at least once each day. Shortly thereafter, a few other cast members emerged. Then came Cameron.

Delilah was transported back almost a year to when she waited for him outside the television studio in London. Now, she watched him smile demurely and sign playbills. He occasionally leaned in to listen to a comment or laughed politely. He was wrapped in a perfectly tailored, charcoal Burberry coat with a deep green scarf. The light picked up the silver in his hair. As she watched him, she became certain that if she intended for things to be over for good, she should walk away. If she was done with him, with the relationship, it would only hurt them both for him to see her. There could be no more back and forth after this. They knew each other inside and out. If it was over, it really had to be over.

Delilah wrenched her gaze away and turned to leave. Pulling her coat around herself, she tried to be inconspicuous as she slowly made her way through the crowd and away from Cameron. She just made it past the last few autograph seekers and onto the open sidewalk when she felt a hand on her shoulder. She turned, expecting to see someone who recognized her or perhaps another fan wanting to share a comment. Instead, she was looking directly at Cameron. He must have jogged over, she decided, to cover the space so quickly. Behind him Delilah could see the crowd of confused and surprised fans. She took off her sunglasses so she could see him clearly. Her hair was spilling from the confines of her hat, giving her away.

Leaning down to speak softly into her ear, Cameron said, "Come in the car with me. So we can talk. Please? Can we just…talk?"

Delilah started to say no, but the look in his eyes was desperate. There was no manipulation or coy charm—just open need.

Damn you, Cameron Burke, she said to herself without conviction.

She nodded her concession.

He started to lead her away, but she gestured to the fans, "Finish what you started. They waited a long time."

He gave her a half-smile and turned back to the fans. Someone on security detail from the show ushered Delilah to Cameron's waiting car.

Having overheard what she said, someone called out, "We love you, Delilah!"

It was a strange thing, celebrity.

21
As You Are

I do not love you as if you were salt-rose, or topaz,
polished sterling silver or halls of marble, grand.
I cannot love you as things kept. Instead, as jazz,
quiet and wafting on balmy August evenings, as sand
kissed by oceans, caressing toes, ankles, the soft
in the arches of feet—not as lilies, tulips, orchids—
rather, as the wishes made on milkweed seeds aloft
breezes, made on twilight's first stars amid
indigo sky-fields littered with tangerine cumulus.
Nor do I love you as the sun itself—to me, you
are its rising and falling and the hues strewn across
horizons, vibrantly tossed, ever changing and new.
My love for you is not constant and unchanging,
for you are not. So I love you as you are: living.

—"I Do Not Love You" by Julie Ann Cook
After Pablo Neruda's Sonnet "XVII"

Cameron was on edge for the entire ride back to his flat. It wasn't a long trip, but Delilah stared at her hands or out the window for the entirety of it. He had no idea why she came to see him today, but he was determined not to let her go until they had a chance to talk. The past few months made him sure of one thing—he needed Delilah. For Delilah, he would give up fame. He would go back to Chatfield and spend his days living in a cottage and taking lunch at the pub if that's what she wanted. After four months without her, without even the promise of seeing her again, he was sure. But telling her was another thing entirely.

When they arrived at his building, Cameron helped Delilah from the car. Making a quick decision, he led the way across the street into the park instead of inside to his flat. He wanted to give her neutral ground for this conversation. They crossed the loop, avoiding the evening traffic, and followed the paths through the trees and past massive rock outcroppings that hinted at the bedrock beneath the island of Manhattan. They walked until they found a bench in a fairly secluded area. Cameron sat down and Delilah joined him. She looked around, studying the leaves in the fading light. She pulled her hat back on against the chill in the air. No one had followed or was lingering to stare at them, yet.

Cameron asked, "What made you come to see me today?"

Delilah pulled herself up straighter. "I believe it was my complete inability to be without you, Cameron. Even though logic and good judgment says I should have stayed away."

"Perhaps you should have," he threw out before he could stop himself.

"And yet here we are."

The rustling of leaves and the noise of the city around them filled the silence between their words.

Delilah finally asked, "Cameron, why did you come back here? Why are you doing this play?"

He hesitated, trying to decide what she was really asking. Then he said, "It felt like the right thing to do."

Delilah was more direct, "Did you come here because of me?"

"Perhaps." He struggled for a bit with what else he wanted to say. "Delilah, what I did to Marianne…I know it was wrong. It was selfish and childish and I know I should probably be telling her this, but…I'm sorry. I'm truly sorry." He went on, "I also never meant to keep it all from you. I assumed when you unearthed that I have a son, you also read about what specifically happened between me and Marianne. But I should have told you myself."

"I guess there are several things we should have told one another," Delilah replied softly.

"I wish..." he struggled again, "I wish you could have told me that what you have is so serious."

She sensed what he wasn't saying. When she spoke again, her voice was stronger. "I didn't tell you, because I'm not dying, Cameron. I don't have cancer or another disease with a specific progression. I'm young and otherwise healthy. I could go on like this for years and I will probably qualify for a lung transplant eventually. One of the reasons I shut myself in my house in Branton was because no one understood that. Once I was diagnosed, I became 'Delilah who's dying' to everyone who knew me. And I was already 'Delilah who lost her sister on nine-eleven.' I was getting enough heavy-handed pity already, and I didn't want that. Not from them, and certainly not from you. One of the best things about us is that we don't see in each other what everyone else sees. I don't look at you and see 'Cameron the playboy' or 'Cameron the sexiest man alive.'"

"Well, I wouldn't mind..." he interjected.

She gave him a withering look and went on, "In my life, I've been ready to die. I've *wished* to die. That was easy. But living is much harder. Living means creating a future out of the ashes of what I had. It means accepting my new weaknesses. I mean, let's face it Cameron, in our situation I am far more likely to bury you, someday. And *living* means being able to stand over a grave and keep on going. And that is a far scarier prospect than death."

Cameron stared at her for a long time, trying to decide what to say. He didn't want to sound patronizing or gushy, but he understood. Nothing about the two of them had ever been typical. Nothing about this was easy, and no future is ever certain.

Delilah went on, "I simply want to live. Not 'live like I'm dying' or some other platitude from a motivational poster. And I don't want you doing things with me or *for* me like we're checking off some sort of bucket list. I just want a life. A real life. Not one of the romance novels I read to *escape* life."

In spite of himself, Cameron smiled. She really did have a way with words. Delilah smiled as well, but she kept looking at him in that way that made him think she could read his mind.

"I am sorry, Delilah," he repeated. "I'm sorry for who I was and what I've done. I don't deserve you."

She continued to stare at him, searching, and he suddenly wanted, more than anything, to have the chance to prove he was more than the sum of his behavior thus far.

After another minute, Delilah carefully asked, "What are we, Cameron?"

They posed the question enough times now that he knew what she was asking. Looking off into the twilight sky, he answered, "We are two ships in the night. We are two selfish romantics who shouldn't be trusted with one another. We are too old for all this drama and we should both know better." Turning back and looking at her intently, he stated, "We are in love. Madly, fiercely, stupidly in love. And we are at the mercy of it, come what may."

Delilah tipped her head sideways. "We are stupid, aren't we?"

"Most lovers are."

After another minute, Delilah slid closer to him on the bench and leaned her head against his shoulder. "You really are wonderful in the play."

Cameron murmured his gratitude. He had so many other things he wanted to tell her, but the words wouldn't come. He was an actor. Other people had been telling him what to say for thirty-five years.

As they sat there, the air grew colder. Eventually, Cameron leaned in and said softly to her, "Delilah, I love you blindly, not knowing what will come. I love you boldly, not caring what the world thinks. And I love you without bounds, because there is no amount of time or distance that can cut it off or contain it. I will follow you, and I will fight with you, till my last breath."

"That's a hefty promise, Cameron."

He didn't argue, because she was right.

"Are you sure you love me?"

"Absolutely."

"You know," she added, "those lines from the book, they sound like a vow."

"I think they were meant to be."

Delilah met his eyes. "Since you're making vows, I suppose I should make things easier for us and just marry you."

Cameron kissed her fiercely, because he really was terrible with words.

When they left the park, Delilah decided to go home with Cameron rather than return to her place. As much as she kept her distance before, she now wanted to be with him. Once in his apartment, she wrestled with a flood of memories as she took a long, hot shower. She hadn't been in this place since their week of isolation the previous summer. The last time they shared a bed here, they were impulsive lovers. Now, they were impulsive lovers who agreed to get married. Alone in the shower with her thoughts, Delilah found she was afraid of the commitment she just made. She had no way of knowing if either of them was really ready, but she knew one thing for certain. She never wanted someone in her life the way she wanted Cameron.

Stepping out of the shower, she pulled her hair loose from the elastic holding it up and wrapped a towel around herself. She found Cameron standing by the tall bedroom windows, staring at the glittering city. It was night now, and the skyline was lit by the moon. Delilah studied his frame in the low light. He wore only pajama bottoms, as was his way, and his stance looked pensive. Coming to stand behind him, she raised her hands to his shoulders. He startled a little at her touch, then relaxed. It had been so long since they last touched that Delilah felt like she needed to rediscover him. She ran her fingers over his bare skin, tracing the line of his shoulders, then down his back. She applied more pressure, finding the muscles beneath his skin and kneading them. She followed the line of his spine back up to his shoulders and raked her fingers through his hair.

Up close, the silver in his hair seemed to be natural, and she said, "This is nice. It suits you."

He chuckled gruffly. "Because I'm an old man?"

With her fingers still in his hair, she returned, "Because it's *you*. I don't need perfection, Cameron."

She stepped back, dropped her towel, then stepped in to press her body against his back. He twitched slightly but didn't move.

Wrapping her arms around him so they were skin to skin, she said, "I just need you."

Cameron closed his eyes and sighed at her touch. Delilah could feel how much he missed her. She trailed her fingers up his stomach to his chest, exploring the familiar landscape of his body. She ran her hands down his sides to his hips as she kissed his shoulder blades. Delilah continued this gentle exploration, reacquainting herself with him. Sliding her hands to Cameron's hips again, she easily divested him of his pants. He let them puddle on the floor, and she pressed her abdomen against his bare buttocks. He moaned a little, and she slid her hands down to his groin.

With one hand pressed against his stomach, she touched him, and he put both hands on the window frame to steady himself. She found the hard length of him both erotic and familiar. There was something sacred in the moment, in realizing they were both committing to touch only each other's bodies for the rest of their lives. For some reason, she needed to feel him, to find every perfect curve and every flaw and to claim them. After a while, Cameron shuddered and turned around, forcing her to release him.

Gently holding her arms, he said, "I need you to know that there was no one else. Not Gabby, not anyone, no matter what the tabloids say. There's been no one but you since last March. Since we first met in the pub, really."

If she was unsure before, she believed him now. Raising her hands, Delilah traced his jawline, finding the slight stubble there. She followed the lines and creases to his high cheekbones. She touched the prominence of his nose and smiled at how he raised an eyebrow in response to her exploration. His eyes were greener in this light. No matter what costume he wore or what makeup was used, Cameron's eyes never changed. She could always find the real him in his eyes. With a finger, she traced the line of his mouth, which smirked so perfectly. Then she pulled herself up and kissed him lightly, their skin touching from lips to toes. Delilah gasped slightly when he lifted her. She twined her legs around his waist, and he carried her to the bed. Throwing the duvet back, he laid her on the sheets. Cameron drew in a sharp breath.

Looking at her body, he winced. "What in bloody hell, Delilah?"

Glancing down, she understood his concern. Small bruises in various stages of healing were clustered on her thighs near her groin, under her arms, and across her ribcage. She had several fabric burns, as well.

She took his face in her hands. "It's okay. It's from the silks and the lyra."

"Fabric does all this?"

"Yes," she answered, "and the lyra is a metal hoop."

Cameron kissed her deeply, accepting her answer. As she did for him, he worked his hands over her body, following his fingers with his lips. He was slow and deliberate, moving over the bones of her hips and following the line of her legs to the arches of her feet. His lips caressed her, his teeth occasionally grazing skin as he left no curve untasted. She clutched the sheets as his mouth lingered between her thighs. His kisses eventually found the hollow in her neck, then he captured her mouth again.

Their bodies moved together in a slow rhythm of give and take, like a call and response in their private *pas de deux*. In the dim light of a single lamp, they saw only one another. In this intimate space, they were equal in every way, and in the haze of lovemaking, Delilah forgot where she ended and Cameron began. Fingers clutched hair and their sighs were warm on each other's skin. He was familiar. His body was both hard and soft and fitted perfectly against her. She realized now how much she had missed him. Cameron slowed, perhaps to prolong the reunion, and Delilah looked up at him. She pulled him closer, so they were a tangle of arms and legs, skin to skin from chest to toes. She could feel his heartbeat.

Kissing the spot just below his ear, she said softly, "I love you, Cameron."

He pulled back enough to meet her eyes, and his face held a thousand emotions. There was a shift, an understanding between them, as they passed from éros to agapé.

Cameron didn't answer with words, but her confession seemed to set him in motion again. Delilah felt like the shore beneath the surf. He drove against her like strong waves against hot sand. She let herself fall open to him.

Clocks ticked.

The moon rose.

The city flowed around them in a cacophony of light and sound.

Unison cries pierced the night, and Delilah held tightly to Cameron. Even after all their time apart, she was surprised at how hard he fell over the edge. She took deep breaths, forcing her lungs to work.

Cameron whispered, "I love you, Delilah MacClare."

This time, she did not doubt him.

Delilah struggled into Cameron's apartment three days later with an armload of bags. Her new friend from work, Lexi, followed her in with more boxes and bags.

Dropping everything just inside the living room, Delilah said, "Thanks for helping me. I couldn't have made more than one trip up here." She leaned on the kitchen counter, breathing heavily.

Lexi, a fellow aerial dance teacher, was average height, but with sinewy arms and legs, jet black hair, and several colorful tattoos. She set down everything she carried and asked, "Doesn't this building have people who carry shit?"

Delilah laughed. "Yes, but I'm not that pretentious yet."

Rubbing her arms, Lexi replied, "Carry a few more loads of stuff up here and, even with the elevator, you'll become pretentious very quickly."

Delilah laughed harder.

Lexi walked slowly around the living room, taking in the view and the adjacent kitchen. She glanced in the spare bedroom. "Holy fuck. This really is Cameron Burke's apartment."

Delilah rolled her eyes. Lexi, she was learning, had a way with words.

Lexi went on, "You're probably sick of everyone making such a big deal out of all of it, aren't you?"

Delilah crossed to the couch and dropped onto it. "A little."

Lexi sat next to her. "Understood. He's not really my type anyway."

Delilah relaxed a little more. Although Lexi was at least ten years younger, she was proving to be a good friend. Standing back up from the sofa, Delilah went to the refrigerator and came back with two waters. She handed one to Lexi, and they proceeded to spend the next hour talking about everything from work to local restaurants to how far behind they both were on every popular television show.

Finishing her water, Delilah stated, "I'm glad we've gotten to know each other. We have more in common than I realized."

Lexi took a long swig of her water.

Delilah broke the silence, "What made you decide to teach? I mean, when I was your age, I was still hopping from one gig to another, dancing or climbing."

Lexi didn't answer right away. When she spoke, her tone was serious. "I needed something more stable than performing that would keep me in the city. My father lives here, and I'm his caregiver."

Delilah listened. She didn't want to pry.

Lexi explained, "He was a firefighter, but he can't work now. His lungs are fucked up."

She didn't have to say anything else. Delilah understood. A thousand things passed between them in spite of the newness of their friendship.

Delilah simply said, "I understand."

Softly, Lexi stated, "I know you do. I didn't want to say anything, though. Kind of a weird thing to mention when you first meet someone. I read the story about your sister last summer in a magazine."

"They got most of the story right, I suppose."

"When you said you couldn't do as much, physically, I just assumed it was from…"

Delilah spoke so Lexi wouldn't have to finish, "I'm glad to be back in it, though. I'm learning there are other ways to be part of what I love. New ways."

Lexi added, "After his diagnosis, my father became a chaplain. He uses a wheelchair because he can't walk far, but he does counseling and things. He found a new way, too."

There was something incredibly cathartic for Delilah in knowing, for sure, she was not the only one who was finding a new way to live.

Lexi took another sip of water. "Well, that got really heavy, really fucking fast."

Delilah laughed in spite of herself.

At that moment, Cameron came through the door. Both Delilah and Lexi looked up. He smiled, but it was obvious he wasn't used to finding other people in his home.

Standing up, Delilah said, "This is Lexi. She's helping me get my stuff from my place and bring it over here."

Lexi stood and nodded.

Cameron crossed the space, shook her hand, and said, "Lovely to meet you. And thank you for helping."

Lexi, despite her statement about Cameron not being her type, had no words.

Seeing her friend's star struck face, Delilah stated with heavy sarcasm, "Lexi will be back with us in a minute."

Lexi shook herself. "Sorry. Involuntary reaction to a famous actor shaking my hand. I'm good now."

Cameron laughed as Lexi gathered her purse and jacket. Delilah walked her out of the building, giving her a quick hug of thanks.

When she returned to the apartment, she found Cameron on the sofa. He had a couple of hours before call time for the show. As she dropped down beside him, he asked, "New friend?"

"Yeah, I think so. We brought a lot of my stuff over here. We came in the back, so I don't think anyone noticed."

"They will eventually."

"True," Delilah softly agreed.

Rising from the couch, Delilah retrieved her shoulder bag. As she sat back down, she pulled out several magazines and a new spiral notebook. She purchased them on her way to her apartment that morning. Armed with scissors and glue, she flipped through the magazines. In at least two, she found snapshots of her and Cameron in the park the day they reconciled. Today, Delilah decided it was time to start a new journal.

Cameron went to the kitchen to make himself a pot of tea, and when he returned to the sofa, he looked at what she was doing and laughed. "You know, if you *buy* the magazines, it only encourages them."

While cutting out photos, Delilah explained, "This time, their invasion of our privacy provided me with engagement pictures. I think we won this round."

Cameron laughed again. Then he asked more seriously, "Have you given any thought to the actual getting married part of all this?"

She returned, "Have you?"

Cameron set his tea down and rested his elbows on his knees. "I think we should do it quickly."

"Are you afraid I'll change my mind?" Delilah teased.

Cameron shook his head. "No. But I think if we do it before anyone figures out our intentions, we have a chance of it being private."

Pausing from her cutting and gluing, Delilah stated, "I'm fairly certain the paparazzi are not allowed in City Hall."

With genuine surprise, Cameron asked, "Is that really what you want? To be married in a courthouse?"

Delilah laughed lightly. "Since I never planned on getting married, I don't know what I want."

Cameron nodded and they sat there, both lost in thought.

Finally, Delilah asked, "What was your wedding like? To Marianne."

"Well, it was a Hollywood wedding, so it was enormous. There are pictures out there somewhere. We invited the press and let them photograph every bit of it. It seemed to make sense, because we spent the year before making a film together. Our entire relationship played out in front of cameras. When we left for our honeymoon, it felt like the first time we'd ever been alone. It wasn't, obviously, but it felt that way. We quickly realized we were better in front of the cameras."

Leaning into him, Delilah said, "I understand."

Cameron gestured toward the magazines. "I don't want to share you with the media. They are not part of this. This is…different."

She returned, "They're already part of this," she indicated the magazines, "whether we like it or not."

Cameron conceded her point.

Delilah stopped cutting out pictures and looked out the tall windows. Then she broke the silence. "I was twenty-three when Anna and Preston got married. The ceremony was close to home, in Virginia. They rented out a huge barn and covered everything in wildflowers. Her dress was perfectly white, with lots of lace. Vintage.

They got married under the oak trees outside the barn, then threw the kind of reception you see in movies about country weddings— dancing inside, picnic tables and lots of kids outside. Our little cousins wore ruffled dresses and linen suits, and the boys ran around without shoes on. I remember telling my dad that he should get ready for his yard to look like that, covered in toys and shoes from all his grandchildren…"

She let her words dissipate.

Cameron pulled her close. "We need to make our own memories. Different memories."

"We need to find a new way," she echoed the words from earlier.

Cameron added, "I'm glad you're moving here. I know you love your studio, but this is safer."

Delilah sighed. "I know. But I'm going to miss that tiny place. The whole building, really. I have good neighbors."

Smiling, Cameron hugged her close. "We can keep it. You can let Jenna or your dad use it when they come."

"Or I can run away over there if you start to drive me crazy," Delilah teased.

Cameron laughed and kissed her forehead.

She started to go back to her cutting and pasting when something occurred to her. Turning back to Cameron, she said, "They wouldn't look for us there."

Confusion furrowed his brow.

She kept on, "Even if they see me move my stuff here, they have no idea that we want to get married. They wouldn't expect it to be soon, or…there."

"Where?"

Delilah smiled. "The roof of my place in Turtle Bay. The residents have made a makeshift terrace out of the roof. If we showed up one night without saying anything and just, got married, no one would have time to tip anyone off. It would be impulsive and…different, just like us. And the only people who might be up there are the people who live in the building. The ones I've met are great and the rest are probably not crazy."

Cameron stared at her and laughed heartily. "Probably not crazy?"

Delilah shrugged and smiled.

Cameron hesitated. "Is that what you want? To get married on a roof in front of people who are 'probably not crazy?'"

And suddenly, she did. It was absolutely what she wanted.

Ten days later, on the first of April, Cameron and Delilah stood on the roof of her apartment building. Strings of lights hung off the gables and chimneys and even up the ladder to the ancient water tank. A few chairs were scattered around. In the fading sunset, Marcy, the librarian from the second floor, Talia, the artist with long, rope-like braids and flawless skin, and Dan and Kevin, a young couple from the fourth floor, stood by the wall bordering the terrace to witness Cameron and Delilah's wedding.

Delilah wore a filmy dress in deep purple. Rhinestones and beadwork covered the fitted bodice from the left shoulder to her right hip. The tiny straps left her arms bare, and the feathery skirt floated gracefully when she moved. It was a dancer's dress rather than a wedding dress, complete with shorts underneath, but it suited her. Delilah's hair was piled on her head with rhinestone pins securing the loose curls. On her feet, she wore her old ballroom shoes, because, tonight, Delilah intended to dance until she fainted. Courtesy of Jenna's iPod and an old guitar amp, Delilah's favorite 80's ballads played softly.

In addition to her four neighbors, Jenna, Jason, her father, Libby, and Lexi were present. At Delilah's request, Lexi's father, Carl, would be officiating. He was stocky, with dark hair and work-worn hands, and he moved slowly, using a cane. Delilah was honored that he agreed to marry her and Cameron, because he understood what it was like to struggle every day to breathe.

Delilah cleared her throat, and Jenna turned the music down. "I would like to ask you, as my neighbors, not to video this. Except for Jenna. I've asked her to do so. However, we would love for you to take pictures. My only request is that you send them to me before forwarding them to your friends. Or putting them on Facebook."

Nodding their consent, the handful of guests sat down in the mismatched collection of chairs. Delilah turned and waved for Cameron to come closer. He was dressed in dark pants and a dark sport coat, with his shirt open at the collar, per usual.

They turned to face Carl, who leaned on his cane for support. Without any pomp or pretense, he said a few heartfelt words about love and commitment. Then, he looked at Cameron and Delilah and asked, "Have you prepared anything you want to say?"

Delilah held Cameron's hands and looked up at him, trying to put together the right words. Finally, she said, "I promise you Italian red wine and trips to the English West Country. I promise you pub food, Yorkshire Tea, and late-night walks in the snow. I promise to laugh with you, to argue with you, to cry with you, and I promise never, ever to say what you expect."

Cameron smiled, picking up on all the references to their time in Chatfield. He returned, "I promise to never make you drink my tea. I promise you poetry and sappy romance novels. I promise to listen, and to never take you for granted. I promise that I will never, ever love anyone else the way I love you. And," he appeared to struggle, "I promise to be there for you. No matter what."

Delilah's was taken aback by how hard his words hit. Those were the most raw, unfiltered sentiments Cameron had ever shared. And they weren't scripted. They were *his* words.

Carl asked, "Do you have rings?"

Delilah started to say no, but Cameron reached into his pocket. He pulled out a box, opened it, and produced two rings. Holding one out to her, he said, "I know we said we didn't need these because we both can't wear them most of the time, but I wanted to do it anyway. I wanted us to have one traditional thing."

Delilah took his platinum ring, and it felt heavy with symbolism. At Carl's prompting, she slid the ring onto Cameron's finger. He did the same for her, and she studied her left hand. Her ring held a cushion cut diamond with smaller stones graduated down the sides. The platinum was intricately carved around the stones to look like vines. It was stunning.

Cameron explained, "I had to get it. The jeweler called it, *The Delilah.*"

Standing there, holding his hand as the sun set between the skyscrapers, Delilah spontaneously asked, "What are we?"

Cameron smiled. "We're husband and wife."

She didn't wait for Carl's prompting. Delilah put her hands around Cameron's neck and kissed him. Then Jenna played the song that turned them into lovers in a terraced house in Chatfield. The music filled the rooftop space and carried out into the city around them.

Take my breath away…

Cameron took her in his arms, and they danced slowly as the sky faded to purple and revealed a dusting of stars. During the next song, Delilah danced with her father. She wanted to give him one traditional thing, too. Stephen held her close and kissed the top of her head when the song drew to a close.

Before he let her go, he whispered, "I'm so proud of you."

She hugged him tightly, crushing his good Sunday suit.

For the next hour, Jenna played some of her and Delilah's favorite old songs, and they passed around champagne. Jenna and Delilah danced with each other, and Lexi joined in. They let themselves be silly while the others chatted and got to know one another. Marcy snapped what felt like hundreds of pictures. Talia watched the action while sketching on a thick pad of paper. Cameron stood a few paces away with a slight smile on his face until Jenna picked one last song. The synthesizer chords filled the air, and Delilah crossed to him, took his hands, and pulled him close. They moved together, and Pat Benatar's voice filled the air.

We belong together.

Delilah laughed as Cameron spun her out and back in to him, using a few moves from their first dance together, the tango. At the end, he lifted her over his head, and she threw her head back in unabashed joy.

Cameron took Delilah dancing after their wedding ceremony, just as she asked. By the next morning, pictures and video of their night out were all over the social media sites. They made the cover of *USA Now* later that week, in the center of the sidebar, with an extreme close-up of their wedding bands dominating the coverage inside. There was speculation that Delilah was pregnant or simply after Cameron's money. Talk show hosts weighed in on what they thought Cameron's motivation might be. The world simply could not imagine a scenario where he and Delilah simply fell in love and wanted to be together.

They were both pleasantly surprised, however, when none of Delilah's neighbors sold any of the pictures from their ceremony. Marcy covered her Facebook feed with the shots, and the media found and used them. But no one sought profit. It made Cameron feel just a touch better about people in general. Jenna sent Delilah the video she made of that night, and they also received a sketch from Talia. It was a beautiful charcoal piece of the two of them making their vows. With it was a note:

I kept a copy, but this is for you.

Delilah had it framed and hung in the lounge.

About two weeks later, while Cameron was having a cup of tea before heading to the theater, Delilah pulled out The Notebook, as he called it, and started cutting out more photos from the tabloids. She also had several wedding snapshots Jenna sent her laid out on the coffee table. She looked like a child when she worked, with her hair falling around her as she uncapped a glue stick.

Watching from behind the kitchen counter, Cameron said, "I still say you're encouraging them when you buy their gossip."

Her deadpan reply was, "These are my wedding photos and announcements. Like I said, sometimes we win. I figure, if they're going to print them, I'm going to make something good out of them."

For a while, she worked silently and he sipped tea. Then, Delilah picked up Cameron's tablet and started scrolling.

"What are you looking for now?"

"Anything online I might want to print."

He smiled, remembering the stack of notebooks she let him look through during his first trip to her house in Branton. Delilah's old journals were filled with newspaper clippings and pictures of school events, as well as printed or partially written poems. For whatever reason, this made her happy.

"This site has pictures of me getting coffee, with a discussion of how I'm hiding a 'baby bump,'" Delilah called out after a few minutes. "If only they really knew how impossible that is."

Still leaning on the counter, Cameron offered, "You know, there's one way for them to really know what's true."

Delilah raised an eyebrow.

"We talk to them."

She rolled her eyes.

He went on, "I have no less than five requests for interviews. It's not time for the summer films to take over the press, yet. It's not awards season, so they're looking for stories. We can pick the magazine we like the best, give them our story, and set everyone straight."

Growing suddenly serious, Delilah asked, "Should we have to do that?"

"No," Cameron stated, "but if it makes them back off, we can."

She stared at him, contemplative. Then she went back to the tablet without answering. After another few minutes, she laughed.

Cameron looked up from his tea again. "What now?"

"I've found the comments section on one of the videos from the club the night we got married."

"I'm afraid to let you continue."

"This person writes, 'I would sell my soul to be Delilah MacClare tonight.' Well, that seems a little extreme," she stated. "Here's another gem, 'For years, I thought that Cameron's hotness would fade, but it never does. It just morphs.'"

Cameron shook his head. "They sound like adolescents."

She threw back, "This person says, 'Can we just take a moment to appreciate the great wonder that is Cameron Burke?' And this one was crafted by a great wordsmith, 'Shag me, Cameron Burke. Just, literally. Now.'"

Cameron was speechless.

Delilah added with a chuckle, "It's no wonder you've never had any self-esteem troubles."

He came to sit beside her. "Not until I met you."

Still reading, Delilah added, "Wow. Some of these are like little porn sentences."

Cameron smirked. "Do they use the porn words you used to keep on your refrigerator?"

Delilah slapped him lightly on the arm. "Actually, some of them do. CrazyForCameron156 says, 'I would be happy to let him…'"

"And we're done with the comments." He turned off the screen and took the tablet away.

Delilah rolled her eyes at him.

"You never answered. Do you want to talk to the press? I'm leaving it up to you."

Delilah lost herself in thought for a minute or two. Finally, she conceded, "One interview. Both of us. Print not television. We tell our story our way, and we answer nothing we don't agree to in advance."

"Done," Cameron said, picking up his phone.

22
Many Little Secrets

By reason of her marriage to a gentleman in power,
Delilah was acquainted with the gossip of the hour;
And many little secrets, of the half-official kind,
Were whispered to Delilah, and she bore them all in mind.

—*From "Delilah" by Rudyard Kipling*

They gave their interview to *Film Magazine*, and the issue with their photo on the cover was out by the end of April. As much as she hated catering to the press, Delilah was glad to have a professional photo, rather than grainy paparazzi shots, in print for a change. Overall, it was a decent article. She respected *Film*. They kept things professional, were accurate in their writing, and didn't take cheap shots to sell their product. The wild rumors died down, but Delilah noticed the attention on Cameron spiked.

He kept a standing reserved ticket for her at will-call for his show. As a newlywed couple with opposite schedules, it was often the only way for them to spend time together before midnight. On the days she used the ticket, Delilah enjoyed watching Cameron on stage. Afterward, she would meet him backstage. Sometimes she playfully gave him notes, and they would walk out the stage door together. There was always a crowd, but after the *Film* article was released, the crowds grew larger. More fans learned Cameron Burke was doing a play and wanted to see it before the end of his run. Delilah usually walked just behind him as he signed playbills and took the occasional picture. She watched the people who came to see her husband, trying to imagine what it might have been like to be his fan and meet him this way.

Delilah also noticed that the fans came in three varieties. There were the women, young and old, who stared at him with fascinated admiration. They giggled and said nice things. They were sweet. There were the men and teenage boys who knew him only from *Fyrelords* and *Heir of Taivas*. They usually came with movie posters to be signed and quoted Cameron's most memorable, most heroic phrases. Then, there was the third group. The ones with "hungry eyes." Delilah could almost hear Eric Carmen singing as she thought about it. They would stare Cameron down, and Delilah felt like, if he gave the slightest indication of interest, they would be in his dressing room with their skirts hiked up. It reminded her of his story about the one girl from years ago whom he *did* take back to his hotel. It made Delilah realize that he still had that option. He had lots of options. It was one thing to read about how his fans felt on the internet, but it was another to see them standing in front of her.

On the nights when the fans were especially demanding, Delilah would slide close to him in their bed. Their kisses would start out lazy and sleepy, then intensify as Cameron's hands wandered over her body under the covers. Despite how tired they both were, they would find themselves making love gently, a natural end to the day.

On one of those nights, as Cameron ran his hands up her sides and lifted her nightshirt, Delilah asked softly, "Do you see how they look at you? You know some of them would shag you in a heartbeat, if you let them."

Kissing her neck, Cameron said, "Let them dream. *This* is what I want."

On the first Thursday in May, just after midday, Cameron's phone rang while he was checking his email. Recognizing the number of Delilah's school, he answered quickly.

Immediately, Libby said, "I need you to come down here."

Feeling a stab of alarm, Cameron asked, "What's happened?"

With a sigh, Libby explained, "Delilah fainted. She was working on a piece for the spring show with Lexi. The teachers perform in that one. They were doing lyra together, and she passed out. She won't let us call anyone else."

"Is she okay?"

"I think so," Libby answered. "Lexi caught her. I think she's just shaken."

Feeling less panicked, Cameron said, "I'll be there shortly."

Living with Delilah over the past month, rather than having an on-again, off-again affair, forced Cameron to see realities about her illness he missed before. He watched her take a handful of pills every morning, and she had two inhalers, one for everyday use and one for when she was sick. Once, while she was asleep, he read over the labels on all the pill bottles and inhalers:

Alprazolam.

Sertraline.

Guaifenesin.

Prednisone

Albuterol.

Budesonide.

It was foreboding to see it all at once, but Delilah usually took it in stride, refusing to spend much time discussing the details of her disease. Some days, she could make him forget she was sick. Today, however, was not one of those days.

When he arrived at the school, Libby led him through the hallways to the largest studio in the corner of the second floor. The silks were hoisted overhead like colorful ribbons and only the lyra hung free. Delilah was sitting on the Marley floor, leaning against the mirrors and looking out of the floor-to-ceiling windows across the room. Lexi was sitting next to her, her jet-black hair pulled into a tight bun and her features arranged in a worried pout. When Cameron entered, Lexi stood up, gave Delilah a quick smile of encouragement, and left the room. Libby left as well, leaving the couple alone. Cameron crossed the space and lowered his long-limbed frame to sit next to Delilah. He could see in her profile, by the way her jaw was set, that she was more angry and frustrated than hurt or sick.

He asked, "Are you all right?"

Delilah nodded slightly. "Yes. Lexi caught me."

"What happened?"

"We were partnering with each other, and I just pushed too hard."

"You're sure that's all it was?" He pressed.

Annoyed, she shot back, "Yes. It's the same reason I haven't performed in six years. I'm a 'fall risk.'"

Cameron returned carefully, "You can't ask your body to do what it can't do."

She turned to look him in the eyes. "I know that, Cameron. But you don't understand what it's like to have the one thing you love to do, your livelihood, the thing you're most passionate about, slowly taken away."

He conceded, "You're right. I don't."

Disarmed by his agreement, Delilah leaned into him. She sounded unusually vulnerable when she explained, "I can't climb for more than two minutes. I can't run. Any tempo other than 'slow' feels impossible…"

Cameron wrapped his arms around her and pulled her close. "Then, dance for two minutes. Make it the best two minutes anyone has ever seen."

"What if I want to quit?" Delilah's expression was troubled.

"If that's really what you want, I'll support you," he answered. Then he asked carefully, "Should you come home?"

She shook her head. "No. I've got about ten minutes to work before the next class comes in. I'll be fine."

"Are you sure?"

"Yes. And I'll be home late tonight."

"Then, I'll see you after my show."

Cameron kissed her quickly and rose to leave, checking his phone for messages as he walked toward the door. Behind him, he could hear Delilah manipulating the different apparatus. He glanced back and saw that she dropped a bright red silk to the floor. He stopped in the doorway and watched her climb. Since she wore only knee-length leggings and an open-back leotard, he could see the strain in the long lines of her back and arm muscles. He knew, without a doubt, that she was stronger than him. Cameron watched her twist the fabric around her legs so her body was pulled into a perfect, vertical split. He watched her climb higher and wrap herself in the silk so she was suspended horizontally, like a bird in flight. When she unwrapped herself and slid back to the ground, breathing hard and fast because she couldn't continue, Cameron suddenly *felt* her loss. In a sharp, unexpected way, he found empathy. To see her literally grounded by her disease hit him hard. When she looked up and realized he was watching, Delilah glanced away to hide her tears.

Crossing to her, Cameron wrapped her in his arms again. With the red silk tangled around their feet, he kissed her softly, slowly. Looking down into her eyes, he said, "I love you, with or without this. Whether you climb or not. Whether you dance or not. I love you."

It was all he could think to say.

After leaving the studio, Cameron hurried from the building. He was almost late for his lunch date with Meg. She asked to meet with him before the show that night, and now he was barely going to make it to the restaurant.

Fifteen minutes later, he dropped into a chair opposite her in an airy café.

Meg set her menu on the table in front of her and smiled at him. She was perfectly dressed, as always, in tailored trousers and a flowing top.

With a half-smile, he said, "I hope you haven't brought me here to tell me we're closing."

Meg shook her head. "No, Cameron. Unashamedly using your name has certainly increased ticket sales."

"Well, good. Even if it was…what word did you use? Whorish?"

Meg laughed. "That it was. I won't deny it. I wish all people could simply appreciate the art of theater and give it an unbiased chance without having to be baited, but that is not the world we live in."

"No, it's not," Cameron agreed as the waiter arrived to take their order.

They ordered soup and sandwiches and turned their menus over to the wait staff.

Sipping water, Cameron asked, "So, if I'm not being sacked today, what brings us here?"

Meg stared at him, her expression unreadable. "I've been nominated for the Tony for Best Direction of a Play."

Sitting back in his chair, Cameron was genuinely happy. "Congratulations."

Sipping her drink, Meg went on, "I won't win. I'm up against Mark Jacobson and his show about the Holocaust children."

Cocking his head, Cameron stated, "It's been a year of rather dark subject matter on The Great White Way, has it not?"

Meg chuckled. "I suppose. I asked you here to tell you my news in person, and to thank you."

"For what?"

"For being the whore. For dusting off your stage skills and doing a play almost no one had heard of for a fraction of what you could get making another film. Thank you for thinking with your heart, finally."

Cameron smiled. "And what have I been thinking with until now?"

Meg gave him an amused look. "Your wallet, mostly."

Cameron shook his head. "I can't deny that. Not to you."

"I wish I could convince you to renew," Meg said softly.

Cameron sighed. "Part of me wants to say yes, but Delilah and I need some time together this summer. Alone. More time than the eight-a-week schedule allows. Besides, you don't need me. Not anymore."

Meg smiled. "Darren is going to be great."

"He should be." Cameron smirked. "We hand-picked him. I think those blokes from Telsey want to kill me for interfering."

Meg laughed heartily. "He's you. But younger."

"Well, there's no substitute for the sharp English tongue," Cameron threw back.

Growing serious again, Meg stated, "I hope you'll do more of this, Cameron. You don't need more money or another magazine cover. Do things that matter. You've already had the world's attention. Now, give the world *your* attention."

Delilah's spring show with her dance school was on the first Saturday in June at a theater in Brooklyn. Because he took his last curtain call in *Anonymous* the Sunday before, Cameron was able to attend. He waited until almost show time to slip into his seat, wanting to create as little a distraction as possible. When the lights went down, it didn't appear anyone had noticed his presence.

The show, which featured the instructors and the senior students, began with a large group number using several different kinds of apparatus as well as floor work. As the production progressed, Cameron followed his program. The theme of the show was relationships, both concrete and abstract. One piece stood out clearly as Delilah's choreography. It featured several couples and their relationships at different ages. There was a boy and a girl in preadolescence, their partnering innocent and playful. There were two teenagers jockeying each other in wild emotion. The movement played on as one of the other teachers, obviously in early pregnancy, danced with her partner, their choreography delicate and light. Two of the most senior students from one of the adult classes moved fluidly together, ageless in beauty.

The final piece before the show finale was entitled, *Dust*. Reading his program again, Cameron was surprised to see that Delilah would be performing. For the piece, a row of mirrors was set upstage to reflect Delilah as she entered from stage left. She stopped to face the mirrors as the music began. The song started with a contemplative piano solo that was soon joined by the rich swell of strings. Delilah moved before the mirrors, intentionally ignoring the audience as though in her own, internal space. She would pull away from her reflection, as though trying to reach the fourth wall, but she was quickly drawn back upstage in a call and response with her own reflection. After about a minute, the music shifted, and a large group of dancers dressed in street clothes entered from both sides of the stage. The crowd and the chaos caught Delilah. Their movements were frantic and unsynchronized. When they cleared the stage, the mirrors were gone and Delilah was on her knees, alone, with just one white silk. She slowly pulled herself to her feet, searching for the mirrors.

As Delilah put her grief into simple but exquisite choreography, Cameron felt a sharp pang in his chest. Looking down at the program, he read: *Music written and recorded by Anna MacClare*. He took a heavy breath as Delilah continued to dance. She slowly began to climb the silk, twisting and inverting herself to try and reach the single light at the top. The higher she climbed, the harder it became. She dropped and began again a few times. Finally, she almost reached the light, but she took heavy breaths and slowly slid back to the floor. She sat there, legs splayed beautifully, toes pointed and her arms reaching up toward the light. On the scrim upstage appeared an image of swirling dust. It was not an identifiable image. There were no buildings or people, but the dust was enough. Delilah continued to look upward into the one spotlight until the stage went dark. On the screen, the image faded to leave only two lines of text:

For Anna.

March 28, 1971 – September 11, 2001.

The audience was still, as if collectively holding their breath. Cameron heard sniffling. Then applause erupted—reverent applause that stretched on for some time. He glanced at the time and realized she did exactly what he said.

She danced for two minutes.

The following Sunday, Delilah had the great privilege of attending the Tony Awards ceremony. She went once before, the year that *Rent* won Best Musical. Her boyfriend at the time was playing Munkustrap in *Cats* and gave her the tickets for her birthday. Those seats were in the back of the house. This time, she got to walk the red carpet and sit near the front with the cast of *Anonymous*. The Beacon Theater, in all its red and gold glory, was packed with famous faces. Delilah, despite spending every day with a celebrity, found herself quite star struck. She also recognized a few faces from years earlier when she worked in the city. The capstone of the evening came when Meg, surprisingly, won. In an emotional gesture, she pulled the small cast up on stage with her, and Delilah watched as Cameron tried to stay out of Meg's spotlight.

At the after-party at the Plaza Hotel, Meg was quickly swept away by friends and admirers. Cameron and Delilah did a turn around the room so he could shake hands with all the right people. Then they nursed their drinks on an expensive couch, watching actors, directors, and producers vie for each other's attention. As they discussed going home, Delilah looked up to see a tall, classically beautiful woman approach. She wore a long, intricately beaded red dress, and her deep brown curls tumbled over one shoulder. Her lips were a darker shade than her dress and her lashes were thick. She looked older than fifty, but that was Delilah's best guess.

Stopping in front of them, she said, "Hello, Cameron."

He looked up and gave her a measured gaze. "Hello, Marianne."

Delilah felt her stomach clench.

"I see you've brought your newest conquest," Marianne stated, her eyes fixed on Delilah.

Delilah felt a flash of anger.

Taking a sip of her drink, the dark-haired woman went on, "Hopefully she won't find you upstairs later fucking a waitress with great headshots."

Delilah could feel Cameron tense, but his voice stayed even as he said, "I thought you moved back to Hollywood years ago. Isn't live theater beneath you now?"

Turning her eyes on him, she replied, "I occasionally produce for the stage, too. I like to come out and rub shoulders with the people I'm paying."

"Or," Cameron threw back, "you knew I would be here."

"That is an unfortunate coincidence."

Watching them interact, Delilah was taken aback. She always pictured Marianne as being timid. Perhaps because Cameron admitted to treating her so poorly, Delilah imagined a damaged victim. It hadn't occurred to her that Marianne was not a soft-spoken saint.

"I noticed you're working with Gabby." Marianne went on, "I suppose that means you're finally fucking women at least close to your age? In addition to this one, of course."

"Marianne," Cameron warned.

Taking another swig of champagne, she kept on, "I just want to make sure that she knows what it means to be Mrs. Cameron Burke." She addressed Delilah, "You might have a ring, but that doesn't mean you won't have to hear secondhand about who's blowing him in the dressing room."

Standing up, Cameron warned, "Marianne, this is entirely unnecessary and not good for either one of us."

Laughing harshly, she spat, "*Good* for us? When have you ever been concerned about what was *good* for us? Or even for me? I don't remember ever feeling much of your *concern*."

Looking her in the eyes, he said, "I was wrong. But this is not the place for that apology."

His sincerity seemed to throw her, and she shot back, "And where is the place, Cameron? It's been almost thirty years. You've gotten married again, God knows why, and I've yet to hear this apology."

Delilah glanced around, noting that people were beginning to stare.

Cameron held his ground. "I'd be happy for you to hear it, but not here."

Setting her glass down, Marianne crossed her arms over her chest. "I don't need your apology."

"Then why are you here?" Cameron demanded.

Looking back at Delilah, she stated, "Because I wanted to see *her*. In person. I wanted to look her in the eyes and tell her that she should have a good lawyer ready, because you can only keep up the act for so long. And to tell her to please, by any means necessary, do not get pregnant. Or sick."

Delilah inhaled sharply. She couldn't tell how much Marianne had to drink, but she was not slurring like a woman scorned and drowning her sorrow. Marianne chose her insults carefully, making sure they cut to the bone.

Speaking up, Delilah asked, "Who would want to be with someone who says such vicious things?"

Eyes flashing, Marianne asked rhetorically, "But is it vicious if it's true?"

"Sometimes," Delilah said sharply, "truth can change."

Marianne threw back her head and laughed. The attention of a small crowd was now on them as she said, "Cameron doesn't change. He lies, he manipulates, and he'll say anything you want to hear to get you out of your clothes. But once the sex is over, which, I must say, is certainly not as great as all the hype, all those promises will be as good as dust."

Perhaps it was the word choice or the way Marianne inserted herself into the most private parts of Delilah's life, but she snapped. Standing up, Delilah threw her nearly full glass of red wine onto Marianne's Donna Karan dress. Then, like so many of the actresses in the room, she exited dramatically stage right.

She was pacing the hallway outside the banquet hall when Cameron found her. "Well, that's going to make *Entertainment Review* tomorrow."

Delilah tried to laugh, but it caught in her throat. "That can't be the craziest thing that happened tonight. It's a party full of actors."

"Marianne Agrietta told me I was bad in bed at the Tony Awards after-party. That's tabloid gold." He shook his head. "And to pour diamonds on that gold, my current wife threw red wine on my ex-wife, who is also the producer of *Barking Mad*."

Meeting his eyes, Delilah asked, "You mean the play about the man who thinks he's a dog and falls in love with his therapist?"

Cameron's eyes sparked with laughter as he nodded.

"How could that possibly have been nominated next to Meg's show? Or Mark Jacobson's show?"

Cameron shrugged. "Someone is shagging someone in the American Theater Wing?"

Delilah couldn't help laughing.

Cameron went on, "I'm sure she wasn't here to support the play. She was here to see me and you."

"Do you think she would listen if you were to apologize in private?" Delilah asked. She twisted her wedding ring on her finger.

Running his hand through his hair, Cameron said, "She does deserve an apology, a real apology, because her bitterness is mostly my fault. All the scenarios she referenced in there are true. I treated her terribly. But she has no right to take it out on you."

Churning with emotion, Delilah watched him wrestle with what to say next.

Finally, he stated, "I don't deserve you, Delilah."

She tipped her head to the side. "We've done this already."

Cameron smiled in spite of himself. "Let's get out of here. Not just tonight, but for a while. Let's take the summer and go wherever you want to go, alone. Places without crowds and cameras and posh parties. Call it a honeymoon, if you like, but let's just…go."

Delilah wholeheartedly agreed.

Their first stop was Paris. Delilah raved about the City of Light like the tourist she was. A week later, they drove the open roads through Germany and into Switzerland with Cameron at the wheel of his Bentley. Delilah thought it was particularly American that he loved to drive so much. He explained that he learned to love it from driving the Pacific Coast Highway during his early film career in Hollywood. As they crisscrossed Europe, rather than staying in the typical celebrity suites, they picked tiny hotels along the way and stayed in one place until someone inevitably recognized them. On sunny days, while they drove, Delilah would insist Cameron put the top down so her hair could fly around her like brushfire. In Italy, they went wine tasting, and he bought her an '85 Sassicaia without blinking at the four-figure price tag. They shared it on a balcony overlooking the vineyards of Tenuta San Guido and the wine was, as Delilah read in the description, "perfect."

While they were gone, Marianne decided, on the heels of their interaction at the Tonys after-party, to start giving interviews. Under the guise of promoting a film she was co-producing, she took every opportunity to slander Cameron. For some reason beyond Delilah's understanding, after years of silence, she decided it was time to dredge up the past. Amelia, Cameron's publicist, had a full-time job dealing with the repercussions.

Once, when they stopped for fuel and Delilah caught a glimpse of the magazine rack, she asked, "Why is Marianne doing this?"

Cameron sighed. "Because I have you."

Delilah tried to understand.

In the middle of June, they went to Edinburgh for the International Film Festival. After ten days of films and local food, they drove up into the eastern Highlands. There, Cameron reminded Delilah how they once compared the mountains of West Virginia to the Scottish landscape. Seeing it for herself, she decided there were similarities, but the mountains at home nurtured thick forests of dark pines and black oaks that turned brilliant shades of crimson and tangerine every fall. These mountains were covered in scrubby grasses in shades of green more brilliant than Delilah had ever seen. They were cut through with serpentine lochs and rocky outcroppings that were sometimes hard to differentiate from the ruins of ancient castles that dotted the landscape. For Delilah, it conjured up scenes from *Heir of Taivas*, part of which was filmed here, and made her feel like real magic might lurk in the Cairngorms.

Following the same routine they established in Europe, she and Cameron rented a room at an inn and spent their days exploring the little town of Strathloch. When people started to get curious, they rented horses from a local barn and took them out into the hills. Delilah was a decent rider, since taking lessons was almost required in West Virginia, but Cameron was incredible. She marveled at his poise, his form, and the wildness he displayed when the rocky paths would open into flatlands and he would spur his stallion into a full gallop. Watching him ride on-screen, as Marcus Eperra, was wonderful, but watching him ride as just Cameron, free of any expectation, was breathtaking. This, she realized, was his dance, the thing he shared with the world but was really just for him. She understood it completely.

One evening in early July, they sat at the edge of a tiny, isolated loch, taking advantage of the extended summer daylight and the unusually warm weather.

Breaking the silence, Delilah threw out, "I got a call from Libby last week. Someone saw my performance at the spring show, and they want me to perform *Dust* at the September Peace Concert this fall."

Cameron turned to her and looked surprised.

"I told them yes."

There was a long, silence.

"I didn't tell you right away because," she struggled, "for some reason telling you makes it real. It means I'm really going to do it. Even though that makes no sense, because saying 'yes' meant I'm doing it."

He smiled at her. "Some things don't have to make sense."

Delilah appreciated his wisdom. "I think...I'm trying to let Anna go. 'Move on,' as everyone says. I even had a counselor say that to me once." She hesitated. "What they don't understand is, I can't move on. Not like they think. I can keep going forward. I can make a new way, but I can't get on with the life I had before. And not just because I'm sick. Even if I was perfectly healthy, I will never be the person I was before September the eleventh. That life is gone. That is what I've learned about grief. It's not about turning the page. It's about writing a new book."

Delilah stopped and thought over what she wanted to say, and Cameron held her hand silently.

After another minute, she went on, "I've also realized I'm grieving two different things. I'm grieving the loss of my health and the innocence I used to have. I can't go back and unsee what I saw. I can't remove the experience from my mind, and I can't fix my lungs. When I have nightmares about that day, they are self-focused, rooted in my own fears and anxieties. They are violent dreams. But the nightmares about Anna are desperate and hollow and, strangely enough, I no longer dream about her and the violence at the same time. The nightmares about my sister are just full of her absence." She paused. "But I think I know what I have to do. I have to actively share her. I have to put so much of her out into the world that it comes back to me and surrounds me. It feels like a paradox, but it is the only way I know to let her go."

Squeezing her hand, Cameron said, "You have an incredible way with words. And you are stronger than anyone I know."

Delilah shook her head. "No, I'm not. It's not about strength. I've just...I've found the wind."

Cameron met her eyes. "What?"

Delilah explained, "Just something my dad used to say. I'm...moving forward again. Filming the interview with Katie last winter was the first step. Dancing in the show last spring...another step. This concert will be the next."

Cameron asked carefully, "When does the interview air?"

"Early September," Delilah replied. "And it will be part of the archive on Katie's website."

She waited, but he didn't ask anything else.

After spending a few more days in Scotland, Cameron surprised Delilah with another leg to their journey. She was expecting to go back to London for a month, but they left the car there and flew to Dubai instead. From there, they went to Thailand, then on to New Zealand. The summer was a whirlwind of places she wanted to visit before her life fell apart. As they sat on one of the many crescent shaped beaches on Waiheke Island, Delilah told Cameron stories about how she had always wanted to study with Aerial Artists in Australia and perform on the beach. The closest she ever got was taking trapeze class in Hudson River Park, or the time she was dared to hang her silk from the Chesapeake Bay Bridge in Virginia. Luckily for her, someone talked her out of that. Cameron shared stories about filming parts of the first *Heir of Taivas* movie in New Zealand, before computer graphics took over and the settings could be digitally created with a blue screen. Delilah could tell he mourned the loss of the adventure of filming everything on location. They talked for hours on the beach that day, and Delilah pretended they were alone in the world. She let herself imagine, for a short time, that nothing else existed but them.

No matter how far they traveled, however, they couldn't escape Marianne's newfound determination to dredge up the story of her and Cameron's relationship and its demise. Delilah was sure she fueled the fire by throwing wine at Marianne, but she wasn't exactly sorry. Every store Delilah ran into featured magazines with fuzzy clips of her and Cameron on a beach or eating out in Dubai, with captions speculating on his fidelity and whether she was crazy for marrying him.

At the beginning of August, they flew back to the States to spend a week in West Virginia. Delilah promised her father she would visit, and she wanted to spend some time with him before his school year began. She wasn't sure how long they could stay before someone realized Cameron was in town and started stalking her house. She hoped, if they were discreet, it would be at least a week.

On their third day in Branton, Stephen left in the morning to attend a planning meeting for the upcoming school year, leaving Delilah and Cameron in the house alone. They spent the morning sprawled together on the sofa watching cartoons, because Delilah couldn't find the remote control for the television to change the channel. As much as she enjoyed all the traveling, she was glad to just be sitting in her own home in her pajamas. Suddenly, her phone buzzed, and she pulled herself out of Cameron's lap to find it.

Picking it up, she read a text and stated, "It's Jenna. She says, 'I'm coming over. Put on clothes.'"

Cameron laughed, and she looked back at him, asking, "Why would I not be wearing clothes?"

Shaking his head, Cameron returned, "Well, this whole summer was meant to be our honeymoon, but it's lovely that you've forgotten already."

She threw a decorative pillow at him and rolled her eyes. "I plan to wear these pajamas all day. Jenna will have to deal with it."

"Then I shall be equally as poorly dressed," Cameron stated, referencing his usual pajama bottoms and old t-shirt.

With a sudden spark in her eyes, Delilah went back to the couch and curled back into his lap. Running her fingers through his hair she said, "Maybe I won't wear them *all* day…"

Cameron pulled her closer and kissed her, and she savored the moment. He had just deepened the kiss when the doorbell rang. Pulling back a little, he said, "Your friend has impeccable timing."

Climbing off his lap, Delilah laughed. "She must've texted from the car. I've told her not to do that."

She went to answer the door and returned with Jenna.

The tall brunette surveyed both of them. "Thanks for dressing up for me."

Delilah threw the same decorative pillow at her friend.

Cameron moved to leave the room as though he anticipated girl talk. However, Jenna stopped him.

"I think you should see this, too," she stated, suddenly serious.

Concerned, Cameron sat back down on the couch. Delilah dropped next to him, and Jenna sat down in the chair.

She slapped a magazine on the table. "This came out today."

It was a copy of *Film Magazine*. Marianne was on the cover of the August issue looking stunning with her hair straightened and her face airbrushed. The tagline promised a revealing article about Marianne and her relationship with Cameron. Delilah was sure the choice of publication was intentional, and she was sure this would not be good.

Staring at the magazine, Delilah asked, "How do you find these things so fast, Jenna? You might as well be a publicist."

Looking at her friend, Jenna returned, "Like I've told you, I'm at the store *every* day. Every. Single. Day. All my children do in the summer is eat."

Picking up the magazine, Delilah found the article and scanned it. She inhaled sharply and instinctively whispered, "Cameron..."

"What is it?" He asked wearily. "Are there nude photos I don't know about? Perhaps there's a story about me taking puppies away from orphans or a sex tape I don't remember filming?"

Delilah didn't answer. Instead, she started to read. After several paragraphs describing Marianne's career and her relationship with Cameron, the journalist wrote:

According to Agrietta, her son, Andrew, is, in fact, Cameron Burke's child. Andrew is now thirty and lives in North Carolina. She won't expound on exactly why she kept the truth from the public for so long, but would only state, "Cameron would not have been a good father. It was for the best." People can only speculate that, given their explosive breakup and Burke's admitted infidelity, children were never part of his plan. When asked if Burke and his son have any contact now, she said simply, "No."

Delilah finished the article, which consisted of a few more paragraphs and a question-and-answer session with Marianne. There was a grainy photo on the right side of the spread that had to be Andrew. His profile was enough like Cameron's that Delilah could identify him immediately. Someone snapped the picture as he was coming out of what looked like an office building. There was no accompanying quote anywhere, so Delilah could only assume he had declined an interview.

When she looked up, Cameron took the magazine from her. They all sat in heavy silence until he finished reading. When he was done, he closed the magazine and laid it on the coffee table. He didn't say anything for some time. It was obvious they were all thinking the same thing. The other interviews were superficial and catty. This was manipulative and mean.

Eventually, Delilah asked, "Why would she do that?"

Looking up at her, Cameron said darkly, "She's never gotten over what happened between us. You know that. She played the victim for a while, even after she was well again. And please understand, I say that knowing she *was* a victim of my bad behavior, and she survived a terrible illness, but she also made sure the media knew all about it. Eventually, she ran out of ammunition against me and stopped talking. I assume she felt some sense of protection for her child and that kept her from exploiting him when he was young. Now, however, she's playing the last card she has. Andrew."

Looking at the pictures again, Delilah asked, "How did no one recognize him until now? This profile is…you."

Cameron stated, "There was speculation, but without confirmation, rumor dies out fairly quickly. And Andrew has stayed completely out of the spotlight."

Delilah could see the turmoil in her husband. When he dropped his face in his hands, she slid closer and put her arms around his shoulders.

She said softly, "You can't take it back, Cameron. It's where we go from here that matters."

After another minute or so he got up, wordlessly, and went out to the back patio. Delilah watched him and wished she could fix the mess, but she understood all too well that there are some things that cannot be repaired.

———

Ten million dollars.

That was the most recent offer Charlie relayed to Cameron to appear in the reboot of the *Fyrelords* franchise. It was the thirteenth of August, and Cameron was back home in his Manhattan flat mulling over whether the money was worth having to work with his ex-lover Naomi again. Principal photography for the film was scheduled to begin in just two months, so he had to make a decision. He could only imagine how the production team must feel, having their whole project hinging on his decision. For the first time in his life, it felt wrong to be wielding such power. His role wasn't even technically a lead. He, Robert Chesney, Chad Logan, and Naomi would be making appearances to please the fans and transition the story from one generation to another. The others already signed contracts. Cameron wondered if they were also made such lucrative offers. In the end, however, it was not the money that made Cameron say yes—it was his feeling of possession over his role. He wasn't willing to let it go. So he agreed despite his trepidation about working with Naomi again, and filming was scheduled for the fall.

As August became September, the news that Cameron would be returning to *Fyrelords* became public. The fans tweeted their excitement. Meg congratulated him. And Marianne continued to talk about her son. A few more pictures appeared in the tabloids, mostly of Andrew leaving his place of business or running in a local park. There were no interviews, however. As far as Cameron could tell, his son refused to acknowledge the press. He was proud of Andrew's ability to do what his parents had never been able to do—say nothing.

On the eighth of September, the documentary featuring Delilah's interview with Katie Brooks aired. That evening, she and Cameron watched it together while curled up on the sofa in what was now *their* Manhattan flat. The program included interviews without any journalistic commentary or gratuitous video footage. Cameron learned from Delilah that the practice of replaying footage from September 11 was traumatizing to families who were forced to watch their loved ones perish over and over again. Whether it was video of the twin towers, the Pentagon, or a field in Pennsylvania, it was considered the equivalent of showing uncensored murder scenes. Katie used no such footage, making it solely about survivors, family members, and the people they wanted to remember.

When the program was over, Cameron said nothing when Delilah went to the bedroom and shut the door, leaving him alone on the sofa. He left the television on, letting it be background noise as he made a pot of tea. Sitting back down with a steaming cup of Yorkshire Gold, he saw that another documentary had begun. He meant to change the channel, but he found himself unable. The current program was compiled from raw footage filmed on the streets that day. After a couple of hours, Cameron wasn't sure why he was still watching. Searching his thoughts, he decided it was because he was so unaffected when the tragedy actually happened. He was caught up in his career, and it was so easy to think of it as a terrible moment in history and to stand stoically while memorials were made. It was so simple to use words like "bravery" and "sacrifice" when neither were asked of you. Now, Cameron needed to really see it. He wanted to try and grasp, just briefly, what Delilah went through and now lived with every day. It put into perspective how stressed he was over his recent poor publicity. Staring at the television, Cameron thought about Delilah's dance. He thought about Anna. He tried to imagine that his wife was reduced to nothing but gray, billowing dust. Cameron did not usually cry, but the image brought hot tears to his eyes.

Turning off the television, he went to the bedroom and found Delilah asleep on the bed in her clothes. He curled beside her and pulled her close. She stirred but didn't wake. He felt certain she took some of her medication in order to sleep so soundly. He also noticed her notebook was open on her chest, the same notebook where she pasted their tabloid engagement photos. It looked like she was writing when she fell asleep. Lifting it carefully from her sleeping form, he considered looking at it. Instead, he closed it, not wanting to be intrusive. Even his wife deserved a place for her private thoughts. Then he fell asleep beside her.

On the evening of September 11, Cameron discretely joined the crowd at Rumsey Playfield for the Peace Concert. Stephen was with him, and they stood shoulder to shoulder without saying much. Jenna and Jason also made the trip to the city and stood a few paces away. After scanning the crowd, Cameron spotted Lexi and her father, as well as a couple other staff members from Delilah's school.

The concert began at seven o'clock, and the musical styles ranged from classic to contemporary to rock, appealing to the varied audience in a gesture of unity. The New York Symphony was featured and accompanied several vocalists. A group of children from a local dance school performed a modern piece while a soloist sang. As the concert went on, the sun set and ushered in a sky full of stars. Toward the end, just as a crisp breeze began to blow, Delilah took the stage. This time, the symphony was playing her sister's music, with the first chair violinist on the solo. Delilah and her company danced her piece, *Dust*, just as they did at the spring show. At the end, the only sounds were the rustling of the trees and the distant noise of the city. Then thunderous applause erupted.

After the last song of the night, a young man from a local high school got up and said a few words. Then he turned the microphone over to a couple of other students. Cameron deduced that their teachers had challenged them to write about peace, and these were the ones selected to present their work. To Cameron's surprise, Delilah came up next. She didn't mention she was going to say something. Taking the microphone and stepping to the front of the podium because she was so short, she referenced some note cards in her hand.

She began, "My name is Delilah MacClare, and I lost my sister, Anna, on September eleventh. She was not, and will most likely never be, found. She was one of the many in the dust. And because of that dust, I struggle every day to breathe.

"I lost a lot of things that day. I lost my sister. I lost my work. And I lost my way. But I will not be terrorized anymore. I will not live in fear, and I will not be overcome by hate. Because every seed of hate that we plant grows into something bigger and uglier until it destroys us. When we allow ourselves to believe, for one moment, that we are better, holier, and more deserving of life than someone else, we are doomed to destroy one another.

"I want my sister to be remembered. May every victim of September the eleventh remind us that the enemy is *never* one another. The enemy is hate, and its propagation is man's greatest scourge. The object of terrorism is to instill terror, or fear, and fear gives birth to division and isolation. We can never allow fear to cause us to stop reaching out, to stop helping one another. We can't allow our grief to stop us from sharing stories of those we lost."

She hesitated.

"In spite of everything, I believe in a God who loves us more than we love each other most of the time. We must remember that the greatest commandment is to love, without stipulation or exception. If my sister was here tonight, she would quote the book of

Romans and say, '*Do not be overcome by evil, but overcome evil with good.*' Peace is achieved by choosing to love one another unconditionally, by choosing, every day, to overcome evil with immeasurable good.

"I'm going to leave you with a quote by author Joseph Warwick."

"We go on, not because we are strong, but because we carry those who are gone with us. We are the guardians of their memory and the propagators of their legacy. So we must live, and we must live fully, but we will never forget them. They will be part of every moment of joy, and we will hear them in every cry of new life. We will carve something new out of this blood-soaked rock and we will stand, unafraid. We will strive to be better, to be kinder, and to show full measures of compassion. And even though the price of love may be loss, we will pay. No matter the cost, we will love blindly, boldly, and without bounds."

23
By Virtue Fall

Well, heaven forgive him! and forgive us all!
Some rise by sin, and some by virtue fall:
Some run from brakes of ice, and answer none:
And some condemned for a fault alone.

—*From Measure for Measure by William Shakespeare*

Cameron was too old to be thrilled with birthdays anymore. When he was a boy, he loved to be surprised with parties or outings. Now, he generally liked to pretend he stopped aging at around fifty. On the night of September 22, however, he was at the mercy of Delilah's plans. She made reservations at one of his favorite restaurants and presented him with tickets to an off-Broadway show they both wanted to see. He still wasn't keen on birthdays, but Delilah made it worth acknowledging he was a year older. Unfortunately, the paparazzi were especially aggressive that night, accosting them at both the restaurant and the theater afterward. In order to get rid of them, Cameron had Adam drive around until they lost them in heavy, Saturday evening traffic.

They found themselves in the Lower East Side and, on impulse, Delilah asked to walk the promenade across the Brooklyn Bridge. Cameron was sure she wouldn't make it all the way, since it was a little over a mile from end to end, but he agreed anyway. Adam dropped them off across from City Hall, and they tried to remain inconspicuous as they joined the other pedestrians. Luckily, it was dark. As they walked, Delilah confessed she always meant to make this journey. It was on her to-do list when she moved to the city for the first time.

"But, in all those years, I never did it," she admitted, looking out at the skyline as they walked.

They only got about a third of the way across before Delilah's lungs started to protest. Cameron could tell she was struggling, though she said nothing. He slowed his pace and led her over to the wooden railing overlooking the motorway and the water beyond. The East River was still and glassy, with ferries and other watercraft dotting the surface. They were facing north, so the Manhattan Bridge cut across their view of the Lower East Side. Cameron tried to be unassuming. They both wore black overcoats, and he thought they might continue to blend into the darkness if they didn't speak. Cameron knew his voice tended to give him away. Delilah must have sensed what he was thinking, because she said nothing. They stared out at the river for another few minutes.

In spite of himself, Cameron leaned close to her and said, "Thank you, for tonight."

Delilah looked up, smiled mischievously and said softly, "It's not over yet."

He leaned down and kissed her. She responded, and Cameron could feel the focus shift around them. Lovers kissing at the handrail would attract anyone's attention and, in most circumstances, people would look, smile, and move on. However, they were not just any couple. One public display of affection might as well have been a spotlight on them. Another couple a few paces away started whispering. Footsteps stopped. Cameron heard someone say, "It's them." Then he heard the clicking of camera phones behind them. He turned around and Delilah followed. The murmuring intensified. Cameron saw people debating whether to come over and he was trying to figure out the most diplomatic way of asking them to sod off. He was sure there had to be a way of preserving this night without looking like a prick.

Suddenly, from one of the piers just up the river, came the sharp report of fireworks. Cameron had no idea what sort of event might be taking place or what the celebratory cause was. All he knew is that it startled him. Delilah, however, was more than startled. Much as she had on New Year's Eve just after they met, she reacted as though someone struck her. She didn't even turn to find out for sure what the noise was. Dropping to her knees, she pulled into a ball, putting her hands over her ears.

Cameron knelt down beside her and said, "It's just fireworks. Horribly timed fireworks."

It took several minutes before she could stand. When she did, she was trembling so badly Cameron was sure she wouldn't be able to walk.

He whispered, "Do you have your medicine?"

Delilah shook her head. "I didn't think I needed it."

Her answer was a paradox, showing how far she'd come and yet how deep the wounds ran.

Considering his options, Cameron decided to forget discretion. Scooping Delilah up into his arms, he carried her back toward Manhattan. The camera phones continued snapping around them as he made his way back to where Adam agreed to wait with the car. Cameron was infinitely glad they didn't take public transportation. He was also incredibly grateful for Adam, who never asked questions. He simply drove home.

When they were back in their flat, Cameron shed his coat, helped Delilah out of hers, and pulled her to the sofa. He sat her down and brought her medication and some water to her. Then he sat and wrapped his arms around her, holding her close.

She explained, "I thought I was past things like that. It's been a long time since I've panicked outright…"

Softly, Cameron said, "It's like you said, some things don't go away."

Delilah laughed dryly. "Maybe, but I'm really trying not to be crazy, for you."

"You don't have to be different for me."

She returned, "But *you* are different for me."

"How so?"

She laughed. "Think of your last relationship, or even your last date, before me. What would you have done if she lost her shit on the Brooklyn Bridge?"

Cameron thought about it and confessed, "I probably would have seen her home, then run away."

More seriously, she asked, "What did you do when I panicked in the pub in Chatfield?"

He admitted, "I ran."

Delilah pulled closer, looked him in the eyes, and said, "Don't you see? You are not that man anymore. You are different."

He understood.

Ten days later, Cameron flew out to Hollywood to spend three weeks filming *Fyrelords*. Subtitled *The New City,* this film focused on the next generation's struggle to overthrow the last remaining dystopian settlement on a futuristic planet Earth. As requested, Cameron was staying in a luxury hotel. If he was going to be away from Delilah, at least it would be a comfortable trip. His one remaining concern was having to see Naomi again. Naomi Ruiz-Sosa played Elianna, Cyrus Whitkey's love interest in the original trilogy. She and Cameron fell for each other during principal photography for the first film and slept together on and off. Naomi believed it was exclusive, but their time together was constantly overshadowed by rumor of his infidelity. Just after the premiere of the final film, she caught him with another actress, and he was forced to admit the rumors were true. As with Marianne, the breakup was all over the tabloids. Given their history, Cameron was concerned about their ability to work together. Charlie promised that the director would be sensitive to their relationship, but he wasn't sure it was going to help.

While he read over his script on set the first day, Naomi arrived. Glancing up, he saw her from across the massive studio. When she got closer, he noticed she had changed little. Naomi was stunning, with thick, jet black hair and skin like smooth toffee. Cameron remembered being smitten by her exotic beauty. On-screen, her voice dripped with sexuality, and she would occasionally launch into streams of Spanish. He felt suddenly guilty that he thought of her as "exotic" but couldn't remember where she was originally from. He also considered, for the first time, whether it was fair that she was having to return to a role that typecast her as a voluptuous, Latin American heroine with a stereotypical, fiery personality, but who needed a man to save her. Pushing the questions to the back of his mind, he smiled when she approached.

Standing in front of him, Naomi flicked her hair back and fixed him with her dark eyes. Eventually, she asked, "Can we go somewhere and talk?"

Cameron felt sudden dread, but he nodded. Checking his watch, he saw they had some time. Standing, he led the way out of the main studio and down the hall to an empty meeting room. Inside, they faced off. He waited for her to start berating him.

Instead, she looked him over carefully and said, "I wanted to let you know, I'm not angry. The past is the past, and I'm ready to make this film with you."

He stared at her, dumbfounded.

Smiling, she went on, "We're adults, Cameron. Things happened. We never would have lasted, long-term. I'm happy. You're obviously happy. Let's just make a good movie."

Cameron still wasn't sure what to say.

Naomi added, "I saw the pictures of you online, carrying your wife off the Brooklyn Bridge. Very heroic."

"They're online?" It was all he could think to say.

"Yep," she replied. "*Studio Zone.*"

"Well, I could use a little good publicity at this point."

Naomi tipped her head. "Yeah, you could. Marianne is angry. If you're happy, I think she feels like she's getting screwed all over again."

Surprised, Cameron asked, "Do you know each other?"

Naomi explained, "We did a movie together some years back. It wasn't great. I think it was the last thing she did on-screen. Then she started directing and eventually producing."

Cameron took a deep breath. "I'm sorry for what happened between you and me. My actions were…inexcusable. It's good of you to let it go. I appreciate it."

She smiled. "We're playing lovers. And we both know how claustrophobic filmmaking is. We'll be around each other day and night. I even think we're in the same hotel. I thought it would be best if we're not ready to kill one another."

Humbly impressed with everything she was saying, Cameron replied, "I absolutely agree."

Like responsible adults, they shook on it for solidarity.

With things settled between him and Naomi, the three weeks went by quickly for Cameron. He worked long days and spent nights catching up with Robert Chesney, a fellow Brit. Like Cameron, he was tall and could fill a theater with his voice, but Robert had sandy gray hair, blue eyes, and a contagious smile. They were quick to become friends more than ten years ago, and now they picked up much where they left off. One afternoon, during their lunch break, Cameron approached Robert in his dressing room to ask if he wanted to go for drinks later. Robert was deep in thought over a sheaf of papers in front of him.

When he recognized that Cameron was in the doorway, he said, "Sorry mate. I'm a bit preoccupied by this right now."

Cameron's expression was curious.

Dropping his pen, Robert explained, "I'm editing a script. Friend of mine's niece wants to be a playwright."

Cameron wasn't sure what to say, because it seemed so far beneath someone of Robert's caliber. All he could say was, "When do you have time for all this? You've done as many films as I have since we wrapped *Fyrelords*, but you've done as many plays as well. You talk about going to see everything at The National. You give notes or assistance to everyone who asks you, and since we've been here, I've witnessed you *personally* responding to a letter from a drama school student in London. How is there time?"

"I make time," Robert returned.

Cameron was at a loss for words.

Robert went on, "I like to say, no one ever became famous unless someone gave them a chance." He looked thoughtful. "One of the greatest things you can do is give someone an opportunity. Fame is fleeting. Legacy lives on."

Cameron stood there, suddenly feeling inadequate as an actor, as a friend, and as a human being in general.

That night, instead of going out, Cameron called Delilah via video chat. He felt homesick, but more for her than for Manhattan or his flat. He listened as she filled him in on how her fall choreography was coming along. Then she launched into an animated story about an after-school class she was teaching at a community center uptown. Where his days were filled with running from imaginary enemies that would be digitally added later, hers were filled with classes and meetings. Just before he left for California, she had joined the board of Katie Brooks' nonprofit company, and she was now actively helping to collect and organize hundreds more nine-eleven stories like her own.

With light in her eyes, she said, "I met someone, working on the website, who wants me to give another speech. It's at an event for first responders and others affected physically by that day."

"Wonderful," Cameron replied softly. "Are you going to dance there, as well?"

She shook her head, and he saw her hesitate. "No. It's probably just the cold weather, but...I can't right now."

Even through a computer screen, he could see she was upset. But she changed the subject abruptly, so Cameron let it go. He knew that if Delilah wanted to talk, she eventually would. He listened to her describe the routine she was working on for her youngest students. Watching her across the miles between them, he took stock of the differences in her. He realized she had started taming her hair into waves more often than not. It also looked like she had cut off a few inches since he left. She looked lovely, as usual, but Cameron realized she was no longer the messy woman in knitted hats and old sweaters whom he met two years ago. Somewhere along the way, she left her sister's wardrobe behind. She no longer needed to see Anna in the mirror. She was Delilah again.

A week later, filming for *The New City* concluded. Cameron returned to his hotel room late that evening and took a long shower. Tomorrow, he had a leisure day, then he would fly back to New York on Monday, the twenty-ninth of October. He was more than ready to see his wife again, but he was also pleased with this trip. It had been a long time since he had such a pleasant filming experience. He was thrilled to have reconnected with Robert, and he and Naomi were, if not friends, at least colleagues again. Cameron was proud of his work and grateful for the chance to make amends.

After his shower, he pulled on his standard pajamas. Just then, there was a knock at the hotel room door. When Cameron opened it, he found himself staring at Naomi. Her dark hair was piled on top of her head, and she was dressed in one of the hotel's plush bathrobes and her own expensive flip flops. She looked like she had been at the pool.

With an apologetic smile, she said, "I'm sorry to bother you. I was down at the spa and people recognized me. Now they're loitering around my room. Could I come in until security takes care of it?"

Cameron smiled compassionately. He was not a woman, but he was a celebrity, so he understood her concern.

"Certainly," he replied, opening the door to let her in.

Looking around, she said, "This looks exactly like my room."

Cameron chuckled. "I think that's the idea, with hotels."

Naomi smiled in return. She looked around again and crossed to the French doors leading out to the balcony. He followed her outside.

Leaning on the iron railing, she said, "You have a better view."

Standing next to her, he looked down into the courtyard and shrugged.

Silence stretched. Then she stated, "This has gone well, yes?"

He replied, "Yes, it has. Thank you again for your willingness to leave the past in the past."

She gave him a long look. "Well, that was one of the things I hoped to accomplish…to even things out between us."

Cameron thought her response was odd, but he shook off the feeling. Naomi stepped back from the railing and, in one motion, untied her thick bathrobe and dropped it to the floor. Underneath, she was not wearing a bathing suit as he anticipated. Instead, she wore only black, lace knickers. As he stood there in shock, she stepped in and kissed him full on the mouth. Her hands went around his neck and her breasts pressed against him.

As quickly as he realized what was happening, he stepped back. Naomi looked him over.

Standing in front of him mostly naked, she purred, "Come on Cameron. No one's here. We've been on this set long enough for you to remember how good we were together." She stepped closer and whispered next to his ear, "Remember that night in Cabo?"

He did remember.

She put her hands on his hips and whispered, "No one will know."

Cameron stepped back again and said with great intention, "You need to go."

She stared at him as though she hadn't understood.

"I mean it, Naomi." He repeated, "You have to leave."

She stood there as if she never considered a scenario where he would reject her. Finally, she picked up her bathrobe and pulled it back on in a huff. Crossing back through the room to the door, she stopped with her hand on the door handle and threw back with a smirk, "Your loss. I've got what I need. You could've at least taken me to bed. Either way, you're fucked."

With that, she exited, letting the door slam behind her.

It took Cameron a moment to understand what she said. He turned around and looked back through the open doors leading to the balcony. Crossing the room, he walked back outside and scanned the hotel courtyard and all the other balconies surrounding it. He saw no one, but he was sure there was someone out there with a telephoto lens. Someone had photos of him and Naomi kissing, with her in only black lace knickers.

Turning around, Cameron went back into his room and slammed the French doors. He pulled the curtains closed and silently cursed fame. He had been caught a lot of times doing a lot of things, but he had never before felt this absolute panic. It took him seconds to remember that Naomi was friends with Marianne and to deduce that this had to be his ex-wife's doing. He knew she was absolutely capable of orchestrating something like this. Dropping onto the sofa, he considered all his options. He was sure those photos would be in the hands of the highest bidder by morning. Cameron thought about all his previous reactions to being caught. He could deny it. He could ignore it. He could run away somewhere and let it blow over. Then he remembered he hadn't actually done anything wrong. He picked up the phone and rang Delilah.

It was two in the morning on the east coast, but she answered on the fourth ring. Groggy, she asked, "Cameron?"

"Yes," he replied. "I'm sorry to wake you, but this is important."

It only took a few minutes to explain to her what had just transpired.

"Do you believe me?" He asked across the miles between them.

"Yes, I do."

Cameron was shocked at her immediate acceptance of his story.

"What are you going to do?" She asked softly.

Initially, he wanted to get on social media and rip Marianne apart. He wanted to give an interview about all her faults and shortcomings, to play her game against her. However, Delilah's immediate acceptance of his version of the events tempered his anger.

He said, "I don't know. I think I'll decide in the morning."

The line was quiet. Then Delilah returned with, "Cameron? I love you. I trust you. Thank you for telling me."

He swallowed hard and strained to speak over the lump in his throat. "I love you, too," he managed.

The next morning, Cameron rang his sister first thing. When Mara answered, drowsy from sleeping off her night shift, he stated, "I need Marianne's telephone number."

Taken aback, she replied, "It's lovely to speak with you, too."

With a sigh, Cameron said, "I'm sorry, but this is important. I need to contact her."

There was silence before she asked, "Why?"

Cameron started to explain, but he stopped himself. He was certain she wouldn't give out Marianne's number if she heard the story. Mara would never believe him. So he said, "I want to apologize."

There was no answer again.

"I'm serious, Mara. And I need her telephone number."

She conceded, "All right."

After no less than five attempts to ring her, Marianne answered late that evening. She agreed to meet him the following day in a chic little wine bar in Studio City. At just after 4 p.m., Cameron found her sitting in the corner at a round, bar height table, looking out the row of windows that provided an unbroken view of the pavement outside. She wore a designer pantsuit, and her hair was cut and styled in waves around her face. On the back of her chair, expensive sunglasses were tucked into her Coach bag. He took the tall, awkward chair across from her and wished more than anything that he was flying home to his wife today, as planned, rather than doing this.

Marianne smiled, set her drink on the table between them, and said, "Cameron."

"Marianne."

He shifted in the chair, certain that she had picked this table, in this place, to make him as uncomfortable as possible. They were on display to both the entire room and the people passing outside, and the minimalist furniture offered no place to hide. He also noticed the bar was filling up for happy hour, giving Marianne a room full of witnesses. She sipped white wine, which she used to throw back like water when they were first married.

Marianne drew out the silence, then asked, "What do you want, Cameron?"

Taking another beat, he said, "I came to apologize."

She looked suddenly off balance, and her smirk faltered.

It had taken Cameron the better part of the last two days to decide what to say. Now, he went on, "I need you to know that I understand what I did to you was abhorrent. I've realized it for some time, but I haven't made the effort to say it directly. I am sorry. I should have been with you while you were unwell instead of shagging everyone who looked at me. It was incredibly selfish of me to leave you alone through that and there is no excuse. I was wrong, and I admit that wholly."

Marianne sipped her drink and stared at him, her eyes stormy. Eventually, she asked, "It's only taken you thirty years to come to this revelation?"

With a sigh, Cameron said, "I suppose it has. And for that, I am also sorry."

Marianne simply scoffed.

Taking a breath, he went on, "I also want you to know that I would have supported Andrew. If I had known…"

Marianne worked her jaw, then stated, "You didn't deserve him."

Holding back other things, Cameron agreed. "That is probably true."

Stalemate.

Cameron leaned in. "All that said, I need you to know that what you're doing to Andrew has to stop now. You have shoved our son into the spotlight for no reason other than to spite me and you've done it without any regard for his feelings. You have used him against me long enough, and he deserves better. From both of us."

She started to speak, but his expression stopped her.

"Also, what you tried to do to me with Naomi is unacceptable. It was vindictive and disgusting and I would hope both of us would be better than that by now. I did not sleep with Naomi, no matter what people are going to print and say. I didn't even consider it. I'm assuming you thought I would, but either way you have your photos. And that is what you really wanted, is it not?"

Marianne held his gaze and did not deny it.

Setting his jaw, Cameron continued, "I am not that man anymore. I love Delilah, and I wish it hadn't taken me this long to understand what that means. I am truly sorry for what I did. I wish you happiness and peace, and I wish those things for our son. I hope you can find a way to forgive me. Regardless, this must stop. Don't set me up again. Stop using our son for your vendetta. Let's move on. Because if you keep this up, it's called slander. And, at the risk of sounding very American, that's what lawyers are for."

He gave her a long look. Then, he got up and left the bar without looking back.

Delilah saw the pictures two days later. They were published in *Spotlight!* and shared all over social media. She discreetly bought a copy and studied the grainy images. As Cameron said, the setting was a hotel balcony. Naomi was clearly topless, and her body was bare except for lacy panties. To most people, it would look like she and Cameron were locked in a passionate embrace, but Delilah saw differently. Cameron's arms were by his sides, his fingers tensed in surprise. He looked anything but relaxed. In another shot, where she leaned in toward Cameron as if whispering, his hand was on the balcony rail and he did not look seduced. Or even happy. Delilah threw the magazine away without telling him she saw it.

The premiere for the final *Heir of Taivas* film, *The Reaping Stone*, was held on the twelfth of November. Delilah found herself on the red carpet again, this time at a Hollywood theater, with Cameron by her side. She could sense his tension as the reporters asked carefully worded questions. None of them were bold enough to ask about the photos with Naomi directly, but Delilah knew the rumors were circulating. Even some of the fans looked at both of them with uncertainty.

Delilah held tightly to Cameron's hand and refused to let her smile falter. It was her turn to support him. Once they were settled in the theater, they both immersed themselves in the film. The ending left Delilah in tears as she watched Marcus Eperra die a hero's death. She wept for the character, but also because it was Cameron up there. She was certain that, no matter how long they were together, love scenes and death scenes would not get easier.

When they returned to New York two days later, Delilah threw herself fully back into her work. Her school's Christmas show loomed, and she had two group numbers to finish. The stress of the last month also manifested itself in Cameron. What started as a cold that he blamed on air travel gradually turned into a cough that wouldn't ease. Delilah teased him that she was supposed to be the one coughing, and he laughed and resigned himself to several days in bed. By the end of November, however, he still wasn't well.

On the Tuesday after Thanksgiving, Delilah got an unexpected call at the studio. Taking it in one of the offices, she realized it was Cameron on the other end.

Going on her own intuition, she immediately asked, "What's wrong?"

Sounding less than himself, he answered, "It seems that I have the flu, along with bronchitis and a touch of pneumonia."

Delilah was confused, "You finally went to the doctor?"

"Yes," he admitted. "I'm afraid I had to. I nearly fainted in the car and Adam insisted."

Delilah took a beat. "Do I need to come home?"

"No," came a soft reply. "They're keeping me in hospital."

Delilah felt a blade of fear pierce her.

An hour later, she was asking about him at Mt. Sinai. At first, they wouldn't confirm he was there, and Adam wasn't answering Delilah's calls. After going through several employees, someone found him and brought him down to verify her identity. He rescued her from the lobby and took her up to the eleventh floor. Delilah followed him down the hall and into a room. Looking around, she was surprised. She hadn't spent a lot of time in Manhattan hospitals—her treatments were in Virginia—but she visited a few friends with injuries over the years. She knew most patient rooms were small, often double occupancy. This room, however, was more like a hotel suite. There was a wide window and what looked like mahogany furniture. At the sight of Cameron, however, the room was forgotten. Delilah crossed to the bed, noting he looked tired, perhaps a little disheveled, but otherwise normal. An IV line ran into his left arm. He looked up at her and smiled.

"Hey," she said softly.

"Hello yourself," he returned.

Delilah tried to formulate a question, but there were so many things running through her head, and she knew she wasn't thinking clearly.

When she said nothing, Cameron stated, "This is only for a day or two. I need stronger medication than I can take at home. Pneumonia is apparently sneaky."

"I know," Delilah said softly, remembering.

Sensing her distress, he said, "I'll be fine. Some antibiotics and some rest and all will be well. I've just let it go for too long, that's all."

She tried to look nonchalant.

Gesturing at the surroundings, Cameron teased, "This is where they put the patients whom they don't want disrupting the entire hospital."

Relaxing a little, Delilah replied with sarcasm, "Aw, poor you."

Cameron laughed, and she felt a touch less afraid.

In the wee hours that night, she lay awake, listening to him breathe. She refused to go home, and even Xanax hadn't helped her sleep. Logically, she knew he should be all right. She had been in the hospital herself with pneumonia, and she knew that if it was more serious, he would be in intensive care. He would be on constant oxygen support. Delilah knew plenty about respiratory illness, and that was why she couldn't sleep. She understood better than most how unpredictable it was. She knew she probably shouldn't be here now, risking infection, but she couldn't leave him. More than ever before, she understood that Cameron wasn't young. He was strong and certainly virile, but he was still sixty-three. Delilah thought about her own struggle to breathe and how painfully ironic it would be if respiratory illness took him instead of her. Then she banished the thought. Under the light of a crescent moon, she listened to Cameron's even breathing and felt the frailty of life. The fragile uncertainty was real, tonight.

And so, Delilah did not sleep.

24
When I Have Fears

When I have fears that I may cease to be
before my pen has glean'd my teeming brain,
before high-piled books, in charact'ry,
hold like rich garners the full-ripen'd grain;
When I behold, upon the night's starr'd face,
huge cloudy symbols of a high romance,
And think that I may never live to trace
their shadows, with the magic hand of chance;
And when I feel, fair creature of an hour!
That I shall never look upon thee more,
never have relish in the faery power
of unreflecting love! --then on the shore
of the wide world I stand alone, and think
till Love and Fame to nothingness do sink.

— *"When I Have Fears that I May Cease to Be" by John Keats*

Cameron was discharged two days later, exactly as predicted. Delilah listened as his doctors insisted he rest over the next few weeks. He seemed rather put off by it all, but she understood the seriousness better than he did. Delilah cancelled their plans to travel to London for Christmas and insisted they spend the holiday in their apartment together. Cameron grumbled but made the phone call to tell Mara they would not be coming. Delilah was certain he was more upset about not being able to visit London than not seeing his sister. Things had been especially tense between them this past year, and all of Marianne's interfering hadn't helped matters. Delilah hoped that someday they would make amends and stop allowing Marianne Agrietta to drive a wedge between them. In Delilah's opinion, she wasn't worth it. However, it was not her place to interfere. Delilah cancelled all her extra commitments and focused only on her work and taking care of her husband. She ignored the complaints of her own body and insisted he stay in bed while she made meals and even learned to make his tea. She relied on Adam for errands and such, and he was a silent hero, as always.

By Christmas Eve, Cameron was significantly better. He insisted they go out for at least part of the day, so they went to the park and watched the skaters on Wollman Rink. They stayed just far enough away to maintain anonymity. Delilah marveled at how people could forget from year to year how bad they were at ice skating, insist on trying it, then have such a good time falling. Delilah wasn't willing to do it herself. She might be able to hang by her ankles from the lyra but trying to stay upright on ice was beyond her skill set.

Later, they took a slow walk down to Rockefeller Center to see the Christmas tree, if only because neither one of them felt like finding and decorating their own. Instead, Delilah covered the apartment in Christmas lights that she might or might not get around to taking down. Ever. They mostly avoided recognition by the public until they stopped at the usual coffee shop Delilah frequented in Midtown. There they were recognized by a group of theatergoers visiting from Appleton, Wisconsin. They had been in the city for four days and were afraid to ride the subway. Also, Grandma didn't enjoy the ferry. Delilah knew all of that because they came over and shared that much information before asking for autographs and photos. Graciously, Cameron acquiesced, and Delilah had to admit, they seemed to be decent people.

Christmas Day, Delilah talked with her father on the phone. She wished him a merry Christmas and apologized for not visiting.

"It's all right, Delilah," Stephen insisted. "I won't be alone. I do have friends."

She wasn't exactly sure who he meant, but she was glad he seemed happy enough. Stephen's only request for the holidays was that she try and make it home for New Year's Eve. He explained he was hosting a gathering at his house for some of his fellow faculty members and their families.

Delilah's response was, "A party? You're having a party?"

Stephen expounded, "I'm sure this is going to be far from your definition of a party. It's going to be teachers and their kids. More Kool-Aid and sandwiches than champagne and *hors d'oeuvres*. It was my turn to host."

Delilah laughed heartily. "Of course I'll come. I'd rather not be in the city that night anyway."

Cameron, who was almost back to his usual self after six weeks of coughing, surprised her and agreed to come, as well. Meg invited them to an exclusive party in the city, and Delilah assumed he would want to go. However, he agreed to come home with her instead.

The night of the party, Delilah dressed in a casual, black dress and Cameron wore the deep green shirt from the night they became lovers. Looking him over, she said, "That's cheeky of you."

"Cheeky?" He asked.

She shrugged. "It's a good word. You Brits have much better slang than we do."

"Good to know." He laughed, and they headed out into the backyard of Delilah's house.

The night was unusually warm for the mountains of West Virginia, so they were able to host the party outside. However, "warm" meant barely forty degrees, so Stephen had a friend of his set up a bonfire.

To say no one knew what to think about or say to Cameron was an understatement. Delilah watched a couple of female teachers start preening and forget their husbands were yards away. She saw others glance around nervously in whispered conversation. After making the rounds for polite introductions, they headed back toward the house to take refuge in the kitchen, using Delilah's complaining lungs as an excuse. Just as they crossed the patio, which was strung with colorful lanterns that illuminated a table of sandwiches and hot cider, Stephen intercepted them. A step behind him stood a slender woman with kind eyes and straight, gray-blonde hair that brushed her shoulders.

Smiling, Stephen said, "Delilah, I would like for you to meet Natalie."

Delilah looked them over. Cameron hung back, hands in his pockets. Extending her hand, Delilah offered warmly, "It's nice to meet you."

They shook hands and Stephen said, "This is my daughter, Delilah, and her husband, Cameron."

Natalie looked past Delilah to Cameron. She smiled and extended her hand to him as well. He stepped forward and shook her hand, and she didn't so much as blink when she said, "It's lovely to meet you both."

Delilah looked from her father to Natalie and sensed there was more to be said. Stephen, however, offered nothing more than, "We're both teaching twelfth grade now. Natalie's just down the hall trying to explain Physics to teenagers."

Delilah laughed, and her father let her and Cameron pass.

They stayed in the kitchen most of the night drinking cheap wine and talking about their plans for the spring. When they went to bed, just after midnight, Delilah knew this was not the type of holiday Cameron was used to. He told her stories about the parties in New York and Los Angeles and London that he attended over the years. He was used to rubbing elbows with people who had more money than time to spend it, not being stared at by the staff of Branton County High School. Delilah knew this was a change he was making for her, and change was the theme of the year.

The next morning, just as the sun crested the horizon, Delilah stood in the doorway of her and Anna's bedroom. She lingered there in thought. Then, without a word to her father or her husband, she took a stack of boxes and plastic totes from the guest room closet and set about packing up the room's contents. She left some pictures on the walls and books on the shelves, but she carefully packed everything else away. She separated it into things to keep and things to donate. She had already taken her own clothes months before, but she finally emptied her sister's closet. What she would wear, she kept. What she wouldn't, she packed for charity. She didn't want to erase the fact that they ever occupied this room, but it was time for the space to have new memories. She sat with her sister's violin, still in its worn case, for a long time. Eventually, she decided to put it on the shelf above the clothing rod. Before she returned for her next visit, she vowed to start looking for someone, the right someone, who could use it.

When Delilah finished, she stacked the boxes and took a long, deep breath. She sat on the floor and pulled one small box toward her. It contained all of Anna's journals, as well as her composition cassettes and CDs. She took out a notebook and flipped it open, then another and another. She tried to read her sister's music compositions, then smiled at her inability. There were some journal entries, but Anna had been more about putting her feelings into music. In the middle of one notebook, Delilah read a few stanzas of a song her sister wrote at about seventeen years old. It was around the time they were both making decisions about college. After the lyrics Anna had written:

> *I am so afraid of making the wrong decision. I wish, sometimes, that I could be a little more like Delilah. She doesn't think this hard. She feels something deep inside and she just…goes. She's going to New York for circus training, and she has no worries. The future is wide open, for her. I wish I was less afraid. I want to be me, but I want to be a little more like my fearless sister.*

Delilah read the passage several times before putting the notebook back in the box. She didn't cry, but she felt an ache in her chest. Before she could let it get the best of her, she continued stacking the boxes by the door. Taking a last look around the room, she found one more box far underneath her old bed. Pulling it out, she realized it was full of VHS tapes. Reading the labels, she remembered the video camera her dad used to point at them every holiday, recital, and birthday. It was a Christmas gift the year before the girls turned twelve, and Stephen was so proud of it. Taking the tapes into the living room, Delilah turned on the television and the old VCR and put in the first tape. After a few seconds of fuzzy tracking, the tape began to play.

Cameron, who was in the kitchen making tea, said, "I didn't hear you get up."

Delilah shrugged. "I've been up for a while. I couldn't sleep."

Coming to sit beside her on the sofa, he watched the television as well.

On the screen, a group of students performed in a school play. They looked to be about twelve years old. Delilah danced in a group with her hair pulled on top of her head in a bouncy ponytail and her legs clad in two colors of legwarmers. She smiled widely. When the camera panned to the piano, Delilah saw that Anna was sitting at the old, upright instrument, which dwarfed her. As the upbeat musical piece finished, she began to play. She wore leggings and a black dress, and her hair fell in curls down her back. Unlike Delilah, she never looked at the audience. Her hands moved over the keys as she played, and she sang in a clear, rich soprano. Delilah watched, mesmerized.

After a minute, she said, "Anna wrote that song. It was the first piece she ever wrote and performed herself. The show was terrible, though. I guess that's what happens when you let sixth graders write a musical."

Cameron smiled.

Over the next few hours, Delilah let the tapes play. About forty-five minutes in, Stephen joined them. He didn't say a word or ask a question. He just sat down and watched. The first tapes included Delilah and Anna's mother, Kitty, who was petite like her daughters, but who had dark hair and deep amber eyes. In a video clip of her singing in the kitchen along with her children, Delilah remembered where Anna's musical ability came from. Stephen, when he wasn't behind the camera, looked not only younger but less burdened in these glimpses into their past life. As the clips played, the girls got older, blowing out candles on their birthday cakes and rolling their eyes at their father and his camera. Eventually, Kitty was no longer present, and the videos were mostly of just Delilah and her sister.

Late in the afternoon, Delilah put in the last tape. This one was obviously from several years later, in the late 1990's when Delilah first trained to perform with Cirque. The twins were now adults, and they were in the woods behind the house filming the tree with Delilah's silk. Anna was behind the camera encouraging her sister as she climbed. Delilah, with her hair in a messy knot and wearing worn leggings and a sports bra, climbed the fabric effortlessly. She was quickly some twenty feet in the air. Setting the camera down on something, Anna came around and stood at the base of the silk.

Over-exaggerating the tone of a newscaster, she said, "This is my sister, Delilah MacClare, and she is either going to perform her first ever dive-star, or she's going to kill herself. We're filming it as either a demo tape, or as evidence that she chose to do this stunt willingly." Coming closer to the camera, Anna added, "Dad, if you ever see this, this was her idea."

Stepping back, she looked up to where Delilah was wrapped at the top of the silk. Despite her teasing, Anna's fear was evident. Delilah let go and plunged forward then twisted, spinning downward in the fabric with her legs perfectly split. She stopped just feet from the ground, her back arched and her toes together and pointed. Delilah laughed gleefully and Anna relaxed. Unwrapping herself, Delilah dropped to the ground. Noticing her sister's obvious relief, she walked over and threw an arm around Anna.

With a teasing smile, Delilah looked at her sister and said, "Never be afraid. Never."

Anna rolled her eyes and playfully shoved her sister. Delilah disappeared from the frame and the clip ended.

Reaching forward for the remote control, Delilah turned off the VCR. No one spoke for a long time.

Eventually, Stephen rose from his seat and said, "It's almost supper time. I'm going to make a sandwich."

Delilah said, "I'll join you."

Sometimes, she decided, there just isn't room inside an experience for words.

Cameron excused himself to make a few phone calls. Twenty minutes later, Delilah sat with her father at the familiar round table in the kitchen. They ate in silence for a while.

Delilah eventually explained, "I packed up our room. I know you've never asked me to, and I don't really want to talk about it, but I did it. That's where I found the tapes."

Stephen smiled. "I'm glad we still have them."

Another few minutes passed.

Stephen spoke up again. "I meant to tell you, I finished the books you gave me."

"*Heir of Taivas?* When?" Delilah asked curiously.

"Couple of months ago. I had to intersperse them with Pre-World War II literature, on principle," he teased.

Delilah rolled her eyes. "And?"

He cocked his head, "They…"

"Are not without literary merit?" She finished for him.

Stephen laughed. "It is a beautiful story." As he took the last bite of his sandwich, he asked, "How are things? You know, how is life being married to a movie star?"

Delilah smiled in spite of herself. "It's hard sometimes, because my work is in the city and his is wherever filming takes him. But we knew it would be this way. We knew we wouldn't have a normal life. Neither one of us ever has."

Stephen appeared to struggle before asking, "Does his past ever worry you? I mean, do you…trust him?"

Delilah realized her father must have seen the magazines with the pictures of Cameron and Naomi. Never one to pry, this was his way of voicing his concerns. Delilah wasn't offended, though. She was grateful, because he wasn't tiptoeing around her anymore.

Meeting Stephen's eyes, she said, "I do trust him. Over the past year, he could have cheated on me many times, and he has not. But life is not without risk. You told me that once. I'm willing to take the risk, for him."

Stephen's expression softened. With a slight smile, he said, "I know, but I feel compelled to ask these things. I'm your father, after all."

Taking tiny bites of her sandwich, Delilah said, "I'm glad you feel like you can ask me this stuff again. You know," she teased, "preach at me a little."

Stephen agreed, "Me too. I also don't tell you enough how much I love you. *You*, Lilah. I know you think your sister was your better half, but I've never thought that. Yes, you gave us hell and pushed every button and boundary, but love is not conditional. Not real love. If I've preached at you, it's out of love."

Delilah thought it over. "I did push you. And mom. I know you haven't loved all my choices, but," she struggled, "I've never lost my faith, Dad."

He smiled and his eyes took on a faraway look when he said, "I remember your mother dressing you and Anna in those matching pink dresses on Sunday. I remember your First Communion and your Confirmation…"

Gently, Delilah replied, "All that's still there, Dad. Remember what you used to say? 'Have faith like a mustard seed.' I've just," she struggled, "I've had a lot of mountains to move."

"We both have, you and I."

"Honestly, I've been angry with God, but I'm finding my way back."

"I can understand that," Stephen stated.

Perhaps because of the intimate honesty of the moment, Delilah felt a nagging in the back of her mind. She wrestled with it for a minute before deciding it was time for all the cards to be on the table.

"Dad? There's something I need to tell you."

He looked at her, curious.

Delilah said, "It has bothered me for a long time that you and Preston stopped talking to one another. I know he got married again and that was hard, but you stopped talking long before that. I know how close the two of you were and I hate that you lost that friendship."

Stephen studied his hands. "I wasn't going to force him to talk to me. Everyone deals with things differently."

Delilah went on, "I know, but you have had literally no one through all this. With Mom gone and Preston out of the picture and me nearly losing my mind, I've only just realized how unfair it all was to you."

Smiling in spite of himself, Stephen said, "I do have two sisters, Lilah. And an acceptable number of friends."

"I know, but," she hesitated, "you should have had Preston. The two of you should have been the ones to decide when, or if, to part ways."

Stephen looked at her in confusion.

Drawing up her courage, Delilah said, "It's my fault that he ran away from us. It's my fault, because a year after Anna died, when we were cleaning out the apartment, we slept together."

Stephen stared at her as though the words were foreign.

Plowing ahead, she stated, "We were both such a mess and I know it was about Anna, on both our parts. There was *never* anything going on before that. Preston—he at least had the excuse that she was my twin. He wanted her back so badly he let himself pretend I was her. But for me, my only excuse is that I have used sex as a distraction, as a manipulation, or as revenge for years. And it was wrong. I know it's been a long time, but I thought you should know." She took a deep breath. "You see, Cameron and I both need absolution, it's just that his sins are the ones on the covers of magazines."

When Delilah finished, she watched her father, hoping he wasn't too angry. She hoped he would at least forgive her.

After a minute, Stephen said, "That is something I never would've guessed. Not in my lifetime."

"I'm so sorry," Delilah said softly.

Stephen conceded, "We all make mistakes, Lilah. I think this one is a little too old for me to get angry about."

"Still, I should've told you."

"Maybe..." Stephen looked away. "I suppose that better explains why he wouldn't keep any of the money."

"I think so."

"I always assumed he stopped calling because he felt so guilty about getting out...when she didn't," Stephen added.

"I'm sure there was that, too," Delilah answered softly.

Eventually Stephen said, "Lilah, there's something I haven't told you as well."

Delilah was surprised because he rarely truly opened up to her.

He cleared his throat and went on, "Natalie and I have been dating for some time now."

Delilah had suspected.

Her father went on, "We've known each other for a long time, but we got closer when you went to Chatfield. I was so worried when you left, and she cared. When you went back to London, I asked her on a real date. Then another and another. You were finding yourself again, and we were already such close friends. It was just...easy."

Even having had a suspicion, Delilah wasn't sure what she felt. After some time, she asked, "How serious are you?"

Leaning back in his chair, Stephen said, "We want to get married. Natalie wants to do it next month because, as she says, it won't conflict with anything. She's so practical. I've been trying to find the right way to tell you and over the phone felt wrong."

Delilah let it sink in.

Stephen continued, "I never expected this to happen, but we have similar situations. Natalie has been on her own for some time. Her husband left her with their three kids twenty years ago. We just…make sense together. We laugh. There's less loneliness. I don't think I need to tell you that love can be…unexpected. And ageless."

Delilah thought about all the days she and Cameron spent in the pub talking, laughing, and even arguing. She remembered how unexpected it was to love him, and she did understand. She considered all the other things her father must have hidden all these years, all the grief and loneliness he must've set aside to provide for his children then to walk Delilah through the loss of her sister. His needs, his wants never came first, and she took that for granted.

Searching her father's face, she said, "I think…that February is a lovely month for a wedding."

Stephen's smile lit his whole face.

It was the third of January when Delilah realized her cough was back again. It was right on time, brought on by the winter air that alternated between wet with snow and achingly dry. Her Manhattan doctor worked her in that afternoon, and she was on her way back home when Lexi called with the news that her father passed away. It hit Delilah hard. Even knowing how sick he was, she hadn't expected this so soon, and she didn't think Lexi had, either.

The funeral was four days later. Delilah went without Cameron, because she didn't want her husband to become the focus of the service. Carl DiSalvo was only fifty-seven years old. His cause of death, officially, was "lung cancer with no history of smoking." Pictures taped all over poster boards and displayed in the lobby of the funeral home told his life story. His service to the city of New York was recognized during the memorial, and his effect on the community was evident in those who attended. A book on the small entry table quickly filled with handwritten stories about Carl's impact on those who paid their respects. It was all beautifully done. Still,

Delilah watched Lexi struggle through the whole affair, and all she saw was the senselessness of it. She kept thinking that no one should lose their life by walking into a disaster that didn't have to happen. There were enough terrible things beyond mankind's control.

After the service, Delilah was overcome by all of it. She meant to stay to talk with Lexi, but she found herself unable. She gave her friend a hug, promised to call, then hurried from the funeral home. Over and over, the same thoughts tumbled in Delilah's mind:

They shouldn't have died.

It was so unnecessary.

It was for nothing.

And they're still dying.

Delilah was overwhelmed, and she felt herself falling into a dark place emotionally. Part of her wanted complete distraction and another part wanted to dwell on all of it until she felt stable again. Her mind was cluttered as she took the E train from Queens back into Manhattan. Instead of getting off in Midtown, however, she kept riding south until she was in the financial district. She got off at Chambers Street and walked a couple of blocks to the 911 Memorial. She had been only twice since it opened, both times on the anniversary. Most days, it wasn't a place she wanted to visit, but for some reason her wild emotions brought her here today. The only sense she could make of it was that she couldn't think of any other place to chase down her sister's presence. So she crossed the plaza slowly and sat on a simple stone bench just a few paces from the North Pool.

Knowing he would worry, she texted Cameron:

I needed to be with Anna for
a bit. I'll be home soon.

Then she wrapped her winter coat around herself against the January wind and lost herself in thought.

Much later, when the sun had sunk behind the buildings around her and cast the geometric stone walkways of the memorial plaza in long shadows, Delilah felt someone behind her. Turning, she realized it was Cameron wrapped in his usual coat and scarf. Despite the fading light, he wore sunglasses. He sat beside her and said nothing. Delilah slid closer to him and pulled a hat out of her coat pocket. She pulled it down over her head against the deepening chill.

Delilah eventually said, "I don't know why I came. Usually, I avoid this place. There are days when I can't even look this direction. But...I needed to feel like I was near her, and I feel like...there's something of her, something of all of them, here..."

She gestured at the vast site because she couldn't finish the thought. "Like it says in *The Reaping Stone,* 'This is hallowed ground. A blood-soaked rock where thousands lost their lives.'"

Cameron put his arm around her.

After another few minutes, Delilah said, "Sometimes, I really hate this place. And not just because of what happened here, but because of what it could become. I keep imagining people having picnics here, and I hate the idea of people buying merchandise from this place. But I understand the need for funding. I know the Holocaust Museum in Washington sells things, appropriate things. But you would never build a gift shop on top of a mass gravesite, and that is what this is."

She took a moment to look around.

"Parts of this place are beautiful now, but it will always feel wrong. And I don't mean it's the wrong kind of memorial, because there is no *right* kind of memorial. There is nothing that could be built here that would satisfy all of us left behind. Sometimes I think it would be better to have simply left it as a hole in the ground, because there is no garden or parapet or infinity pool beautiful enough to erase my memories. There is no void great enough to represent the loss. There will always be a hole in the skyline. There will always be a hole in...everything. So, some days, I hate this place. But on days like today, this is the closest I can be to Anna, and I need it."

Delilah stopped to wipe away tears that came unexpectedly. Then she dissolved into a coughing fit.

When she got herself back under control, she let her thoughts wander. She voiced them without thinking, "Someday, when I'm gone, I don't want to lie in a grave somewhere. I want to be cast on the wind over the city. Let what's left of me rest here, like Anna."

Cameron stared at her, his eyes troubled with sadness. He said, "I can't think about losing you, Delilah."

She hated that she was upsetting him, and she explained, "I'm sorry for being so morose. It's just...I've had no choice but to think about these things." She waited a minute before asking softly, "What about you?"

He searched her face. "What about me?"

"Where do you want to end up?" She asked.

Cameron looked away, then said, "I have been all over the world. I have chased fame everywhere. When it comes down to it, though, I want to be in Chatfield. Mara thinks I've left it all behind, but I know where I came from. Deep down, I'll always be a boy from Warwickshire."

Delilah looked him over and found she wasn't surprised. Then she asked, "Do you believe in God?"

He took a minute. "It's taken me a long time, but yes, I do."

Looking around, Delilah said, "In my twenties, I rejected the idea of a deity controlling things, controlling life. But now...I don't believe He controls us. I believe God weeps for us."

The heaviness of the conversation stirred up the fear Delilah felt when Cameron was hospitalized. Even though she was now the one coughing, she still felt the frailty.

Turning toward him, she wound her fingers through his and said, "I've been afraid these past few weeks...of losing you. I've even had nightmares..."

Cameron pulled her in and held her close.

"I need you, Cameron Burke." The words were out before Delilah really thought about it.

When he answered, he stated, "I think...we need one another."

The wind was turning bitingly cold and the sun was fading, but Delilah wasn't ready to leave. Instead, she pulled back and said, "Cameron...I haven't danced since last September. I'm doing more choreographing than teaching because I can't do demonstrations anymore. Everything is getting harder...and my doctor wants me on oxygen therapy." The words all tumbled out, the result of her holding them back for so long.

Cameron turned to look at her profile and asked, "What does that mean?"

"It means I'll use a machine and a cannula to breathe oxygen for at least part of every day. The only reason I've made it this long without it is because they caught the disease so early, but it tends to progress...exponentially."

"How do you feel about it?"

"I think...my doctor is right."

Cameron squeezed her hand.

She leaned her head on his shoulder and said, "I just want to get through the March showcase without it, if I can."

Cameron gently twined his fingers in her hair.

"He also thinks," Delilah went on, "that I should consider trying to qualify for a lung transplant."

Delilah could feel the low vibration of his voice when he asked, "And what do you think?"

"It's risky," Delilah answered, "but it would mean...a cure."

Cameron carefully asked, "What else do you think?"

Delilah took a deep breath. "I think," she hesitated, "I'm afraid it won't work."

Still holding her close, Cameron said, "This from someone who can climb thirty feet in the air and just, let go, trusting that fabric will catch her?"

Delilah realized he was trying to encourage her through metaphor, but she could hear the notes of fear in his voice. She reached down deep into herself, trying to find the girl who once blazed through life with fearless abandon. She searched for the woman who *could* simply let go, confident she would be caught.

With new conviction, she looked up into Cameron's eyes and said, "Never be afraid. Never."

Cameron was surprised at how fast the winter passed. However, while Delilah threw herself into her work and her extracurricular causes, Cameron found himself restless. This lack of purpose had been nagging him since he wrapped *Fyrelords* and ended up with pneumonia. Even as he accepted some voice-over work and filmed a couple of guest roles, he wasn't sure what to set his sights on. He was still receiving projects, and he worked daily to read the scripts and consider the offers. Some of them sounded quite lucrative. There was a time when he would've picked the one that combined the best part with the biggest paycheck. The decisions were so easy before.

Before Delilah.

Now, he didn't want to leave her. For the first time in his life, someone else's happiness, someone else's success, mattered more than his own. He wanted to work, but he didn't want to be away from his wife while their marriage was so new. While he wrestled with his purpose, Delilah was settling into hers. In addition to teaching, she was working with Lexi to set up a support group for people with chronic health problems following September 11. Delilah wanted it to offer both online and in-person meetings, but she was having trouble negotiating space. However, Delilah revealed her biggest mission late one night when neither she nor Cameron could fall asleep.

"Anna wanted to open a clinic that paired music therapy with occupational therapy for kids who've been through trauma, and for those on the Asperger/Autism spectrum or with other behavioral disorders. Years ago, she had a friend who was an occupational therapist who agreed to help her. I think dance could be a part of it as well. I would love to make it happen…for her."

Cameron had no doubt that she could make it happen, if she was well. He imagined all the things she could do with a new set of lungs. And he hoped with all that was in him for that future, but he wouldn't push her. The choices were hard enough without him adding unnecessary pressure.

On the first Saturday in February, Delilah went home for her father's wedding to Natalie. Cameron stayed in the city to avoid diverting attention from the couple. He didn't want Stephen's wedding to be as awkward as the New Year's Eve Party. So, Delilah went alone and returned a day later looking quite content with the whole situation.

Her only comment was, "I'm glad for him. He's…writing a new book."

Cameron smiled. "Your father could *actually* write a book."

Delilah laughed. "True. And Natalie is lovely. She's nothing like my mother, which is somehow…good."

Cameron tipped his head in agreement.

"Although the word 'wedding' was a bit of an overstatement," Delilah added. "They basically took vows in the backyard. Then everyone went inside for cake and hot chocolate because it started snowing."

Laughing, Cameron said, "We got married on a roof. And not even a nice roof."

Delilah laughed with him.

As the month wore on, record amounts of snow fell, forcing Manhattan's residents to trudge through puddles of dirty slush. It was the type of winter that made Cameron want to stay inside with a pot of tea until April or May. The weather was also unkind to Delilah's lungs. The Cough, as she called it, would not abate and she was forced to visit her doctor several more times. Cameron also noticed that when she came home after a full day of work, she was so out of breath she had to lie down. She admitted to having to instruct students while sitting down at work. He often found himself bringing her dinner or breakfast in bed, which would feel romantic if he wasn't so worried about her. He wanted her to take her doctor's advice and accept oxygen support. From what she told him, it would help, and it was time. Cameron understood, however, why it scared her. It scared him, too, knowing this silent disease was progressing inside of her. Yet there was some joy in knowing that, based on all Delilah's recent evaluations, she was prequalified for a lung transplant. It was the worst kind of contradiction, because for her to have a chance to be well again, she had to get worse. So, he took care of her and listened to her if she rang him during the day with what seemed like illogical panic from something she called "air hunger." Cameron even learned how to make her coffee.

At the end of March, to celebrate Delilah's birthday and their anniversary, he surprised her with the trip to London they didn't take in December. They boarded a plane mid-morning on Monday, the twenty-fifth, and filled the next few days with theater, pub food, and making love by a roaring fire in Cameron's London flat. They took a quick trip up to Chatfield to see Flora, and even stopped in to see Mara, who was relatively pleasant.

When they arrived back in New York the next Sunday, it was three o'clock local time, but eight in the evening London time. Despite the early hour, they fell into bed and were asleep immediately. The next morning, Delilah left for work at her usual time. Her student showcase was in five days, and Cameron knew enough about live theater to guess how the week would go. As expected, Delilah came home late each night and struggled out of bed each morning. By Friday, she could barely walk upright, and her cough was deeper, wetter. She waved Cameron off when he told her she needed to call her doctor.

"The showcase is tonight," she threw out between coughing fits.

Cameron made her coffee, feeling rather proud of himself for mastering it, and brought it to her.

Taking a sip, she said, "If I'm not better by Monday, I'll call my doctor."

Cameron felt a twist of uncertainty in his gut, but he knew that Delilah knew more about her disease than he did. She managed it for seven years now, so he decided to trust her.

They agreed it would be best for him not to attend the showcase to avoid being a distraction in the small space. Instead, Cameron went out with Meg and her beau Nathan to a Japanese restaurant. They talked shop as Meg geared up to direct her second film. She expressed her apologies that she didn't have a part to offer but gave him two tickets for Sunday to a brand-new play and asked him to bring Delilah.

By Sunday morning, however, it was obvious Delilah was not going anywhere. She spent the whole day before in bed with Cameron waiting on her, and she sounded dreadful.

Trying to smile, she said, "We're going to have to disinfect this place after the winter we've had."

"Do you want me to stay in?" Cameron offered. "Meg won't mind if I cancel."

Delilah shook her head. "No. You can't sit here with me for days on end. I'm old enough to take care of myself. So, go. Go to brunch and see the show."

Cameron laughed lightly then dressed to leave.

As he was heading out of the bedroom, she called after him, "I love you."

He turned back and crossed to the bed to kiss her gently, then echoed, "I love you, too."

Then he left the flat.

When Cameron returned home in the dark that evening, he felt badly for leaving his wife alone. But he hoped that, with him gone, she might have gotten some sleep. It was what he was always told to do when he was unwell. Sleep. Drink Fluids. Don't go to plays.

"Delilah?" He called her name once he was through the door.

She didn't answer and the flat was dark, so he tried not to disturb her. He put his phone on the kitchen counter and turned on a lamp. Crossing to the bedroom, he peeked inside. Delilah was asleep. She had some books lying beside her in the dark. Cameron went to the bed and sat down opposite her, glad she was resting. He watched her for a couple of minutes, then moved her books to his nightstand. Cameron watched her breathe and realized how fast her breaths were coming. Something was wrong. He lifted her t-shirt and saw how her diaphragm pulled in just below her ribs with every breath. Her clavicle was also sucked into deep relief with every inhalation. He touched her and found she was covered in a sheen of cold sweat. Cameron quickly switched on his bedside lamp. She looked ashen in the light. Her lips were close to purple, and her hair was damp.

"Delilah?" He shook her gently.

She flinched but didn't respond.

"Delilah?" He was more forceful.

Her eyes fluttered.

"Delilah!"

Her eyes opened slightly. "Cameron?" She barely whispered.

Just as quickly, she fell back into sleep. Or what he assumed was sleep. In searing panic, he launched himself off the bed and into the kitchen to get his phone. He called downstairs, told the building staff to get him a taxi immediately, and stuffed his phone and his keys in his pocket.

Returning to the bedroom, he wrapped Delilah in the blanket she cast off in her sleep and scooped her into his arms. Like the night on the bridge, he carried her, this time out of the flat and to the elevator. He cursed it all the way down. Emerging into the lobby, Cameron realized how mad he must look as he demanded of one of the doormen, "Where's the taxi?"

Glancing at Delilah, the older gentlemen said, "Just outside, Mr. Burke."

Cameron didn't reply. He rushed through the front door and onto the pavement. Not paying any attention to the other people who might be staring, he put Delilah into the taxi. She came around just enough to whisper his name again. Tucking in beside her, Cameron slammed the door and barked out the name of the first hospital he could think of. He held Delilah close for the entire journey, asking himself why he hadn't called emergency services for help. He cursed his impulsiveness.

"Delilah?" He nudged her again.

She murmured and stirred, reaching to hold his arm.

Cameron told himself that as long as she was responding, it wasn't a true emergency. She just needed medication or some other treatment. He didn't need an ambulance, just a hospital. The driver, sensing the urgency of the situation, drove quickly and without comment. He said nothing about recognizing Cameron or Delilah. When they pulled up in front of the Mount Sinai emergency department, he said simply, "I hope all is well."

Cameron paid him quickly and slid from the car. Lifting Delilah out, he rushed through the ER doors. Everyone in the crowded waiting room turned to look at him with recognition and concern on their faces. Cameron ignored them and approached the desk. The gray-haired woman behind the counter stared and her mouth dropped open in shock.

"She needs a doctor. Now," was all Cameron could get out.

Still dumbfounded, the woman said, "If you can just fill out these…"

"No!" Cameron cut her off, not wanting to be rude but reacting in desperation.

A nurse who came from triage, possibly to pick up new charts, stopped when she heard Cameron's response. She looked at him, and her face registered shock as well. However, her attention quickly shifted from Cameron to the woman in his arms. She came around the desk in quick strides.

Pulling the blanket back, she took one long look at Delilah and said, "Come with me. Now."

As he followed her, Cameron realized almost everyone in the lobby was either staring or aiming their phones at him. He didn't care. He followed the nurse with curly black hair down a hallway and into the bowels of the ER. Throwing back a curtain, she called out instructions to a couple of other nurses and motioned for him to lay Delilah on the gurney behind the curtain. Cameron caught a glimpse of coherence as Delilah's eyes fluttered open. She tried to touch his face, but he was forced to back away. An alarming number of staff descended on the room. They stripped the blanket away and began taking vitals and a host of other measures that Cameron didn't completely understand. In minutes, Delilah was hooked up to beeping machines and all sorts of terminology was being thrown around.

In the midst of it all, one of the doctors turned around and asked, "Did she not come in by transport?"

Another person replied, "No. He brought her."

Cameron watched the young doctor turn and start to chastise him. When he realized Cameron Burke was standing in front of him, he froze. The doctor said nothing and went back to his work. Feeling panic rise up so strong it made him nauseous, Cameron slowly backed out of the room. Just outside the curtained entryway, he leaned against the wall and closed his eyes. He tried to compose himself, to stop the pounding behind his eyes and slow his breathing. After another couple of minutes, he felt a hand on his arm. Cameron opened his eyes to see the nurse with curly black hair looking at him with compassion.

"Come with me," she said gently.

He obeyed, having temporarily lost the ability to argue. They walked down the hall and around the corner to a tiny room. Once inside, she shut the door. Cameron sat down nervously in one of the chairs.

Sitting across from him, the woman said, "I'm Michelle and I'm one of the ER nurses. Normally, we would ask you to remain in the waiting room until we finish assessing and stabilizing the patient, but I assume you would prefer some privacy?"

Cameron gave a weary smile.

"I just have a few questions," she said softly.

He nodded.

"Her name?"

"Delilah MacClare."

"Age?"

"Forty-two."

"Her doctor or doctors?"

"I believe...Doctor Fleischer."

"Significant medical history?"

Cameron hesitated. He had no idea how to answer. He simply said, "Pulmonary Fibrosis."

He saw the shift in her expression. His stomach twisted painfully. She didn't ask anything else.

Standing up, the nurse said, "That's enough for now. We can get more later. I'll be back as soon as she's settled. Let me know if you need anything, Mr. Burke."

Cameron tried to smile.

Some indefinite amount of time later, he was led back to the curtained room with Delilah. A doctor greeted him and used a lot of medical words, but all Cameron heard was that they were admitting her and that her oxygen levels were dangerously low. The nurse with the curly hair stayed behind after the doctor left.

Sensing Cameron's confusion, she explained again, "She has pneumonia. In both lungs."

He looked at his wife.

Gently she added, "She's very sick, Mr. Burke."

Rubbing his eyes, Cameron said, "Just this morning, she was..."

He couldn't finish.

Sensing what he was trying to say, the nurse stated, "These things can happen quickly."

Looking into her eyes, Cameron asked, "What was your name again?"

"Michelle."

Trying again to smile, he said, "Thank you, Michelle, for your honesty."

Holding his gaze, she said, "We'll be moving her to the ICU soon."

Cameron felt his chest tighten. Michelle left him, and he pulled the one chair over to the gurney-bed. Sitting down, he looked at Delilah. Her face was covered by an oxygen mask and an IV ran into her left arm. Her breathing was still fast and labored, but better than before. They cut her clothes away and dressed her in a loose hospital gown. Cameron took her hand and was glad to feel her gently squeeze in return. She turned her head and opened her eyes just enough to see him. He caught the ghost of a smile on her lips before she closed them again. Still holding her hand, Cameron leaned his head forward, resting it on his forearm, and prayed.

25
Quiet

Only stay quiet while my mind remembers
the beauty of fire from the beauty of embers.

—From *"On Growing Old"* by John Masefield

Delilah died on a Sunday.

It was the twenty-first of April. Cameron would always remember the day and the date. More specifically, however, he would recall the hazy sun as it broke the dawn. It filtered through the curtains and bathed her hospital room in buttery light as he held her hand. The room was quiet, as though all sound had been vacuumed from the space. Cameron sensed that somewhere beyond the glass doors, life continued, but in this room, all was still. The light gave the room a dreamlike quality that made the space feel surreal. It had only been two weeks since he rushed Delilah into the emergency room. One week ago, he discussed her prognosis with her doctor:

Dr. Fleischer explained, "Pneumonia is an exhausting illness, Mr. Burke. And in someone with damaged lungs, it's debilitating. We have to kill the infection, then help her lungs get strong enough to push out the fluid. The type of pulmonary strain she's under stresses her heart, which can lead to cardiac arrest. Being unable to move enough oxygen can also lead to confusion and dementia-like symptoms. These are the problems we face immediately."

Feeling overwhelmed, Cameron asked, "But the medications, the treatment, is working? She will pull through this?"

Dr. Fleischer went on, "Delilah is young, comparatively, as far as lung disease goes, and she is strong. It's a miracle she's made it this long without more aid or intervention. It's a testament to how healthy her lungs were before they were injured, and it gives me great hope for her recovery. But, as expected, things have gotten notably worse over the past year. I do believe that, after this, she will require oxygen support. Most likely all the time. She'll also need rehabilitation and it will be some time before she can find a new normal. And she will be actively awaiting a lung transplant."

Four days ago, on Wednesday, Cameron sat beside her and pushed her tangled hair from her face. Trying to find something familiar in this sterile place and to hear her voice, he asked, "What are we, Delilah?"

With great effort, she pulled the oxygen mask away, licked her dry lips and said, "We *are*, for now. We belong together. And, we are."

It was the last thing she said to him.

Late that night, Cameron ran home to take a quick shower. While he was gone, Delilah's fever spiked and her lungs struggled against the infection. In order to keep her oxygen levels high enough, her doctors needed to put her on a ventilator. Stephen rang with the news and by the time Cameron returned, she was intubated.

He would never forget the moment when he understood he would lose her. Delilah's doctor and his team came in shortly before midnight on Saturday. They used words like "blood gases," "respiratory acidosis," and "septic," but he barely heard them. He was looking at Michelle instead. She stopped by after her shift in the ER, something she had done several times over the past two weeks, and Cameron watched her body language as she listened to the doctor. He saw the shift in her shoulders and the way she glanced away, as though she couldn't look at him. Cameron saw it in Stephen's reaction as well, in the way he dropped his head in defeat.

When the doctors left the room, Michelle said more simply than they could, "No matter how much oxygen we give her, there just isn't enough healthy lung tissue left to absorb it. And she's too sick for an emergency transplant."

A few hours later, the doctors laid out the choices. Stephen wiped away tears as he sat across from Cameron and they were told there was nothing more the doctors could do. They could either wait for a "cardiac event" to take her or remove the ventilation and make her comfortable. Cameron scoffed internally at the use of the words "cardiac event" and "comfortable." Those words were only used to soften the blow. None of this was comfortable. Cameron glanced at Stephen, who looked ready to break down. Asking for some time to think, they sat there together in silence for hours. Delilah had been unresponsive for three days by then, her body paralyzed by drugs to keep her from fighting the breathing tube. There was no flicker of recognition in her face for her husband or her father.

In the wee hours of Sunday morning, Stephen said, "This is no life, Cameron. This," he indicated all the machines, "is for us. And I can't watch her struggle anymore."

The decision was made.

Cameron learned something during Delilah's last hour. Death is not like it's portrayed in films. There was no sorrowful soundtrack, no beeping or whining of monitors. No flatlining. The nurses removed the ventilator and the tubes from her face. They gave her doses of several medications and they turned off all the machines. It took about forty minutes to do it all. When they finished, Delilah's breathing was almost imperceptible. Cameron sat on one side of the bed, her father on the other. Everything seemed to move in slow motion.

Twenty minutes later, she was gone.

Cameron left the room and gave Stephen some time alone with his daughter. Stephen eventually came out and they traded places. Now, Cameron just looked at her. In the morning light, he tried to memorize Delilah.

He looked at her hair, hastily braided by the nurses, and remembered:

Have you always had all that hair?

Cameron studied the now familiar scar circumscribing her right arm.

It took thirty stitches to close it.

He traced her fingers, remembering how she raked them through his hair after he let the silver grow in.

This is nice. It suits you.

Because I'm an old man?

Because it's you. I just need you. I need you, Cameron Burke.

"I need you, Delilah," Cameron said into the quiet.

But she was gone.

Over the next few hours, Cameron was forced to fill out innumerable forms, as though he was completing a bank transaction. It was ludicrous to him how people could know what just happened in his life and yet be so worried about paperwork. Stephen looked as though he wanted to help, and Cameron thought Delilah's father would probably be better at it, but the task fell to Cameron. He was her husband, for better or worse, in sickness and in health. After some indefinite amount of time, someone brought a plastic bag into the tiny consultation room where Cameron was now sitting and handed it to him. The girl looked intimidated, and he couldn't think of a less appropriate time for someone to acknowledge his fame. After she had gone, he opened the bag.

It was Delilah's belongings: The clothes they cut off her in the ER. Her shoes. The blanket he wrapped her in. And in a small plastic bag, her wedding ring.

Cameron couldn't look at any of it. After a cursory glance, he took the bag, made his way out of the ICU and down to the lobby. He backtracked through the corridors, deciding to use the pediatric unit as his exit after seeing photographers camped outside. They had been hungry for photos for the past two weeks, all the while printing wildly speculative snippets about Delilah suffering from a drug overdose. Once they managed to pull their heads out of their arses and remember that she had a debilitating lung disease, their guesses got closer to the truth. Still, Cameron wished them gone more than he ever had before. Sometimes, even the truth could wait to be printed.

Once out of the hospital, he pulled up the hood of his pullover and put on his darkest sunglasses. Hailing a cab, he rode silently home, and the driver was mercifully silent. He left a hefty tip, hoping it would imply discretion, and made his way mindlessly up to his flat. He stood for a long time inside the door. Delilah seemed to hang in the air. Crossing to the sofa, he dropped onto it, putting the bag with her things on the coffee table. He stared at the bag. He assumed there were arrangements to make, that he should talk with Stephen about it, but his mind wasn't ready to process anything, yet. At some point, Cameron crossed to the kitchen and opened the drinks cabinet. Reaching behind the wine, he pulled out a bottle of Blue Label Scotch and a glass tumbler and returned to the sofa. He poured himself a decent portion and drained the glass. Then he sat there, existing in the numbness that comes before indescribable pain.

———————————

On Sunday, the fifth of May, Cameron stood in a field just down the hill from Delilah's home in Branton. The sun was bright, but not yet hot, and the grass was cut through with wildflowers in bright purple and yellow. It was a beautiful place, and he could understand why Stephen chose to have his wife buried here. Kitty MacClare's gravestone was just to the east of a grove of pine and spruce trees, so that the headstone refracted the morning light. The nearly thirty-year-old grave was covered with a thick down of grass. Fresh flowers decorated the headstone, and next to it were two newly excavated plots, like dark puncture wounds in the damp, spring earth.

Looking around, Cameron realized he never asked how much land Stephen owned. It must be a considerable amount if this open field and the wooded area stretching behind the house was any indication. He tried to do math in his head but quickly gave up. He straightened his tie and adjusted his sunglasses. Cameron focused on any detail, any mundane observation, other than the reason he was here.

Stephen wanted to have a funeral service for both of his daughters. He told Cameron, before he left New York, that he felt it was time to memorialize Anna. He admitted to having wanted a service for years, but not doing it because Delilah refused to have any sort of grave without something to bury. Cameron felt that, soon, she would have changed her mind. She would have been ready. Now, the gravesite would be for her, as well. Stephen also expressed that he wanted his daughters buried next to his wife. He wanted them together, and Cameron wasn't one to argue with a man who lost his wife and two children. He did, however, mention Delilah's desire to be where her sister physically was. With great difficulty, Stephen concurred that Delilah had mentioned, on numerous occasions, that she wanted to be cremated.

"She wanted to be dust, like her sister," Stephen explained. "It was horrific to hear, at the time…"

Cameron understood. It was still horrific. All of it was. But it was what she wanted, and so they decided to honor it. Stephen took care of the details. Cameron simply signed forms, because he couldn't even ask questions without fighting the urge to vomit. He had never known what it was like to feel this gutted, this empty. He felt paralyzed. Stephen, however, had walked this road before. He at least knew what to do.

Someone snapped photos of Cameron leaving the funeral home in Manhattan after he picked up Delilah's ashes. They were promptly posted all over the internet. In them, Cameron saw a shell of himself, pale and unkempt. It was voyeurism, he thought, to spy on someone's sorrow like that. After those photos were posted, the details of the funeral service were kept private. Cameron told Mara and Flora, who both insisted on coming despite the cost. They put aside their differences and traveled together. He also extended an invitation to Libby and Lexi. Meg offered to come, but he declined, explaining that more celebrities and more attention was not what they needed. Stephen made sure that only his family and close friends were invited, asking all of them for discretion.

Now, looking around the open field, Cameron took inventory of who arrived. Mara and Flora were standing under a sprawling oak, trying to make small talk. Stephen's sisters, Polly and Margaret as they were introduced, stood with him, talking softly. Natalie stood next to Stephen, holding his hand. Cameron was also quickly introduced to Delilah's cousins—four young men somewhere between thirty and forty, and Mandy, who looked just enough like Delilah to make it impossible for Cameron to speak to her. Lexi wore a flowing, black sundress, her tattoos standing out in the bright sun. She stood next to Libby in silence. There was also a petite, brown-haired woman with a cropped bob and amber colored eyes. Coming over, Stephen introduced her as another cousin, Hayleigh.

"She's the only person," Stephen explained after she walked away, "from my late wife's side of the family who responded to my calls."

Cameron watched her walk away. "Good for her," he added.

Small talk was the game of the day.

Children wandered about, as well. Cameron assumed they belonged to the cousins. There were wives and husbands he had never met. He tried to be congenial, knowing the circumstances didn't erase their natural curiosity about him. He knew some of them were bound to wonder why they weren't invited to his and Delilah's wedding. Cameron wasn't interested in explaining.

Finally, Jenna arrived with Jason and their children behind her. She wore a dark dress and large, dark glasses. The kids were bigger—nearly two years older than when Cameron first met them. He suddenly remembered Delilah's face as she watched Isaac question him. He would have tolerated an infinite number of *Heir of Taivas* questions from a twelve-year-old for her. Now, Jenna glanced at Cameron, and he understood that neither one of them was ready to try to talk. Just as they sat down in the spindly white chairs Stephen rented for the occasion, another young man arrived. He took a seat in the back, and Cameron glanced at him. He had short, sandy-brown hair and wore a well-tailored suit. Cameron couldn't place him, but he looked familiar. Shaking off the questions, Cameron turned his attention to the service.

Stephen's wife, Kitty, came from a staunchly Catholic family. He explained her faith to Cameron one evening over dinner at some point. Delilah confirmed the story, remembering her mother's faith with fondness. Stephen regularly attended mass with her until her passing, then found his own spiritual home in the small Methodist church on the edge of Branton. Now, the pastor of that church was eulogizing his daughters. Cameron didn't know the pastor's name, but he spoke well. He stirred memories of Sunday services from Cameron's childhood, when he and Mara sang hymns alongside their parents. It reminded him of the value of faith and prayer. It made him think about eternity and his place in it.

Eventually, the time came for those present to share something about the twins, if they wished. Cameron listened as Stephen talked, through tears, about his children. He was shaken with the unfairness of it all. No man should have to lose so much, but Stephen was eloquent even in grief. Years immersed in literature and lecturing to students made him so. He told stories both funny and sad. He shared from his heart, and the attendees reached for tissues. A few others shared memories as well. To Cameron's surprise, Flora got up and told a couple of stories about watching Cameron and Delilah face off in the pub. The small crowd laughed through tears, because this was a part of Delilah's life they had never known.

Cameron knew they expected him to speak, and he considered a few things he might say. When it came down to it, however, he couldn't do it. He couldn't think of anything he was willing to share with these people he didn't really know. He didn't want to seem aloof or distant, but any real thing he could share about his wife was stuck beneath the painful lump in his throat. He also didn't want them analyzing his performance, and even the best of people would. To most of them, he was still an actor they watched on-screen, and if he had lines to read, he might have been able to give a passable performance. There was no such script, however. Real emotion muted him. So, he remained silent and hoped that Stephen or Jenna could help everyone else understand why.

Once the service concluded, some people from the local funeral home helped to inter the small, beautifully crafted urn vaults Stephen had chosen. Delilah's contained a portion of her cremated remains. Anna's contained a collection of items Stephen chose. Cameron didn't ask for specifics, not wanting to pry. Now, he focused on making it through the interment. It was so ludicrous that this was happening, that he was burying the woman he loved, that he moved on autopilot. He had to participate. This was necessary, but if he thought too hard or looked too closely at the gravesites, he would break.

Later, while the adults ate tiny sandwiches and the youngest children ran through the field, oblivious to death, Stephen came to stand beside Cameron.

He said, "Thank you, for allowing this. I know your life with her was everywhere but here, but…"

"Stephen," Cameron cut him off, "you're her father. You were her father long before I married her, and this was her home."

"I know," Stephen sighed, "but you could've said no. The husband has the right. And I know that part of her should be in the city, like she wanted. That's where Anna was, for her. But this is where all my memories are. I need to be able to sit with all of them sometimes, you know?"

Cameron stated, "You don't have to explain. And truthfully, I think here is where I first knew I loved her. I thought I was crazy for driving all the way out here, but when she came out of the house that day, I knew…"

Stephen smiled slightly. "I appreciate that. You could've shared that, earlier."

Cameron shook his head. "Not in front of strangers." Changing the subject, he asked, "Who is the young man in the expensive suit?"

Stephen looked across the expansive property to where the person in question spoke with Jenna.

"That's Preston," Stephen stated.

As if sensing their eyes on him, Preston turned. He waved to Stephen and made his way over. Up close, Cameron realized why he looked familiar. He was the boy from Delilah's photo albums. Cameron remembered the snapshots of Anna with her boyfriend-then-husband. In the photos he had long, dirty blonde hair and a few visible tattoos. There was also usually a guitar across his chest. That was clearly another lifetime for Preston. This man looked every bit like he had been groomed by Wall Street.

Giving Stephen a brief hug, Preston said, "Thank you for inviting me."

"Of course," Stephen returned. "Preston, this is Cameron Burke. Cameron…Preston Spratt."

As they shook hands, Preston smiled. "Cameron Burke. I always told Delilah it would take someone incredible to settle her down."

Cameron decided to take that as a compliment.

Turning back to Stephen, Preston said, "I really am glad you called. I always hated the way things went, how we lost touch…"

Cameron saw Stephen flinch, and he wondered if Stephen knew what happened between Preston and Delilah. He also realized that he understood better what they had done. Cameron wasn't sure he would be able to maintain any sort of objective, rational behavior if he was confronted with Delilah's twin right now.

Stephen said, "What matters is that you're here now, and I appreciate it."

Turning to Cameron, Preston said, "I wanted to say, I only realized a few months ago that I work with your son, Andrew. Different departments. It's a large firm, but I see him in passing. Seems like a great guy."

Cameron stared at him, deciding that Preston couldn't possibly know the whole story about Andrew. Otherwise, he wouldn't have spoken so freely.

Nodding, Cameron decided to use his most neutral response, which was, "It's a small world."

"I suppose it is," Preston agreed.

Not wanting to explore that vein of conversation further, Cameron decided to excuse himself and let the pair catch up.

Two hours later, when almost everyone had gone, he sat in the kitchen drinking horrible tea and staring at another, smaller urn. It was made of mosaic glass, with hues of burnt sienna, ruby, and dark honey. This urn was the only detail Cameron had taken care of. He chose it because it reminded him of Delilah's hair. Inside was a portion of her ashes. Part of her would stay in Branton, with her father, and the rest would go to New York to be with her sister. And it was up to Cameron to do it. That was the terrible mission with which he was charged. He had to find a way to cast her ashes over the city where her sister died, and the idea of it wrenched his guts.

These are the things, he realized, *that life can never prepare us for.*

Standing up, Cameron crossed to the window. He looked outside and saw Stephen talking with Jenna and Jason. Natalie listened with her arm around Stephen, her eyes full of compassion. They all looked bleary-eyed and worn. Beyond them, however, the children played. Cameron hadn't noticed before, but one of Natalie's grown sons had come with her. He had two small children of his own who were running in the twilight with Jenna's children. Looking at them, Cameron felt that Delilah would be pleased. They weren't Anna's children playing in the garden, but Stephen had found what she wanted for him. He would not be alone. Natalie had grandchildren, so there would be babies in his arms during holidays. Jenna would visit as well, because they would have this place under the pine trees to remember Delilah. They would carry on together, and Cameron was glad for it. For himself, however, he saw nothing in front of him but the urn. Turning around, he stared at it again on the table. He was still staring at it when the others came inside.

Cameron stayed for dinner, because it was the polite thing to do. He thanked Stephen again for all he had done. He hugged Jenna and promised to keep in touch. He cared about them. He was glad Delilah brought them into his life, but he had to get out of there. So he said his goodbyes and declined several offers to stay the night. He hoped Stephen would understand.

Cameron drove straight back to Manhattan, despite the hour. It was the same route he took the first time he and Delilah drove into the city, but he couldn't compare the urn packed in his things to the woman who rode beside him with the summer wind in her hair.

He cleared his mind and drove, and he didn't stop until he left the car with Adam, who wasn't thrilled to be woken up at three in the morning. Then he went up to his flat and stared at the only liquor left—a bottle of rum Delilah used to make fruity drinks at Christmas. Cameron chose function over sentimentality and threw it back in long swigs.

He spent the next month single-handedly keeping the liquor store on West 55th Street open for business. Cameron tolerated Charlie, who called several times to check up on him. He ignored Amelia, who was dealing with photos of him looking like hell and buying multiple bottles of Scotch at a time. His only response to the photos was to start making Adam buy the liquor. He especially ignored Mara, who called every other day and left concerned messages. Cameron half-watched endless reruns on television and slept more than he was awake. By the end of May, he couldn't stand being in the flat anymore.

It took Delilah eleven years to pack up her sister's things. It took Cameron four hours to remove all signs of his wife's presence from the flat. He probably wasn't ready, but he did it anyway. He simply couldn't look at it anymore. Grief, as he understood it, manifested differently in everyone, and this was his response. Shoving his feelings down so far they formed a heavy knot in his stomach, he packed boxes and bags. Finally, he reached her nightstand in the bedroom. There, Cameron found her well-worn notebook. On the cover, she had scrawled:

Do not open. That means you, Cameron.

She wrote it one day when he threatened to read whatever she was writing. He was only teasing at the time. Now, he *couldn't* open it. Collecting the notebook, along with two other books from the nightstand, he put them in his shoulder bag. He also tucked her wedding ring, still in the little bag from the hospital, in the bag. As he did so, his hand brushed the box that held the urn with her ashes. Cameron hadn't been able to look at it again since he packed it away in Branton after the funeral. There was some dark humor in the fact that his bag, which used to contain dog-eared scripts, schedules, and the occasional novel, was now full of the most morose collection of items possible.

Taking a glance around his flat, he saw nothing else to pack. He called Adam to fetch the car. Calling downstairs for help, he had the building staff load the boxes and bags into his car. They barely fit.

Seven hours later, he stood in Stephen's front hallway. After a couple of trips to the car, his cargo was now stacked up in Stephen's unused front room. Cameron stared at all of it. Six boxes. Three rucksacks. It seemed like there should be more. *She* had been so much more.

Turning to Stephen, he said, "I'm sorry it's late. And that I didn't ring you. But…"

Stephen gave him a compassionate look. "It's okay. We're all still a little irrational."

"I just…I couldn't keep looking at all of it. I'm going back to London, and I thought it would all be safer…here."

Stephen nodded his understanding. Natalie came from the corridor in a bathrobe and asked, "Is everything okay?"

Stephen turned to her and said, "Yes. I was just going to ask Cameron to stay for a drink."

Natalie gave Stephen a little smile, kissed him on the cheek, and went back to bed.

Ten minutes later, Cameron and Stephen sat across from each other at the kitchen table with a bottle of Tennessee bourbon between them. They each had a glass with a generous serving.

Taking a swig, Stephen said, "I hope, someday, we can meet for a drink for another reason than this."

"I hope so, too," Cameron said softly, though he couldn't see past his grief right now.

Stephen took another drink. "I'm having trouble deciding what to put on the stone, for Delilah." He looked toward the window in the direction of the gravesites down the hill. "Anna's was easier, like their mother."

Cameron was too distracted on the day of the funeral to memorize gravestones.

Stephen answered the unspoken question, "Kitty's is Psalm 57:7. *'My heart, O God, is steadfast; my heart is steadfast. I will sing and make music.'"*

Cameron listened.

"For Anna, 1 Corinthians 13," Stephen concluded.

"All from the Bible?"

Stephen shrugged, "We're a family of faith."

Cameron struggled, "I'm not sure I'm the best one to ask for help, especially not with scripture verses. I'm a little afraid that, if I set foot in a church, I would burst into flames."

Stephen smiled. "Fortunately, that's not how God works."

It was a quip, but Cameron knew there was a deeper meaning implied.

"You know," Stephen added, "Kitty liked to point out that the room we've come to call the 'church sanctuary' got the name honestly, because that is what they once offered. There was a time when, no matter who came to the church door, no matter how sick or poor or outcast, if a person asked for sanctuary, they had to be taken in and kept from harm. It came from the idea that God loves us all, accepts us all. Would die for us, all. But so many churches now offer the opposite of sanctuary."

"That's true," Cameron softly agreed.

Stephen went on, "The way we treat one another, whether we shove someone into the rain or offer them sanctuary, those things resonate across eternity. They matter. A lot of people dream about what it would be like to be immortal. What they don't realize is…we are."

Cameron let that roll around in his mind.

Stephen added, "Delilah shared our faith. I was there for her Baptism. Her First Communion. But…I'd just like to put something on the stone that *she* would want."

Cameron looked him over. "I wish I could be of more help. Maybe I can find something…"

Stephen nodded. "Well, there's no rush. I can set the markers whenever I choose, since it's my property."

Glancing away, Cameron asked, "What made you decide to do that…to have your wife buried here?"

Stephen met his eyes. "I suppose I just never liked the idea of grieving in public, and cemeteries are public. It's my land, and her family left her funeral all to me, so…it was right for us. And it's registered as a family cemetery with the county."

Cameron understood. He stared at Stephen as they nursed their drinks. As he clutched the glass, Cameron noticed how work-worn Stephen's hands were, and how his profile echoed Delilah's in the dim light. Watching him and knowing he was thinking of the three graves outside, Cameron was suddenly overwhelmed.

Before he could stop himself, he asked, "How have you done it?"

Stephen turned back. "What?"

Staring into his amber drink, Cameron clarified, "How have you kept going after losing them? How have you done this three times and not..."

He couldn't find the last words.

Stephen set his glass down. He leaned on his fists, thoughtful. "There is no easy way."

"I didn't think so," Cameron sighed, feeling heavy.

Stephen went on, "I don't know if Delilah ever told you, but my grandfather, my mother's father, was a sailor. He sailed from Fleetwood, in Lancashire, in the early twentieth century. It was his whole life. Everything he did and every story he told related back to fishing or sailing.

"His name was Albert, but we called him Grandad. He would tell us about finding the best places for fish and all kinds of things about boats that I've forgotten. But the thing I loved most were his stories about storms. He had stories of all kinds of storms, some terrifying and some rather funny. I remember being surprised, after hearing some of them, that he was still alive. When I got older and wrote a few stories myself, I drew the obvious metaphors. 'Keep your boat at sea during a storm' translates to 'always face your fears.' 'Lash yourself to the mast' means 'find something that keeps you from drowning.' There are so many excellent lessons for life and struggle, and I don't think my grandfather fully realized those deeper meanings when he was telling the stories. But I did. However, when Kitty died, those metaphors didn't help me. You see, when she died, the storm was over. She was gone. All the begging and pleading and hoping were done. And I struggled. Badly. More than my girls knew, for years. However, after a lot of prayer one afternoon, I remembered another story."

Stephen refilled his glass, and Cameron realized this must be what keeps his students' attention—this rich, honest way of communicating with great finesse but no pretense.

Continuing, Stephen said, "Grandad told me once how he was training another young sailor and they encountered a fierce storm.

After it was over, the boy just sat there, too terrified to move. He was clinging to the rail, paralyzed. My grandfather said to him, 'Lad, you've made it through the storm. It's over and you've survived, whether you wanted to or not. Now, you must either sail the boat or sit here, adrift, until you die. I recommend you sail the boat, because drifting until you wither and die is no way to go out of this world.' The boy said, 'I can't do *that* again. I can't.' And Grandad told him, 'You don't think about the last storm, or the next. You sail the boat.' The boy looked around at the twisted rigging and the torn sails and said, 'This boat?' My grandfather said, 'Yes. This is the only boat you've got. Might be rough for wear, but it's what you've got. It's not sunk, so get up. Raise the sails. And find the wind.'"

Cameron was quiet for a long time before saying, "I get the idea of it. You must go on. But that's not so easy."

"No," Stephen shook his head, "it's not. And I thought the same thing. I remembered the story and just kept focusing on moving the boat forward. But, at some point, I realized that wasn't it at all. You see, to sail, you have to find the wind. You must raise the sails, making the boat vulnerable again, and let the wind take you forward. Otherwise, you're just rowing a sailboat, and that's miserable."

Cameron listened, trying to appreciate the wisdom.

Taking another swig of bourbon, Stephen said, "I'm sure Delilah told you that after a loss like this, you are never the same. You will never go back to normal, but you don't have to drift. You don't have to just cling to a broken sailboat. It's what I told her before she left for England. Find something that makes you want to live again, something that carries you forward. Find the wind."

Cameron thought it over for a minute before saying, "That's very poetic, but…"

"I know," Stephen interjected. "It's not easy. But it can be done."

Cameron let it sink in as far as it would, for now. Then he asked, "What was it for you? What was the wind?"

Leaning back in his chair, Stephen said, "After Kitty, it was the girls. Being as present in their lives as I could be. But after Anna, it was work. And not in the throwing-myself-in-as-a-distraction kind of way. After I conceded that Anna was not coming home, I saw all these young faces in front of me every day, and I decided I needed them as much as they needed me. I was considering retiring. Public school is...difficult. But I decided to give them everything I had, to put all the good into this world that I could manage. For Kitty. For Anna. And now, for Delilah."

Cameron swirled the bourbon in the bottom of his glass. Right now, he would give all his wealth for the wisdom and fortitude of Stephen MacClare.

Cameron stayed the night, mostly because he was too exhausted to drive. The next morning, he drove back to the city. By evening, he was on a flight to London. He asked Adam to take care of the car and the flat, then fly over the next day.

Because he arrived in London without his assistant, Cameron took a car service to his flat in Fulham. He was there all of ten minutes before he decided he couldn't stay. The towels he and Delilah used during their anniversary trip were neatly folded on the bed. Two clean wine glasses were in the drying rack. Even though the place was clean, the memories of Delilah lingered. So, despite his body's confusion about the time and the fact that he wasn't exactly sure what day it was, Cameron got his car out of the car park and headed north. He didn't have an exact destination in mind, and he knew he was essentially running from his problems, but he just kept driving. Some subconscious motivation aimed him in the direction of home. Two hours after leaving London, he knocked on the door of his sister's house.

Your house, he reminded himself, because this was home whether he liked it or not.

When Mara didn't answer, he used his key to enter. He realized his sister must be asleep. Checking his watch, which he reset to local time at the airport, it was 10 a.m. Walking slowly upstairs, he set his shoulder bag and small suitcase on the floor of his tiny bedroom. He sat down on the bed and looked around. Something on the dresser caught his eye. Crossing to it, he realized it was the book Delilah gave him just after they first met.

Secrets of the Shore.

The title was written in flowing script. He flipped the pages, and he was suddenly accosted by memories.

I'll read yours, if you read this. He remembered the gleam in her eyes when she said it.

Still holding her book, he sat back down on the bed.

The bed where we first...

It was too much. It was worse than the flat, and he wished he had stayed in London. Cameron realized there was nowhere he could go to escape her. She had permeated every part of his life. He realized, with equal part wonder and agony, that this is love.

And even though the price of love may be loss, we will pay.

The lines from *Heir of Taivas* accosted him. The books that started his relationship with Delilah had brought him full circle. And he understood the words fully now. He would do it all again, to love her.

Cameron's exhaustion accosted him. Even as the sun rose high in the sky, his body insisted it was five in the morning. He had been awake all night. Despite his raging emotions, Cameron fell asleep on the bed with Delilah's book on his chest.

Mara accepted Cameron's sudden appearance without much surprise. She didn't nag or lecture him but gave him clean sheets for his bed and let him stay. In the evenings, as she got ready to leave for work, she gave him long looks as he sat on the sofa nursing whatever drink he could find. He was draining her drinks cabinet of its meager supply, and he knew he couldn't hide it from her. But he didn't care. He went back to his routine of drinking and sleeping alternately.

He was in Chatfield a week before he had to truly face his sister. Seven weeks after Delilah died, he stumbled down the stairs sometime in the early afternoon. He hoped Mara stayed at church to chat with her friends. He had no such luck. When he entered the kitchen, he found her and Flora sitting at the dining table with cups and saucers in front of them. Cameron stood there in shock. He might as well have walked in on Benvolio and Tybalt having tea.

Both women looked up and looked him over.

Recovering from the shock, Cameron crossed to the kitchen cupboard behind them, retrieved a cup, and poured himself some lukewarm tea. He sat down at the table, and they all stared at each other for a minute.

He grumbled, "I'm assuming hell has frozen over, and you've had no choice but to get together and discuss it."

Mara set down her cup. "You assume me to be so snobbish that I wouldn't let Flora into my home?"

Cameron chuckled gruffly. "I assumed Flora would never visit here because you have been calling her names for forty years. Unsavory names."

Tipping her head, Mara added, "When you're stuck on an airplane together for nine hours, it has a way of forcing you to talk."

Cameron nodded, feeling a twist in his gut as he remembered *why* they were on a plane together. His thoughts flashed back to Delilah's funeral, and he stood up in search of whisky to add to his tea.

"Cameron," his sister's voice stopped him, "you can't drink her away. All you're doing is drowning yourself."

Giving her a hard look, he crossed to the refrigerator. He knew the drinks cabinet was empty, so he searched for anything stronger than wine. All he could find was some chardonnay and cheap champagne from holidays gone by.

From behind him, Flora said, "She's right, luv. It i'n't possible t' drink yer sorrows away. And I should know."

Shutting the refrigerator with a bang, he turned around and rubbed his eyes, asking, "And what brilliant advice do you two have to offer, since you've obviously conspired against me here?"

Mara held his gaze. "I did lose my husband, Cameron. I know a thing or two about grief."

He crossed his arms over his chest, unable to imagine his sister, the champion of prudent sensibility, loving someone the way he loved Delilah.

More softly, Mara said, "I know what it is to feel as though the world has fallen out from under you."

In that moment, Cameron saw something in his sister that he had never seen before, or perhaps never looked closely enough to see. Now, in the light of his own loss, he saw her pain. Looking away, Cameron dropped into the chair at the end of the table.

After a long pause, he said, "I'm sorry, Mara. I shouldn't have minimized your grief. Ever."

Flora considered him carefully. "I know ye hurt, luv. And I know it's fierce. But we're all 'ere, puttin' aside our differences and our ages-old arguments, because of Delilah. And that's summat, in't it?"

Rising from her chair, Mara came around the table to where her brother sat. From behind him, she wrapped her arms around his shoulders and held him tightly.

Cameron decided to go back to London three days later. He was glad that his sister and Flora were getting along, but they were making him claustrophobic. He felt like they were hovering, waiting for him to have some kind of emotional revelation. Also, Mara refused to have any more liquor in the house. He appreciated all the effort to help him, just like he appreciated Stephen's wisdom, but he just wanted to drink. Right or wrong, he wanted the vice. The one thing he managed to accept is that he wasn't going to be able to run from Delilah's memory. No matter where he went, he would feel her absence. So he went back to London and faced the flat.

He had Adam stock the drinks cabinet there, so, once he was home, he had little reason to leave. Cameron vaguely realized that, at this rate, he was on his way to becoming an alcoholic, but he didn't care. He wanted to take Stephen's advice and keep sailing. He understood that he was trying to row a sailboat, but he was at a loss as to what could possibly pull him from his misery. Cameron was sure that Stephen MacClare must be drawing on some unseen, superhuman well of strength that Cameron, a mere mortal, could not access. So he drank.

One afternoon in mid-July, about four weeks into his isolation in the London flat, Cameron woke up on the sofa with a massive headache. Taking a swig from the half-empty glass on the coffee table, he looked around the room. He was sure he looked like hell. *Snapshot* would kill for a picture of him stumbling outside like this. They were probably camped out downstairs, he decided, waiting for the chance. He wondered how long they would wait. How many days of staking out his flat would it take before they gave up and chased down some other unfortunate celebrity? He couldn't say.

Reaching for his shoulder bag, he pulled his phone out of the exterior pocket. The battery was dead. He considered plugging it in, but that meant getting up and stumbling across the room. Reaching back into the bag for his tablet, his hand brushed something else. It was the notebook he took from Delilah's nightstand in New York. In the haze of alcohol in which he'd been for weeks now, he forgot he packed it. He stared at the contents of the bag, grazing his fingers over the box with the urn. Her ring was tucked beside it. Cameron still wasn't ready to do anything with them. Instead, he pulled out the other items.

Along with the spiral-bound notebook were a copy of *The Reaping Stone* and the worn book of poetry that Delilah carried around. Flipping through the poetry book, he remembered her saying it was a gift she received right before her mother passed away. It was full of dog-eared pages and highlighted passages. Her favorites were obvious, with scribbled notes and smudged ink. Flipping the pages, he read a few poems, recognizing Longfellow, Brontë, and Lawson. Then something caught his attention. Turning back a page, he read:

Love to faults is always blind
Always is to joy inclin'd
Lawless, wing'd and unconfined
And breaks all chains from every mind

Underneath the poem by William Blake, Delilah had scribbled, *Blindly, Boldly, and Without Bounds,* and underlined the words.

Cameron stared at it. Then, he set down the poetry book and picked up the spiral-bound notebook. There were the words again:

Do not open. That means you, Cameron.

He opened it. It was a glimpse into Delilah's thoughts. She cut out several poems by Sara Teasdale, glued them across a few pages, and made comments about the author's sad life story. She wrote down song lyrics, some he recognized from times they danced together. He found the photos from the magazines that she cut out when they were engaged, along with a few other photos and articles from the past year. She had several shots from their wedding he assumed Jenna took, and there was a photo of them at the final *Heir of Taivas* premiere, smiling. Delilah was beautiful. So beautiful it hurt.

Pouring himself another tumbler of Blue Label, Cameron kept flipping the pages. He smiled without thinking a few times. Somewhere amidst the pictures, something else caught his attention. He read across the top of a page:

September Blue

Cameron remembered her explaining to him what that meant to her, both for good and for bad. Now, he realized the words had become the title of a poem. Glancing over it, he saw no author reference. He wondered how Delilah could have found such a poem. Then he wondered if she wrote it. After he read the first stanza,

Cameron knew they were her words. It was too personal to be coincidental. Feeling his throat tighten, he took a deep breath and read:

September Blue

Remember me when rain-soaked grass
Fills air with earthy musk
When cicadas chant
And leaves glisten red
In the fading light of dusk

Remember me on the lonely road
When you leave the trees behind
As new asphalt carves
The mourning mountains
And the city fills your mind

Remember me in a distant land
Where I sought the silent rain
Where I hoped to live
Quiet and unsung
To make peace my last refrain

Remember me in firelight
In the warmth of reaching flame
As words that fall
From eager lips
And reveal us as the same

Remember me in moonlight
Where new lovers catch their breath
In fingers holding
Sweaty skin
As we die a little death

Remember me in goodness
And let go of all the wrong
Don't dwell upon
The struggle
But recall when I was strong

Remember me in brilliant skies
Of purest cerulean hue
And call them not
As cornflower
But always, September blue

Staring at the paper, Cameron felt her absence with a sharp, blinding pain. He stood up and paced the lounge, trying to calm his raging thoughts.

This, the thought blindsided him, *should be on her gravestone. This is what Stephen was searching for.*

The revelation was not cathartic. The memory of fresh gravesites only stirred Cameron's already tumultuous spirit. Logically, he felt he should call Stephen and share the poem, perhaps do something productive with his feelings. But Cameron wasn't in a logical place. Instead, he paced erratically.

Finally, his pain exploded into anger, and he shouted, "I can't do this Delilah! I can't…I don't know how to do this!"

Picking up his glass again, he drained it, then stared at the empty tumbler. Intense anger swelled in him again. He heaved the glass across the room and watched it explode into shards as it hit the wall.

"Fuck!"

Cameron had no better words. He picked up an empty bottle of Scotch and threw it across the room as well. He was sure if his neighbors could hear him, they would think he had gone mad and maybe call the authorities, or the press. He also knew yelling at the walls would heal no wounds, but he didn't care. He was on the edge of some kind of breakdown, and he wasn't sure which way it was going to go. Crossing into the kitchen, he surveyed the empty bottles and dirty dishes. He shoved them across the counter in the direction of the sink. They rolled and tumbled, making a cacophony of clinking, shrill notes as they shattered. He stared at them, still unsatisfied. Cameron had no idea how he was supposed to do this. He thought about Stephen, who had somehow done this *three* times. Cameron couldn't figure out how to keep breathing, let alone keep sailing. Right now, it felt like a bullshit metaphor.

He dropped onto the couch and put his hands over his face. His head rang with all the things he wanted to scream. Soon, he was up again, this time shouting profanity at the unresponsive walls again. There were no answers, no respite, and no healing. There was simply pain. And loneliness. Sinking back onto the couch, Cameron felt two rogue tears escape. They cut themselves from his eyes and burned like acid down his face. He rubbed them away. A few more fell. Finally, he gave up the fight. He had no more strength left. He put his face in his hands and keened with the force of the sadness within him.

Late the next morning, Cameron woke and forced himself to get up off the sofa. He stood there for a long time, staring at his surroundings. Clothes were strewn haphazardly over the backs of chairs and across the foot of the bed in the bedroom. Empty takeaway containers littered the kitchen counters, and now they were covered in broken glass. Cameron started to estimate how many bottles there were but gave up. He had never been a heavy drinker. This habit of swilling liquor to mute his life was new, and he realized it had to stop. He had no idea what to do with himself, but he knew if he continued down this path, he would be dead as well. For a half-second, that felt like a decent option, but he forced the thought away.

It took him until afternoon teatime to clean the flat, because there was a layer of filth only a month of not giving a shit could cause. Once it was clean, he sat down on the sofa and stared at the walls. He checked his phone messages. There were several from Charlie and a couple from his sister. He went through all of them and wrote down the things Charlie wanted him to consider. Cameron made a mental note to call his sister at some point. Then he found a saved message. Playing it back, he realized it was from Delilah. She called him from work the day after they returned from their anniversary trip at the end of March and said:

Last week was wonderful. We really do belong together, you and me. I was thinking, we should work on something together. Maybe this summer. I mean, with your superior acting abilities and my overwhelming intelligence, we could make something great. But seriously, we should find a project together. Just think about it. Call me later. Love you.

Cameron played the message three times. He wanted to keep listening to her voice, but it conjured up an ache in his chest that grew unbearable. So he put the phone down, and the flat was silent. He felt the emptiness pressing in around him, seeping into him and wiping away the desire to do anything, to feel anything. Even the desire to drink was suppressed by the numbness. He ran from Manhattan to Branton to Chatfield to London. He consumed a year's worth of liquor, but there was no escape. He conceded he could not outrun this or drown this, and there was some healing in the tears he shed the night before. Cameron felt purged, but now there was nothing left. This, he decided, would be his existence. He would sleep. He would eat. He would breathe.

And nothing more.

26
The Wind's Song

I must go down to the seas again, to the lonely sea and the sky,
and all I ask is a tall ship and a star to steer her by;
And the wheel's kick and the wind's song and the white sail's shaking,
and a grey mist on the sea's face, and a grey dawn breaking.

—From "Sea Fever" by John Masefield

Ten days later, Cameron's phone rang shrilly beside him. He was still in bed at 10 a.m., but he had a script that Meg asked him to read over open next to him. So far, he was making more progress at watching every episode of *Lost* than doing any work. Noting that his sister was calling, he answered the phone.

"Cameron?" Mara said softly, "How are you?"

He had absolutely no answer for that and, right now, it felt like the world's stupidest question.

Sensing how he felt, she started again, "I'm sorry. That was the wrong thing to ask."

Relaxing a little, he said, "I've been watching a lot of television. Did you ever watch *Lost*? It's an American drama, I think. Friend of mine had a brief guest spot on it. I have absolutely no idea what the fuck is going on, at this point."

Mara was quiet. Then she laughed. Cameron wasn't sure that he had meant to be funny. Still, it felt good to hear someone laugh.

Growing serious again, she said, "I called because…there's something I need to tell you."

Cameron paused the television, silently thanking God for the invention of Netflix. Concerned, he asked, "What is it?"

Mara hesitated. "Marianne rang me yesterday."

Cameron felt a sinking in his gut. He didn't want to deal with this now.

His sister went on, "She's seen photos of you looking...worse for wear. She sent them to me. I'll be honest, in some of them you look absolutely pissed."

"Mara..." he started to protest.

She cut him off, "I'm not calling to debate that, Cameron. I'm worried about you, but I know it's not my place to mother you."

He was surprised, because she always reveled in mothering him.

"After informing me she thinks you're an alcoholic, Marianne went on to tell me how glad she is that you're finally 'getting what you deserve.'" Mara's tone softened, "I asked her what a person could possibly do to deserve to lose someone they love, and she said, 'If anyone deserves it, Cameron does.'"

He was absolutely floored at his ex-wife's callousness, but he couldn't say he was surprised. Marianne had been reaching for new levels of vindictiveness over the past year. He waited, expecting a lecture from his sister about how he could have avoided all of this by being kinder to Marianne.

Instead, Mara said, "I told her to sod off."

Now, Cameron was surprised.

Taking a breath, Mara went on, "I told her that it's been long enough, and that she crossed a line. I've tried to be her friend. I've sided with her because she went through a lot of terrible things. I was angry with you, Cameron, but only because I love you and I've always believed you are better than how you chose to behave. But no matter what, Marianne has no right to say you deserved...this. No one deserves this. So I told her to sod off."

Cameron felt the wall of resentment Mara built crumble. It should have been a watershed moment, but he was having a hard time appreciating the significance.

Struggling to speak, he said, "I...I appreciate that, Mara."

"I love you, Cameron. I always have. And...I'm here. Anytime."

He nodded, even though she couldn't see him, and said softly, "Thank you."

"And Cameron," she added, "you are more than what they say about you in magazines. No matter what Marianne says, you are more. Delilah saw it. I see it. I won't give you platitudes right now, but just...don't forget that."

Over the next three weeks, Cameron remained in a state of perpetual nothingness. He wasn't throwing things or shouting at the walls, and he refrained from stocking the drinks cabinet. He simply continued to sit, watching television and avoiding everything. Adam came when he called, bringing food and running interference with Amelia, his ever-patient publicist. Cameron found it hard to care what the population of the planet thought of him right now. If he subscribed to the notion that grief could be divided into neat, progressive stages, he would say he was at the bottom of the bell curve. He felt content to not give a shit for the rest of his life. On some level, he thought this might be considered progress, but he also thought telling people how to grieve was psychoanalytical rubbish.

In mid-August, on a day when the weather turned uncomfortably hot and Cameron assumed everyone in their right mind was at the coast, Meg rang him. She asked to take him out for lunch, and she refused to take no for an answer. He put up a half-hearted argument but gave in because he couldn't find the strength to really care. They met at a café in Covent Garden. Meg had her hair streaked with white blonde and pulled up into a messy knot. Her tall frame was clad in some sort of yoga getup. However, she had a way of making workout clothes look elegant. Cameron, on the other hand, knew he looked like shit. His eyes looked better since he quit drinking nonstop, but he hadn't bothered to shave in several days and his complete lack of vanity over the past few months revealed just how silver his hair had gone. Taking a table on the outdoor patio of the restaurant, Cameron greeted Meg and decided to leave his sunglasses on.

As she looked at the menu, he grumbled, "I thought we were in London, not Los Angeles. This sun is brutal."

Meg smirked. "Is it aggravating your perpetual hangover?"

Cameron gave her a long look. "I stopped drinking a month ago, but thank you for being my new sponsor."

Meg scrutinized him as though she was trying to decide if she believed him. He made no argument when she set the drink menu on another table.

Eventually, she said, "Adam tells me you were taking in more Scotch than food for quite a while."

With a heavy sigh, Cameron asked, "What do you expect of me, Meg? After a lifetime of being told I care too little, now I apparently care too much. The world expects me to be out socializing or making another bloody film sequel."

Softening a little, Meg said, "I don't expect that. And it's not possible to care too much."

She went back to the menu.

Looking out into the distance, Cameron softly said, "I miss her voice. I miss her warmth. I miss seeing her hair all tangled in the morning and I miss her clothes being simply everywhere. I even miss the smell of coffee."

He stopped and rubbed at his face, glad for the sunglasses to hide the welling tears. He knew Meg would notice the catch in his voice, even as he tried to sound controlled.

Struggling, he said, "I miss her life in every way."

Meg said nothing but looked at him with sadness in her eyes. Cameron wasn't sure why he was suddenly talking about Delilah. If Meg had asked him to share, he would have brusquely refused. Somehow, it just came out, perhaps because he was shoving so many things down inside himself that something was bound to burst free.

When the waiter returned, Meg ordered cold pasta for both of them. While they waited, Cameron looked around, not sure what else to say. He caught sight of a couple people across the way pointing smartphones in their direction.

Looking the other way, he snapped, "I wonder how they're going to caption those. Perhaps, 'Cameron Burke is completely off his trolley.'"

Meg glanced over her shoulder. "They don't mean to be invasive. They're not thinking."

"I used to say that."

Reaching across the table to touch his hand, she said, "They are the least of your concerns right now. Let them say and post what they will." She hesitated. "I'm worried about you, Cameron."

He pulled away from her. "They're right, you know. All the tabloids. I'm a bloody disaster. I'm an old man who will be remembered as a mediocre actor who treated women terribly and probably got what was coming to him."

"Cameron…" Meg started to argue.

The waiter returned with their food, stopping her. Meg ate silently, watching him pick at his pasta. Her clear, blue eyes had a way of capturing him, not as a lover, but as someone with wisdom to offer.

Eventually, she went on, "Cameron, I can't imagine what you're going through. I would probably be a bloody mess, too, if I was in your position. It breaks *my* heart that Delilah is gone, and she wasn't my wife. I'm not going to tell you to get over it or snap out of it. There's no orderly timeline for this. But," she held his gaze, "this doesn't have to be the end of you, and I would like to think you have much more to leave behind than angry women and empty bottles of Scotch. You are more than that, Cameron."

He stared at her, because she was echoing what Mara said. Eventually, he returned, "That's a lovely sentiment, Meg. And sentiments are easy to offer, but not so easy to live out."

"No one said it was easy."

Cameron rubbed his eyes again and resettled his sunglasses. "What do I do then? Donate everything I have to charity? Write a book? Build a memorial?"

Meg tipped her head to the side. "I know it's in your nature to think of big things, grand things, but those aren't always the *best things*. I've learned that. Over the past few years, I've realized it's the little things that matter most. The tiny rudder that steers the ship, the pebble that ripples the pond, the spark you can snuff out or fan into flame." She looked away. "A few years ago, I realized that I was making the same film over and over again, playing the same role. And I decided the world didn't need to see Meg Abbott as the snippy-yet-sexy British heroine one more time. I didn't need more money. I needed purpose, and that came in the form of *Stones and Arrows*."

Cameron remembered the little indie film. It was her directorial debut, made between two of the *Heir of Taivas* films.

"You refused to let Delilah stop dancing, in whatever way she could. Now, it's time to take your own advice."

He hated Meg a little bit, for being right.

After another moment she said, "Look for the little things. Be the rudder. Nurse the tiniest spark. Be the pebble. That's what Delilah did for you. She unsettled the pond. She stirred up what was lying in the depths of you. And that's how we live on, Cameron, in the ripples."

The next morning, Adam rang the buzzer to Cameron's building at 11 a.m. Cameron initially forgot why he was there, but quickly remembered that he asked him the night before to pick up groceries. After meeting with Meg, he felt it was time to eat something other than Chinese takeaway and toast. She said to do little things, and eating something that wasn't junk was a little thing. Cameron buzzed Adam into the building, then let him into the flat. Adam had a key, but his arms were full of bags. Cameron watched as the young man put things in the cupboards. He considered helping but couldn't find the motivation.

Sitting at the kitchen table, Cameron watched his assistant. If anyone had enough dirt to hang Cameron Burke, it was Adam Carlson. Before Delilah, he picked Cameron up from the back entrance of a multitude of hotels and escorted enough women out of Cameron's residences to fill any one of the tabloids. Adam often physically dealt with the paparazzi, and he had access to Cameron's homes and cars. Still staring at him, Cameron wondered if Adam was storing up information for a tell-all book. Surely these past three months would make a great chapter or two. Cameron realized, for the first time, that he knew virtually nothing about the person who jumped at his every whim.

Tipping his head, Cameron asked, "Adam, why do you do this?"

He looked confused.

"I mean," Cameron went on, "why do you put up with me? Why not cash in on what you know and live off the profit?"

Adam didn't answer right away. He put the grocery bags away in the kitchen, then came around to the dining table. Cameron motioned for him to sit down.

Taking a seat, Adam said, "Because you live how you live, and that's not for me to judge."

Cameron considered him again. He couldn't be more than thirty. Adam worked for Robert Chesney before taking this position, and he came highly recommended. But Cameron didn't know much else about him.

He asked, "What made you decide to put up with actors for a living?"

Adam looked away, as though he didn't want to answer. He pushed his longish hair back from his eyes. He had Grecian features and, although he wasn't rakishly handsome, he was certainly charming when he smiled. Cameron wondered why he wasn't settled down somewhere with a partner.

Adam hesitantly admitted, "I wanted to be an actor. I wanted to be on the stage." He continued, "I applied to drama school in London, and I was accepted. I have an undergraduate degree in theater from Northwestern University, but I wanted to study abroad. I love the stage and I wanted to round out the education. But I couldn't put the money together. My parents were…less than enthusiastic. And I had more student loans than I knew how to handle already."

Cameron was stunned, because he never would've picked Adam as a drama school student. "So, how did you end up in this?" He asked.

Adam looked uncomfortable with sharing his personal story, but went on, "A friend of mine from school went out to Hollywood and ended up in a movie with Robert Chesney. Said he helped him a lot and mentioned he was looking for a trustworthy assistant. My friend wanted nothing to do with it, but he asked if he could pass it on to me. He knew I needed a job, badly. So, I did a couple of interviews and turned in a lot of references. I had experience because I worked as an assistant to a couple of my professors in college. The next thing I knew, I was Robert Chesney's assistant."

Cameron asked, "Did you ever tell him you went to drama school?"

Adam shook his head. "No. It felt solicitous."

Cameron just stared at him. It wasn't that his story was unique. There were thousands of aspiring actors doing whatever work they could to try and make ends meet. What made Cameron speechless was that he had known Adam for five years and they never had this conversation. Adam occasionally worked for Meg, as well, and she had never mentioned any of this, either. Cameron accepted Adam on Robert's recommendation. It was never important that he know anything else about his assistant except that he was trustworthy.

Cameron finally asked, "And you've never wanted to try again?"

Adam looked away. "After a while, the certainty of employment became more appealing than following a dream."

"What drama school accepted you?"

Adam looked decidedly uncomfortable when he said, "The Royal Academy of Dramatic Arts."

Cameron had no words. Adam was accepted into RADA. Adam might very likely be a better actor than he was, and Cameron had been using him as a glorified gopher for five years. They sat there while the clock over the fireplace ticked. Suddenly, Cameron remembered what Meg said.

Look for the little things.

Cameron saw it. Sitting in front of him was a spark, and he had the power to turn it into fire.

Over the next two weeks, Cameron found himself reading through Delilah's notebook over and over, memorizing her words and hearing her voice in her written thoughts. He ached for her. At night, he would dream of seeing her, then wake up in agony at the realization she was still gone. He found himself bargaining with God, promising to give up his career and save starving orphans if he could have his wife back.

Even for just a day, he would plead. *Just one day.*

However, he was forced to accept the harsh reality that death is not in the business of giving back what it has taken.

On the second of September, Cameron received a call from Charlie. After pleasantries, his agent carefully said, "Janine has quite a pile of cards and letters down here. She's done the usual responses, but she wanted me to ring you and see if you wanted to look at some of 'em. Over the past couple of months they've gotten a little more...personal."

Cameron knew what he meant.

"She says she doesn't feel right about getting rid of this batch." Charlie added, "And also, she has another pile of shit you need to sign."

As always, Charlie had an eloquent way of putting things. Janine was the one responsible for answering fan mail. Cameron agreed on a standard response to most of it years ago, and he only came in to sign the piles of fan photographs when it became absolutely necessary. Right now, he couldn't think of anything he wanted to do less. Usually, he would have Adam go get it all and bring it to his flat so he could sign it in the privacy of his home, but Adam was in the States at the moment.

So, somewhat begrudgingly, Cameron pulled himself out of his morose thoughts and made the trip northeast to Bloomsbury. The talent agency office was in a modern, four-story building with square windows and not much character. Once inside, Cameron made his way up to Charlie's office. Janine sat in the outer vestibule.

She smiled at him. "Everything's in there with Charlie. It was cluttering things up out here."

Cameron returned the smile and went in to see Charlie. His agent's office had as much personality as the man who occupied it. There were posters tacked up everywhere with signatures from the actors he represented, both past and present. His desk was overflowing with stacks of papers and the credenza behind him held a multitude of family photos. He looked up and smiled broadly at Cameron.

Charlie stood and shook Cameron's hand heartily. "Good to see you, mate. Good to see you." He made no mention of Delilah. Instead, he said, "You've made Amelia earn her paycheck this summer, that's for certain."

Cameron shrugged, not willing to deny or defend his erratic behavior.

Clearing his throat, Charlie explained, "Those are your boxes by the door. That's everything Janine found too special to toss out."

Cameron looked over and saw the cardboard boxes. Plump and silver-haired, Janine had worked for the agency as long as Charlie, and she had a stubborn streak. She was also a tad sentimental. The combination meant that Cameron was periodically handed a box of fan mail she refused to throw in the bin. Usually, he gave the things a cursory glance and tossed them out himself.

"Top two are recent," Charlie explained. "The box on the bottom is one I found when I cleaned out this closet. No idea how long it's been there."

Cameron was not in the least bit surprised.

With a sigh, he sat down in the one extra chair and pulled the boxes over. He opened the top one, hoping if he acted like he had looked through all of it, Janine would get rid of it. He did not want to carry three boxes out to the bins himself. The first card contained a lovely sympathy poem. The second was also a bereavement card, but it contained a more personal message:

> Mr. Burke,
>
> I lost my husband this year. So, when I heard about your Delilah, I was devastated for you. It is a terrible feeling, this limbo. This lost place. It's unbearable some days, but I just keep going. I keep cooking, because it was our passion. I can imagine that, at a time like this, fame doesn't matter. I imagine you feel lost, too. Just know, you're not alone. We have all been lost at some point. I hope this is not too personal, but I wanted to offer something uplifting. I wanted to say…when I think about Frank, I try not to be sad that he's gone, but glad that we had the chance to love one another. I hope you'll keep creating beautiful characters.
>
> Your fan,
>
> Margie

She hadn't said anything especially profound, but there was something in her open honesty that affected him. Placing the card back in the top box, Cameron cleared his throat. "I'm going to take these back home with me. I'd like a little more time to look through them."

Charlie stared at him, confused, because his client never asked for more quality time with his fan mail.

Cameron didn't have the energy to explain himself. Instead, he arranged for a courier to bring them over, then left the office. At home in his flat that night, he read letter after letter from the boxes of mail. There were piles of bereavement cards with kind notes, and there were handwritten letters expressing grief over Delilah's death. Cameron was amazed that this was only a selection of the mail he actually received. He was also struck by how his fans, who were usually gushing over his latest performance, were so affected by Delilah. Even from a distance, they saw the goodness in her. They recognized that she changed him, even if they only hinted at it in their letters. They also, it seemed, had truly been impacted by his work. He realized, as he opened envelope after envelope, that he didn't deserve their sympathy.

Late that night, Cameron opened the third box. This one contained a random assortment of items. He assumed Janine must have been throwing things in for him and, at some point, Charlie shoved the box into the closet. All of it was years old, some of it dating back to 1999, when he first started working with Charlie. There were letters asking for help with drama school or advice on pursuing a career in acting. There were others expressing how one of his films affected someone's life. There was also a stack of scripts and screenplays. The agency itself wouldn't process unsolicited material, but obviously Janine found some of it worth reading. He assumed, at some point, she gave up on passing these kinds of things along to him because he showed no interest. Cameron looked them over now, chuckling at a few of the titles and creatively written cover letters. Finally, his hands fell on a thick, spiral-bound sheaf of papers. If there was a cover letter, it was gone. He read the title page and froze.

The Empty Place

written by

Andrew Agrietta

It was too great a coincidence to be by anyone other than his son. Some unknown number of years ago, Andrew wrote a screenplay and sent it to him. Cameron tried to guess at his son's motivation. He wondered if it was written and mailed out of anger, as a way of reaching out, or as a method of crossing the abyss between them. Finally, he stopped wondering and turned to the first page.

He didn't stop reading until dawn broke over the horizon.

Cameron was staring at the urn again.

He held it up, and it caught the morning sun, refracting amber bands of light. The morning of September 20 dawned clear and brisk, and Cameron stood on the makeshift rooftop terrace where he and Delilah were married. Talia let him into the building without asking any questions. Looking east, toward the sun that was not yet full in the sky, he felt a strong breeze ruffle his hair. He wanted to believe Delilah chose today for what he was planning to do by sending the strong winds. Holding the urn, he was working up the courage to let her go. He wasn't sure what he should feel. Cameron read about people spreading their loved one's ashes. He saw it in films. Somberly, he thought:

Ashes to ashes, dust to dust.

The words were so much prettier when they were merely symbolism. Reality, he realized, wasn't so beautiful. Reality was a beautiful person reduced to dust.

Someday, when I'm gone, I don't want to lie in a grave somewhere. I want to be cast on the wind over the city. Let what's left of me rest here, like Anna.

Cameron took a deep, shuddering breath and carefully unscrewed the lid from the urn. He swallowed over the lump in his throat and closed his eyes. After waiting for the wind to shift and blow hard southeast, he tipped the urn into it. The handful of fine ashes were immediately aloft, taking flight over the low rooftops toward the East River and the Atlantic beyond. He watched them for a long time, until they disappeared from sight. Then he looked down at the urn and thought to himself:

I'm casting you into the world, Delilah. Now, I need you to come back and surround me.

He held up the urn and let the light catch it once more. Just then, a gust swept around the terrace and whipped his hair around. Smoothing it down, he remembered:

Find the wind.

It would come in gusts, he realized, with lulls of stillness in between. He might not always move at a swift and steady pace, but Cameron was ready to stop rowing the sailboat. A week ago, he made several phone calls, one of which was to fire Adam.

"I have to let you go," he explained, "because you are going back to drama school."

Adam was speechless.

Cameron smiled to himself, remembering his assistant's humble gratitude. It was what Delilah would have told him to do. He also made another phone call a few days before, this one to Stephen. He asked for a way to contact Preston and hopefully discover who Anna's friend was who worked as an occupational therapist. Cameron was hoping they could help him realize Delilah's desire to open a clinic in memory of her sister. All these things were the first gust for Cameron, the first push that implied there was more to be done. There were seas yet to sail. There were books yet to be written.

Two days later, Cameron was sitting in a booth in a trendy diner in uptown Charlotte, North Carolina. For all his world traveling, this was a place he never visited. It seemed nice enough, if more urban than he anticipated, and the waitress was certainly friendly. Cameron couldn't tell if she recognized him, or if she was just that perky with everyone. Either way, she brought water and a menu, and he pretended to read it to have something to focus on. After several more minutes, the sound of a clearing throat made him look up. Cameron locked eyes with his son.

How Marianne ever thought she could deny his paternity for any length of time was a mystery to Cameron. The last time they were together, Andrew was just out of adolescence. Now, he had grown into himself. His almost black hair had the same disheveled sweep as his father's. He was tall and carried himself with confidence. He held Cameron in a piercing gaze that made him understand what people meant when they called him intimidating. Andrew's eyes were brown, though, like Marianne's.

Indicating the other side of the booth, Cameron said, "Please, sit."

Andrew obliged.

Cameron added, "Thank you for coming."

"Thank you for calling me," his son returned, "and for coming down here."

Cameron stated, "This…seems like a nice place to live."

Andrew shrugged. "I work in wealth management. And if you work with other people's money, this is the city for it."

Cameron studied his son a little more, noting his accent was muddled. He couldn't blame the young man, though. He was raised in London by an American mother but had been living in the States for more than ten years now. That would've muddled anyone.

After another minute, Andrew said softly, "I'm so sorry for what happened. Delilah seemed like a beautiful person."

Cameron swallowed hard. "She was."

Reaching into his jacket, Andrew pulled out an envelope and slid it across the table. "I hope this is all right. It's not much, but I wanted to do something."

Cameron was expecting a bereavement card. Instead, he opened the envelope to find a tasteful birthday card. Today was, in fact, Cameron's birthday, but he almost managed to forget the whole thing.

All Cameron could say was, "How did you know?"

Andrew smiled. "I've always known."

Cameron couldn't immediately respond.

Andrew cleared his throat again. "I want to apologize for what I said the last time we met."

Cameron shook his head. "I probably deserved it."

They stared at each other, and the waitress brought water for Andrew. Neither spoke for some time.

Cameron broke the silence. "I should apologize as well, but…I don't know where to start."

Andrew replied, "Some things are better off left in the past."

Cameron was humbly grateful. Taking a deep breath, he pulled a sheaf of papers out of his shoulder bag. Setting the dog-eared screenplay on the table between them, he said, "I called you, because of this."

Andrew stared at it in shock and pulled the bound papers toward himself. He flipped through the pages before speaking, "I never thought I would see this again…"

"How old is it?"

Andrew thought it over and answered, "Twelve years."

Cameron explained, "I found this recently, when I was going through some things I neglected over the years."

His son continued to flip the pages.

Leaning on his hands, Cameron added, "I read it."

Andrew looked up slowly.

Cameron went on, "A young man is abandoned by his father and has to deal with the unresolved issues between them?"

With a roll of his eyes, Andrew stated, "I know it's melancholy and terribly self-serving. I would be afraid to hear a Freudian evaluation of it. It's total crap."

Cameron leaned back in the booth. "I'm not going to argue with the Freudian nature of the subject, and it shows the age of its author. But the writing is good. The pacing, the bones… it's good."

Andrew stared at him as though he was waiting for the punchline.

"Why have you not written anything else?" Cameron asked carefully.

His son sighed. "I wrote that for a screenwriting class at university. It was an elective. I've always loved to write, but mum wanted me as far away from the film industry as possible."

Cameron looked away. "I can understand that."

Andrew sipped his water. "Also, I think…I've always been afraid of the risk, which is ironic, because I analyze risk for a living."

Holding his son's gaze, Cameron said, "I would like another screenplay from you. I want to produce it. And I have a director in mind."

Andrew stared at him, his mouth slightly open. "I don't know that I can…"

Cameron looked his son in the eyes, and he could almost feel the wind at his back as he said, "Never be afraid, Andrew. Never."

At this time, over 1,100 of the 2, 977 victims of 9/11
have never been identified.

The World Trade Center Health Program currently has more than
70,000 registered patients, with more than 20,000 diagnosed with
specific conditions directly related to 9/11.
This number continues to rise.

CAT WHITNEY

ACKNOWLEDGMENTS

This is the part of the book where I make an effort to acknowledge everyone who has helped make this book possible. That seems a rather large task, since it's quite a long list. I will try, however, to be concise.

First, to Lynn Pickles, who took on the editing of this novel when it was still very much a rough draft, I thank you. You said yes to a monumental task and for someone you'd never met. Thank you for the hours of reading, editing, and answering of emails. Our conversations about England have been delightful. I owe you a debt of gratitude for making Chatfield come to life, for making Flora sound like a true, Yorkshire lass, and for helping me give Cameron solid English roots. Your input has been invaluable, and this novel would never have come together without you. I look forward to someday having a proper cup of tea together as friends.

Second, I owe a huge thank you to Joe Dittmar for sharing his 9/11 story with me and for continuing to share it with the world. Joe, your commitment to making sure that we never forget what happened that day, and remember the victims of that day, is a beautiful thing. As we discussed, it is not an easy subject, but your willingness to share your story is reaching a new generation. Thank you for helping to make sure Delilah and Anna's 9/11 story accurately represents the events of that day. For those who would like to learn more about Joe's story or donate to his memorial project, his website can be found at **www.wtceskp.com.**

Next, thank you to Bethel Caram for helping me write about the great city of New York. Bethel, it was an honor being your House Manager for a summer, and I'm so glad we've stayed in touch. You remain one of the coolest people I know. Thank you for believing in a writer who had never published anything, for encouraging me along the way, and for offering thorough, insightful feedback. You are one in a million.

Amy Witschey, BSRT, RRT, RCP, I sincerely appreciate you taking time to help me understand Pulmonary Fibrosis. I know you have a busy schedule. Thank you for answering the call of a friend of a friend. You have helped me better represent lung disease and the patients that struggle every day to breathe.

Another thank you to Gabrielle Rutherford, APRN, for helping me to write about the pulmonary ICU and the way these patients leave this world. Thank you for helping me write about the quiet.

Courtney Clayton, thank you for being the first person to pick up my manuscript and read it from start to finish. At a time when I was drowning in details and wondering if any of it would come together, you read the first draft and reminded me why I write. Your emotional investment helped me to believe this was a story worth sharing.

To Mia Warshofsky, for being my very first fan. You were the encouragement that I needed eight years ago to "pick up the pen." Thank you for all the positive comments, late-night chats, and general silliness. You were awesome at thirteen, and you are more awesome now.

Finally, a massive thank you to my editor-in-chief, my sister-by-choice, my crazy neighbor, and my partner in crime, Julie Ann Cook. The reason this book has made it out of the bowels of my computer is because you said, essentially, "Enough with the fanfiction. It's time to publish something." You gave me the shove that I needed to take the risk and publish my work. You have also walked this entire journey with me, from the first sprig of an idea to the final page proofs. I cannot say enough how much I appreciate you listening to me ramble on about plot ideas, characters, and word choice. We have spent endless hours workshopping scenes, cutting the unnecessary bits, and otherwise refining this thing with red pens and sometimes even scissors. You have cut out at least 3000 unnecessary commas. You are the other half of my brain, the counterweight to my tendency to fly into crazyland, and the belay on my life so I can climb higher and higher. You are an amazing poet, and I am honored to have your work represented in my novel. Because of you, this has come to be. There aren't enough words of thanks for all you have done. So, this one's for you.

SOURCES

"World Trade Center Health Program Annual Statistics (March 31, 2016.)" *World Trade Center Health Program.* CDC, 31 March 2016. Web. 13 July 2016.
<http://www.cdc.gov/wtc/pdfs/wtchp_stats033116.pdf>

Pearson, Erica. "Thousands Suffer from 9/11 Illnesses Years Later." *New York Daily News.* 10 September 2015. Web. 13 July 2016.
<http://www.nydailynews.com/new-york/thousands-suffer-9-11-illnesses-14-years-article-1.2356281>

"September 11 Attack Timeline." *911Memorial.org.* Web. 13 July 2016.
<http://timeline.911memorial.org/#Timeline/2>

"9/11 10th Anniversary: America Remembers." *The Guardian.* 11 September 2011. Web. 25 August 2015.
<https://www.theguardian.com/world/blog/2011/sep/11/9-11-10th-anniversary-america-live>

Dittmar, Joe. Personal Interview. 23 May 2016.

Witschey, Amy, BSRT, RRT, RCP. Personal Interview. 31 May 2016.

www.ingramcontent.com/pod-product-compliance
Lightning Source LLC
Chambersburg PA
CBHW030534260626
47157CB00006B/2033